Acclaim for

DEATH, TAXES, AND A SKINNY NO-WHIP LATTE

"Readers will find Kelly's protagonist a kindred spirit to Stephanie Plum: feisty and tenacious, with a self-deprecating sense of humor. Tara is flung into some unnerving situations, including encounters with hired thugs, would-be muggers, and head lice. The laughs lighten up the scary bits, and the nonstop action and snappy dialogue keep the standard plot moving along at a good place." —*RT Book Reviews*

"Readers should be prepared for a laugh-fest. The writer is first-class and there is a lot of humor contained in this series. It is a definite keeper." —*Night Owl Romance*

"A quirky, fun tale that pulls you in with its witty heroine and outlandish situations . . . You'll laugh at Tara's predicaments, and cheer her on as she nearly single-handedly tackles the case." —*Romance Reviews Today*

"It is hard not to notice a sexy CPA with a proclivity for weapons. Kelly's sophomore series title . . . has huge romance crossover appeal." —*Library Journal*

"An exciting, fun new mystery series with quirky characters and a twist . . . . Who would have ever guessed IRS investigators could be so cool?" —*Guilty Pleasures Book Reviews*

"Kelly's novel is off to a fast start and never slows down. There is suspense but also laugh-out-loud moments. If you enjoy Stephanie Plum in the Evanovich novels, you will love Tara Holloway!" —*Reader to Reader Reviews*

"Diane Kelly gives the

bursti

DEATH, TAXES, AND A FRENCH MANICURE

"Keep your eye on Diane Kelly—her writing is tight, smart, and laugh-out-loud funny."

—Kristan Higgins, *New York Times* and
USA Today bestselling author

"A hilarious, sexy, heart-pounding ride that will keep you on the edge of your seat. Tara Holloway is the IRS's answer to Stephanie Plum—smart, sassy, and so much fun. Kelly's debut has definitely earned her a spot on my keeper shelf!"

—*New York Times* bestselling author Gemma Halliday

"The subject of taxation usually makes people cry, but prepare to laugh your assets off with Diane Kelly's hilarious debut." —Jana DeLeon, author of the Ghost-in-Law series

"Quirky, sexy, and downright fabulous. Zany characters you can't help but love, and a plot that will knock your socks off. This is the most fun I've had reading in forever!"

—*New York Times* bestselling author Christie Craig

"With a quirky cast of characters, snappy dialogue, and a Bernie Madoff–style pyramid scheme—hunting down tax cheats has never added up to so much fun!"

—Robin Kaye, award-winning author of
the Domestic Gods series

Death, Taxes, and Peach Sangria

DIANE KELLY

St. Martin's Paperbacks

This is a work of fiction. All of the characters, organizations, and events portrayed in this novel are either products of the author's imagination or are used fictitiously.

DEATH, TAXES, AND PEACH SANGRIA

Copyright © 2013 by Diane Kelly.
Excerpt from *Death, Taxes, and Hot-Pink Leg Warmers* copyright © 2013 by Diane Kelly.

For information address St. Martin's Press, 175 Fifth Avenue, New York, NY 10010.

ISBN: 978-1-250-02306-3

Printed in the United States of America

St. Martin's Paperbacks edition / February 2013

St. Martin's Paperbacks are published by St. Martin's Press, 175 Fifth Avenue, New York, NY 10010.

10 9 8 7 6 5 4 3 2 1

To Jan Fall, my eighth-grade Language Arts teacher at Noel Grisham Middle School, and to Virginia Anderson, my sophomore English teacher at Westwood High School. I've never forgotten your kind and encouraging words about my writing. Thank you! And to Coach Harlan Holloway from Noel Grisham Middle School. Thanks for looking out for me!

Acknowledgments

Big thanks to my wonderful team at St. Martin's Paperbacks! To my editor, Holly Blanck, for your insightful editorial comments. I'm lucky to have such a nice "boss." Thanks to Eileen Rothschild and Aleksandra Mencel for building buzz about my books. Thanks to Danielle Fiorella and Monika Roe for the fun and eye-catching covers. And to everyone else at St. Martin's who played a role in bringing my books to readers, thanks for all you do!

Thanks to my agent, Helen Breitwieser, for your part in making this series a continuing success. You're smart, hardworking, and encouraging. I'm so glad to have you on my team!

To authors Trinity Blake, Celya Bowers, Angela Cavener, Cheryl Hathaway, Angela Hicks, and Kennedy Shaw for your feedback, support, and friendship.

To Liz Bemis and Sienna Condy of Bemis Promotions, thanks for making my Web site and newsletters rock!

Thanks to the wonderful members of my Street Team! I appreciate all you do in introducing Tara and her cohorts to your friends and fellow readers.

To the IRS special agents, thanks for sharing your fascinating world with me and for all you do on behalf of honest taxpayers. Please forgive Tara for being such a naughty agent and breaking the rules. I tried to make her behave like a special agent should, but she refused to cooperate. Shame on her!

Finally, thanks to my readers! I hope you'll enjoy your time with Tara and the gang and that this book will bring you lots of laughs.

$\mathcal{B}$onnie Pratt's Easy-Peasy Peach Sangria Recipe

Ingredients

1 peach, sliced
½ cup raspberries
1 small orange, sliced
1 bottle of your favorite white zinfandel wine
1½ cups peach schnapps
½ cup frozen pink lemonade concentrate
1½ cups lemon-lime soda

Place fruit in a pitcher. Add wine, schnapps, and lemonade concentrate. Stir well. Refrigerate at least one hour. Add soda just before serving and stir again. Serve over ice, enjoy with friends, and forget your troubles!

chapter one

$\mathcal{D}$eductive Reasoning

On a Monday morning in late September, Eddie Bardin and I donned our ballistic vests, slid our Glocks into our ankle holsters, and headed out of downtown Dallas in a plain white government-issue sedan that smelled faintly of French fries.

Eddie leaned toward the door and checked himself in the side mirror. "How do I look?"

What my response lacked in decorum it made up for in sincerity. "Like an idiot."

"Then it's the perfect disguise."

With the shiny gold chains, sagging jeans that exposed polka-dot boxers, and untied high-top basketball shoes, he looked like a hip-hop singer or a wannabe gangster. The disguise was a far cry from Eddie's usual attire of classic business suits and silk ties. I, too, wore a disguise, though mine was far more subtle. In blue jeans, sneakers, and a Dallas Mavericks T-shirt, I was undercover as a retail sales associate from a sporting goods store at a nearby mall. As a final touch, I'd pulled my chestnut-brown hair into a ponytail and topped it with a Texas Rangers baseball cap. Go, team!

We were two IRS special agents on a mission. Today's mission would be taking down a tax preparer who called herself the Deduction Diva. According to her glittery red advertising flyer, she provided clients with massage chairs and a complimentary glass of champagne while their returns were prepared. Hoity-toity, huh?

With tax law growing increasingly complex, more people were turning to professional preparers. Entrepreneurs looking for a niche figured they'd cash in on the trend. Unfortunately, too many had jumped on the bandwagon. Tax preparation services had become a crowded market and preparers had resorted to gimmicks to grab the attention of potential clients. But where these people came up with the gimmicks God only knows.

After merging onto the freeway, I glanced over at my partner. "Don't you dare touch that stereo."

I slapped his hand away as he attempted to eject my Tim McGraw CD and slip in some soft jazz. Eddie might be African-American, but he was much more Kenny G than P. Diddy. I, on the other hand, was much more Lady Antebellum than Lady Gaga.

Yep, in many ways Eddie and I were polar opposites. He was tall and dark, a father of two, who'd grown up and was now raising his family in the affluent North Dallas suburbs. I was a petite white woman, a recovering tomboy who'd grown up climbing trees, shooting BB guns, and swimming in the muddy creeks of the East Texas piney woods.

Dig a little deeper, though, and you'd find Eddie and I shared quite a few similarities. We'd both kicked academic ass in college, graduating at the top of our classes. We'd both taken jobs as special agents in IRS Criminal Investigations when we'd discovered that sitting at a desk all day didn't suit us. And we both wanted to see tax cheats get their due. Especially the Deduction Diva. She'd been cheating the government for years. The Diva's due was long *overdue*.

Twenty minutes later, I pulled the car into the lot of the suburban office park where the Diva's business was located and took a spot in the second row.

"Break a leg," I said. Given that my partner was in costume, the sentiment seemed appropriate.

Eddie opened the door and climbed out, a phony W-2 clutched in his hand. I sat in the car, snickering as he shuffled across the parking lot in his saggy jeans and entered the glass-front office space.

The audit department had referred the Diva's case to Criminal Investigations after examinations of several of her clients revealed a disturbing pattern. Each of their returns showed a significant loss on a vague "consulting" business. Suspiciously, the loss in each case was just enough to offset the client's other income, resulting in a refund of all taxes the client had paid in. When questioned by auditors, the clients pointed fingers at their tax preparer, claiming the Deduction Diva had devised the fraudulent scheme.

Though the Diva's clients were hardly innocent, as long as they made good on the taxes owed we'd let them slide with a stern warning. Criminal Investigations was more interested in nailing the preparer who'd perpetrated the fraud on a wide-scale basis. Besides, we'd need the clients to testify against the Diva should she plead *not guilty*. But just in case our potential witnesses decided to assert their Fifth Amendment right to remain silent, we were here to collect direct evidence of the Diva's fraud.

Catching tax cheats red-handed was always a hoot. There's nothing quite as satisfying as seeing that *oh-shit-they-got-me!* look in their eyes.

The Deduction Diva wasn't the only abusive preparer in the Dallas area. There were dozens on the IRS radar and hundreds more across the country. Abuse had become so prevalent, in fact, that the agency had enacted a number of measures to crack down on preparer fraud, including background checks and competency testing. Whether these new regulations would reduce fraud remained to be seen.

Our boss, Lu "the Lobo" Lobozinski, had decided that the most efficient way to deal with these cheats was to perform an intense, concentrated sweep. She'd paired up the special agents in the office and handed each team a list of preparers to investigate and arrest. Eddie and I were half-way through our list. We'd already taken down several abusive preparers, including a moron who called himself the Weapon of Mass Deductions and advertised on television, wearing combat fatigues and army boots in his cheesy commercial.

With the October 15th extension deadline rapidly approaching, the summer lull was over. Tax preparers were busy with clients who'd requested more time to file their returns, some because their finances were extensive and complicated, others because they couldn't get their act together by the April deadline. I suspected most of the Diva's clients were of the latter variety.

While the Deduction Diva prepared my partner's tax return, I sat in the car playing Scrabble on my cell phone and tried not to think of the major case Eddie and I had pending. We'd dealt with some pretty nasty people in our investigations, but these guys were by far the nastiest we'd faced. They were heartless, cruel, and extremely violent, killing hundreds, perhaps thousands, in their attacks, with no thought to the lives they'd ruined, to the innocents maimed and killed as collateral damage.

Terrorists.

Just the thought gave me acid reflux.

A half hour later, I'd just earned a triple score with the word "FUNGUS" when Eddie emerged from the Diva's office, walked around the corner of the building, and sent me a text.

4K refund.

The Diva had done it again. Eddie'd gone into her office with a decoy W-2 showing thirty-five thousand in earnings from a purported job as a DJ at a local nightclub. Given the amount of tax withholding on the W-2, Eddie should have owed $38.76 in additional tax had the Diva properly prepared his return.

Busted.

I tugged on the hem of my jeans to make sure my ankle holster wasn't exposed, slid my phone into my purse, and headed inside with my false W-2. Mine showed I'd earned twenty-eight grand, with just enough withholding to cover my income taxes. If the Diva prepared my return correctly, I'd be due a whopping fourteen-cent refund.

I pushed open the glass door and stepped inside.

Whoa.

The office looked like a brothel. The walls were painted a deep scarlet. The cushy black velvet massage chairs featured red satin pillows. A pole lamp with a red fringed shade stood between the chairs. Over the gray industrial carpet lay a large fluffy red rug. Barry White's deep voice crooned softly from a stereo in the corner.

A young African-American receptionist sat at a desk chewing on the end of a yellow highlighter, a college textbook open in front of her. Accounting 101, an introductory class. She wouldn't have learned enough yet to know her boss was up to no good. The girl's casual coed attire clashed with the seductive office motif, but for ten bucks an hour who wanted to suffer in heels and panty hose? On the corner of her desk was a silver champagne bucket that contained partially melted ice and a half-empty bottle of cheap champagne.

Behind the receptionist were two doors. The one that read "Diva" in sparkling red paint was closed. The other one, which was unmarked, was cracked open a few inches. Through the open door I could see a trio of young girls seated at long portable tables, earbuds in their ears as they input data into computers. The Diva's production staff, no doubt.

The receptionist removed the highlighter from her mouth. "Can I help you?"

I held up my W-2. "I need to have my tax return prepared."

"Fifty dollars per form," the girl recited. "Ten percent discount if you pay cash."

I had a sneaking suspicion the fees paid in cash went unreported. "Great. Can it be done while I wait?"

"No problem. It'll just take a few minutes." She reached into a small cabinet behind her, retrieved a plastic champagne flute, and poured me a glass of bargain-brand bubbly. "Enjoy."

"Thanks." I traded my W-2 for the champagne. As I took a seat in one of the massage chairs, the girl carried my W-2 through the open door.

I looked down at the magazine offerings on the coffee table. *Ebony. Essence.* Oprah's magazine, *O.* I picked up the *O* magazine. I had a lot of respect for Oprah Winfrey. She was a ballsy yet classy broad, fighting for justice and fairness and generally making the world a better place. Though I shared her admirable aspirations, I could never be as classy as Oprah. I found it hard to be consistently well behaved.

I jabbed the button on the chair control and the entire seat began to vibrate. The movement made it a little difficult to sip the champagne without spilling it on myself, but I wasn't going to let that stop me from enjoying the stuff. It reminded me of the spiked 7UP my friends and I used to drink back in college.

"This is g-g-great," I told the receptionist, my voice quivering along with the chair.

She smiled. "Sometimes clients fall asleep there."

I could see why. Between the effects of the champagne and the gentle rocking, I was tempted to take a nap myself. The Diva was definitely on to something here.

I was halfway through an article on the merits of regular colonoscopies when one of the girls from the back room came out of her door with a piece of paper in her hand. A draft of my return. She pulled a black earbud out of one ear. Katy Perry's voice came through the tiny device, singing about hickeys, streaking through a park, and dancing on tabletops. Been there, done that, got the T-shirt. The girl rapped softly on the Diva's door.

A husky woman's voice called, "Come in!"

The coed stepped inside for a moment, then came back out, closing the Diva's door behind her. She returned to her spot at the portable table.

Not long after, the receptionist's phone buzzed. A voice came over the speaker. "Miss Henry's return is ready."

Yep, my alias was Anne Henry, a combination of the names of my two cats. I'd wanted to go with something more clever like Gwen Down, a veiled take on "Going Down," but Eddie'd feared it might be too obvious.

The receptionist slipped into the Diva's office and came back with my tax return.

I turned off the massage chair and looked over the paperwork she handed me. The return showed I was due a refund of fourteen cents. *Damn!* The Diva had computed my taxes correctly. I felt cheated that I hadn't been cheated. Silly, huh? But it didn't matter that she'd prepared my return accurately. We had more than enough evidence of her large-scale fraud to take her in.

"That'll be fifty dollars for the preparation service," the receptionist said as she slid back into her chair. "We can e-file it for you for another twenty-five."

"No thanks."

I stood, pulled out my phone, and texted Eddie. *14 cent refund.*

He texted back. *U want a big refund, u gotta ask for it.*

So that was where I'd gone wrong.

I'm coming in, he added.

The receptionist stared up at me, waiting for me to pay my bill.

"You said fifty dollars, right?" I asked, stalling for time as Eddie returned to the office.

The girl nodded.

I reached into my purse, but instead of removing my wallet I pulled out the leather holder that contained my special agent badge. Eddie opened the door and came back inside, his badge at the ready.

"We're from the IRS," I told the receptionist. "We need to see the Diva."

"Uh . . . okay." The girl's expression was equal parts confused and surprised as we knocked on the Diva's door.

"Come in!" the woman called.

We opened the door and stepped inside. The Diva's office was just as gaudy as her foyer. Red wallpaper with thick gold stripes graced the walls, and her windows were covered with red satin curtains. She sat behind a shiny black lacquer desk in a high-backed red leather chair.

The Diva was a light-skinned black woman, with shiny swirls of dark hair swept into an elegant, curly updo on her head, like a pile of chocolate shavings. Her makeup was heavy yet impeccable, from her perfectly lined crimson lips to her glimmering burgundy eyelids. Her long acrylic fingernails were painted a shiny ruby color. Her voluptuous body was packed into a low-cut red dress, the bustline around her double Ds trimmed with black faux fur.

She looked like a movie star on Oscar night. But she wouldn't be going home with a bag of pricey swag or a gold, man-shaped trophy, her photo featured on the cover of *People* magazine. Nope, the only things she'd get today would be a mug shot, a body cavity search, and a one-size-fits-nobody jumpsuit.

Neener-neener.

At our unexpected intrusion, the Diva stood from her chair, her expression as surprised and confused as her receptionist's. "May I help you?"

Eddie and I flashed our badges.

"We're from the IRS," I said. "Criminal Investigations Division."

Now her expression was only surprised. The confusion was gone. She knew exactly why we were here. But that knowledge wasn't going to prevent her from feigning innocence.

"What do you want with me?" She put one hand to her chest, pointing to herself. The other hand went for her bulky electric stapler.

At point-blank proximity, I wasn't able to fully avoid the stapler she hurled at me. I only had time to duck. The device bounced off my back and onto the floor. Thanks to the padded Kevlar vest under my Mavericks tee, I hardly felt the impact.

She flung a box of paper clips at Eddie. He batted them away with both hands.

I reached down my leg and pulled my gun from my ankle holster. I really didn't want to draw on the woman, but the way she was acting left me no choice. "Put your hands up!"

She yanked open her desk drawer and pulled out a metal letter opener, clutching it in a loose fist, her long fingernails preventing her from fully closing her hand.

I aimed my gun at her. "Drop it, Diva!"

"No!" She swung the blade around as if she were a Jet and Eddie and I were Sharks. But this was East Dallas, not *West Side Story.* And I certainly hoped none of us would end up dead like Riff, Bernardo, or Tony. I preferred happy endings.

In a move that would make Chuck Norris proud, Eddie stepped forward and brought up his right arm, knocking the letter opener out of the Diva's hand. The blade sailed through the air, bouncing off the wall and falling back to the fluffy rug. Before she could retrieve it, Eddie ran around one side of the desk, I ran around the other, and together we tackled the Diva to the floor.

On her back now, she kicked and rolled side to side, trying to loosen our hold on her. Her boobs swung side to side, too, though they followed a second or two after the rest of her body. Eddie slapped them away just as he'd done with the paper clips.

"You touched my breasts!" she shrieked at Eddie.

It was kind of hard not to touch them given that there was so much fur-trimmed cleavage heaving to and fro. She raised a knee and rammed it into Eddie's groin. He rolled aside, retching and grabbing his crotch in agony.

Poor guy. Looked like his wife wouldn't be getting any for a while. It also looked like I'd have to handle the Diva by myself now.

The woman spun away from Eddie. Once she'd gotten herself up on all fours, I grabbed her right wrist from the back and yanked it out from under her. *Ha!* Roughhousing with my two older brothers as a kid had taught me some good moves.

The Diva fell onto her face on the rug, sputtering and

spitting fuzz out of her mouth. I climbed onto her back, straddling her as I grabbed her arms and pulled them up behind her.

"Let me go!" she yelled, squirming under me.

"Yeah," I said, "that's not gonna happen." Two *clicks* later, I had her hands cuffed.

The Diva's four employees stood in the open doorway, mouths hanging open.

"OMG," one of them said.

"Totally," said another.

The third nodded her head in agreement. "Totally OMG."

"Does this mean we won't get our paychecks?" asked the receptionist.

The Diva had ripped off the IRS, but I didn't want these hardworking college kids to get ripped off, too. It hadn't been all that long ago that I'd been a starving student, eating ramen noodles for dinner three times a week. "I'll let her make out your checks before we go. But cash them immediately. We'll be freezing her accounts later today."

Realizing she was now in deep doo-doo, the Diva switched tactics, boo-hooing and promising to be a good little girl from now on if we'd only let her go. "I'll pay back every penny!" she cried. "I swear!"

Eddie shot her a pointed look from where he stood, hunched over, hands on his knees. "You should've thought about that before you busted my balls."

Was it just my imagination or was his voice an octave higher?

I removed the right handcuff so the Diva could make out her employees' paychecks, clicking the cuff onto the arm of her chair lest she attempt a last-ditch effort to escape.

While the Diva made out the payroll, my phone beeped, indicating an incoming text. I checked the screen. The message was from Nick, a coworker on whom I had a hopeless crush. The text included a discreetly snapped photo of a man dressed in an Elvis costume wearing handcuffs. The man was being led out to a marshal's car. A sign on the office building behind him read: "REFUND-A-RAMA."

Can u believe this shit? the text read. *One more idiot and I will lose it.*

Nick wasn't exactly known for his tact. What he was known for were his spectacular pecs, whiskey-colored eyes, and take-charge style. I texted him back: *Eddie took a knee to the nuts.*

The reply came back in seconds. *I'll count my blessings.*

Once the Diva finished, I cuffed her wrists back together and handed out the paychecks.

"Sorry about this, girls," I said. "But let this be a lesson to you. Keep your noses clean."

chapter two

If You Cast a Wide Net, You're Bound to Catch a Fish or Two

Once the Diva had been hauled off to jail for processing, Eddie and I headed to the downtown medical clinic. Normally I was the one with injuries, so it was no surprise that Dr. Ajay Maju focused on me when he entered the examination room.

The doc was an attractive Indian-American guy, only a year or two older than my twenty-seven years. His white lab coat was unbuttoned, the gap revealing a printed tee underneath. *Open wide and say aah.*

"What is it this time?" he asked, looking me up and down, searching for evidence of injury.

"Eddie's nuts," I said, hiking a thumb at my partner. "He took a knee to the family jewels."

"Dude." He turned to my partner and shook his head in sympathy. "Ouch." He pushed a button on the wall-mounted intercom. "I need an ice pack in room three. Stat."

The nurse arrived seconds later with a plastic-wrapped blue ice pack. Eddie promptly dropped it down the front of his pants, carefully moving it into place.

Eddie's balls now mercifully frozen, we drove back to the federal building, sidetracking through a Chinese drive-through and picking up lunch on the way. I suggested he order a pair of egg dumplings to replace his damaged set of *huevos,* but he didn't think it was funny.

"Too soon, huh, buddy?"

His only response was a scowl.

We climbed off the elevator with our take-out bags. Our boss stood by her secretary's desk at the end of the hall. Lu sported a pinkish-orange beehive, false eyelashes, and bright orange lipstick, a look she'd perfected back in the sixties and stuck with ever since. She'd recently undergone chemotherapy for lung cancer and temporarily lost weight. Once she'd completed her treatments she'd rebounded quickly, packing on all the weight she'd lost and then some. The neon-pink pantsuit she wore looked as if it might burst at the seams at any moment.

Lu used a Slim Jim to stir the can of strawberry-flavored Slim-Fast! in her hand and looked up at me and Eddie. "Did you get the Diva?"

"Yep," I said. "Just three more to go."

One of our remaining targets was an older man, a former IRS auditor no less. He'd started his own tax practice years ago after electing early retirement in lieu of being fired from the Service for excessive absences, incompetency, and, according to the handwritten note in his personnel file, being a "weird-ass crackpot." He called himself the Tax Wizard and claimed he could make taxes magically disappear. As if.

The remaining abusive preparers on our list were both men in their early forties. The first, Richard Wallace Beauregard III, operated an insurance, investment, and tax business called Beauregard Financial Services. The other was a man named Jimmy John McClure, who ran an outfit called Bulls-Eye Taxidermy and Tax Processing. Apparently he processed both deer and tax returns.

"We'll have them rounded up by the October fifteenth deadline," I assured Lu.

"See to it," she said. "I want those frauds taken down

ASAP." She pulled the meat stick out of the shake and stuck it in her mouth, licking off the strawberry liquid. *Urk.* How she could find that combination appetizing was beyond me. But I supposed it was a fairly balanced meal. Three of the four food groups were represented.

Eddie and I parted in the hall. He limped back to his office. Why any woman had penis envy I'd never know. Guy nards were way too vulnerable.

I entered my office, pushed aside the files on the terrorist case, and set my lunch bag on my desk. As I sat down in my rolling chair, I couldn't help myself. I glanced across the hall at my coworker, Senior Special Agent Nick Pratt, a bad-ass bad boy if ever there was one. He was the kind of guy your mother warned you about, but also the kind she'd happily hop into bed with if she were in your shoes. She wouldn't regret it, either. Mothers can be such hypocrites, can't they?

Nick had dark hair, currently cut short. His eyes were the color of Jack Daniel's whiskey and caused the same slow burn in a woman's gut, or perhaps an inch or two lower. He leaned back in his chair, his brown cowboy boots propped on his desk, a silver belt buckle in the shape of a coiled diamondback rattler gleaming from the waist of his navy-blue Dockers. His strong hand worked his ever-present blue stress ball.

Sitting next to Nick, wearing his standard khakis and blue button-down, was Josh, another special agent, one whom I had mixed feelings about. Josh could be whiny, competitive, and arrogant, but he'd saved my ass on a couple of cases when his superior high-tech skills were needed. Gotta take the good with the bad, huh?

The two had been assigned to work together on the sweep. While Josh could put the fear of God in a computer, with his short stature, cherubic blond curls, and baby-blue eyes he failed to intimidate tax cheats. Nick, on the other hand, stood an easy six feet, two inches, with the broad shoulders and *don't-fuck-with-me* demeanor of a former high-school linebacker. He was clearly a force to be reckoned with. With their complementary skills, Nick and Josh made a good team.

They stared at the screen of Josh's laptop while Josh pecked at the keyboard and maneuvered the mouse. Probably reviewing files downloaded from one of the preparers' offices.

After scarfing down an egg roll and a paper container of Buddha's delight, I cracked open my fortune cookie, shoved the dry, sugary fragments in my mouth, and smoothed out the white paper slip.

Live a life of wonder.

Hmm. Not bad advice, I supposed. Then again, whenever I'd wondered about something I'd always sought an answer. I'd never been left to wonder long.

But there was something—or should I say *someone*—I found myself constantly wondering about these days. And that someone sat across the hall wearing boots and a snake-shaped belt buckle.

Nick returned the sentiment, too. He'd let me know he was interested, that he'd like to see if the two of us might make a good couple, that all I had to do was *just say the word*. After much debate, not only with myself but with two close friends as well, I decided not to risk my relationship with my boyfriend, Brett, by pursuing things with Nick. Brett was a great guy and things between us were going well. Taking a chance with Nick had seemed like too big a gamble.

Unfortunately, while my mind had made that logical decision, my heart still couldn't be convinced to let Nick go. Certain other parts of me refused to give up on him, too.

Nick pulled his legs off his desk and leaned in to look more closely at the computer screen. "I don't know," he said to Josh. "You think that'll get a woman's attention?"

He had a woman's attention right now.

Mine.

Nick looked up from across the hall, caught me watching him—*damn!*—and waved me over. "Come here, Tara. We need a female perspective."

Men asking a woman's opinion? That was a rare thing indeed. "Okay," I said as I stood. "But if you don't like my opinion just remember you asked for it." I made my way to

Nick's office and stepped behind them, turning my attention
to the computer screen.

The two were logged on to the Internet. They'd pulled up
a Web site for Big D Dating Service, a business that, according to the information in the sidebar, was dedicated to helping residents of the Dallas area find true love, or at least a
reasonably acceptable substitute.

"What are y'all doing on this site?" I asked.

"Trying to get Josh laid." Nick clapped a hand on Josh's
shoulder. "We'll make a man of him yet."

When Nick, Josh, and I had recently worked a case together, Josh had downed a few too many drinks at a strip club
while spying on a target. When he'd returned to the car afterward, he'd metaphorically spilled his guts, revealing to me
and Nick that he was a virgin. He'd then spilled his guts literally, filling the parking lot with ninety-proof puke.

Oh, such sweet memories.

Though I didn't find Josh attractive in the least, there's
someone for everyone, right? Dallas was a heavily populated city. Lots of fish in the sea. Surely Josh could catch one
using the Net.

Josh pointed to a section of the screen in which he'd in-
putted a short bio. "How does that sound?"

I read the entry.

> *I am a government technology specialist who en-
> joys video games, science-fiction novels, and spy
> movies. I am seeking a woman who likes those things,
> too, and who will want to spend time with me.*

Josh looked up at me, a slight blush on his cheeks, a
hopeful look in his baby blue eyes. "What do you think?
Would it make a girl want to date me?"

Honestly? The bio made him sound like a desperate geek.
But I couldn't very well say that, could I? "Let's tweak it just
a little."

I pulled over one of the wing chairs and took a seat,
glancing at Josh. How could I make the nerdy twerp sound

interesting? I thought back to the marketing class I'd taken in college. According to the professor, advertising was all about spin.

Time to turn Josh into a human dreidel.

I swiveled his laptop my way and, after a few minutes of typing, deleting, revising, and retyping, came up with what I felt was a fairly good sales job.

Federal agent specializing in high-tech espionage seeks an adventurous woman who shares an interest in traveling together to other worlds via video games, sci-fi books, and spy movies.

"How's that?" I asked, turning the computer so Josh and Nick could read the screen.

Nick nodded. "Better."

Josh turned to Nick. "You should sign up, too. Maybe we could double-date."

"No!" The word shot out of my mouth before I could stop it. The mere thought of Nick dating someone else filled me with pure jealousy.

I felt sick. Terrified. Frantic.

Nick eyed me intently as I sputtered, trying to cover for myself.

I turned to Josh to avoid Nick's gaze. "Um . . . I mean Nick doesn't need to join a dating service to meet someone. He could meet someone the traditional way. You know, at a bar or something."

Fat chance. We put in a lot of overtime and Nick had little free time to go searching for his soul mate.

"I'm not into the bar scene," Nick said. "Burned myself out on that years ago. Maybe I should try this online thing. Seems to work for a lot of people." He stared at me, one brow raised, a challenge in his eyes. He was sending me a message loud and clear. *This is your last chance, Tara. Stop wondering what we might be like together and find out for yourself.*

My stomach felt hollow and queasy. But Nick's implied ultimatum had me feeling angry, too. Not that I had any right whatsoever to be angry, but that wasn't going to stop me.

Josh turned the computer toward himself again and began pecking at his keyboard, setting up an account for Nick. "What kind of woman are you looking for?"

Nick looked up in thought. "Well, she needs to be reasonably pretty, of course."

I rolled my eyes. "Wow. You're deep."

He ignored my jibe, looking directly at me again. "I want a woman with brains and gumption. One who's independent and speaks her mind. One who won't get all girlie and upset when I occasionally act like an asshole."

Josh chuckled. "You just described Tara."

Nick raised the second brow. *I mean it, Tara,* said the brow. *This is your last chance.*

I stared back at him for a moment.

And in that instant I knew.

Nick is a chance I have to take.

I'd been miserable and heartbroken since that day, weeks ago, when I'd told Nick that I'd chosen to stay with Brett. I had made the wrong choice. I should've taken the gamble. I knew that now with absolute certainty.

But the thought of losing Brett made me feel sick, terrified, and frantic, too. He was a great catch. Sweet, smart, and successful, too. He was not only an up-and-coming landscape architect at the prestigious firm of Wakefield Designs, but he'd also recently started a nursery business. I admired his work ethic, respected his entrepreneurial spirit. We shared many common interests, like watching goofy British comedies on television and sampling diverse ethnic cuisine at area restaurants.

But was Brett *The One*?

Early on, he'd seemed like a good candidate, more so than any other guy I'd ever dated. But lately? I'd begun to have some doubts. Still, I wasn't sure whether those doubts were real or I was merely confused by my intense, almost desperate, attraction to Nick.

A life of wonder sounded great, but not if I spent the rest of my life wondering whether I'd chosen the right mate, whether I might have been happier with another man, whether the man I was with might have been better suited for a different woman. A life of these wonders would be no life at all. I wouldn't be doing Brett any favors by living a lie, either. He deserved a woman who would give herself to him wholeheartedly. Until I was convinced Nick wasn't the better choice for me, I'd never be able to give myself entirely to Brett.

I'd spent weeks slogging through this emotional wet cement. Frankly, I'd grown damn tired of it. Yep, it was high time to pull myself out of the muck and take action.

Before I took a chance with Nick, though, I had to give Brett a heads-up, talk things through, come to some sort of agreement on the terms of our trial separation. It was the right thing to do. Plus, I wanted to make damn sure the door was left open with Brett in case things didn't work out with Nick. But would Brett agree to take me back if Nick and I proved to be a bad match? Maybe. Maybe not. Nobody liked to play second fiddle or be the fallback.

Still, dating at this age wasn't just fun and games anymore. People our age were looking for lifelong mates, someone to settle down with. It was only smart to do everything possible to make sure that choice was made wisely, right? I hoped Brett would understand.

I broke eye contact with Nick and glanced down at my lap, trying to corral my rampaging thoughts. Brett was coming over for dinner tomorrow night. I'd talk to him then. It wasn't going to be easy. Brett was a nice guy and the thought of hurting him made me feel horrible. But the thought of Nick slipping through my fingers, of never knowing what might have been, made me feel even worse.

When I looked back, Nick had turned to Josh, apparently taking my averted eyes as a sign that I'd passed on his final offer. "Sign me up." He pulled out his credit card and plunked it down on the desk in front of Josh.

Josh quickly input the information, then slid the card back to Nick.

"Let me write your bio, too," I told Nick.

He shrugged. "What the hell. You made Josh sound like James Bond. Go ahead. Take a stab at it."

I pulled the computer toward me and stared at the screen. How could I sabotage Nick's chances of meeting an attractive woman without making it obvious? After some thought and tinkering, I formulated a bio sure to turn women off.

Avid sports fan and fishing enthusiast seeks a woman who is attractive, self-reliant, and tolerant.

Any woman with half a brain would read between the lines and form a vision of Nick as a guy who'd neglect his girlfriend in favor of watching ESPN and spending weekends on the lake with his fishing buddies and a case of beer. Not to mention that the term "self-reliant" implied he'd be a poor provider who'd expect her to go Dutch on their dates and "tolerant" equated with "I don't want to listen to any bitching about my bad habits."

Nick and Josh read what I'd written. I mentally crossed my fingers, hoping they wouldn't catch on to my subterfuge.

"You think it says enough about me?" Nick asked.

"Less is more," I said. "Women like a little mystery."

Josh handed me his phone to snap photos of the two of them for their profiles. Getting a decent photo of Josh took several attempts. In the first, his open-mouth smile made him look like the Gerber Baby. He looked pouty in the second. The third would do.

I snapped several photos of Nick, trying to get his bad side. Unfortunately, Nick didn't seem to have a bad side. He looked manly and sexy and absolutely gorgeous in each and every shot. *Damn him.*

Finally, he ran out of patience and shot me an exasperated look. "Aren't you done yet?"

Snap.

"This is the one," I said, holding out the phone.

Nick took a look and frowned. "I look grumpy."

"No, you don't," I lied. "You look dark and dangerous. That's what women like."

He took another look at the photo, his expression skeptical. "If you say so."

Lu poked her head in the door. "Y'all having a party in here or what?"

"Nick and Josh are signing up for an online dating service," I said, standing from my seat. "They needed a female opinion on their profiles."

Lu crossed her arms over her ample bosom. "Uncle Sam doesn't pay you boys to chase skirts," she snapped at Nick and Josh. "He pays you to hunt down tax evaders and squeeze 'em dry."

"Speaking of dry," Nick said, motioning the Lobo into his office, "you've been in a dry spell for too long, Lu. Your husband's been dead for, what, ten years? It's time for you to get back in the game. Let's get you signed up, too."

Lu's face flashed surprise. "Me?" She blinked her false lashes. "Really?"

"Sure," Nick said. "There's men of all ages on here looking for love. A woman as hot as you? Heck, you'd have to beat them off with a stick."

Lu's bright-orange lips fought a smile. "You're as full of crap as the bull pen at the rodeo," she said. "But God bless you for it." She shooed me out of the way and plunked her plump butt down in the chair I'd just vacated. "Okay, boys, how does this online dating thing work?"

chapter three

The Wheels on the Bus Don't Always Go Round and Round

At home that evening, I ignored the dirty laundry spilling out of my hamper and sat down on my couch to watch some television and take a fresh look at the information on the terrorist case.

A half hour later I closed the file Lu had given me and shut my eyes, shaking my head as if I could dislodge the horrifying images in my brain. The file had been compiled by the CIA and Homeland Security and contained a number of photos depicting the aftermath of terror plots. Homes destroyed, the families' personal belongings strewn about. Bodies covered with blood-soaked blankets and lined up on the ground, awaiting identification and burial by grief-stricken relatives. A yellow school bus, the bright color at odds with the gaping hole in its side and the tattered young bodies being pulled from the wreckage.

The worst thing I'd faced in elementary school was an oversized bully intent on robbing me of my lunch money. I hadn't considered myself lucky when my arm had been pulled up painfully behind me, but everything's relative, isn't it? I'd take a bully over a roadside bomb any day.

I'd faced some scary people in the few months I'd worked for the IRS, but none quite as heartless, as ruthless, *as soulless* as these terrorists.

They had to be stopped.

And the way to stop them was by cutting off their money supply.

Agents at the CIA and Homeland Security knew that money had been sent from the United States to fund terror cells in the Middle East, Asia, and Africa. After receiving tips from undercover agents overseas, they were able to identify some of the financiers. Several lived right here in Dallas and had been arrested after weeks of careful surveillance. E-mails and text messages found on the computers and cell phones of the men linked them to terror cells in Syria.

Unfortunately, the men had been far more cautious about covering their financial tracks. Despite their best efforts, the agents had been unable to track down the money trail and determine how the men had managed to move the funds.

Someone had helped them do it. Someone with the ability to transfer large sums of money undetected.

That's where Eddie and I came in.

As special agents for the Internal Revenue Service, we were among the best-trained financial sleuths in the country. We could trace an extensive series of payments and money transfers back to the original source. We could find assets hidden under multiple layers of corporations, partnerships, and complex trusts. We were financial bloodhounds, able to sniff out even a single copper penny.

Given our mad money skills, we had been solicited to assist the other agencies in finding the financiers' resources and staunching the flow of funds. Unfortunately, none of the information in the file gave me a clue as to how these men were funneling their money out of the United States and into the hands of their coconspirators. Eddie and I had an appointment tomorrow to meet with a CIA operative and a

Homeland Security financial specialist. We hoped they would be able to provide us with more documentation and information that would lead us to the money trail.

My skinny, cream-colored cat, Anne, trotted after me as I went to my kitchen, removed a glass pitcher of homemade peach sangria from the top shelf of my refrigerator, and poured myself a full glass over ice. Nick's mother had given me the sangria recipe. I'd modified it slightly, adding two or three spiced peaches to the other fresh fruit in the mix. Brett had brought me a dozen jars of the peaches when he'd returned after a monthlong project at a country club in Atlanta. The club's chef had prepared them and they were, well, absolutely peachy. Apparently all the food at the club had been superb. Weeks later, Brett still blathered on about the wonderful meals he'd enjoyed there.

Thinking of Brett caused a flood of guilt to flow through me. He'd be blindsided tomorrow when I told him I wanted to put the brakes on our relationship, at least temporarily. For all I knew, once Nick and I started dating we might realize we weren't right for each other after all. If that happened, I could only hope Brett would be willing to give things a second chance. If not, well, I'd end up alone again, back at square one. Hell, maybe I'd be the next one signing up for the Big D Dating Service.

I gulped down the glass of fruity wine and poured myself another, hoping if I drank enough it would wash away the horrible, tragic images burned into my mind and the guilt gnawing at my insides. But I feared there wasn't enough sangria in the world to make me feel better.

"Ready?" asked Eddie from the doorway of my office the next morning at eleven. Eddie held his briefcase in his left hand, his gray suit jacket slung over his right shoulder.

"Ready as I'll ever be." I took a deep breath to steady myself, shoved the file and a legal pad into my briefcase, and grabbed my purse from the bottom drawer of my desk.

Although we'd been granted a brief reprieve in the terrorism case when one of the men who'd been arrested had agreed to talk in return for leniency, the lawyers hadn't worked out the details fast enough and word spread through the jailhouse grapevine that the man was going to spill the beans. His tongue had been promptly cut out, presumably by one of his coconspirators. Needless to say, his offer to talk was no longer on the table. We'd have to hunt down the clues ourselves.

My head throbbed as I followed Eddie down the hall to the elevators. In retrospect, three glasses of sangria last night might have been a bad idea. Not only did I have a headache now, but I'd had to get up twice during the night to pee. On the bright side, though, I'd received my recommended daily allowance of vitamin C.

We exited the building and walked in silence the few blocks to the Homeland Security field office on Main. Eddie had obviously found the information and photos in the file as disturbing as I had, perhaps even more so. His young daughters normally rode a bus to school, but I had a sneaking suspicion he'd driven them to school that morning himself.

We made our way through the security line on the first floor, took the stairs up one flight, and continued down the hall, checking the nameplates on the doors. We found the name we were looking for on the third door on the left.

Chung Wang.

Eddie rapped twice on the door, opening it when a male voice from within called out, inviting us to enter.

The office was small, white, and windowless, lit by a rectangular fluorescent fixture on the ceiling. The walls were lined with gray filing cabinets, which, judging from the stacks of files on top of them, were insufficient to hold Wang's workload. He stood from his seat behind his desk and extended his hand over yet another pile of files on his desk.

"Special Agent Tara Holloway," I said, taking his hand and giving it a firm shake.

Wang had the typical Chinese build, slightly shorter than average, lean but wiry. He appeared to be around thirty years of age, no gray yet in his short black hair. He wore a standard white dress shirt, the sleeves rolled up to the elbows. Working hard, no doubt.

Eddie took Wang's hand next.

A knock sounded behind us, the fourth of our party, the agent from the CIA, having arrived. Eddie and I stepped aside to allow him in.

Like Chung Wang, this agent had black hair, brown skin, and appeared to be in his early thirties. He wore wire-framed glasses and an argyle sweater-vest in green and blue over a short-sleeved white cotton shirt. He looked like a Persian Urkel. I mentally dubbed him Perkel.

"Azad Zardooz," the guy said, extending his hand and stepping forward.

So not Perkel, then.

I shook his hand and glanced around at the dark-haired, dark-skinned men. "Wow, I feel awfully—"

"Pale?" Eddie provided, shooting me a look.

He'd hit the nail on the head, but once he'd put it out in the open I realized how politically incorrect it sounded, even if there was no malicious intent behind it. I decided to go with "female" instead.

"Don't worry," Zardooz assured me as he shook Eddie's hand next. "This isn't a boys' club."

I raised a fist in celebration. "Hooray for ovaries!"

His brows drew together. He looked at Eddie. "Is she always like this?"

"Twenty-four-seven," Eddie said. "She's the most embarrassing partner I've ever had."

"Maybe so." I pointed a finger in his face. "But I'm the best with a gun."

Eddie lifted his chin in acquiescence. "I have to give you that."

Agent Wang invited us to take seats around his desk and handed each of us a second file, this one far thicker and heavier than the initial file we'd been provided. I looked inside and found copies of bank statements, credit card bills, check registers, ATM receipts, and other miscellaneous financial information, including a pay stub from a small biotech company and another from Texas Instruments, one of the area's major employers. There was even a grocery store receipt that included Oreo cookies.

"I've been through all the documentation," Wang said, "and it led me nowhere. These guys operate primarily on a cash basis. You'll notice that several large withdrawals were made from their accounts each month, but there was nothing to tell me how they got that money out of the country."

Agent Wang was intelligent and well trained, too, so I wasn't sure whether Eddie and I would have any more luck than he had. But it never hurt to have a fresh set of eyes look things over.

Zardooz glanced at his watch. "I'd like to give you two some background on the men involved. How about we discuss this further over lunch?"

"Sure," Eddie said.

"Works for me," Wang said, standing from his chair.

"Any suggestions?" Zardooz asked.

The men turned to me. As I looked at Azad and Chung, the federal government's answer to Harold and Kumar, a particular restaurant came to mind.

Eddie held up a hand. "Don't you dare say 'White Castle.'"

Sheez. The guy could read my mind.

"Dallas doesn't have White Castle," I shot back. "How about Twisted Root?" The place had an awesome black bean burger, not to mention their yummy sweet potato chips and fried pickles.

"Is that the place that serves kangaroo?" Wang asked.

"Only when it's in season." I replied. They also served alligator, venison, boar, and ostrich, not that there were many takers from what I'd seen. The downtown crowd didn't want to chow down on a Bambi or Big Bird burger.

"Let's hit it," Zardooz said.

We loaded our new files in our briefcases and headed out.

Over lunch, Zardooz shared some intriguing bits of information. In his younger days, he'd infiltrated an Al-Qaeda training camp and learned some of their techniques firsthand. He showed us a photo of himself from a decade earlier. With his turban, full beard, and machine gun he looked nothing like the nerdy agent who sat before us sipping a Coke and dipping his French fries in ketchup.

"Those camps are crazy places," he said. He went on to explain that the strategy of the camp leaders was to visit poor villages where they could easily recruit young men and boys who had little or no prospects for the future. They'd move the recruits to remote camps in wilderness areas. Once at the camps, the recruits were deprived of sleep, exercised to the point of exhaustion, and fed a steady diet of lies to incite them against the rest of the world.

The tactics were similar to those used by cults. Isolation. Sleep deprivation. Brainwashing. I had to admit there were some eerie similarities to a summer church camp I'd once attended in Louisiana. Whatever spell the staff had cast over us campers was broken, however, when we caught the head counselor in the woods with a copy of *Playboy* in one hand and his ding-dong in the other.

Zardooz continued. "The leaders convince the recruits they're doing something worthy and heroic when they're only being used to further a horribly warped interpretation of Islam." Sadly, many volunteered for suicide missions, hoping to become martyrs. "These extremists haven't just given Islam a bad name," he said. "They've made life very hard for mainstream Muslims. A man once ripped off my wife's hijab when she was shopping in Walmart."

No man had a right to touch any woman without her permission, especially to do something as heinous as tearing off her head scarf. I wish I could say the reprehensible act surprised me, but alas it did not. For a country founded on religious freedom, America was full of ignorance, intolerance, and distrust. I felt bad for Zardooz and other Muslims who'd suffered prejudice due to the acts of a small faction of extremists. It was no different from judging all Christians based on the radical few who murdered abortion doctors or judging all Jewish people based on the bombings carried out by the Jewish Defense League.

Zardooz reached into his back pocket and removed a small envelope. Inside the envelope were wallet-sized photos of the three men who'd been arrested here in Dallas. Zardooz handed one set to me, another to Eddie.

I spread the photos out on the table in front of me and looked them over. I wasn't sure what I had expected to see, but it certainly wasn't the ordinary-looking men in the photos. All three were clean shaven, with short dark hair and light brown skin. They appeared to be in their late twenties, around my age. One wore a business suit and tie in his photo; the other two wore dress shirts. Though none smiled, their expressions were in no way threatening. Had I not known these benign-looking men were terrorists, I would've assumed they were no different from the thousands of other immigrants who had come to the United States seeking education, work, and a better life.

Agent Zardooz pointed to each photo in turn. "Their names are Radwan Algafari, Karam Homsi, and Hani Nasser."

While the sounds rolled off his tongue, I knew I'd stumble over the unfamiliar names.

"All three men were raised in very rigid, fundamentalist families," Zardooz continued. "They went to school together in Syria, then immigrated to the United States to attend college at the University of Texas."

Whoa. These guys had attended UT, my alma mater? Scary to think I might have crossed paths with terrorists on campus. Then again, the university was no stranger to terror. In 1966, a student named Charles Whitman purchased scopes and an arsenal of rifles, murdered his wife and mother in their home, then ascended to the observation deck of the administration building tower and proceeded shooting randomly at those down on the campus and streets below. In the end, sixteen people lay dead and more than thirty others were wounded. More recently, in 2010, a student with an AK-47 opened fire on campus. The university was better prepared this time and went into immediate lockdown mode. Fortunately, no others were injured this time around, though the shooter took his own life in the main library. I'd been lucky there'd been no incidents during my period of attendance.

"Algafari was an engineering major," Zardooz informed us. "Nasser studied chemistry and Homsi majored in physics."

Smart guys, huh? Too bad they didn't use their intelligence for good instead of evil.

Zardooz went on to tell us that Algafari and Nasser obtained jobs in Dallas after completing college, while Homsi went to work for a small start-up company in neighboring Fort Worth. They'd stayed in close contact and sometimes prayed together. They traveled back to Syria often and maintained close ties to their relatives and homeland. The CIA had obtained extensive evidence linking them to acts of terror that had taken place in and around Syria at the times the men were visiting their native country. One of those acts involved the school bus.

A queasiness invaded my stomach at the mention of the bus. Luckily, the agent spared us the gory details and moved on to other matters.

Zardooz looked from me to Eddie. "How much do you two know about Arab history?"

Eddie and I exchanged glances. Sure, we heard snippets about events in the Arab world all the time on the news. Another car bomb had exploded; another embassy had been firebombed; another political leader had been assassinated. The snippets failed to provide a complete picture, however. What information was available seemed confusing and contradictory, complicated and conflicting. To make matters worse, allegiances were tenuous and constantly shifting. Countries that fought side by side in one war would be at each other's throats not long afterward.

Admittedly I'd never bothered to research the issues in detail. It wasn't that I didn't care; it's just that I got my fill of violence on my job. I lived in Dallas, thousands of miles away from these Arab countries, and had no control over the events that took place there. Heck, I paid just as little attention to the political unrest here in America. I never did quite get that whole "Occupy Wall Street" movement. I hated corporate fat cats as much as the next guy, but where would the little guy be if his bank went kaput? Honestly, I couldn't tell who was right and who was wrong in many cases. I didn't have the answers. Plus, Neiman's was usually having a shoe sale. A 30 percent discount could be quite distracting. No doubt Eddie also found little time to devote to world politics. Between his job as a special agent and his duties as a husband, father of twin girls, and soccer coach the guy was lucky to find a spare ten minutes to take a peek at a Mavericks game.

Yep, as ashamed as I was to admit it, to a certain degree I was one of those people who'd rather stick her head in the sand and pretend the world is a happy, sunshiny place full of nice people. I knew it was naïve and wrong, but the alternative was to be upset and depressed all the time, wasn't it? Who wants to live like that? Besides, it wasn't like I was doing nothing. I contributed to human rights groups. Just take a look at the charitable deductions on my last tax return.

"What do we know about Arab history?" I repeated, eyeing Zardooz. "Try squat."

"Okay," Zardooz said, thankfully accepting our ignorance without an eye roll or sigh. "Back in the seventh century, the prophet Muhammad—"

Zardooz was interrupted when Agent Wang tossed a fried green bean at him. "We don't have all day, dude. Bring it up to this century, at least."

Zardooz picked up the green bean, dipped it into Wang's chipotle ranch sauce, and took a bite. "All right. You two have heard of the 'Arab Spring,' right?"

Eddie and I nodded. Our heads had not been *completely* up our asses.

Zardooz gave us a quick rundown. In recent months, many of those living in the Arab world had reached the limits of their tolerance and revolted against their country's oppressive regimes. This so-called Arab Spring led to rulers being forced from power in Tunisia, Egypt, Libya, and Yemen. While lesser protests took place in Algeria, Iraq, Jordan, Kuwait, and Morocco, serious civil uprisings occurred in Bahrain and Syria. The clashes were often violent, with thousands killed as a result.

Militant groups took advantage of the recent unrest to unleash further terror across the Arab world. But attacking thousands of people ain't cheap. When they needed funds for weapons and bomb-making materials, they'd hit up their cohorts here in Dallas, playing on their emotions, reminding the men that while they lived in their cushy apartments in the relatively safe United States their family members were risking their lives overseas. It was like some type of sick, sadistic soap opera, with psychological manipulation, constant strife, and goals and motivations that were far from clear.

Still, despite what I'd been told and the evidence I'd been given, I didn't want to accept the facts. The men who'd been arrested lived and worked in this country, interacted with Americans on a daily basis, ate Oreos just like the rest of us. How could they enjoy the freedoms this country offered while supporting radicals who murdered their former neighbors and countrymen back in their homelands? Couldn't they see that, by and large, people all over the world were basically good?

I supposed it was pointless to even try to make sense of their thinking. Their acts could never be rationalized or justified.

Our history lesson now completed, I turned to Wang. "What have you done so far in the investigation?"

"The usual. Searched their homes and cars. Talked to their coworkers and neighbors. Visited their banks." He took a sip of his iced tea. "Our next step is to visit MSBs near their homes and workplaces, see if any of them sent the funds overseas."

Treasury regulations not only included provisions to prevent and detect money laundering, but they also prohibited trade between Americans and certain foreign persons and entities suspected in the promotion of terrorism. Money services businesses, often referred to as MSBs, were subject to extensive regulation to prevent illegal financing. The regulations covered a wide range of financial transactions and gave the government broad authority over any business that cashed checks, performed wire transfers, or sold money orders, traveler's checks, or foreign currency.

In most legitimate financial transactions, funds were transferred directly from the payer's account at one institution to the recipient's account at another, with neither party actually handling cash. In such cases, banking records provided a clear money trail. Cash, however, was an entirely different matter. Large cash transactions were unusual these days and, therefore, suspicious. Because cash was essentially untraceable, it was often used in criminal activity. Thus, the Bank Secrecy Act required MSBs to report cash transactions involving amounts of ten thousand dollars or more.

Recent legislation had been passed to cover loopholes related to the sale or redemption of prepaid stored-value cards, which could easily be purchased in the United States and sent overseas to prohibited parties for redemption. Cash-for-gold transactions were also now subject to record-keeping requirements after it was discovered that gold bars and jewelry had been used as a means of illegally moving assets between the United States and foreign countries. Unfortunately, regulations were often reactive rather than proactive, with the laws put in place only after a scheme had been discovered.

Agent Wang pulled out three copies of a computer-generated map and an accompanying list with addresses for local MSBs. The list covered a diverse range of businesses, including liquor stores, tobacco shops, travel agencies, gas stations, grocery stores, convenience stores, and bus terminals. Heck, there was even a state correctional facility on the list.

"I've divided up the list," Wang said. "With three of us working on this, we should be able to visit each of the businesses within the next few weeks."

I took my copy from him and ran my eyes over it. Many of the MSBs were located in the North Dallas sector that surrounded the TI location where one of the men arrested had worked as a product engineer. *Sheesh*. I wondered if any of his coworkers had suspected him of links to terror cells overseas. I hoped he hadn't programmed any of the products to explode. It would be an awful shame for some high school sophomore to be working on his geometry homework and have his TI calculator burst into flaming shards.

The cosine of B = *KABLOOEY!*

"Be careful," Zardooz warned. "We know that whoever helped the men move their money is on the loose, but it's possible there are others still out there, too."

Eddie's brows drew together. "Say what?"

"We're not certain we got all the terrorists," Zardooz clarified. "Some of the communications we intercepted implied there was another here in the Dallas area, but we feared we'd lose the main targets if we waited any longer to bring them in. They had plans to return to Syria shortly."

"These men don't play games and they don't like getting caught." Wang shot us a meaningful look. "Don't let your guard down."

chapter four

O ld Flames

Eddie and I returned to the IRS office and stepped off the elevator. Voices from down the hall drew my attention to Lu's office, where she sat in her high-backed chair behind her enormous desk, Josh and Nick flanking her on either side. The three huddled, looking down at her computer screen.

While Eddie headed back to his office, curiosity led me to the Lobo's digs. I stopped in the doorway. "What's up?"

Lu glanced up through her false eyelashes. "We're checking the results from Big D Dating Service, seeing if we've got any hits."

I stepped into her office, taking a place next to Nick. He glanced down at me. Though I gave him a smile, his face remained impassive. Surely his response would be different if he knew I planned to talk to Brett tonight, to make arrangements to take Nick for a test-drive.

The three checked Josh's account first.

His cherubic face lit up when he noted he'd had a response. Just one, but that was all he needed, right? He reached down and maneuvered the mouse, clicking on the link. The screen brought up a photo of a skinny young woman with white-blond hair pulled up into two long pigtails on either side of her head. Her blue eyes were opened wide, giving her a youthful, innocent look. She wore a white short-sleeved sailor-style top with a blue collar that ended in a big red bow over her chest.

"Does she work for a cruise line?" I asked.

"No." Josh rolled his eyes. "She's dressed as Sailor Moon."

"Sailor *who*?"

"Sailor Moon," he repeated. "She's an anime character."

No wonder I hadn't recognized her. I knew less than squat about anime, though I could quote Homer Simpson, Hank Hill, and SpongeBob SquarePants verbatim. Hey, I'm not totally uncultured.

"She fights evil by moonlight," Josh said, "and wins love by daylight."

"The girl who responded to your ad?"

"No!" Another eye roll. "Sailor Moon."

"Oh." I supposed I was a bit like Sailor Moon, though I generally fought evil between 8:00 AM and 5:00 PM and preferred to win my love in the more romantic evening hours.

Josh read from the screen. "The bio says her name is Kira and she's a freelance Web designer."

Another tech nerd. "She sounds perfect for you, Josh."

Lu took control of the mouse and pulled up her account next. She'd received three responses. The first was from a forty-year-old man with greasy hair and a sleazy grin. "No thanks," Lu told the screen. "I'm not a tiger mom."

"I think you mean cougar," I said.

She waved a hand dismissively. "Whatever. I'm not dating someone my son's age." She clicked on the second link. This potential suitor had the opposite problem. He was a man in his late eighties looking for a "nurturing" woman. Lu's lips pursed in disgust. "That's just a nice way of saying he wants someone to change his diapers."

While Nick, Josh, and I leaned in, she pulled up the third

respondent. This guy was sixty-five, which made him age appropriate for Lu. The bio indicated his name was Carl. He wore a navy-blue polyester leisure suit with visible white stitching around the collar and buttonholes, along with black plastic horn-rimmed eyeglasses.

"He's very fashionable," Lü said, gesturing at the screen. "He's wearing those new stylish glasses that are so popular."

Nick and I exchanged glances. Carl's glasses weren't the geek chic look that was in vogue today. No, his were definitely original horn-rims from the 1950s. To make matters worse, the guy had a horrid comb-over. Well, maybe "comb-over" was the wrong word. "Comb-forward/comb-across" would be more precise. His hair, which appeared to originate on the back and sides of his neck, had been combed up and over his bald dome in a sort of crisscross pattern, like a hairnet made of real hair. He'd glued the stuff in place with Brylcreem.

I looked at Lu, taking in her pinkish-orange beehive, false eyelashes, and lemon-yellow dress trimmed in purple rickrack. Perhaps I shouldn't be so hard on Comb-over Carl. He could be just the guy for Lu.

Josh put a hand on the mouse. "Let's check your responses, Nick."

As Nick leaned in closer to the screen, a slight twinge of guilt tightened my gut. Poor guy. He still didn't realize I'd sabotaged him with that horrible bio and angry photo. I hoped he wouldn't feel bad when he learned there'd been no interest.

Josh clicked the mouse. "Holy crap!" he cried, his eyes wide as he turned from the screen to look up at Nick. "You've got seventy-three responses."

What!?!

I leaned in closer now, too. Yep, sure enough, seventy-three women had responded to Nick's ad. Well, make that seventy-two women and one guy named Sergio who encouraged Nick to "be open to new experiences" and "take a walk on the wild side."

To my surprise, Nick didn't look so much excited by the

responses as exhausted. Josh clicked on each of them in turn, taking us through a long line of women with abundant cleavage, excessive lip gloss, and biographies containing far too many exclamation points.

Maddie, a blue-eyed blonde, was a "party girl!!!" who was sure she and Nick would "hit it off!!!"

Kaitlyn was a green-eyed redhead who "enjoyed wine! Music! Dancing!" and thought Nick looked "sexy and fun!"

Shea was an African-American woman with cute short curls. She was a "Dallas Mavericks Dancer and a big sports fan!" who thought she and Nick would have "an awesome time together!"

No fewer than a third of the bios noted that the woman enjoyed long walks on the beach. Seriously? Dallas was three hundred miles from the nearest beach. That was indeed a long walk.

"If I were you," I told Nick, "I'd give Sergio a try. Look at those biceps. He definitely works out."

Nick shot me a look before turning back to Josh. "They're all running together. Is there a way to sort them?"

"How about by IQ?" I suggested, my sarcasm earning me another exasperated look from Nick. Hey, he was the one who said he wanted a woman with some brains.

"Try sorting them by breast size," he told Josh, earning himself an indignant grunt from me.

"I thought you were an ass man," I said. He'd told me so himself after a well-endowed reporter named Trish Le-Grande had made me feel inadequate when Nick and I were working together on an earlier case.

Nick eyed me again and shrugged. "Maybe my tastes have changed."

Ouch. That hurt. Like a knife in the heart. He wasn't over me already, was he? Just when I'd decided to take a shot with him?

Josh pulled up the next potential candidate and Nick sat bolt upright, his eyes wide.

What was that about?

Lu squinted at the screen. "Natalie. She looks like a nice

girl." Lu glanced up at Nick, then back at the screen, then back at Nick. "Wait a minute. Isn't she that woman you almost married?"

Nick nodded, his gaze still locked on the screen, a faraway look in his eyes.

The knife in my heart turned and twisted, like a sharp corkscrew working its way to my core. I knew Nick had been engaged years ago, but he'd never talked much about it other than to say his job as a special agent had been a problem in their relationship, just as it was sometimes a problem in my relationship with Brett. Our jobs were demanding and risky and often took us away at inopportune times. Not everyone could deal with it.

Nick's reaction was strange. Did he still have feelings for this woman? And did she still have feelings for him? Of course she did. Why else would she have responded to his ad?

Did Natalie want Nick back?

I looked at the screen. The photo showed a dark-haired girl with sweet brown eyes, a scattering of freckles, and a figure that bordered between voluptuous and pleasantly plump. She was dressed modestly in a pink cotton blouse buttoned high enough to keep her cleavage completely under wraps.

If ever there was a girl-next-door, Natalie was her. I was more like the girl down the block with bare feet and a frog in her pocket, hanging upside down from a tree branch.

I looked back at Nick. He stood stock-still, as if transfixed.

Dammit! I was about to dump Brett for him. Was he still hung up on his ex-fiancée? Was I about to make a big mistake?

I couldn't take it. I had to get out of that office. "Good luck with the dates," I managed as I bolted from the room, blinking back tears of frustration.

Just when I thought I had things sorted out they got all screwed up again.

I'd better move fast or I could lose Nick forever and spend the rest of my life wondering what might have been.

chapter five

$\mathcal{B}$reaking Up Is Hard to Do

Tuesday after work, I stopped by a neighborhood Italian restaurant and picked up two orders of manicotti to take home. I was about to break Brett's heart. The least I could do was fill his stomach first.

Despite the delicious smells emanating from the take-out bag, I wasn't sure I'd be able to eat. My stomach had shrunk into a tight little ball.

Brett and I had been dating for a few months now, ever since last spring when we'd met at a charity event at the Dallas Arboretum. The firm he worked for had sponsored the event. Brett had taken my ticket and captured my interest. For several months things had seemed nearly perfect. But then Nick came along and got me all discombobulated.

I greeted my cats as I came through the door with my briefcase in one hand and the bag of food in the other. Henry, my oversized Maine coon, glanced my way from atop the TV cabinet with his usual look of disdain. Anne scampered out from under the couch and followed me to the kitchen, interrogating me all the while. *Meow? Meow? Meow?*

I glanced down at her. "You ask too many questions, you know that, Annie girl?" Despite the third degree she'd given me, I fed her a tuna treat and ruffled her ears affectionately once I'd deposited my briefcase and the food on the counter.

On my drive home, I had convinced myself that Nick's reaction to seeing Natalie's photograph was perfectly natural and didn't mean anything. He hadn't seen her since they'd called off their engagement shortly before a violent money launderer forced Nick into a three-year exile in Mexico. If she'd still meant anything to him, he would have looked her up himself, right? Sure. It had only been the surprise of seeing her face come up on the screen that had set him aback. No sense postponing my *let's-take-a-break* discussion with Brett.

It had been a while since I'd broken up with a guy, so I was a little out of practice. One of my college boyfriends had made breaking up with him easy. Telling someone you never wanted to see him again was fairly easy when he showed up at your door with a hickey on his neck that you hadn't put there. *Jeez.* Did the guy think I was blind? Most of my other breakups had been relatively amicable, the fact that the relationship wasn't going anywhere obvious to both of us. But with Brett things would be difficult, especially since I wasn't exactly breaking up with him for good. Rather, I'd just be seeking permission to date another man and evaluate my feelings before making a more definite decision.

I was scared, to be honest. Part of me still wondered whether it could be a mistake, whether raising the subject would backfire on me. There would be things about Brett I'd miss, like playing with his dogs at the park, laughing together over ridiculous British comedies, daringly sampling unusual ethnic foods. Heck, Nick thought an egg roll was an extreme culinary adventure.

Still, as much as I adored Brett, there was no denying that Nick and I were more alike at the core, that we understood better what made each other tick. The fact that I could totally be myself with Nick said a lot, too. It wasn't that I had to hide my feisty side from Brett, because he often found my unconventional nature to be exciting. But he worried about me, too. Despite my pledge to be honest with him, I found myself conveniently leaving out the details of my job that would cause him anxiety. And as classy and sophisticated as Brett's parents were, they could sometimes be a tad too conventional. Nick's mother, on the other hand, was warm and open and down-to-earth, the kind of woman who would make a wonderful mother-in-law and grandmother.

I dragged myself upstairs and changed into a pair of wrinkled jeans I scrounged from the floor. I really needed to get on my laundry. The pile had expanded from the hamper to a laundry basket beside it.

I slid out of my work shirt and into a T-shirt I'd picked up at a Toby Keith concert a couple of years ago. I didn't bother freshening up my makeup or brushing my hair. If I didn't look too good, maybe Brett would find it easier to let me go.

I went back downstairs to wait, pouring a tumbler of peach sangria to fortify myself. I simultaneously dreaded what I had to do and wanted to get it over with as soon as possible. I wished someone would invent a time machine so I could fast-forward to tomorrow morning, when I'd tell Nick I was a free woman and wanted to give the two of us a try.

I wondered how Nick would react when he heard the news. Would he grab me in a hug? Maybe plant a big ol' kiss on me?

Dare I dream of more?

I glanced at the clock. Brett wouldn't be here for a quarter hour. Just enough time to call my mother and fill her in. She'd encouraged me to give Nick a shot when she'd met him a few weeks back. She'd be glad to hear I was finally heeding her advice.

I dialed my parents' home number, and after the usual preliminaries—"I'm fine," "the cats are fine," "the weather's fine"—I told Mom about my plans to put Brett on the back burner.

"I know it'll be hard, hon," she said, "but you're doing the right thing."

"I hope so."

"I *know* so."

Sounded like Mom was speaking from experience. "Oh, yeah?"

"Yeah," she said. "Did I ever tell you about Candy Cummings?"

"Sounds like a stripper name."

"It does, doesn't it?" My mother harrumphed. "Candy was this cute little thing on the drill team. Your dad had a crush on her our senior year of high school."

What? My parents had been high-school sweethearts. They'd met their sophomore year in biology class and married just a year after their graduation. They seemed so content, so perfect for each other, that I'd assumed their relationship had been smooth sailing from the start. Had this Candy been a bump in their road?

Mom sighed. "I caught your father sneaking glances at Candy several times in the cafeteria. She was a total twit, but something about her got your father's motor running."

Urk. I didn't want to think about my father's motor, running or not.

"Anyway, I knew if he didn't take Candy for a whirl he'd spend the rest of his life pining for that high-kicking nitwit. I wanted him to be sure about me. So I cut him loose for a while."

"If you love something, set it free?"

"Exactly."

"And what happened?" I asked.

"The two of them fell in love, moved to a castle, and lived happily ever after."

Obviously that didn't happen or I wouldn't have been having this conversation. "Smart-ass."

For once, Mom didn't threaten to break out the Ivory soap and wash my mouth. She must've realized she'd earned the curse. "Your dad took Candy out on a couple of dates. Meanwhile, I went out a few times with the captain of the chess club, a boy named Randall. Smart as a whip. He'd grown a few inches over the summer and gotten his braces off, and heck if he hadn't become quite the catch. He had all kinds of potential, too. Ended up becoming a research scientist. Last I heard he was working on a new treatment for diabetes."

I glanced at the clock. Only five minutes now until Brett's ETA. "Can you get to the point, Mom?"

"Okay, hon. Point is, once your dad spent some time with Candy, he realized that as cute as she was, she wasn't the right girl for him. She was shallow and spiteful and full of herself. He came running back to me."

"And you welcomed him back with open arms?"

"Heck, no! I made him beg and plead and make a fool of himself for me first."

Mom might be forgiving, but she wasn't a pushover. "Good for you." The fact that Dad groveled said a lot, too. He was a proud man, not prone to displays of humility. If he'd been willing to beg to get her back, he must have known, without a doubt, that Mom was the girl for him.

I hoped that Brett would be as understanding as my mother had been when I asked for a chance to try things out with Nick. I also hoped Brett would give me a second chance if things with Nick didn't pan out. I hoped, too, that I wasn't being overly hopeful.

"You know," Mom said, "I should look up that Randall on Facebook."

Dad might have gotten over Candy, but that wistful note in my mother's voice told me Randall might be the one she thought about on those cold and lonely winter nights when Dad and my brothers went off to the deer lease. Maybe she dreamed about Randall putting her in checkmate or capturing her queen.

"Speaking of high school," she said. "We've got our forty-year reunion coming up. I was thinking I'd come to Dallas on Saturday to look for a new dress to wear."

"So you can look good for Randall?" I teased.

"So I can look good *for your father*," she said, after a brief pause adding, "okay, maybe for Randall, too."

A knock sounded at the door and, despite my mother's pep talk, a sick feeling came over me.

"Gotta go, Mom. See you Saturday." I ended the call,

shoved the phone into my pocket, and opened the door to find Brett on the porch. With his sandy hair, boyish good looks, and lean but muscular build, he was easy on the eyes.

Brett wore a suit tonight. His job as a landscape architect required him to be two people—a smart businessman who could land high-dollar contracts for major landscaping projects and an artist of sorts who used foliage as his medium. He was good at both sides of the business, earning him a reputation as the must-have landscape designer in Dallas. His reputation was beginning to spread nationwide as well. The country club gig he'd recently completed in Atlanta had put him on the short list of potential landscapers for an extensive job at a resort in Palm Springs that was undergoing renovation.

As we sat at my kitchen table eating our manicotti—well, Brett was eating his while I was merely poking mine with a fork and moving it around on my plate—I took a good, hard look at him, knowing it might be one of my last. Brett was a caring and thoughtful guy, intelligent and hardworking, too. His skills in the sack weren't bad, either.

But whether he was *The One* remained to be seen.

Still, even though I'd fortified myself with a glass of sangria, I felt my conviction slipping as I looked at Brett. I drank another glass, only half-listening to Brett prattle on about a big new gig he'd landed with the city of Grand Prairie's Parks and Recreation Department, the upcoming fall planting season, expected rainfall amounts predicted by *The Old Farmer's Almanac*. My thoughts now loosened somewhat by the alcohol, I realized if I wasn't convinced by now that Brett was the man I was meant to spend my life with, I owed it to myself to take a chance with Nick. Yep, as hard as it would be, telling Brett we needed to take a break was the right thing to do.

When we finished the manicotti, I rinsed the dishes and stuck them in the dishwasher. Despite the two glasses of sangria I'd polished off, my nerves were still on edge. I led Brett to the living room, but rather than sitting next to him on the couch for our usual presex make-out session, I took a seat on one of the chairs. He cocked his head and gave me a questioning look.

Damn! Did he have to look so sweet and concerned and unsuspecting? I felt as if I were about to kick a puppy.

I took a deep breath, looked at Brett, looked away, looked back at him. No sense putting things off any longer. This wasn't going to get any easier. It was now or never, Tara. "Brett, I—"

Bam!

My front door flew open and banged against the wall of the foyer as my best friend, Alicia Shenkman, stormed in. As always, Alicia was impeccably dressed in designer jeans, wedges, and a black tunic-style top with a red sash around her waist. Her platinum hair hung in asymmetrical, angular lines on either side of her face. Ultrachic.

As much as I loved Alicia, her timing tonight totally sucked. I regretted giving her a key to my place, at least until I saw her face contort in grief. Something was wrong. Something big. She rarely cried. She didn't like to risk runny mascara.

I stood from my chair. "What's wrong, Alicia?"

"Men suck!" she shrieked.

I looked from her to Brett. He looked from me to Alicia. Alicia looked from me to Brett.

"Sorry," Alicia told Brett, choking out her words. "I didn't realize you were here."

"Some kids were tossing a football in the street earlier," he said. "I parked down the block."

Tears began to stream down Alicia's cheeks, leaving the dreaded dark, mascara-tinted rivulets on her skin.

Tears. The cue for any man in the vicinity to hightail it to safer territory.

Brett slowly rose from the couch. "Um . . . I think I'll go, give you two some time alone."

"Thanks, Brett." Alicia flopped onto the couch as soon as he vacated it.

I walked him to the door and he gave me a quick kiss on the forehead.

"We'll talk soon," he said.

I forced a smile I didn't feel. "Sure." He'd told me earlier that he'd be tied up the rest of the week. I wouldn't be able to see him in person again until Friday evening, but I wasn't about to put things on hold with him by phone. That would be disrespectful and wimpy. Unfortunately, this delay meant I'd have to put off telling Nick that I was available.

Damn. Damn, damn, damn!

chapter six

A Friend in Need

As soon as I'd shut the door on Brett, Alicia broke out into an all-out wail. "Three years!" she sobbed. "Three years I've been dating Daniel! And for what? He's never going to marry me!"

She began blubbering so profusely I couldn't understand most of what she was saying, though I made out that Daniel was somehow both "a miserable son of a bitch" and the man of her dreams who she hoped would "rot in hell" yet also "realize what a mistake he'd made and come crawling back."

How long a crawl would it be from hell?

I went to the kitchen, poured Alicia a big glass of peach sangria, and grabbed some napkins. I brought the drink and napkins to her, taking a seat beside her on the couch.

She slugged back the drink in ten seconds flat. Impressive. I hadn't seen her do that since back in our college days when we'd gone barhopping on Sixth Street in Austin.

"My mother was right!" she cried, setting the glass on the coffee table. "Why would a man buy a cow when she's giving away the milk for free?" She bent over, sobbing into the wad of napkins clutched in her hands.

"Come on." I put a hand on her back. "You know that's not true. Marriage isn't just about sex." Heck, from what I could glean from my married coworkers, marriage was hardly about sex at all. Seemed like once people said "I do" they didn't actually *do it* anymore. "Daniel's not like that. He loves you."

"Oh, yeah?" she spat, glancing over at me. "Then why did he freak out when I told him I was tired of shacking up and wanted to get married?"

"You told him that?" I knew Alicia wanted to marry Daniel someday, but I'd never felt any sense of urgency on her part. She loved the yuppie lifestyle, having a professional career, living in a downtown loft, spending her big paychecks on nice clothes at Neiman Marcus and fancy meals at trendy restaurants.

"It just sort of slipped out," she said. "Our neighbor's sister was visiting with her new baby and we saw them on the elevator and something came over me." She dabbed at her eyes. "I realized I'm ready for the next phase, Tara." She dabbed again. "It's clear Daniel isn't."

"He'll come around," I said. "Just give him some time."

She shrugged. "I don't know. We've been together for years. How much more time does he need?" She sighed and slumped back on the sofa, her tears dwindling to a mere trickle. "I'm thinking about putting myself back on the market."

I wasn't sure what to tell her. What did I know about love and relationships? Not much. Fortunately, she was only looking for a sympathetic ear, not advice.

"I've got some news, too." I gave her the full scoop. That I'd decided to give Nick a try. That I'd planned to break things off, at least temporarily, with Brett. That I'd planned to tell Brett tonight.

Her eyes grew wide and she sat up. "Oh, shit. Did I screw that up?"

Royally. "It's fine. I can tell him later." And meanwhile I would pray that Nick hadn't reconciled with Natalie or started something with one of the seventy-one other women who'd expressed an interest in dating him. Of course there was always Sergio, too. Those biceps had indeed been impressive. Maybe if things didn't work out with Nick or Brett, I could convince Sergio to switch teams.

My doorbell rang. "I wonder who that is?" I hadn't expected this many people to come to my door until later in the month for Halloween trick-or-treating.

Alicia put a hand on my arm. "If that's Daniel, tell him I don't want to talk to him. That I need some time to think." Despite her words, her eyes gleamed with hope. She wanted Daniel to track her down here, to prove how much he cared.

I went to the door and put my eye to the peephole.

"Is it Daniel?" Alicia whispered. She'd stood from the sofa and was looking at me expectantly.

I shook my head.

"Figures!" She flopped back onto the couch and began to wail again, muttering about the "stupid jerk" whom she was "so in love with" who she'd hoped would "drop dead" and/or "get his shit together and grow up."

I opened the door. DEA Agent Christina Marquez stood on my porch, her long black hair hanging loose over a zipped purple hoodie. She wore yoga pants and a pair of cheap black flip-flops. Christina was tall, busty, and gutsy. She and I had teamed up recently to take down a drug-dealing, tax-cheating ice-cream man, and we'd remained friends ever since. She'd even helped me out on a later case, acting as bait for a bunch of thugs sent by my target, a violent loan shark.

She pushed past me into my place. "Got any of that peach sangria handy?"

I closed the door. "Just made a fresh pitcher."

She turned in my foyer and held out her left hand. Her ring finger bore a huge diamond roughly the size of a shotgun shell. Surrounding the diamond was a circle of brilliant blue sapphires.

"Oh, my God!" I cried. "Ajay popped the question?"

Alicia shrieked, alerting Christina to her presence. I'd introduced the two of them weeks before and we'd all gone out together as couples several times since.

Alicia rushed over and looked at the ring. "Ajay proposed to you?"

Christina nodded.

My mouth contorted, half of it trying to smile in congratulations at Christina, the other trying to frown in empathy for Alicia.

"But you've only been dating a few months," Alicia said, fresh tears forming in her eyes as she held Christina's hand and took in the beautiful ring.

"I know," Christina said. "That's the problem. It's too soon, isn't it? I told Ajay that, but he told me to wear the ring for a while, to see how it feels." When Alicia released her hand, Christina held her hand up in front of her face and eyed the gorgeous ring. "I'm just not sure."

Alicia threw her ring-less hands in the air. "Oh, boo-fucking-hoo! Your boyfriend cares too much about you and wants to marry you! What a horrible, awful problem!" Alicia turned, snatched her empty glass from the coffee table, and stormed into the kitchen for more sangria.

Christina raised a brow at me.

"She and Daniel are having problems," I said, keeping my voice low. "She's ready to tie the knot and he's not."

Christina grimaced, realizing that her timing, too, was off. "Sorry."

"This is life. We'll deal with it." With a little help from Nick's mother's sangria recipe and a mason jar of spiced Georgia peaches.

The three of us sat at my kitchen table for the next hour, drinking peach sangria and taking turns lamenting our man problems.

"Men," I said, shaking my head. "You can't live with 'em, and you can't shoot 'em."

"You've shot men plenty of times," Alicia said.

"I've shot *at* them many times," I corrected, "but I only actually put bullets in three of them." I took the left nut off

the first and got the other two in the leg. But don't worry.
They totally deserved it.

When we finished off the first pitcher of sangria, I made
another. Alicia drank most of the second pitcher herself.
Before Christina prepared to leave she helped me drag Alicia and her overnight bag upstairs to my guest room.

"By the way," Christina said as she turned at my front
door to go. "Ajay and I are planning a Halloween party at
the rec room at his condos. Tell Alicia she's invited. And
you can bring Nick. . . . or Brett, or . . . whoever."

"Whoever" was right. With the luck Alicia and I were
having, we might have to be each other's dates for the party.

chapter seven

$\mathcal{P}$seudocelebrities

Wednesday morning, I arrived at work only to have Viola, Lu's gray-haired secretary, immediately summon me to the Lobo's office. To my surprise, I found Trish LeGrande already seated inside. Trish was a butterscotch blonde with excessive tenacity and enormous tits. She worked as a reporter for a local TV station and had been a thorn in my side for several weeks now, not only because she'd put me on the spot and made me look like an idiot on camera but also because she'd openly flirted with Brett and inched her way into his life via volunteering for the same Habitat for Humanity project on which he'd been installing the landscaping.

Damn! For the first time it hit me that if I told Brett I wanted to take time off from our relationship to give things a try with Nick, he might seize the opportunity to seize Trish. The thought of Brett with this pushy, brazen, big-breasted woman made me sick. Brett had assured me time and time again that he had no interest in Trish, but that could change after our talk, couldn't it? All bets would be off then.

Ugh.

Seated next to Trish was a middle-aged man with muscular shoulders, a large black case at his feet. I recognized him as the cameraman who'd taken footage of me putting my foot in my mouth on a recent case against an errant minister. I fought the urge to kick him in the shins.

Lu jerked her beehive-topped head at Trish. "Tara, you remember Trish LeGrande, right?"

How could I forget the bosomy bitch? "Sure," I told Lu. I turned to Trish then. "Hello, Trish." I didn't bother saying, *Nice to see you.* A lie that huge would make my nose grow to the size of an anteater's.

Trish used to do the happy feel-good segment on the late news but had recently been promoted to a position as a business reporter. Now it seemed she was constantly up in *my* business.

Trish cocked her head and looked me up and down, her lips quirking to indicate she was less than impressed with my poly-blend pantsuit. Hey, I wasn't crazy about it, either, but it's hard to say no to a half-price sale and it wasn't like my job required me to dress like a supermodel. Besides, I hadn't done laundry or made a run to the dry cleaner's in a while and this was one of the few clean outfits I had left. I'd paired the suit with my cherry-red Doc Martens, my takedown shoes as I thought of them. They had thick rubber soles that provided good traction, as well as steel toes. Perfect for kicking or serving as a doorstop if the need arose.

Trish finally raised her eyes to mine. "Hello, Tara."

"Trish has heard about our sweep of abusive preparers," Lu said. "She wants to do a piece on the issue."

Was it actually possible that Trish and I could be on the same side for once? If she ran a feature on the news about abusive preparers, it could not only strike some fear into those who might be considering fudging their returns but also educate the public on the issue. Still, I didn't trust the woman as far as I could throw her.

Lu waved a hand. "Get her set up in the conference room and round up some agents for her to interview."

"Will do," I said.

"And don't make any lunch plans for tomorrow," Lu added. "You and Nick are coming with me to meet Carl."

Trish looked at me and raised an accusing brow.

"This way," I told Trish, ignoring the brow and jerking my head toward the door.

Trish and her cameraman followed me down the hall to the conference room.

"Good news about Brett's contract with the city of Grand Prairie, right?" Trish said from behind me. "Landscaping all of the city parks is a huge deal." Though her tone sounded innocent, the bitch knew exactly what she was doing. The question was her way of letting me know she was still in touch with Brett despite my recent request that he cut off contact with her.

I was glad she couldn't see my face, as I'm sure my expression showed the hurt and betrayal I felt. I managed to continue on, not breaking stride. "I'm sure Brett will do a great job." If I didn't kill him first.

While they set up their equipment, I headed to the kitchen and offices, rounding up special agents and sending them down to the conference room to be interviewed.

As I approached Nick's office, I heard voices coming from within and stopped a few feet short of his door to eavesdrop on a conversation taking place between him and Josh. Apparently Nick had wasted no time and invited Shea, the cute Mavericks dancer, out for drinks last night. Although she was "smoking hot" with "a body that wouldn't quit," according to Nick, she'd seemed a bit immature. Not surprising since she was only in her early twenties.

So Nick hadn't made a love connection. I glanced upward. *Thank you, Lord Jesus!*

"I e-mailed Kira," Josh told Nick. "She asked me to meet her for coffee after work today." The quiver in his voice told me the prospect had him quaking in his Buster Brown loafers.

Nick must have noticed it, too. "Need a wingman?" he offered.

"That would be great."

Great? Apparently Josh didn't realize that having Nick along would only make him pale by comparison. Then again, Kira was a techie sci-fi nerd and anime enthusiast. Maybe a badass cowboy like Nick wouldn't be her type.

Aw, hell. Who was I trying to fool? Nick was *every* woman's type.

I stepped into the doorway of Nick's office.

He looked up and caught my eye. "Want to join us for coffee after work?" he asked. "Josh is meeting up with a woman from the Big D site and wants me to be his wingman. It'll be less awkward if we've got another woman with us."

"So I'll be your date?" I tossed my head coyly.

His eyes narrowed. "In a manner of speaking."

I was thrilled by the thought of being Nick's date, whether officially or not. "Count me in."

Eddie appeared in the hallway. "Ready to nab Richard Beauregard?"

"Almost." I told Eddie, Josh, and Nick about Trish and her cameraman waiting in the conference room.

"How do I look?" Eddie asked, turning his face side to side. "Do I need some powder? How's my hair?"

I rolled my eyes and led the entourage down the hall.

Trish had arranged two chairs in front of a bookcase that contained the seemingly endless volumes of the Internal Revenue Code and the extensive regulations promulgated thereunder. She sat in the chair on the left, leaving the right chair open for the interviewees.

Trish ran her eyes down the most recent recruits, smiling up at Nick and putting a hand on his shoulder. "Let's get you in the chair," she said. "Your face was made to be on camera."

It was bad enough that she'd put the moves on Brett, but the bitch was flirting with Nick now, too?

Nick cut his eyes my way, took in the pissed-off look on my face, and grinned down at Trish. "I bet you say that to all the boys."

Grrr. Nick's name was so going on my *people-to-kill-today* list, too.

Trish asked Nick some remarkably well-prepared questions and Nick provided a series of sound bites in return, clever, witty comebacks sure to make us IRS special agents appear smart and sharp. Eddie performed well, too, explaining that fraudulent tax returns not only cost honest taxpayers hundreds of millions of dollars in unreported taxes due but also caused significant costs for enforcement personnel. Josh went next, but Trish quickly wrapped up his interview when Josh turned pink and began to sweat and stammer.

As I slid into the seat, Trish said, "No need, Tara. We've got what we need already. Besides," she scrunched her nose as she eyed my suit again, "cheap fabrics don't film well."

I stood, doing my best to remain calm. "You're right, Trish," I said. "Cheap things look awful on camera." I punctuated my words with a pointed look and a snide smile before raising my head high and walking out.

My cell phone vibrated in my pocket a few seconds later. I checked the readout. It was a text from Nick.

Good one.

I smiled to myself. He'd earned his way back off my list. He'd live to see another day.

chapter eight

*B*eau on the Geau

The interviews now completed, Eddie and I hopped into our basic white G-ride and headed out to arrest Richard Wallace Beauregard III. Beau, as he was known, had been an exceptionally naughty boy. He'd sold his clients interests in a fuel company, which he claimed entitled them to fuel tax credits on their returns. Problem was, the fuel company didn't actually exist and the interests were bogus.

I supposed I couldn't blame his clients for falling so easily for his song and dance. Energy companies had recently discovered they could use a fracturing technique to exploit the natural gas reserves trapped in the Barnett Shale formation that lay under the Dallas–Fort Worth metroplex. Thanks to "fracking," the tight rock formation that had once been deemed too difficult and expensive to drill in could now produce natural gas at significant profits. Hundreds of oil and gas companies had descended on the area, offering property owners a pretty penny for leases on their mineral rights. Once the drilling began, property owners enjoyed further income in the form of royalties.

Though the drilling had been a boon to some, others had suffered, claiming benzene and other carcinogens had seeped into their groundwater as a result of the gas companies' fracking activities. A few lawsuits were making their way through the courts now. It wasn't clear where the cards would fall at the end of the day. Still, North Texans overall had renewed their love affair with oil and gas, each expecting to become the next Jed Clampett. *If you don't own a well,* went the wisdom, *get one!* Beauregard had apparently realized the gas fervor could work in his favor and devised the fraudulent scheme.

As if ripping off his unsuspecting clients in the gas well scam weren't bad enough, he'd also hijacked their personal data and filed amended tax returns in their names and Social Security numbers. The amended returns generated over seven hundred thousand dollars in phony tax refunds. Because Beau'd had the additional refunds directly deposited into his own bank account, most of his clients had no idea he'd amended their returns without their authorization.

The IRS had caught on to his identity theft ploy when a taxpayer had responded to a notice questioning an entry on his amended return. When the taxpayer indicated he'd filed no such amended return, the audit department had looked to the preparer for explanation. The one Beau offered the auditor had been flimsy and evasive. Thus the case had been transferred to Criminal Investigations. A little bit of digging into the amended returns, a few phone calls to his clients, and we'd built the case against him easy peasy without his knowledge. Yep, our visit to his office today with our arrest warrant would be a surprise.

I pulled into the parking lot of a three-story stucco office building painted the color of pistachio ice cream. A yard sign stuck in the empty flower bed let potential tenants know "Executive Suites Available—First Month Free." We exited the car onto a parking lot covered with oil stains and cigarette butts.

A beat-up beige Chevy Suburban was parked near the doors. The windshield was cracked and the back bumper

was held on by baling wire. The tires appeared mismatched.
The driver's door featured a magnetic sign that read:

BEAUREGARD FINANCIAL SERVICES
TRUST YOUR FUNDS TO US
(555) 837-BEAU

The door buzzed as Eddie and I entered. I glanced
around. The building appeared to be a typical arrangement.
A dozen office suites on each floor, most housing small one-
man or one-woman operations. The tenants shared a common copy room, conference room, and kitchen, as well as the
services of a receptionist/secretary.

The receptionist didn't look up from her built-in horseshoe-
shaped desk as I approached. From the top of her graying
head all I could tell about her was that her part was crooked
and that she suffered a mild case of dandruff.

I stepped up to the desk. She still didn't look up from
the *National Enquirer* she was reading. I couldn't much
blame her, though. The article about alien remains found
in the freezer at a grade-school cafeteria looked intriguing.

"Excuse me," I said.

She glanced up, a slightly annoyed look on her wrinkled
face. "Can I help you?"

Eddie and I slid our cards onto the countertop in front of
her.

"We're looking for Richard Beauregard," I said.

She turned and glanced down the hallway behind her to a
door marked with black stick-on letters that spelled "BEAU-
REGARD FINANCIAL SERVICES." "His door's closed,
which means he's with a client. But I'll let him know you're
here."

While she buzzed Beau on the intercom, Eddie and I
took seats on the cheap vinyl couch.

"Some people from the IRS are here to see you," the receptionist said into her phone. She paused a moment as she
listened to Beauregard's response. "Okay."

She hung up her phone and turned back to us. "He said he'll be with you shortly."

Eddie nodded. "Thanks."

We waited for a moment or two. Eddie used the downtime as an opportunity to read conservative political blogs on his phone while I played another game of Scrabble. Despite my double word score with the word "violin," the program beat me with a triple word score for "quizzes."

Eventually the door to Beauregard Financial Services opened and a man in dark-blue work pants and a short-sleeved blue work shirt emerged. He had a ball cap in his hand and a perplexed expression on his face. He walked up to the receptionist's desk. "I don't know what the hell happened in there," he said. "One minute I'm talking to Mr. Beauregard about my taxes and the next minute he's climbing out the window."

Eddie and I leaped from our seats. "You check the office," Eddie said. "I'll head outside."

Eddie ran to the building's doors and yanked them open. The sound of tires squealing came through loud and clear, followed by the stench of dust and burning rubber. Eddie turned around and I tossed him the keys to our fleet car. He ran back outside, hopped into the car, and took off after Beauregard. I headed down the hall to see what I could find in Beau's office.

The space was spare. A basic wood desk sat in the middle of the room with a lateral filing cabinet stretching across the wall behind it. Two cheap metal chairs with black vinyl seats faced the desk. The built-in white bookcases were mostly bare, the only items on them an outdated copy of a tax primer, a stack of pamphlets promoting the fictitious fuel company, and a glass candy dish containing a handful of plastic-wrapped peppermints.

The windows consisted of a large plate-glass rectangle with narrow vertical glass panels on each side. For safety reasons only the vertical panels could be opened. The one to the left of the center panel was ajar, the screen punched out.

I stepped to the window and took a quick look. How the heck a grown man had wriggled out through the ten-inch space was beyond me.

I walked around the desk where Beau's laptop sat open, his screen displaying a list of e-mails. I hit the space bar to keep the machine active and took a seat in his rolling chair.

The man with the ball cap had followed me back to Beauregard's office. He stood in the doorway, his head cocked. "You know anything about taxes?"

"I work for the IRS," I said. "So, yeah, I know a little about taxes."

He pulled a folded piece of paper from the breast pocket of his shirt. "Can you tell me what this mumbo jumbo means?"

I took the paper from him and read over the notice he'd received from the IRS. It informed him that his fuel tax credit had been denied.

"It means Beauregard duped you." I offered him a consoling smile. "That gas well he sold you? It doesn't actually exist. Sorry."

"Well, I'll be a monkey's uncle," the man said, crossing his arms over his chest. "I paid good money for that well." He glared at the open window, then looked back at me. "What are the chances I'll get that money back?"

"Honestly?" I said. "Slim to none." I opened the drawers to Beau's desk and found a dollar and thirty-seven cents inside. I handed it to the man. "Here. Buy yourself something from the vending machine." Maybe some chocolate would cheer him up.

After the man left the room, I rummaged through the rest of the drawers. I found more pamphlets detailing the benefits of financial planning, as well as application forms for insurance policies and forms to open investment accounts. I'd never heard of the insurance company, Alltex Allied Mutual Incorporated, or the investment company, Gulf States Portfolio Management. Chances were good they were bogus companies, too.

Eddie came into the office then, a pissed-off look on his

face. "I lost him," he said. "I've called Dallas PD so they can keep an eye out for him."

I returned my attention to the computer, looking over Beau's e-mail in-box. Eddie stepped up behind me to read over my shoulder. Most of the e-mails were typical spam from businesses trying to sell him promotional items. An e-mail from his cell phone provider reminded him that his bill was past due. A communication from his bank warned his account was overdrawn. He'd racked up over three hundred dollars in overdraft fees. Some financial planner he was.

I looked up at Eddie. "How can the guy be broke?" After all, he'd cheated the government out of over half a million dollars in the last year alone. That was like, what, forty thousand dollars a month? "What could he have spent all that money on?"

"My guess would be drugs, gambling, or hookers," Eddie said.

As I continued to scroll down Beau's e-mail in-box, we found an e-ticket for a flight from Dallas to Las Vegas.

"That narrows it down to gambling and hookers," Eddie said.

The flight was scheduled to leave late in the day on the October 15 extended tax deadline. Beau planned to treat himself to some fun after the mad rush, huh? Too bad for him that Eddie and I had come along to play party poopers.

While I forwarded all of the e-mails to my account at the IRS, Eddie looked through the filing cabinet. Other than a few paper copies of tax returns, there wasn't much there. Together Eddie and I packed up Beau's things. We instructed the receptionist to give us a call immediately if he returned to his office.

After we carried his things out to the car, I pulled up directions to Beau's house on my phone. Our search warrant gave us the right not only to seize evidence from his office but to search his home as well.

We climbed back into our G-ride and headed farther

south into the suburb of Duncanville. A few turns and the
blue dot on my phone indicated we were getting close. The
blue dot met up with the red dot right as we pulled up in
front of a trailer park. A hand-lettered sign in the front window of the first trailer read: "MANAGEMENT."

"Here we are," I said.

Eddie turned in. While many trailer parks were well kept
and tidy, this one was not. Broken toys and trash bags sat in
the yards of many of the homes, some of which were unan-
chored travel trailers. We slowly made our way down the
cracked asphalt drive, looking for space thirteen.

"There it is," I said, pointing.

A rusty mailbox sunk into a plastic bucket filled with
cement marked the spot. The spot, however, was empty. Well,
not totally empty. A cheap red barbecue grill lay on its side at
the back of the space, alongside a faded canvas lawn chair and
a metal TV tray. Beau's former backyard cookout spot, no
doubt. Several gray cinder blocks lay at odd angles to the
sides of the space, as if they'd been slung aside in haste.

We drove back to the entrance and pulled to the side,
parking near the manager's trailer. Three quick raps on the
door frame rousted him.

He yanked his door open. "Yeah?"

The manager wore a short-sleeved shirt hanging open
over his pasty, hairless chest and belly, along with a pair of
boxer shorts and ratty house slippers. Unusual sounds came
from the television playing in the background. Lots of "oohs"
and "aahs" and cheesy music.

Sheesh. The guy was watching porn in the middle of the
afternoon? *Ew.*

Eddie and I flashed our badges. "We're from the IRS,"
Eddie said. "We're looking for Richard Beauregard."

The man chortled. "You and everyone else," he spat.
"That deadbeat's been served with lawsuits three times in
the past month."

"His space is empty," I said. "You know anything about
that?"

The man nodded. "He hooked up his camper and hauled

out about an hour ago. Saved me the hassle of evicting his sorry ass. He owes me two months' rent plus late fees."

Eddie and I exchanged glances. "Any idea where he might have gone?" I asked.

The man raised a finger. "Just a minute." He disappeared and came back a few seconds later with a piece of paper in his hand. He held it out to me, but I didn't want to touch it. Who knew where the manager's hands had been before we knocked on his door?

Eddie shot me a look and took the paper, holding it where I could read it, too. It was Beau's rental application. In the emergency contact blank he'd listed his mother, who also lived in Duncanville. I plugged her address into my phone's navigation system.

"Thanks," Eddie said, handing the paper back to him.

"You find him," the man called after us, "you tell him to bring me my rent!"

"Will do!" I called back.

Ten minutes later, Eddie and I pulled up to Beau's mother's house, a two-story redbrick home in a respectable, though modest, neighborhood. She was a tall woman, her once-dark hair now much more salt than pepper. Though she was open and friendly, she was no help.

She rolled her eyes. "I know a mother shouldn't say this about her own son," she said, "but Richard just can't seem to get it together. He's borrowed over sixty grand from me over the years and hasn't paid back a penny. I'm seventy-two and still having to waitress at the Waffle Hut just to keep my bills paid."

"Any chance you've got a photograph of him handy?" I asked. If we were going to have to pursue the guy, we'd need to know what he looked like. The auditor who'd referred the case had described Beau as looking like Woody from *Toy Story*. Unless Beauregard had a pull string in his back, I wasn't sure that was enough to go on.

Beau's mother removed a large framed photo from the foyer wall. "Here you go."

The photo was a picture of a man who indeed looked like Woody. Unlike Woody, though, this man had a virtual unibrow. They hadn't quite grown together, but the two wide, flat brows sported a distinct tuft in the middle, as if they were spelling out the letter K in Morse code. Beau was dressed in a tux and stood at an altar next to a tiny blonde in a puffy-sleeved white wedding dress with a wide, bell-shaped skirt.

Mrs. Beauregard waved her hand. "You can keep that. Richard's wife left him years ago after he lost all their money at that Indian casino just over the Oklahoma border. Damn shame. She was a sweet girl, crazy about him. He managed to screw that up, too."

So Beau was single. Perhaps he had indeed spent some of the money he'd stolen from Uncle Sam on hookers. With those gangly limbs and that unibrow, Beau probably wasn't getting laid for free.

chapter nine

$\mathcal{D}$ouble Date, Double Espresso

Since we were already out, Eddie and I figured we might as well pay a visit to a few of the money transmitters on the lists Wang had given us.

The first was a payday loan place that ran a brisk business despite the outrageous interest rates and fees they charged. The business was part of a chain with a corporate headquarters that implemented strict procedures and kept a close eye on its branches. As expected, everything was in order there.

The second was a jewelry store that paid cash for gold jewelry. Everything was in order there, too, though I was a bit disturbed by the man next to us who'd produced a handful of teeth and asked how much he could get for the gold fillings. Eddie and I had made a note of his license plate and put in a discreet call to local law enforcement.

Our final stop was a convenience store operated by a pleasant middle-aged Muslim couple. Like Zardooz, they'd suffered bigotry thanks to the radical terrorists. After 9-11 someone had spray-painted "Go home, towelheads!" on the side wall of their store.

"I was born and raised in Texas," the man said. "I *am* home."

Their records were in good order, fully compliant, nothing suspicious. There was no flicker of recognition when I showed them the photos of the local men who'd been arrested, either.

"Sorry we couldn't be of help," the wife said as I slid the photos back into my briefcase.

I thanked them and bought a Lotto scratch-off and a package of peanut butter crackers.

On the drive back to the IRS building, I shared my crackers with Eddie and took a penny to the scratch-off ticket. "Hey! I won five bucks!"

"Don't forget to report the winnings on your tax return," Eddie said.

"Party pooper." I put the winning ticket in my wallet to redeem later and called Wang to update him on our investigation. He'd had no luck with the money transmitters he'd visited, either.

Whoever had helped the terrorists move their money was still out there, waiting to be discovered. I pictured him as a bearded man with dark hair and squinty eyes that reflected a crazed rage. Sheesh, even I was falling for the stereotypes and I should know better. After all, most of the people we arrested for tax evasion looked like normal, upstanding citizens.

Back at the office, I logged into the tax-reporting system and suspended Richard Beauregard's e-filing privileges. We may not have brought the cheat in, but at least we could prevent him from filing any more fraudulent returns and stealing further from the government's coffers.

At a quarter after five, Nick stepped into my office. "You ready to head to the coffee shop?"

I looked up at Nick. "No flowers or candy?" I quipped. "Way to make our first date special."

Of course he had no way of knowing that this was, in

fact, sort of our first date. He had no idea I planned to put Brett on the back burner for him.

"If you put out," Nick replied, a sexy grin spreading across his lips, "I'll bring you all kinds of flowers and candy."

At least he was flirting with me again rather than acting angry. That was a step in the right direction.

We rounded up Josh and the three of us headed out to Nick's truck, an older, hail-dented pickup that I'd bought to smuggle Nick out of Mexico a few months ago. He'd taken the thing off my hands when we'd returned, even paid me a premium for it. The truck might not look like much, but it ran well and had enough towing power to pull a bass boat, an item that was on Nick's wish list.

I sat between Nick and Josh on the bench seat. Josh fidgeted with nervous energy the entire way.

"Relax," I told him. "Everything will be fine. It's just coffee. No big deal."

Easy for me to say. He had a lot riding on this date. While Nick had received more than fifty additional inquiries today—*dammit!*—no other women had responded to Josh's ad on the dating site. It was Kira or nobody.

Nick parked the truck in the side lot of the coffee shop and we made our way inside. Josh carried his personal laptop bag with him.

"You're bringing your computer?" I asked.

"I thought I'd show it to Kira," Josh replied.

Sheez. What a hopeless geek.

The three of us stopped inside the door and scanned the area. No blue-eyed blondes in sight.

"She's not here," Josh said, his voice tinged with panic.

I checked my watch. "It's not even five thirty yet. She'll be here."

We got in line and ordered drinks, Nick's treat. I went for a caramel *macchiato*. I'd work off the calories by spending an extra twenty minutes on the exercise bike at the gym tomorrow.

We took seats at a square table in the middle of the room

where we could keep an eye on the door. As we waited for
Kira, I told Nick and Josh about Richard Beauregard, about
our visits to his office, the trailer park, his mother's house.

Nick snorted. "Sounds like Beau's the family fuckup."

The front door opened then, and a young woman stepped
inside. She was tall, with white-blonde hair. Although she
was clearly the Kira from the dating site, she looked almost
nothing like the innocent-eyed girl in the photo.

Her white-blonde hair didn't hang in pigtails today.
Rather, it was shaved short over the ear on one side, the rest
of it hanging in chunky clumps around her face. Not quite
dreadlocks, but close. The wide blue eyes from the snapshot
were now rimmed with black smudges, the uniformity of the
circles indicating they were intentional. Her lipstick, likewise, was black. She was thin, almost painfully so, with
long, gangly limbs, like a Tim Burton character come to life.
Gone was the sailor suit, replaced by a tight black belly top,
a black leather miniskirt with white netting underneath, torn
fishnet hose, and thigh-high black leather boots.

"Boy howdy," Nick said, giving a low whistle and turning
to Josh. "That girl is going to eat you alive."

Josh emitted a sound like the whimper of a puppy.

Kira's flat chest was crisscrossed by the straps of a laptop
bag draped diagonally over one shoulder and a messenger
bag. She removed the laptop bag and glanced around the
room, her eyes stopping and locking on Josh. She stood
there for a moment, her head tilting first one way, then the
other as she assessed him. Her eyes narrowed for a moment.
Was she thinking about turning around and walking back
out the door? For Josh's sake I hoped not. Or maybe for his
sake I should hope she would. Heck, I had no idea what to
make of her.

Finally, she stepped forward and came to our table.

"Uhh . . . h-h-hi," Josh said, his voice breathy and weak
as he looked up at her.

Josh's trepidation brought an openmouthed smile to Kira's
dark lips, as if she enjoyed the fact that he was afraid of her.

In contrast to her ebony lipstick, her teeth appeared an almost blinding white, with oddly long and pointed canines.

Kira laid her laptop bag on the table and followed it with the messenger bag. Up close, additional features were apparent. Her belly button was pierced, as were her nose, one brow, that little dimple under her bottom lip, and her tongue. Given all that metal, it was a wonder her face wasn't constantly drawn to magnetic north. She had a small tattoo on her upper hip, the standard yellow happy face wearing a black hood and carrying a sickle. What the hell was that? The grin reaper?

Nick and I stood, introduced ourselves, and shook her hand. Josh just sat there, his mouth hanging open, dumbfounded.

Given that Josh was totally dropping the ball, Nick asked Kira what she'd like to drink and set off for the bar to place her order for a double espresso. I invited her to take a seat, giving Josh a nudge with my knee as I sat, trying to dislodge him from his stupor.

"Nick and I work with Josh at the IRS," I told Kira, explaining that we were special agents who pursued tax evaders. "Josh is the department's cybercrimes specialist."

"A crime fighter," she said in a slightly nasal voice, turning her gaze on Josh. "Cool."

At her eye contact he made the puppy whimper sound again. I half-expected him to drop to the floor, roll over onto his back, and pee on himself.

She turned to me. "He seems nervous. What's his deal?"

"He hasn't dated much," I said. "Plus, he's a virgin."

"Tara!" Josh shrieked, turning purple with embarrassment. But at least he was talking now.

Kira laughed. She probably assumed I was joking. She leaned across the table toward Josh. "I don't bite, you know. At least not on the first date." She ran her tongue over her lips, laughing again when Josh turned an even darker shade of purple.

Josh said little for the next minute or so while Kira and I

got to know each other. Although we clearly had totally different tastes in fashion, we hit it off, having other things in common. We were both nonconformists with a rebellious streak. We both thought iced coffee was an abomination. Coffee should be taken hot, the way God intended. We were both cat lovers. She had three to my two. COBOL, Delphi, and Fortran, all named after computer languages.

Nick returned with Kira's espresso and the three of us chatted amiably. Josh simply stared at Kira the entire time. She pulled an artist's sketchbook out of her messenger bag and showed us some of the logos she'd designed for her clients' Web sites, including one for a local punk rock band called the STDs. The shape of the T was somewhat phallic and the pink D was suspiciously reminiscent of a woman's nether regions, but I suppose you have to give the clients what they want, huh?

She pulled up some of the Web sites on her iPad. Most of the others were less provocative, though no less unique. She'd designed a cute site for a vegan restaurant that featured a singing carrot, as well as one for a shoe repair service with a dancing cobbler. The woman not only knew computers and HTML; she was a creative genius, too.

Josh eventually found the courage to speak. "Your sites are awesome."

"Thanks." She gave him another smile and this time he managed to maintain eye contact. Good for him. It was a baby step, but it was progress.

Josh pulled his laptop from his bag and set it on the table, punching the button to boot up the machine.

Kira noted the bug-eyed logo on the back of his screen. "Alienware?" Her brows rose as she looked his machine over. "Wow. You've got some really nice equipment."

Josh managed a small smile. "Thanks."

I supposed to a computer geek like him showing off his expensive hardware was the equivalent of an alpha male flexing his muscles. Kira seemed impressed, so Josh's strategy appeared to be working.

Kira pulled her chair up closer next to Josh and the two

began to compare computers. Just as Kira had admired Josh's hardware, he complimented her on her software, which ranged from an extended version of Flash, to Photoshop, to some type of moviemaking program.

When the two began communicating in technical lingo and computer jargon, Nick and I could no longer join in the conversation. They might as well have been speaking a foreign language.

Nick and I eyed each other over our coffee, neither of us saying anything for a while, not wanting to risk throwing Josh off his tenuous game. Eventually, the conversation steered back to Josh's job.

"So you hack into computers?" Kira asked Josh.

Now that she was looking at him instead of the computer screen, he seemed to shrink again. He nodded.

Might as well help the poor squirt out, huh? "Josh is amazing," I said. "He can hack into any system." It was true. Josh hadn't met a firewall yet that he couldn't break through and he could decrypt code in less time than it took me to log on.

Nick played his part as wingman, piling on. "I don't know what we'd do without Josh's tech skills."

Also true, though I could do without his sometimes sniveling attitude.

"I'm a bit of a hacker myself," Kira said. "Haven't met anyone yet who's better than me." She narrowed her eyes at Josh. "You up for a challenge?"

Josh shrugged. "Okay."

Kira gestured to a businessman in the corner. "See that guy on his laptop? First one to hack his system wins."

"Piece of cake." Josh grinned. "You're on."

The two of them began pecking away on their keyboards and running their fingers over their mouse pads, presumably accessing the coffee shop's Wi-Fi system and manipulating their way into the guy's machine. It was a geek-off.

As Nick and I watched their frantic movements, I sent him a discreet text. *Is this some type of nerd foreplay?*

Nick checked his phone when it buzzed with my

incoming text. A slight smile crossed his lips. *Hell if I know,* he replied.

"Watch," Josh whispered a few seconds later. "I'll open his CD drive." He punched a few more keys and, sure enough, the CD port on the man's computer slid open. The man looked down, frowned, and pushed it back closed.

Nick and I exchanged glances. Knowing Josh could so easily infiltrate a stranger's system had me wondering what else he might have hacked into. Our banking records? Personnel files? Personal e-mails? I'd considered him little more than a pesky twerp, but perhaps he was much more of a threat than I'd realized.

Kira raised her hands and bowed forward to Josh. "All hail the mighty hacker, supreme lord of cyberspace."

Josh leaned back in his chair now, all cocky confidence.

When our cups ran dry, Josh and Kira packed up their computers and we stood to go.

Kira slid her bags back over her shoulders, the straps once again making an X across her chest. "It was nice meeting all of you."

Nick and I both gave Josh the eye. He took the hint.

"Um . . . how about a movie this weekend?" Josh asked Kira.

"That would be great," she replied, suggesting the latest superhero flick. I knew Josh had already seen it, twice in fact, but at least he had the good sense not to mention it. He programmed her cell number into his phone and we parted ways.

Josh beamed as we made our way back to Nick's truck. "I nailed it!"

Nick and I exchanged glances. If not for our early intervention, Kira probably would've gone on her merry way after two seconds. But no sense ruining Josh's newfound confidence.

"Way to go, dude." Nick raised his hand, offering Josh a high five.

Josh slapped Nick's palm, then pulled his hand down to his hip in a victorious fist. "Yes-s-s!"

I noticed Nick check his watch as he drove Josh and me back to our cars at the office.

"Late for dinner?" I asked. Nick had lived with his mother since he'd returned from Mexico, though lately he'd been making noises about finding a place of his own.

"No," he said. "I've got another date."

"Another date?" *Sheez.* That made two nights in a row. Nick was a man slut! A hot flare of anger lit up in me. "You don't waste any time, do you?"

Nick shot me a meaningful look. "I've wasted quite a bit of time, Tara."

I wanted to tell him that his time spent waiting for me to make up my mind had not been wasted. That I had come around. That as soon as I could get Brett alone and have a heart-to-heart with him, Nick and I would be free to explore our relationship. But I couldn't very well do that with Josh sitting next to me. I didn't want the entire office knowing our business.

I was worried, though. I'd seen those girls on the Big D site. All of them were attractive. Some were younger than me; many were prettier. All of them had bigger breasts. Not hard to outdo a 32A. No doubt a few of them might be interesting to a guy like Nick. The angry flare in me blazed into rage-fueled fear.

"You trying someone new tomorrow night, too?" I spat.

"Nope," Nick replied.

Good. "I'm sure your mother will be glad to have you home for a change."

"I didn't say I didn't have a date," Nick said. "I just said I wasn't trying someone new."

I shot him a questioning look.

His eyes locked on mine. "I'm having dinner with my fiancée tomorrow night."

"*Ex*-fiancée," I corrected.

He shrugged and looked away, as if the "ex" were irrelevant.

Damn! I needed to move fast or Nick might reconcile with the woman. Things just kept getting worse!

As Nick pulled into the lot, I dug in my purse for my keys. My fingers brushed against a cool piece of plastic the size of dice. It was Josh's GPS device that the three of us had used on a recent case. I'd been meaning to return it to Josh but kept forgetting. Things tended to get lost in the deep recesses of my purse. For all I knew, the Holy Grail was down in the bottom somewhere, along with that Perfectly Plum lipstick I couldn't seem to find.

I closed my fingers around the GPS and, as discreetly as possible, eased it from my purse. I reached my hand behind me and shoved the gadget into the crevice between the seat and backrest. I might not have been able to sabotage Nick's venture on the Big D Dating site, but I'd find a way to sabotage his date tonight. I had to. I couldn't risk losing Nick before I even got a chance with him.

I climbed into my car, started the engine, and drove out of the parking lot, giving Nick and Josh time to leave as I circled around the block. Once I verified they'd left the lot, I pulled back in and parked. I scurried into the building and up to Josh's office, where I searched through his box of spy gadgets until I found the instructions for the GPS device. I loaded the app on my cell phone and programmed in the unique code for the unit.

I supposed I should have felt guilty. Following Nick and trying to ruin his date would be a horrible, rotten, no-good thing to do. But I needed to buy myself some time. Besides, all's fair in love and war, right?

I wasn't sure whether this was love, but it was definitely war.

chapter ten

Operation: First-Date Flop

I arrived home to find Alicia lying prone on my couch. She was dressed in her usual sophisticated office attire, which she hadn't bothered to change out of. Her black silk blouse was wrinkled, as were her gray linen pants. The pumps she'd kicked off lay at haphazard angles on the floor next to the couch.

Also crumpled on the floor was the gorgeous Monique Lhuillier wedding gown she'd scored for a mere seventy-five bucks at a resale shop. I'd dragged her to the thrift store when I needed some cheap undercover outfits. At first, Alicia had been appalled by the idea of secondhand clothing. But when she realized what amazing deals she could get on barely worn designer items she'd gone nuts, filling her entire trunk with bags of bargains.

Alicia's eyes were closed. She didn't bother to open them when she heard me come in. She simply sighed loudly to acknowledge my presence and to alert me to her mood, which apparently hadn't changed since she'd moved in with me the night before.

The pitcher of sangria sat on the coffee table, mostly empty, only a few orange and peach slices left in the bottom. Next to the pitcher was a glass with a half inch of reddish liquid in the bottom. Alicia hadn't wasted any time getting wasted.

"Alcohol isn't the answer," I told her.

She opened one bloodshot eye. "It is if the question is 'how can I get shit faced and forget about my dumb-ass boyfriend?'"

"Ah," I said. "You're right." She'd always been smarter than me.

I picked up the rumpled wedding gown, held it by the shoulders, and gave it a good shake to fluff it out. Once the dress had settled back into shape, I slid it onto the hanger and hung it in my coat closet.

"You might as well throw that dress in the trash," she said. "I'm never going to wear it. I'm going to die an old maid and it's all Daniel's fault. He stole the best years of my life."

He didn't so much steal them as take what she had willingly offered. Still, no need to point that out, right? She felt bad enough already.

"As long as you're in a man-hating mood, wanna do me a favor?"

"Sure." She pushed herself up to a sitting position. "What do you need me to do?"

"I need you to derail Nick's date tonight. Make sure things go bad."

She nodded. "I'd be happy to help. Nobody should fall in love. It's too painful. Love is just an illusion, anyway. It's like a rainbow. There for a moment, then suddenly—" She splayed her fingers in the air. "Poof! It's gone."

Apparently the sangria had made her philosophical as well as shit faced.

I called Christina. I was in luck. She was available, too.

I changed into jeans and a sweatshirt and led Alicia out to my BMW, depositing her in the backseat, where she promptly lay down again. I drove to Christina's apartment, texting her from the lot when I arrived. She'd thrown on a lightweight shapeless sweater that somehow still managed to show off her perfect body. If she wasn't such a great person I'd really love to hate her.

We decided to take Christina's car, since Nick would be more likely to recognize my BMW than her Volvo. We transferred the drunken blob that was Alicia to the backseat of the Volvo and took our seats up front.

I held out my phone and showed Christina the GPS app.

"That's handy," she said. "But I'm glad they didn't have those things back when I was in high school. My father would have tracked my every move."

The red dot on the map was in motion, indicating that Nick's truck had left his mother's house and was heading north. We hopped onto the freeway and headed after him.

I looked over at Christina, eyeing her left hand on the steering wheel. "You're not wearing the ring today."

She glanced back at Alicia, who was sound asleep, her face smushed against the leather seat. No need to worry about upsetting our friend at the moment. "The ring felt, I don't know," Christina said, "like a lot of pressure?"

I nodded. At the moment, none of us seemed to be in synch with the men in our lives. But if my mom and dad had managed to bounce back from the Candy Cummings/Randall the chess master incident, there was hope the rest of us would work things out, too, right?

"Take the next exit," I instructed Christina, my eyes on the GPS map on my phone. "He's stopped a couple of miles from here, on Greenville."

She pulled off the freeway and continued down the surface street. As we neared the red dot on the map, I pulled the owner's manual from the glove box and opened it, holding it up to cover my face. I peeked discreetly over the top.

"There he is." Christina kept her hand low but gestured to the apartment building to our right.

I glanced that way to see Nick in the parking lot, opening his passenger door for a woman with wavy brown hair. She wore jeans over boots, along with a western-cut woman's shirt pulled tight across her sizable bust. She was tall, probably five foot nine or so, a good match for Nick's six-foot-two-inch frame. She looked strong and capable, like a woman who'd know how to gut a fish and field dress a deer.

"Damn," I muttered. "She looks like Nick's type." I suppose I shouldn't have been surprised by that. After all, the two had prescreened each other and it's not like Nick would've chosen someone who was clearly *not* his type.

Christina narrowed her eyes as she looked at the two of them. "Don't worry your pretty little head, Tara. Ain't nobody fallin' for nobody tonight. Not on my watch."

Did I have great friends or what?

She drove past the apartment complex and pulled into the parking lot of a used-car dealership next door where we wouldn't be spotted. We shooed away the three salesmen stampeding toward us, waited until the GPS indicated Nick had a five-block lead, then turned to follow him, maintaining a good distance.

Alicia sat up in the backseat, eyed herself in the rearview mirror, and said, "No wonder Daniel doesn't want to marry me. I look like crap."

I knew Alicia. There was no sense arguing with her when she was in this kind of mood.

She picked up her purse from the floorboard and retrieved a comb, running it through her hair to smooth it into place. She put on a coat of lipstick and patted her nose with pressed powder.

After a few miles, the GPS indicated Nick had turned into the parking lot of Del Frisco's.

I shrieked. "He's taking her to a pricey steak house on their first date?" Their porterhouse cost over fifty bucks. "He must be trying to impress her." *Damn!* All he'd bought me today was a cup of coffee.

We made the block, stopping at an ATM so I could withdraw a couple of hundred dollars to cover Alicia and Christina's dinner. There went my manicure budget for the next two months. But the least I could do was pay for their meals since they'd be spying for me.

We returned to the restaurant. Christina parked around

the side, where I'd be out of sight of Nick's truck. I handed Christina the stack of twenties and she and Alicia headed inside, Alicia wobbling slightly on her heels.

I sat in the car with the windows rolled down a few inches, waiting. After a few minutes, I received a brief text from Christina.

2 tables over.

Good. They'd been seated close to Nick and his date.

She texted me again. *Ordered a bottle of cabernet.*

I wasn't sure if Christina was referring to herself and Alicia or to Nick and his date. Alicia definitely didn't need any more to drink.

My phone sat silent and still for an agonizing hour, but it might look suspicious if Christina was texting me a play-by-play. What was happening inside? Was Nick meeting the woman of his dreams? Laughing and bonding over red wine and red meat? Or were my friends successfully interfering with his date?

Finally, I received another text from Christina. *Mission accomplished.*

I pulled up the map on my phone. According to the GPS app, Nick and his date had left the parking lot and were on their way back to the woman's apartment. No sign of Christina and Alicia yet. I supposed I couldn't expect them to pass up dessert, though I'd hoped to follow Nick back to the woman's apartment to make sure he didn't go inside.

I debated sending Christina and Alicia a text and instructing them to bring their wine bottle in case I needed to lob a Molotov cocktail through the woman's window. Of course I didn't actually know how to make a Molotov cocktail, but I Googled it while I waited. *Hmm.* It sounded fairly simple. All you needed was a bottle, some flammable liquid, and a small swatch of fabric. I could siphon gas from Christina's tank and tuck my panties into the top of the bottle. I'm nothing if not resourceful. Besides, the pair of underwear I was wearing had definitely seen better days. It was an old pair from a days-of-the-week set my mother had bought me for college years ago. Despite the fact that it was currently

Wednesday, my panties read: "FRIDAY." Yep, I definitely needed to get on that laundry.

Ten minutes later, Christina and Alicia returned to the car, doggie bags in hand.

"So?" I asked as they climbed into the Volvo. "What happened?"

Christina grinned. "Alicia pulled a chair up to their table and turned on the waterworks. She told Nick that she and Daniel had split up because Daniel wouldn't make a commitment. She asked Nick for advice."

"As if I'd take advice from a man," Alicia said, waving a hand dismissively. "Those idiots don't know what they want. Other than sex, of course."

"Of course," Christina said.

"But women want sex, too, don't we?" I knew I did. I'd been without it for several days now and was feeling the strain. I guess I hadn't realized how much I relied on the act to relieve the tension accumulated on my job. "I mean, we don't have to pretend that it's just for men anymore, right?" The sexual revolution of the 1970s had moved us beyond that.

"Please," Alicia said. "Don't even mention sex. As busy as Daniel's been, I'm lucky to get a little something-something once a month."

"Brett and I have had a bit of a dry spell, too," I said, though I only had myself to blame for that. Admittedly, I'd been avoiding intimacy. Given my feelings for Nick, I couldn't enjoy sex with Brett like I used to. I felt too guilty afterward. Too bad I wasn't a slut who could do the deed without any emotional connection.

"You know what you two need?" Christina slid us a sly grin. "A B.O.B."

"Who's Bob?" Alicia asked.

"He's not a *who*," Christina said. "He's *a what*. A Battery-Operated Boyfriend."

"You've got to be kidding," I said. I'd sooner take up jogging to relieve my tension than use one of those things. And I hated jogging.

Christina shrugged. "We found one in a drawer on a bust the other day. It was enormous." She held up her hands to indicate length, like a fisherman describing the one that got away. Her hands were at least two feet apart.

Both Alicia and I cringed and shrank back against our seats. "Ouch!"

Christina looked down at her widely splayed hands. "Okay, maybe I was a little off there. But you get my point."

I didn't want to think anymore about the *point* she was trying to make. Time to get this conversation back on track. "Tell me more about what happened in the restaurant."

"It was *so-o-o* awkward," Christina said. "The girl just sat there looking uncomfortable while Alicia blubbered on Nick's shoulder."

Alicia chuckled. "I stayed at their table a full twenty minutes."

Nick was too nice to tell her to buzz off. He could be sort of sweet on occasion.

I took each of their hands in mine and gave them a squeeze. "Thanks, you two. I owe you."

"No you don't," Christina said. "That dinner was delicious."

Alicia agreed. "Besides, all you have at your place is cereal and SpaghettiOs."

My stomach growled in response and for the first time I realized I hadn't eaten yet. I'd been so worried about Nick that my stomach had been in knots. I'd fix a bowl of Fruity Pebbles at home later.

As we pulled out of the restaurant's parking lot, I checked the GPS app again. Nick's truck was already on its way back to his mother's house. He hadn't gone into the woman's apartment.

I heaved a huge sigh of relief. Much better than heaving a Molotov cocktail, huh?

chapter eleven

*T*ricked Out

Alicia and I watched the ten o'clock news. Trish's report on abusive tax preparers was fair and informative. Nick made a great impression, letting the public know the IRS was on their side.

Once the women of Dallas saw Nick on television, it wouldn't surprise me if a dozen or so called the office volunteering to be audited. Heck, I'd gladly let Nick get his hands on my files.

Brett and I spoke briefly after the newscast. I asked how Trish knew about his new gig for the Grand Prairie Parks and Recreation Department, but he claimed ignorance, telling me that she'd probably heard it from someone else on their volunteer team. He said the two of them hadn't communicated directly in a while, since I'd asked him to sever ties with her.

I supposed I didn't have any right to accuse Brett of improper interactions with another woman given my plans to put him on the back burner and start something up with Nick. I also supposed I sought the information as much to figure out whether Brett had honored my request to cease communication with Trish as to catch him doing something wrong. It would be so much easier for me to make a definitive decision if he'd screw up in a major way. But Brett being Brett, he played nice and did his best to try to keep me happy.

So why was I so *un*happy?

At the office Thursday morning I checked my voice mails and completed some paperwork on a smaller case involving a painting contractor who'd accepted quite a bit of unreported cash under the table. He'd hired a smart attorney who realized the case was a sure win for the IRS. They'd offered a plea deal to pay all taxes and interest owed. The contractor would avoid jail time, but in return he'd pay a steep civil penalty. I hoped he'd learned his lesson.

You don't mess with the IRS.

Neener-neener.

At eleven thirty, Nick stepped into my doorway. "Ready for lunch?"

"Yep." Seemed Nick and I had become the official first-date chaperones. On our walk to Lu's office, I figured I might as well seize the opportunity to fish for information about Nick's date the preceding night.

"I heard Christina and Alicia ran into you at Del Frisco's," I said. "Your date must've been something special if you were willing to drop such a big chunk of change."

Nick shrugged. "I was in the mood for a good steak."

Nick had a craving for red meat? That's all it was? I supposed I shouldn't have been surprised. Women were constantly reading too much into men's actions. Men were actually fairly straightforward creatures. If they want steak, they eat steak. I felt a surge of relief.

We arrived at Lu's office to find her all aflutter. "How's my hair?" she asked, spraying her wig with another coat of her imported extra-hold hairspray.

"Perfect," I said.

She eyed herself in her mirrored compact. "Makeup?"

"Perfect, too," I said.

She tugged on her blue polyester-blend dress. "What about the dress?" She didn't give us time to answer before adding, "It's all wrong, isn't it? I should've worn my black pantsuit."

"Relax, Lu," Nick said, putting a hand on her shoulder. "You look great."

She looked up into his face. "Really?"

"Really. No need to get yourself all worked up."

Lu snapped her compact closed and stashed it in her purse. "I can't help being nervous. I haven't had a first date with a man in over forty years."

"Just be yourself." Nick shot her a wink. "No man will be able to resist that."

Twenty minutes later we walked into a small bistro on the edge of downtown. Carl stood in the foyer, dressed in another leisure suit and white bucks he'd obviously had freshly shined for the occasion. He held a small box of chocolates in his hand. The instant he saw Lu, his face ignited like a propane grill at a tailgate party. He stepped toward her, extending the candy. "I hope I don't sound too forward, Luella, but you are even more beautiful in person."

For a man with fishnet hair, Carl was quite the charmer.

"Thank you." Lu blushed, her face turning as pink as her hair. "I hope you don't mind that I brought a couple of my staff with me. They didn't have lunch plans and asked to join us."

"That's not how I remember it," Nick said, earning him two elbows in the ribs, one Lu's, one mine.

Nick held out his hand to shake Carl's, introducing both himself and me. A moment later, the hostess led us to a round table. Carl stood behind the Lobo's chair and pushed it in for her as she sat. Not to be outdone, Nick did the same for me, his fingers brushing my shoulder as he turned to take his seat.

Over lunch, Carl asked Lu about herself, showing interest in her children and grandchildren, her work, her souvenir spoon collection. "Over three hundred, you say?"

Lu nodded. "From Niagara Falls to Tijuana and lots of places in between."

Not only was Carl a charmer; he was a witty conversationalist, too. He'd spent years in hotel management and entertained us with funny stories of wacky guests, including a troupe of circus sideshow performers and a group of nudists he'd found skinny-dipping in the swimming pool.

"They argued that the posted rules said nothing about a bathing suit being required," he said. "I had to threaten to call the cops to get them out of the water."

His wife passed away a few years ago from heart troubles, but he'd only recently begun dating. "It's kind of hard to get back on the horse after all those years of being married."

"Tell me about it," Lu said. "You're the first date I've had in over four decades."

"Is that right?" Carl sat up straighter and smiled. "Golly. I sure am honored you picked me, Luella."

When the Lobo blushed Nick and I exchanged glances. We'd never seen this side of Lu before. We were used to her barking orders, bossing everyone around, kicking our butts when needed. Who knew she had a girlie side?

When lunch ended, Carl insisted on picking up the tab for all of us. We thanked him and made our way outside onto the sidewalk. Nick and I stepped aside to give Carl and Lu a little privacy.

Carl asked Lu if she might like to get together again. He leaned toward her and whispered, "Maybe just the two of us next time?" He shot Nick and me a wink.

"That would be lovely," Lu said.

Lovely? Was this the same woman who, mere hours ago, had threatened to put her shoe in Josh's ass for blowing the circuit breaker with all his high-tech gadgetry?

Carl took Lu's hand, raised it to his lips, and gave it a quick peck. "I'll be in touch."

After lunch I hopped into my G-ride, left downtown, and headed northwest into Grapevine, a quaint suburban city just north of the sprawling Dallas/Fort Worth International Airport. The town was known for its wineries and wine festivals. It was also home to Winston Wisbrock, aka the Tax Wizard, the next abusive preparer on the list Lu had assigned to Eddie and me.

I parallel parked on Main, having to ease forward and back five times before managing to bring my car close enough to the curb. If I'd been in my BMW I wouldn't have had any problem, but these government fleet cars didn't have the best handling. Gotta spend the taxpayers' dollars wisely, right?

Eddie'd been out scouting MSBs for the terrorist case and taken his own car. He met me on the sidewalk, pointing across the street. "That's the place."

I looked across the road. The Tax Wizard's office was a narrow space lodged between a cupcake shop and a women's clothing boutique. Purple curtains trimmed with gold fringe hung in the window. According to the information in the file, Wisbrock subleased his space from a psychic, utilizing the front half of the unit while the psychic occupied the back.

"What exactly is a wizard anyway?" I asked Eddie. "A magician with a pointed hat?"

"No," Eddie said. "I think wizards are like witches, except they're men."

"Nah. Male witches are called warlocks."

Eddie frowned. "What's a female wizard called, then?"

"I don't know. A fairy?"

"I don't think so."

Eddie and I crossed the street and approached the Tax Wizard's office. On closer inspection we noticed the words "MADAM MAGNOLIA, PSYCHIC CONSULTANT" spelled out in gold lettering on the glass door. I rolled my eyes. I supposed "PSYCHIC CONSULTANT" sounded better than "FRAUD." But, really, what kind of people believed in that ridiculous stuff?

A hand-lettered white poster board sat in the front window.

TAX WIZARD
I MAKE TAXES DISAPPEAR!
ALSO AVAILABLE FOR CHILDREN'S BIRTHDAY
PARTIES

Sheesh.

We pulled the glass door open and stepped through a beaded curtain that rattled as it fell back into place. The smell of incense, or perhaps patchouli, greeted us.

We discovered the Tax Wizard seated behind a cheap metal desk, a trio of four-drawer filing cabinets standing side by side behind him. The Wizard wore a long white beard, a pointy hat, and a dark-blue cape covered with shiny silver stars. Clearly, he'd read a little too much *Harry Potter.* Or perhaps he'd been snorting fairy dust.

He spread his hands. "Welcome to the Wizard's secret lair."

"Secret?" I hiked a thumb at the sign in the window. "You've got a sign. Right there." Obviously this guy was no good at keeping secrets. That could work to our benefit.

The Wizard ignored me, picking up a deck of cards from his desk and fanning them. He held them out to me. "Pick a card."

I glanced at Eddie. He shrugged.

What the hell. I was game. I reached out, eased a card from the deck, and took a quick look. The card was upside down, but once I'd turned it the right way I saw it depicted a fool.

A woman with straight black hair and dangly earrings poked her head out of a curtained doorway behind the Wizard. She said nothing, just watched us.

I handed the card back to Wisbrock, who slid it back into the deck. He shuffled the cards, cut them, and pulled one from the deck. "Is this your card?" He looked at me, white brows raised, a gleam of hope in his rheumy eyes.

The card he held up depicted a pretty woman tending to a lion.

"Um . . . no. That's not my card."

The dark-haired woman crossed her arms over her chest, a dozen bangle bracelets giving off a tinkling sound as she did so. "She chose the fool."

The Wizard looked down at the deck, sorting through it until he found the card I'd chosen.

"The card was inverted," the woman said, her gaze fixed on me. "That means you've made some type of impulsive, ill-advised decision."

Yeah, like agreeing to take the card in the first place. Then again, maybe the bad decision was my plan to put Brett on ice while Nick and I explored what might be between us. Maybe fate had been trying to intervene by sending Alicia to interrupt our conversation earlier in the week.

Then again, maybe this was all a bunch of bunk.

The Wizard held the cards out to Eddie now. Eddie snagged one and handed it to the Wiz. The Wiz, in turn, looked up at the woman.

"You've drawn the High Priestess," she said, stepping forward. "She represents intuition, secrets, and mystery."

The only mystery here was what these people had been smoking.

The woman collected the cards from the Wizard. "I've asked you not to take my cards, Mr. Wisbrock, remember? I need them to read for my clients."

The Wizard nodded, then gestured to me and Eddie. "What are they doing here?"

"They're from the IRS," she said. "I told you they were coming today. You should've listened to me."

No doubt the woman was Madam Magnolia. But we hadn't told anyone we were coming here today. How did she know we'd show up? I mean, that psychic stuff was pure hogwash, wasn't it?

Eddie and I showed the Wizard our badges.

"We'll need you to come with us," I said. "We're taking you in on tax fraud charges."

As Eddie began to recite the Miranda rights—"right to remain silent," "right to an attorney," blah, blah blah—the

Tax Wizard slowly stood from his desk. When I saw him go for his pocket, I drew on him. Better safe than sorry, right?

The Wizard removed his hand from his pocket. Though he held something between his fingers, it appeared too small to be a weapon.

"Alakazam!" he cried, throwing his hand into the air.

Poof!

Whatever he'd tossed into the air created an instant smoke screen.

Eddie waved his hand through the smoke. "What the hell?"

We looked at each other, not quite sure how to deal with the situation. We'd been trained to deal with regular wackos, ones who pulled guns or knives or attempted to flee. But there was nothing whatsoever in the IRS Special Agent Training Manual on how to deal with a magical smoke screen. Looked like it was time for an expanded edition. Maybe they should also add sections on how to ride a unicorn and shape-shift into a vampire. That wouldn't be too much of a stretch. People already thought IRS agents were bloodsuckers.

Fortunately, as quickly as the smoke had appeared it dissipated.

We glanced around the room. The Wizard was nowhere to be seen.

"Seriously," Eddie said, repeating himself. "What the hell?"

Richard Beauregard had managed to evade us. Had the Tax Wizard escaped as well? If we'd been outsmarted not only by an idiot with a unibrow but also by a lunatic in a starry cape, we'd be the laughingstocks of the office.

Madam Magnolia hadn't moved from her doorway, so it didn't seem likely that Wisbrock had escaped into her digs. While Eddie rushed outside to see if the Tax Wizard had fled out the door, I stepped around the desk and quickly looked around.

A corner of dark-blue fabric peeked out from behind the filing cabinets.

"Come on out, Mr. Wisbrock," I said. "I know you're behind the filing cabinets. I can see your robe."

The fabric was quickly snatched away.

Gun in hand, I eased toward the cabinets and peeked behind them. The Tax Wizard crouched there, his eyes squeezed
firmly closed and his fingers in his ears, like a child who
thought that if he couldn't see or hear his pursuers they
couldn't see or hear him, either.

I nudged him with my toe and he opened his eyes. He
looked up at me, pulled a wand from the pocket in his robe,
and waved it, chanting some nonsense over and over. "Moo
goo gai pan. Moo goo gai pan."

What kind of spell was he trying to put on me? And why
did his incantation sound familiar?

I took a closer look at Wisbrock's magic wand. *Sheez.* It
was only a cheap wooden chopstick, the kind you get at any
Asian restaurant. Suddenly his words made sense. They appeared on every Chinese take-out menu, under the section
for chicken dishes.

Eddie returned to the office, grabbed the Wizard's ankles,
and dragged him out from behind the filing cabinets. Wisbrock didn't put up a fight and surrendered peacefully.

If only all tax evaders would be so cooperative.

We handcuffed Wisbrock, sat him in his chair, and put a
call in to the marshals' office. While we waited for the marshals to retrieve the Tax Wizard, I rounded up some empty
boxes and four chocolate coconut cupcakes from the bakery
next door. I offered one to Madam Magnolia and one to the
Tax Wiz. I was beginning to think the guy wasn't so much
evil as simply nuts. I'd recommend a psychological evalua-
tion when I spoke with the attorneys from the Justice Department.

I gathered up the Wizard's files and loaded them into the
boxes. When I turned back to the Wizard, I noticed him eating the cupcake with unfettered hands.

"What happened to the handcuffs?" I asked.

He looked down. The cuffs lay in his lap.

I turned to Eddie. "Did you unlock them?"

His eyes went wide. "No. You?"

I shook my head.

Wisbrock just looked up at us and grinned a chocolate-coated grin.

A half hour later, the marshals had taken the Wiz away and Eddie and I gathered up the boxes to leave.

Madam Magnolia helped us carry the boxes out. "Thanks for going easy on the Wizard. He's got a few screws loose, but he doesn't mean any harm."

Despite filing dozens of bogus returns, he hadn't actually caused much harm, either. The returns he'd filed contained such outlandish data they'd been immediately flagged for review before refunds were issued. On one return he'd listed over fifty dependents. On another he'd reported a deduction for postage expenses in the amount of $7 million. People generally trusted their preparers and tended to take only a quick glance at their tax returns. They really needed to look the returns over more carefully.

We slammed the trunk closed.

"Thanks for your help," I told Madam Magnolia.

"No problem," she replied. "By the way, if you want to catch the man with one eyebrow, he's at a campground on Lake Lewisville. But you better hurry. He's planning to move out soon."

Eddie and I exchanged glances. How the heck did this woman know we were after Beauregard? Had we discussed his case while we were inside?

I racked my brain, reviewing our conversation. I didn't remember either of us mentioning Beauregard, and especially not his unibrow. Weird.

"Uh . . . thanks," I said, feeling a little freaked out but trying not to show it.

"My pleasure. Oh, and one more thing." She cast me a knowing smile. "*Neener-neener.*"

I was glad Eddie was driving as we pulled away from the curb, because I felt totally dazed and confused.

"How?" I demanded. "How did she know we were after

Beau?" And how did she know we'd show up today? And how did she know my catchphrase? And why was I asking Eddie these questions when the only one who knew the answers was Madam Magnolia?

"I don't know, Tara," Eddie said. "But there has to be a logical explanation."

Could Beauregard actually be at a campground at Lake Lewisville? It was possible. After all, his camp trailer had to be parked somewhere, right? He hadn't used his credit cards anywhere since we'd tried to arrest him, so we hadn't been able to track him to a hotel. I wasn't sure he'd even be able to use his credit cards. Most were maxed out and all were delinquent. Of course he could be staying at one of those sleazy cash-only motels that rented rooms by the hour.

I glanced out the window, then looked back at Eddie. "You think we should try the campground?"

Eddie shrugged. "Couldn't hurt."

"A-ha! So you *do* think Madam Magnolia could be on to something."

Eddie shot me an exasperated look. "No," he insisted. "I just think it would be nice to take a drive out to the lake."

"Bullshit."

As if to prove he didn't believe in Madam Magnolia's purported gift of prophecy, Eddie stopped to fill the car with gas, then took a detour through a coffeehouse drive-through. He ordered his usual black coffee while I opted for a caramel-drizzled extra-whip latte. Hey, winter was coming. I could hide any extra fat under sweaters and coats for the next few months, right?

We made our way out to Lake Lewisville and drove through the campgrounds, paying careful attention to the spaces with electrical and water hookups for campers. According to the DMV's vehicle registration records, Beauregard's trailer was a Palomino fifth-wheel-style travel camper, the Puma model. Unfortunately, none of the trailers on-site bore the Puma logo. Beau was nowhere to be found.

"See?" Eddie said as we drove toward the exit. "Madam Magnolia is just as bonkers as the Tax Wizard."

I pointed to the park ranger's shack. "Pull over. I want to talk to them."

Eddie emitted a snort of derision but nonetheless eased to a stop by the small structure.

A ranger slid the glass window open and tipped his pith helmet in greeting. "Howdy, folks."

We explained who we were, flashed our badges, and asked whether they'd had a camper by the name of Richard Beauregard.

The ranger consulted a sheet of paper on his clipboard. "Looks like he checked out of here a half hour ago. You just missed him."

Damn! We might have caught him if we hadn't stopped for gas and coffee.

I raised a brow at Eddie. "Think we should go ask Madam Magnolia where Beauregard's headed off to?"

"Hell, no," Eddie said. "I've got a reputation to uphold."

I could probably have gotten away with it. People at the office already thought I was a little kooky. Shooting a man in the nuts tends to earn one some notoriety. Still, I didn't want to put Eddie's good name at risk. I'd check in with Madam Magnolia later on my own.

chapter twelve

$\mathcal{L}$ooking for the Money Trail

I retrieved my G-ride and spent the rest of the afternoon visiting money transmitters, hoping for a lead in the terrorism case.

According to the data in the file Agent Wang had given me, the men who'd been arrested here in Dallas had maintained accounts in a number of banks and credit unions, keeping their balances relatively low to avoid catching the attention of bank personnel. They had a standard MO. Just prior to transferring funds overseas, they'd make a series of cash withdrawals from their accounts, each in the two-thousand-to three-thousand-dollar range. They probably thought that by spreading the funds among several banks they'd enable their multiple withdrawals to go unnoticed and unreported.

About a year ago, one of the banks had bought one of the others, though the terrorists were apparently unaware of the pending consolidation. During the merger process, a keen teller clued in to the fact that one of the men had made significant cash withdrawals from both banks within a half hour of each other. A Suspicious Activity Report was filed and an investigation ensued, though at first nothing came of it. It wasn't until agents in Syria received information from an informant there that the government put two and two together and realized the man who'd made the suspicious withdrawals here in Dallas was financing the terrorists overseas. Although surveillance helped federal agents identify the man and most of his cohorts, they never could determine who had helped them transfer the funds.

My first stop was Zippy's Liquor, a small, grubby place in dire need of a thorough scrubbing. As I reviewed the store's wire transfer records, I found several errors and discrepancies. While most were minor transgressions that appeared unintentional, the records included several large transfers to Honduras, including three made on a single night to the same party, each in the amount of four thousand dollars.

It was obvious the transactions had been intentionally structured to keep each transfer under the ten-thousand-dollar cash-transaction reporting threshold. Still, banking regulations required MSBs to observe not only the letter of the law but also the spirit. If an MSB suspected a client of manipulating their transactions to avoid the cash-transaction reporting requirements, the MSB was supposed to file a Suspicious Activity Report. In this case, no such report had been filed.

Hmm . . .

Was it possible that the terrorists had filtered their money through someone in Honduras who had then forwarded the funds to Syria? Having their funds sent to a straw man in a seemingly innocuous country would be a good way to avoid detection.

I showed the staff on duty the photographs of the men who'd been arrested, but none of them claimed to recognize Algafari, Nasser, or Homsi. Hard to say whether they were telling me the truth. Perhaps I should hire Madam Magnolia as a consultant to read their minds. Then again, there was no way in hell the tight asses in the IRS accounting department would reimburse the cost of a psychic consultant.

I pulled the manager aside and asked who had handled the transfers to Honduras. He glanced at the records. Though he could not tell for certain who had handled the transfers, he noted they'd been performed in the evenings by the staff who worked the 6:00 to 10:00 PM shift.

"How many people work in the evenings?" I asked.

"Four," he said. "Two per shift." He counted them off on his fingers. "Dottie, Israel, Jesús, and Gloria."

I jotted down their full names and Social Security numbers and informed the manager I'd come back at a later time to speak with them.

On my way to my next MSB, I spotted a sign up ahead.

PARADISE TRAILER PARK—STAY FOR A DAY
OR STAY FOR A LIFETIME.

Might as well check it out, huh? Beau had to move his camper somewhere after he left the lake. Perhaps he'd driven it to Paradise.

I pulled into the park, driving slowly down each row, searching for his camper. I eyed the trailers, looking for the telltale Puma logo. One had a hawk on the side; another featured a deer. But nope, no big cats here. The closest I got was a stray orange tom popping a squat in a kid's sandbox. There'd be an unpleasant surprise in Little Johnny's sand castle tomorrow.

I stopped at the management office and left my business card with the woman who ran the place, asking her to give me a call if Richard Beauregard happened to show his face.

My last official stop for the day was a bus station. As I approached the place, I noticed that the parking lot was virtually empty of cars. Not surprising, I supposed. People who owned cars didn't need bus service, right?

I pulled into the lot. The darn thing looked like a minefield, potholes all over the place. I drove slowly to avoid hitting one and damaging a tire. I parked near the front glass doors and climbed out of my car.

Two young men in hoodies and ripped jeans leaned

against the exterior wall, smoking cigarettes. They eyed my car and exchanged glances. I could virtually see their minds computing how much cash they could get at a chop shop for my hubcaps and engine parts.

I whipped my badge from my purse and held it up. "I'm a federal agent. You lay one finger on my car, boys, and you will be sorry."

They glared at me, not even bothering to pretend they'd simply been admiring my car for its power or appearance.

I pulled open one of the glass doors and stepped inside. Sheesh, the place was depressing. The lobby smelled of urine, stale cigarettes, and coffee left too long on a burner.

A few people sat in the cheap plastic chairs, waiting until it was time to load their buses. A Latina woman was on her cell phone, having a heated argument with someone in Spanish while her two young girls chased each other in circles around the bank of chairs. A twentysomething black man stared droopy eyed into space, slowly bobbing his head to music playing through his earbuds. A stoop-shouldered elderly white man mumbled to himself while eating a ham-and-cheese sandwich he'd bought from the refrigerated vending machine. Some dinner.

A blonde in a frayed denim miniskirt stood near the doors, strumming a guitar and singing a horribly botched version of a Taylor Swift song. A quick glance into the open guitar case at her feet showed her efforts had earned her a whopping twenty-three cents so far. I was tempted to offer her a dollar to stop her off-key caterwauling, but who was I to kill a young girl's dream of stardom? I dropped the bill into her guitar case anyway, hoping she'd apply the money toward voice lessons.

I made my way across the mismatched tile floor to the booth. A large bald black man sat behind a pane of thick glass I suspected was bulletproof. He appeared to be in his mid- to late fifties, his expansive forehead wrinkled with age, making him resemble a shar-pei. He was reading a Tom Clancy novel.

"Hi," I said, flipping my badge open. "I'm Special Agent

Tara Holloway with the IRS. I need to take a look at the records for wire transfers, money orders, and traveler's checks."

The man lifted his chin in acknowledgment, extended his hand through the small window at the bottom of the glass panel, and pointed to a door a few feet away. I stepped over to the door and he opened it to let me in, locking it behind me.

He introduced himself only as Mack. Given his size, his last name might as well have been Truck.

Mack walked with the confident gait of a man who knew how to handle himself. I followed him back to the ticket booth, which turned out to be merely a small nook in what was otherwise a fairly large administrative area. Four built-in desks ran along the walls. Two of them were occupied by older women wearing headsets connected to multiline telephones, while a young man in a mechanic's uniform sat at another, surfing the Web with grease-stained fingers.

Mack directed me to the empty desk and showed me how to log into their system and access the information I sought. I thanked him and he returned to his nook and his book.

I was immersed in data a half hour later when I heard a commotion at the ticket booth. I looked up to see a young kid standing on the other side of the glass, aiming a pistol at the ticket booth attendant. The boy had bright orange hair, braces on his buck teeth, and looked all of twelve years old. He held the gun on its side, gangster-style.

"Give me all your money," the kid said, his voice cracking with puberty hormones. "Or else." His hand shook uncontrollably, telling me this was likely his first stickup.

Mack barely glanced up from his novel. "Or else what?"

The kid looked confused. Apparently he hadn't expected questions.

"I'm not interested in playing cops and robbers." Mack waved his open book at the boy, shooing him. "Buzz off, squirt."

The boy stood there for a moment, unsure what to do. He pulled out a cell phone, dialed a number, and told the person on the other end of the line what had taken place. The kid listened intently, shoved the phone back into his pocket, and banged his adolescent fist on the glass. "Give me your money or I'll shoot you and everyone else, too!"

His raised voice caught the attention of those in the lobby. The woman with the guitar fled out the door, the old man on her heels. The Latina woman gathered up her girls and followed the others, rolling her bags behind her. Only the man listening to music through his earbuds didn't move. He probably hadn't heard a thing.

"I don't believe a word you're saying, you little carrot-topped shit." Mack banged his fist on the inside of the glass, imitating the little twerp, laughing when the boy flinched. "I bet you don't even have bullets in that gun."

I glanced around me. Back here, behind the glass, everyone was nonplussed. The women on the phone continued to take calls, answering questions about bus schedules and taking seat reservations. The mechanic didn't bother to look up from his computer.

I put in a quick call to 911, rose from my seat, and made my way to the ticket booth. As I did, the kid said, "Last chance, futhermucker."

"Futhermucker?" The ticket seller threw his head back and laughed. "Kid, you got no business pulling a stunt like this. Go back home to your scooter and your G.I. Joe."

The kid's face clouded with anger. He raised the gun level with the man's face and pulled the trigger.

Bang!

The bullet hit the glass and was absorbed into it, thin cracks spreading like a spiderweb over the surface. The kid shrieked, but the ticket seller didn't even blink. Forget buns of steel. This guy had titanium testicles.

Mack's arm shot out, reached through the small opening for passing cash and tickets back and forth, and grabbed the front of the kid's jacket. He yanked the boy forward, slamming the kid's face against the glass. The gun clattered to the floor at the boy's feet as he now used both hands to resist having his face smashed to bits.

Knowing I was useless on this side of the glass, I ran

down the hall, out the door, and into the lobby. The attendant continued to yank forcibly on the boy's jacket, give the kid just enough slack for him to back up a few inches, then yank the kid forward again. The boy's face repeatedly hit the glass.

Bam!

Bam!

Bam!

I got the distinct feeling this wasn't the first time Mack had used this particular technique to subdue a would-be bandit.

I snatched the boy's gun from the floor and shoved it into my pocket. I pulled out my cuffs and clicked them onto the boy's wrists while his hands were stretched up against the glass in his futile resistance effort. His puny preteen muscles were no match for the man on the other side of the glass.

Mack let go of the boy's jacket and I shoved the kid to the floor. "Don't move!"

The kid struggled to a sitting position and looked up at me, terror and desperation in his eyes. "I didn't know the gun was loaded!"

"Really. Then why did you pull the trigger?"

" 'Cause he made fun of me!"

I crossed my arms over my chest and rolled my eyes. "Tell it to the judge, kid."

"If you let me go," the boy said, tears welling up in his eyes, "my dad will pay for the window."

I looked down at him and shook my head. "Kid, that window is the least of your problems right now."

The boy began to cry. "I want my mommy!"

If I'd pulled something like this as a child, my mother would be the last person I'd want. She'd tan my hide.

I looked up, my gaze meeting Mack's through the cracked glass. "Nice moves," I said. "Former military?"

He shook his head. "Former Black Panther."

Twenty minutes later, Dallas PD had hauled the boy off to the juvenile detention facility. They'd also sent officers out to arrest the boy's eighteen-year-old brother, who'd needed quick funds to replace beer he'd snitched from the family fridge and put the kid up to the stunt rather than risk adding to his own rap sheet. With any luck, the boy would learn his lesson and wouldn't follow in his brother's dirty footsteps.

I returned to my review of the bus station's records, but just like the kid's attempt to rob the place, my search was futile. I thanked the attendant for his time and headed out, hoping Eddie or Agent Wang had more luck than I'd had today.

chapter thirteen

$\mathcal{B}$argain Hunting

Frustrated by my lack of success, I phoned Eddie to see if he'd had any more luck at the money transmitters than I had. He hadn't. And we still had a slew of MSBs left to visit. It could take weeks to hit them all. Working our way down a list seemed horribly inefficient. There had to be a better approach, didn't there?

Eddie exhaled sharply into his phone. "We could spend weeks spinning our wheels."

It had happened before and it was frustrating as hell. Eddie and I didn't mind working hard, but we didn't want our efforts to be in vain. Our time was too important.

"Think there's any point in paying a visit to the men who were arrested?" I asked. "See if they'll open up?"

Eddie and I knew their attorneys had instructed them to remain silent. Hell, Homsi, the one who'd originally offered to turn state's witness in return for leniency, couldn't talk now even if he wanted to. Can't form words without a tongue. I supposed he could write, though. I wondered how he managed to eat in prison. Maybe they brought him jars of baby food. I imagined him eating that pinkish-gray guck that purported to be some type of meat.

Urk.

Yeah, visiting the jail would likely be another waste of our time. Still, it wasn't unheard of for someone who'd been arrested to have a change of heart after spending some time in the slammer. Using the toilet with an audience couldn't be fun, and once a man had suffered a few dozen lousy meals, spent restless nights on a painfully thin mattress, and fought off repeated amorous advances from a big and burly guy named Crazy Al, he could sometimes be more easily convinced to cooperate in order to whittle time off his sentence.

"You never know," Eddie said. "Sometimes a person who won't open up to one agent will spill their guts to another."

"Let's give it a shot then," I said. "What have we got to lose?"

I phoned the terrorists' attorneys and arranged meetings at the jail. All of them told me they'd instructed their clients not to talk unless a very generous plea deal was offered. Heck, it would probably be malpractice if the lawyers had done otherwise. But I suspected each attorney secretly hoped his client would decide to cop a plea. Better to collect their legal fees and move on to the next case than spend precious time preparing for a trial they were sure to lose.

At five thirty, I was headed home when I drove past a pawnshop. The store was called Strike-it-Rich Pawn and featured a rusty fifteen-foot oil derrick atop the roof. A large sign in the window caught my eye.

Gun Sale

I braked and made an illegal U-turn. It's not like a cop would give me a ticket. I was on official federal government business.

Sort of.

Many women collected teacups or figurines or rare books. I, however, owned a sizable handgun collection. To each her own, right?

I'd been worrying about Nick all day, whether he'd fall for one of the women from the dating site before I had a chance to break up with Brett. I needed something to lift my spirits. A new gun would be just the thing. Besides, Dallas rush-hour traffic was a bitch. Might as well go check out the guns and let the gridlock ease up a bit.

I pulled into the drive. The only vehicles in the lot were a Harley with high-arching handlebars parked near the door and an ancient wood-paneled station wagon parked at the end. I took a spot next to the motorcycle.

Metal burglar bars covered the front windows and glass door, which bore a sign that read: "FAMILY OWNED AND OPERATED SINCE 1952." A string of bells hung from the inside door rail, giving off a tinny tinkle as I entered. The place smelled like dust and rose petals. Dust because the place was dusty, rose petals because of the large glass bowl of potpourri perched on a pedestal near the door.

The place contained the usual amalgamation of odds and ends sacrificed by desperate owners needing quick cash. Guitars in both acoustic and electric varieties lined one wall, along with amplifiers and an electronic keyboard. Televisions of all sizes took up at least a quarter of the room, followed by stereo and computer equipment.

I wandered farther into the store. Toward the back of the space was a wide selection of exercise equipment, most of it nearly new, abandoned by owners who'd long since given up on their New Year's resolutions to get in shape. Treadmills, exercise bikes, stair steppers, elliptical machines. Heck, there was even a first-generation NordicTrack with the pull ropes.

Near the register was an assortment of sports equipment. Golf clubs, hockey sticks, tennis rackets. A wooden rack displayed both snow skis and water skis. Whether you wanted to ski on frozen or melted H_2O, this place could trick you out.

Each of the items bore a round orange price sticker with the store's oil derrick logo printed on it in black. The prices were handwritten below the derricks.

I approached the register. Behind it was a short woman who appeared to be in her mid- to late fifties, around my mother's age. Her soft brown curls were tinged with streaks of gray. She had the roundish figure of a woman who'd borne several children. She wore a loose cotton shirt untucked over a pair of well-worn corduroy pants. White canvas sneakers graced her small feet.

When the woman looked down at a stack of paperwork on the counter, her pink plastic-framed reading glasses threatened to slide off the end of her nose. She put her index finger on the nosepiece to push the glasses back into place. She appeared flustered as she rifled through the documents. No wonder. A man wearing a black leather vest with no shirt, dirty blue jeans, biker boots, and a bandana wrapped around his shaved head stood at the counter, staring her down. His arms, adorned with sleeve tattoos, were crossed over his chest, his underarm hair fluffed out around his pits as if his upper arms were wearing brown tutus.

The man's language was as colorful as his tattooed arms. "I've paid off my fucking loan. I want my goddamn guitar back."

The woman's eyes shone with fear as she looked up at the man. "I'm sorry. I can't seem to put my hands on your paperwork. But it's got to be here somewhere if you'll just bear with me." She set aside the stack she'd been sorting through and pulled a box out from under the counter. "Maybe it's in here." She dumped the contents of the box onto the counter and began sifting through the stack.

The pawnshop still used old-fashioned paper records? A bit surprising in these days of computerized data storage. The outdated record-keeping method had probably been in place since the store opened in 1952.

The man waited a couple more minutes, though his tapping boot made it clear his patience was growing thin. "Look, lady. You're wasting my time and screwing me over. I've paid back every cent I owe you." He pointed to a shiny black electric guitar on display. "That's my guitar right there. I want it back. *Now.*"

The woman's glasses slid down her nose again and once again she pushed them back. The man appeared to have a legitimate beef, but at the same time this poor woman seemed to be in over her head.

I stepped up to the counter, noting that the man smelled faintly, though undoubtedly, of marijuana. You'd think a stoner would be a bit more mellow, huh?

I pulled back my blazer to reveal the gun holstered at my waist in case the biker had any thoughts of getting violent. "I'm Special Agent Tara Holloway with the IRS. Can I be of help here?"

Now the man's eyes bore a slight tinge of fear. Unreported income from pot sales, perhaps? He backed away a step or two, as if wanting to put some distance between us. "We're good," he said, probably hoping I'd step away.

He didn't know me very well, did he?

I stayed at the counter, looking around. On a shelf behind the register was an official Major League Baseball bat autographed by Texas Rangers star Josh Hamilton. Next to it was an autographed baseball signed by Rangers legend Nolan Ryan. My father would love the ball and Christmas was coming in a couple of months. I squinted to read the price sticker on the plastic box. One hundred and fifty bucks. That was doable.

"Phew!" the woman said, her tense features softening in relief as she pulled a loan agreement from the pile. "Found it." She stamped each page of the man's triplicate form with a rubber stamp that read: "PAID IN FULL" and handed him the yellow copy. He snatched the paper out of her hand and turned to leave, grabbing his guitar from the wall as he left.

"Thanks for your help with that man." The woman gave me a grateful look as she restacked the paperwork. "He got me all flustered."

"Glad to help."

The woman scooped up the papers and plopped them back into the box. "Can I help you with something, hon?"

"I saw the sign in the window. I'm interested in seeing the guns you've got on sale."

The woman gestured for me to walk down to a glass display case at the other end of the counter. Several guns in the case caught my eye.

On the top shelf was a nice Beretta 3032 Tomcat. I'd shot one before. Great accuracy. Next to it sat a Ruger Super Redhawk revolver. The gun's disproportionately long skinny barrel gave it a comical look, as if a white flag reading: "BANG!" would pop out when the gun was fired.

"Could you show me the Cobra?" The Cobra CA380 pistol was cherry red, my signature color. It was also lightweight and compact, the perfect gun for a woman.

The woman pulled a stretchy coiled key chain from her wrist. The plastic bracelet seemed like a good way to keep her keys handy. Maybe I should get a key chain like that for when I went jogging.

Oh, who the hell was I kidding? I never actually went jogging.

The woman reached into the case, retrieved the weapon, and held it out to me. "Here you go."

Like the other items in the store, it bore an orange label with the oil derrick logo. I took it in my right hand, gripping it and pretending to take aim at the clock mounted on the wall behind the counter, testing its feel. *Hmm. Not bad.* The piece would cost about eighty bucks brand-new. According to the price tag on this secondhand model, it was on sale for thirty dollars.

While I was examining the gun, the bells on the door tinkled behind me. A UPS courier in a brown uniform headed toward us, a large cardboard box in his hand.

"Got a package for you, Margie," he said, holding the box out to her.

She pushed her glasses back once again and glanced at the return address, a smile spreading across her face. "Oh, good. That's the toy train I ordered for my grandson's birthday. He's going to love it." She took the box and thanked the man, calling, "Take care!" as he headed back out the door to the large brown truck parked out front.

After she stashed the box under the counter, the woman I now knew as Margie returned her attention to me and the gun in my hand. "What do you think?"

I engaged in a brief mental debate. I already owned a .38, a pretty pearl-handled model. But thirty bucks was an awfully good deal. *What the hell,* I decided. Between Nick dating other women, Beauregard escaping out his window, and me striking out at the money transmitter offices, it had been a frustrating week. Why not treat myself to a little pick-me-up? "I'll take it."

"Okeydokey," Margie said, stepping back to look under the counter. "I'll need you to fill out a form first." She pulled out a manila file folder and peeked inside. "Nope. That's not it."

This woman was friendly enough, but she really needed some help in here, someone with good organization skills. After five minutes of searching, she finally found the required Form 4473 Firearms Transactions Record in a two-drawer filing cabinet pushed up against the back wall. "Here you go." She handed me the form and a ballpoint pen.

We chatted as I filled out the form. She told me she had five grandchildren, two boys and three girls, all under the age of ten. The grandson who would be the happy recipient of the toy train was turning seven on Saturday. She showed me his most recent school photo, which she carried in her wallet. He was an endearing kid, all freckles, with a gap-toothed grin.

I pronounced him a "cutie-pie."

She gazed lovingly at the photograph. "He's growing like a weed."

My mother said the exact same thing about my nieces and nephews.

"What's it like working for the IRS?" Margie asked as she put her wallet away.

"Never a dull moment," I lied. Actually, there were lots of dull moments. Like all afternoon when I'd been looking through transaction records at the money transmitter offices. *Urk.* Talk about tedious. Still, among my job's many dull moments were some interesting ones, too. Some thrilling, some even terrifying. I'd been attacked with a box cutter and shot at several times during my short tenure with the IRS. But, hey, I'd lived to tell about it. All's well that ends well, right?

"I can't imagine all the paperwork you have to deal with," she said.

"Luckily, most things are computerized these days." I cocked my head. "Have you considered updating your record-keeping systems here? It might make things easier to find if you kept your records on a computer."

"Oh, honey, I'm a hopeless case. My son once hooked up a computer in here, but it was a complete disaster." She shook her head and rolled her eyes in a self-deprecating manner. "I tried and tried, but I couldn't get the hang of it. Like they say, you can't teach an old dog new tricks."

"You're not such an old dog." I offered her a smile.

She offered me one right back. "That's kind of you to say. Me and technology, though, we simply don't get along. Sometimes I think I was born in the wrong century."

Once I'd completed the form, she pulled a telephone out from under the counter. Holy moly, the old-timey thing had a rotary dial. Coming into this shop was like stepping back in time.

The woman dialed into the National Instant Criminal Background Check System, otherwise known as NICS, as required by the Brady Bill. The law required her to verify that I was not a convicted felon, drug addict, or adjudicated psychiatric risk, and thus eligible to purchase a gun.

The Brady Bill came into being after Jim Brady, President Reagan's press secretary, was shot along with the president and two others in an assassination attempt. The shooter, John Hinckley, Jr., bought the revolver he used in the shooting at a pawnshop right here in Dallas. Weird how the city had so many links to presidential assassinations, huh? Something in the water here must make people want to kill government officials. Hinckley had given a false home address and used an old Texas driver's license as proof he lived in the state.

The guy had been arrested four days prior to the shooting at an airport in Nashville when he'd attempted to board an American Airlines flight bound for New York with three handguns and ammunition in his carry-on bag. Hinckley had also been under psychiatric care before he'd bought the gun.

Though many people believed a three-day waiting period was required to purchase a gun, such was not actually the case. After intense lobbying by the NRA, lawmakers had caved and replaced the proposed waiting period with the instant background check system. Thus I could take my gun home with me today. The gun nut in me was happy about that. The law enforcement agent in me thought that perhaps a waiting period wouldn't be such a bad idea.

Margie and I chatted while she was on hold with NICS.

"I noticed the sign on the door," I said. "This place has been in your family for over sixty years?"

She nodded. "My grandpappy started the business back in the day; then my father took over. I'm an only child, so when Daddy got too old to take care of the store he turned it over to me and my husband to run."

I wondered if Nick and I would get tired of each other if we not only worked together but also dated. "Does it get tiresome?" I asked. "Working with your husband?"

"I never thought so," she said wryly. "He must've felt differently, though. He took off two years ago with some floozy he met right here in the store. She came in to look at our jewelry selection and the next day he left me a note on the cash register telling me he needed to go 'find himself.'"

"Let me guess. He 'found himself' between the floozy's thighs?"

"Exactly."

We laughed together about her man troubles. Maybe someday I'd be able to laugh about mine. Right now? Not so much.

The woman raised a finger to let me know an NICS agent had finally picked up the line. She identified herself as Margie Bainbridge, the owner of Strike-it-Rich, then read my information into the phone, rattling off my name, gender, and date and place of birth. She was silent for a moment as she waited for a response. A few seconds later she jotted down a transaction number and hung up the phone. "Good news," she said. "You're approved."

Goody, goody gumdrops.

I paid for my gun in cash.

"Nice chatting with you," she said as she handed me a plastic bag with my gun in it.

"You, too. Have fun at your grandson's birthday party." I bade the woman a fond farewell.

chapter fourteen

Second Chances

Thursday evening, Alicia and I headed out in her sleek black Audi, once again tracking Nick. Tonight he'd be taking out his ex-fiancée, Natalie. Nick had once loved the woman enough to propose to her. I had to do what I could to make sure he didn't fall in love with her again.

I filled a thermos with peach sangria and brought it with me, sipping it as I pulled up the GPS app on my phone. The dot on the map led us to a neighborhood of starter homes in Irving. Nick's truck was parked at the curb in front of Natalie's house, a one-story model with salmon-colored brick. White picket fencing outlined the flower beds underneath her front windows. A whitewashed rocking chair sat on her front porch next to a terra-cotta pot filled with yellow pansies. The front door bore a wreath of autumn-colored silk leaves adorned with plastic pumpkins and wooden letters that spelled: "HAPPY FALL, Y'ALL!"

Everything about the place indicated that Natalie was the Suzy Q Homemaker type. In other words, my complete opposite.

Alicia and I drove by the house, circled the block, and drove by it again.

I narrowed my eyes as I looked at the pristine house. "I bet Natalie's fridge is full of fresh vegetables and homemade apple pie and milk that's still within its expiration date." My fridge contained only a pitcher of peach sangria, a quart of skim milk that smelled iffy, and something green and fuzzy that had once been either a lemon or a kiwi. I'd gone to throw it out earlier but had instead slammed the crisper closed when the thing seemed to move on its own.

I turned to my friend as we drove past the house a third time. "You think that's what Nick wants? A woman who will take care of him? Cook and clean and all that?" If so, our relationship would be doomed. I could hit a target from a hundred yards and take down a man half again my size, but when it came to domestic skills I was sorely lacking.

"I don't know," Alicia said. "He does still live with his mother, so yeah, maybe that's what he wants."

I cut angry eyes her way. "Lie to me next time, okay?"

"Absolutely not." She cut her eyes back at me. "Best friends are always honest with each other. Even when it hurts."

Natalie's front door opened and she and Nick walked out onto the porch. Natalie was dressed in ballet flats, a long skirt that flowed loosely around her ankles, and a white sweater set. She looked prim and proper, perhaps even prudish.

Nick had once planned to spend the rest of his life with this woman. Why? If you asked me, she looked straightlaced and boring.

Alicia punched the gas before they could spot us. We turned the corner and waited on the next block with the engine running. A couple minutes later we consulted the GPS map and headed after them, following them to a nearby Tex-Mex restaurant. Apparently Nick had a hankering for chimichangas tonight. I hoped the night wouldn't end with him slipping Natalie his beef enchilada.

We sat at the end of the lot and watched them walk inside. Nick held the door open for Natalie and put a hand on her lower back as he followed her in. A familiar gesture. Not surprising, I guess. The two had once been very familiar with each other.

I felt a twinge of pain at the thought of Nick being intimate with another woman, that corkscrew in my heart again. *It didn't work out between them before,* I reminded myself. *Maybe they're only getting together to talk about old times.* Unfortunately, I wasn't much good at convincing myself this date would go nowhere. Maybe the timing had been wrong earlier, but now it would be right. Maybe whatever had gone wrong had reconciled itself. Maybe things had changed and their relationship would work the second time around. It happened often enough, right? Heck, my own parents had split up for a while before tying the knot.

Was it possible I wasn't the woman for Nick, after all? Was it possible I was only his Candy Cummings?

What a kick in the pants that would be.

Alicia and I debated tactics, deciding it would be too suspicious if either of us went inside the restaurant. Running into Nick two nights in a row in a city as big as Dallas could never be passed off as mere coincidence. But thanks to modern technology, I could interrupt his date without having to step foot in the place.

Neener-neener, Natalie-ner.

I closed the GPS app and sent Nick a text. *Bought a new gun. Want 2 hit the range tomorrow?*

How's that for chalupas interruptus?

A few seconds later Nick's terse reply arrived. *Sure.*

I texted back: *I'm going to buy ammo. Need any?*

This time his response didn't come for two minutes. *No thanx.*

The new gun's a Cobra .38.

I waited three minutes, but Nick didn't respond. I felt a stirring of panic in my gut. I wished I had an extra-large flyswatter so I could put a quick end to Gnatalie. I put my thumbs to work again. *The gun's red. Really cool.*

No response.

Got a good deal at a pawnshop.

Still no response.

A sick feeling oozed through me. Nick was ignoring me. And not just ignoring me, but ignoring me so that he could interact with his former bride-to-be, the wholesome princess of fresh vegetables and unexpired milk and seasonal door wreaths.

My thumbs desperately worked the keys on my phone. *Only paid 30 bucks.*

Nothing.

Terror wrapped its hand around my throat and squeezed.

"What should I do?" I asked Alicia. "This isn't working." I supposed I could lob a Molotov cocktail into the restaurant. After all, I knew how to make them now and could easily improvise one by shoving my day-of-the-week panties into the top of the sangria-filled thermos and igniting it with the car's cigarette lighter. But I wasn't sure that trying to extinguish Nick's old flame warranted a felony arson conviction.

"Maybe I could call in a bomb threat," I said, thinking out loud. Unfortunately, a bomb threat would also be a felony.

After more thought, I settled for sending Nick a link to a Web site about bedbugs. If he'd had any thoughts about taking Natalie to bed tonight, the thought of those nasty bloodsuckers taking a bite of his bare ass ought to having him thinking twice about getting naked with her. I followed it up with a text that read: *Oops! I meant to send that to someone else.*

"You're an evil genius," Alicia said. "It kind of scares me sometimes."

"It kind of scares me, too." If not for my Baptist upbringing, I probably could have turned to the dark side.

We waited and waited, growing bored and turning to YouTube to occupy our time. We watched all of the Simon's Cat cartoons, viewed some music videos, laughed at some clever movie spoofs. Really, how did people entertain themselves before the Internet and smartphones?

"You know," I said to Alicia, "Nick, Josh, and Lu have had success with that dating service. If you're serious about putting yourself back on the market, maybe you should give it a try."

"You're probably right." She sighed. "I'll think about it."

Rap! The noise of knuckles on the passenger window made both of us jump.

I looked up to find Nick looking in at me. He didn't look happy.

Uh-oh.

He stared—*glared?*—in at me for a moment, then held up the black GPS device between his thumb and index finger.

Busted.

I shrank back against the seat. No need for a cigarette lighter to ignite my cheeks. I could feel them flaming hotter than any Molotov cocktail.

Nick made a motion for me to roll down the window.

I punched the button and the window came down. "Uh . . . hi, Nick," I said, forcing a jovial tone and a smile.

He said nothing, just tossed the device into my lap and walked away.

Damn.

"You know that 'evil genius' comment I made earlier?" Alicia said.

"Yeah?"

"I take it back."

chapter fifteen

$\mathcal{L}$ots of Bull

When I arrived at work Friday morning, I scurried into my office and closed the door, hoping to avoid a confrontation with Nick. No such luck. Just seconds after I'd shut my door he opened it without knocking.

"It's polite to knock," I said.

He leaned against the door frame and crossed his arms over his broad chest. "You've suddenly developed a sense of boundaries?"

Another hot blush raced to my face and ears. Even my scalp felt hot. My hair threatened to melt.

"Eddie got pulled into an urgent case this morning," Nick said, thankfully dropping the subject of my botched attempt to spy on him. "Lu wants me to go out to Bulls-Eye with you."

Despite my embarrassment, my girl parts shouted, *Yee-ha!* Spending the morning with Nick would be an unexpected treat, like an appetizer for the full meal to come once I talked with Brett tonight. My simile assumed, of course, that Nick hadn't decided to take his meals elsewhere, maybe somewhere with fresh vegetables and milk and homemade apple pie.

Nick and I snagged a sedan from the fleet and headed out.

The day was partly cloudy, the sun peeking out, then retreating, unsure and insecure just like me. Was I too late? Had Nick rekindled his flame with Natalie?

Since he'd returned the GPS to me last night, I had no way of knowing whether he'd stayed at her house after their date. I couldn't very well have driven by her house to check. Not after being caught red-handed.

I wondered if he had gone to bed with Natalie when he'd taken her home last night. I'd hardly slept last night thinking about the possibility.

I surreptitiously glanced over at him. The clench in his jaw told me he wasn't a man who'd experienced a recent physical release. Good. Maybe my bedbug scheme had worked.

Nick didn't talk on the drive, didn't ask me why I'd followed him last night. I wasn't sure whether that was good or bad. Didn't he wonder? Didn't he care?

While Eddie and I constantly fought over the radio, Nick and I were totally in tune, both happy to keep the stereo dial set to a country station. Nick sang along with the music as we made our way. While he pulled off a fairly decent imitation of Garth Brooks, his Faith Hill could use some work.

As we drove, I thought about Brett, how my date with him that night could be our last. Then I remembered the evening would also mark Josh's first date with Kira.

"Think Josh will get lucky tonight?" I asked Nick. I wondered what type of birth control two techies would use. The algorithm method?

Nick grunted. "I think it'll be a miracle if Josh gets up the nerve to give Kira a kiss. That boy may know computers, but when it comes to women he's damn near hopeless."

"Maybe you should teach him some of your tricks."

Nick tossed me a naughty grin. "That would be like letting a child play with dynamite. Josh doesn't have my mojo."

Bulls-Eye Taxidermy and Tax Processing was situated in a log cabin on a rural highway southeast of Dallas. We performed a slow drive-by, checking things out. A red-and-white Bulls-Eye was painted on the door. A Rebel flag hung from a pole mounted between the front windows. A marquee sign on wheels sat at the edge of the highway in front of the cabin. The plastic letters read:

WHETHER ITS DEER SEASO OR TAX S ASON
LET BULL EYE DO YOUR ROCESS NG
PENIS

No doubt kids had rearranged the letters on the sign as a prank. But the message was still clear. No matter what hunting season it was—duck, deer, or javelina—it was always tax season at Bulls-Eye.

Two pickups were parked in front of the building. We knew from the plates that the Ford F-350 belonged to Jimmy John McClure, the owner of Bulls-Eye. The other presumably belonged to a client, but whether the client was at Bulls-Eye for tax or taxidermy services was unknown. Either way, we didn't want to put an innocent person in a dangerous situation. Our research indicated Jimmy John owned no fewer than a dozen firearms. No doubt he'd have at least one of them on hand. We'd wait until McClure was alone before confronting him.

There wasn't much else around, other than a taco stand and an XXX-rated book and novelty store. There were two cars at the taco stand, at least a dozen at the sex shop. Barely 11:00 AM and the perverts were already at it.

"Tacos or glory holes," Nick said. "Your call."

Ew. No question here. "Tacos. Definitely tacos."

We drove through the stand and picked up food and soft drinks, parking at the edge of the lot where we could keep watch on the log cabin. We ate in silence, other than the crunch of the taco shells and the squeak of the plastic drinking straws, that is.

While Nick ate he toyed with his phone, sending and

receiving texts, smiling and chuckling at something witty he'd received. I assumed they were from Natalie.

Don't fall for her again! my mind screamed at him. I hoped his subconscious would pick up on my message.

Nick turned his phone so I could see it. "Check this out."

On his screen was a photo of a butternut squash that looked like Jay Leno.

"Hilarious," I said, forcing a smile I didn't feel.

"I don't know where my mother finds this stuff," Nick said.

Okay, feeling the smile now.

We finished our lunch and looked up to see the pickup truck drive out of the Bulls-Eye parking lot. Presumably Jimmy John was alone now.

We drove across the road and into the gravel parking lot. Nick chose a spot near the door. We slid into our ballistic vests and raid jackets and made our way inside.

The interior of the cabin was dimly lit and smelled gamy. A stuffed brown bear posed in an attack stance greeted us as we entered. A flock of stuffed pheasants dangled from the ceiling, aimed upward as if in flight. Along the upper walls hung a wide variety of animal heads affixed to wood mounts. A wild boar with tusks. A twelve-point buck. A bobcat with a Dallas Cowboys cap on his head and a party blower in his mouth. How humiliating.

Jimmy John sat on a stool behind the counter, sorting through a coffee can of glass eyeballs, apparently looking for a matched set. He was a beefy man, nearly as wide as he was tall, and was dressed head to toe in camouflage print. He wore his brown hair in a buzz cut. Behind him was a set of metal shelves on which wood head mounts and tools were arranged.

He glanced up as we approached. "Howdy, folks. How can I help ya?"

The HVAC unit rattled as it kicked on overhead. Nick and I stepped up to the counter and showed Jimmy John our badges.

"We're from IRS Criminal Investigations," Nick said,

taking the lead. "We've got evidence you've prepared a number of fraudulent returns. We're here to take you in for arraignment."

"Say what now?" Jimmy John stood, his close-set, beady eyes flashing with alarm.

"Keep your hands where we can see them," I said, my hand instinctively reaching toward my hip holster.

"You're under arrest," Nick clarified. "Raise your hands and step out from behind that counter."

Jimmy John held up his palms, but only shoulder high. "Hold on just a cotton-pickin' minute here. You telling me you're from the federal government?"

"That's right," Nick said. He placed a copy of the arrest warrant on the counter. "We're authorized to take you in on charges of tax fraud."

"Gimme a minute to take a look." Jimmy John went to pick up the warrant with his left hand, but I noticed his right hand slip under the counter.

I drew on him in an instant. Unfortunately, he was nearly as quick. Both of us had our guns aimed at each other at point-blank range.

"Well, hell." Nick drew his weapon, too. He slanted his eyes at me. "I should've known if I teamed up with you there'd be gunplay."

"It's not my fault," I said. It was *never* my fault. "I have bad luck, that's all."

Jimmy John alternated aiming his gun at my face, then Nick's. *Dang.* A ballistic vest provided no protection for a head shot. Really, someone should invent a ballistic ski mask or maybe some type of bullet-repelling makeup foundation.

"Put your weapon down," I ordered, trying hard to keep my voice calm. Not easy when you're looking down the barrel of a gun.

Jimmy John's upper lip twitched. "Kiss my ass."

Next to me, Nick exhaled sharply. "Do what the lady said," he told McClure. "Set your weapon on the counter, nice and easy."

"You can kiss my ass, too." Jimmy John's nostrils flared. *Ick*. The guy really needed to trim his nose hair.

Nick and I exchanged glances.

"Look," I said, attempting to reason with McClure. "You've got two guns aimed at you. If you shoot one of us, the other will take you out. There's no way you'd get out of this alive."

His left hand shot under the counter and came up gripping another gun. He aimed one weapon at me, the other at Nick. "How do you like me now?"

Damn.

Nick and I exchanged glances again, neither of us sure what to do. We'd be perfectly justified shooting the guy. He'd drawn on us, after all, and with not just one gun, but two. But were his weapons loaded? If we shot the asshole and it turned out his guns were empty, there would be hell to pay. Law enforcement officers were constantly raked over the coals for decisions they'd had to make in the heat of the moment without benefit of complete data. But should we just stand here like sitting ducks? Many a cop had hesitated, given someone the benefit of the doubt, and died as a result. McClure had quick hands and a weapon aimed at each of us. What if he took both Nick and me out? If we survived the shooting, we'd look like idiots. If we didn't survive, well, we'd look like dead idiots.

There was only thing I knew for sure. And that was that I didn't want Nick to die without knowing how I felt about him.

"Nick?" I said, watching him in my peripheral vision. "I need to tell you something."

"What is it?"

"I'm going to break up with Brett for you. I'm planning to tell him tonight. I tried to do it on Monday, but Alicia barged in crying over Daniel and I wasn't able to do it."

Jimmy John snorted. "Well, now. Isn't that special?"

I risked a quick glimpse at Nick. His already-clenched jaw clenched even tighter. He kept his eyes locked on

McClure's hands. "You thought now would be a good time to tell me this?"

"I don't want you to die not knowing how I feel about you. And I don't want to die without telling you."

"You think we might die?"

"Possibly," I said, gesturing at McClure with my weapon. "Look at this guy. He looks stupid enough to shoot us."

Nick cocked his head. "He does look stupid. I bet his parents were cousins."

"They was not!" Jimmy John's eyes flared with anger. "Well, not first cousins, anyway."

Urk. I couldn't imagine having a husband who was also a cousin. What would that make him? A *cousband*?

A bead of sweat rolled down McClure's cheek and onto the collar of his camouflage tee. The guy was getting nervous. Not good.

Nervous people did desperate things.

Our best bet for a good outcome was to put some distance between ourselves and McClure. I was a virtual sharpshooter, but McClure's shots were less likely to hit their target if the target—*us*—was farther away.

I slowly eased backward. Nick's gaze darted in my direction for a split second and returned to McClure, but he eased backward, too.

We'd backed up halfway to the front door when it flew open and a man in gray coveralls stormed in. When he saw Nick and me with our guns trained on McClure, he yanked a gun from his boot and aimed it at Nick. "Don't worry, Jimmy John!" the man hollered. "I got you covered!"

Shit. This arrest was rapidly turning into a major cluster fuck.

"We're federal agents," Nick told the man who'd come in. "IRS Criminal Investigations. Set your weapon down on the ground and go back outside."

"How do I know you're for real?" the man asked, slitting his eyes at us.

I took a quick glance at his coveralls. The patch sewn on

the chest read: "X. PAREDES." "You're Xavier Paredes, right?"

The guy glanced down at his coveralls. "Not exactly hard to guess," he said. "It's not like there's many names that start with *X*."

True. How could I convince this guy we were who we said we were?

I searched my memory banks, trying to pull up a visual of the fraudulent tax return McClure had prepared for this man. "Your wife's name is Gina and you've got three children," I said. "Grace, Angelina, and . . ." What was the name of the other kid? Tyler? Taylor? Tyson? Hell, I couldn't remember. "I forget the other one, but I think his name starts with a *T*."

The man's squinted eyes opened a bit, his gaze darting between me and Jimmy John.

When Xavier looked at me again I said, "Jimmy John claimed thousands of dollars in unreimbursed employee business expenses on your tax return."

"That's right," the man said, his squint totally gone now. "He told us we were entitled to the deductions. It was some new tax law."

"He lied," I said. "Thanks to Jimmy John, you're going to owe at least two grand to the IRS, plus penalties and interest."

"Is that true, Jimmy John?" Xavier turned his gun on McClure now. "Did you fuck up my tax return?"

"I was doing you a favor," McClure spat. "Getting you a bigger refund."

"You got me in trouble is what you did!" Paredes said. "We've already spent our tax refund. Where the hell am I going to get two grand to pay the government?" He jabbed his gun in the air for emphasis.

Great. Now there were four of us in the standoff.

Another car pulled up outside. Before I could get to the door a woman with bleach-blond hair and skintight blue jeans came in, a drooling baby balanced on her hip, a Winnie the Pooh diaper bag hanging from her shoulder, and an IRS notice clutched in her fist. "Jimmy John, I've got a bone to pick with you."

When she noticed all of us with our guns pointed at each other, she reached into her diaper bag, drew out a sawed-off shotgun, and aimed it at me. *Damn.* Nothing like this ever happened in the Hundred Acre Wood. Then again, Jimmy John wasn't exactly Christopher Robin.

"What in the Sam Hill is going on here?" She turned the gun on Nick next, then Xavier. Her baby made a gurgling raspberry sound and began gnawing happily on his fist.

I explained the situation. "Go out to your car," I directed the woman, "and call the police."

She did as she was told. Xavier backed out the door, too. *Good.* At least we wouldn't have to worry about collateral damage now.

"I think we should go, too," I whispered to Nick. Jimmy John's arms were shaking with the strain of holding up the weapons.

"I ain't going to jail!" Jimmy John shrieked. "I know what happens in there!"

Bam!

He sent a bullet sailing between me and Nick, missing us but hitting the bear square in the chest. The bear rocked backward on its mount, bounced off the wall, and fell sideways onto the wooden floor.

In a split second, both Nick and I took aim at Jimmy John and fired.

Bang-bang! Bang-bang!

My shots sent the weapons sailing out of Jimmy John's hands, the force knocking him back against the shelves.

"Son of a bitch!" Jimmy John reflexively grabbed his right shoulder, grimaced, and looked down at his bloody hand. Judging from the two dark spots on his shirt, both of Nick's bullets had found their target, too. The wounds would be painful but not lethal. Jimmy John was lucky we hadn't put a bullet in his head. We'd have been perfectly justified. But the paperwork for a firearm discharge was bad enough. I can only imagine how much red tape would be involved if we actually killed someone.

I glanced over at Nick. "Not bad."

"I'm no Tara Holloway," he said, offering a grin, "but I can hold my own."

We heard the screech of car tires and took a quick glimpse out the window. A police cruiser braked hard on the asphalt highway and whipped onto the gravel lot. A cloud of dust kicked up around the car, hanging in the air. Two officers leaped from the cruiser, weapons in hand, and took up places behind the vehicles.

The sound of glass shattering was the next thing we heard, followed by the hiss of high-pressure gas being released from a canister.

Shit.

The cops had sent tear gas through the window.

In seconds the room was filled with noxious fumes that burned our eyes and seared our throats. Through the haze I caught a glimpse of Jimmy John running through a door into a back room, probably attempting to flee out a back exit. With the gas permeating the space, there was no way Nick and I could go after him. It was all we could do to make it out the front door, coughing and sputtering and blinking to try to clear our burning eyes.

I held my hands up as I tripped over the prone bear and down a step I couldn't see. "Don't shoot!" I fell to my hands and knees in the gravel parking lot. "Federal agents!"

"Get McClure!" Nick hollered to the cops cowering behind their car in the lot. "He's escaping out the back!" He'd barely gotten the words out when his lungs erupted in a coughing fit.

Five minutes later I heard the wail of an ambulance approaching and could make out blurry images of Nick speaking to the cops. McClure sat in the backseat of the cruiser holding one of the baby's burp rags to his wounded shoulder. Handcuffs encircled his wrists and blood poured from his nose.

I wasn't sure how he'd been captured, but with my eyes and lungs burning it gave me pleasure to see he'd suffered some additional damage. If he'd been a good little boy and cooperated with us, he would've been released on bail in a matter of hours. Having fired a weapon at government agents, though, he'd be lucky to be released from jail within the next decade.

Nick and I were led to an examination room at the minor emergency clinic and took seats side by side on the paper-covered exam table. Both my eyes and nose were running. Attractive, huh? Nick's eyes looked a bit pink but not nearly as bad as mine. Lucky him.

Ajay entered the room, our files in his hand. "Tear gas?" The nurse must have already filled him in.

He set the paperwork on the counter and grabbed a bottle of saline solution from a cabinet. "I haven't dealt with tear gas since my residency rotation in the ER. I treated half the SWAT team after a hostage situation. I got to remove a few bullets, too. What a great night."

"Sorry to disappoint you," I said wryly. "We'll try to get shot next time."

"Speak for yourself." Nick grabbed the bottle out of Ajay's hands and squirted it at me.

I threw up my hands to thwart the stream. "Hey!"

The doc had Nick and me take turns lying back on the table and flushed our eyes with the cool, soothing solution.

When Nick was done, he sat up on the table, dabbing his eyes with a tissue. "That feels so much better," he told Ajay, "I'm tempted to kiss you."

Ajay handed him a grape lollipop. "Kiss this instead."

I earned a cherry-flavored sucker for being a big girl and not crying. Well, not crying any more than the tear gas warranted.

On the drive back to the office, I looked over at Nick. He'd said nothing about my major revelation. "So?" I said. "What do you think?"

"About what?"

"About the weather, you idiot." I fought the urge to punch him on the arm. "About you and me dating each other? I laid it all out back there at Bulls-Eye. Remember?"

Nick pulled the car into the federal building's lot and cut the engine before turning to me. "I think your timing is suspicious."

"What do you mean?"

"You weren't willing to let Brett go until I started dating again." He eyed me, his expression wary. "I'm not sure whether you really want me or you just don't want any other woman to have me."

"Oh, my God! Nick! It's not like that at all!" Okay, maybe it was a little. Not the part about me not wanting him, because I totally did. But admittedly part of the reason I'd finally made up my mind was that the risk of losing him to another woman had become real and immediate when he'd signed up for the dating service.

He stared at me for a minute, his gaze flickering from my eyes, to my mouth, to my forehead. Did he want to kiss me? Or was he trying to look into my mind, find out what I really thought and felt? If only he could, he wouldn't doubt my sincerity. He'd realize I wasn't just crazy about him, I was also going crazy without him.

He turned away and looked out the window. "You said you were going to talk to Brett on Monday, but Alicia interrupted you. It's Friday now. You've had all week to do it."

"Brett's busy with a big job," I told Nick. "He wasn't free again until tonight. I couldn't do this by phone. We've been together for months. I owe it to him to tell him in person."

He continued to stare out the window, his jaw working. This was not at all the response I'd expected. Of course I hadn't expected to make my revelation while a dumb-ass redneck had guns pointed in our faces, either. Still, I'd envisioned the scene playing out like something from a romantic movie. I'd tell Nick I could finally be his. He'd take me into his arms and stroke my hair, tell me I'd made him the happiest man alive. He'd hold me a moment; then we'd separate slightly, look into each other's eyes, and come together in a passionate kiss. The kiss would deepen; he'd sweep me up into his arms and take me off to bed for a night of lovemaking.

That would be wonderful.

This, however, sucked.

Nick seemed more annoyed than excited that I wanted to be with him. Had he and Natalie reconciled? Was that why he didn't seem pleased?

I put a hand on his arm, finding myself choked up again, though this time it had nothing to do with the tear gas. "Nick, I . . . I thought you'd be happy about this."

He tossed me a look. "Happy that you've finally come to your senses?"

That wasn't exactly how I'd put it, but . . . whatever. "Yeah."

He looked out the window again, then looked down at my hand on his arm, as if just realizing I was touching him. His gaze went to my face and his rigid posture softened. He exhaled a long, loud breath and looked directly at me now. "Look, Tara. You know I think we'd be good together. But you've made me wait so long. . . . How do I know you really mean this? How do I know you're not toying with me?"

That hurt. I pulled my hand back. "I wouldn't play with your feelings, Nick. I wouldn't do that to you." I might be indecisive, but I wasn't a heartless bitch.

He stared at me another moment, saying nothing.

Panic and grief vied for control of me. "What are you saying, Nick?" My voice had a hysterical edge. "Are you saying it's too late?" *Please, God. Not that!*

Nick watched as tears welled up in my ears. Finally, he flashed me a soft, chipped-tooth smile. "You're exasperating, you know that?"

"I do." My parents had told me that all the time when I was growing up.

A tear broke free and streamed down to my chin. Nick put his warm hand on the side of my face and ran his thumb across my cheek, erasing the tear's trail. "You're a day late and a dollar short, Tara. But I'll make you a deal. As soon as you break things off with Brett, you give me a call. Until then I have to consider myself a free man."

"Fair enough," I said on a breath, lightened with relief. After all, I'd see Brett this evening and we'd have our talk. I'd be giving Nick that call tonight. I gave Nick a smile. "You'll only be a free man for a few more hours. If you've got any more wild oats to sow, you'd better get on it."

chapter sixteen

ℬeetlemania

Friday evening, I arrived at Brett's house with a large mush-room and black olive pizza. He took the box from me at the door. I turned my head when he gave me his usual welcom-ing peck, the kiss landing near my ear rather than on my lips. How could I kiss him with the lips that would soon tell him I wanted to date another man?

His two black dogs, a Rottweiler–pit bull mix named Reggie and a Scottish terrier mix named Napoleon, followed us into the kitchen, their toenails clicking on the floor. Brett opened the pizza box and gave them each a slice, shooing them out the back door lest they attempt to take the greasy, gooey food onto the living room rug.

Brett poured us each a glass of merlot, grabbed a couple of napkins, and joined me at the table. While Brett dug in, hungry after a hard day's physical labor on a landscaping project, I had a hard time getting a bite down. My throat seemed to have closed up. I'd like to blame it on the tear gas, but I knew what was choking me was emotion, not chemicals.

No sense putting off the inevitable, right? "Brett, I need

to talk to you about something important." I could feel my eyes growing misty.

He glanced up mid-bite, freezing in place when he noticed the serious expression on my face. He set his pizza back down. "What is it?" he asked, his voice tentative.

I slugged back some wine to fortify myself. "We've been together for several months now." I hesitated, not sure exactly how to say what I needed to say. Damn, I should've Googled "how to tell your boyfriend you want to take a break."

Brett turned his head slightly, his expression wary. He had no idea what was about to hit him, did he? Heck, for all I knew he was expecting some type of *I-want-to-get-married-and-settle-down* talk, like Alicia had with Daniel. Part of me wondered how Brett would respond if that were the case. Would he freak out like Daniel had and go running for the woods? Or would he acquiesce and agree to go shopping for rings?

I looked down at my wineglass, finding it hard to meet his gaze. "Um . . . we know each other pretty well by now, right?"

"Right?" The word was not only an expression of agreement but a question, too.

"Well, it's just that I wonder if by now we should—"

Brett's cell phone bleeped on the table. He checked the readout. "It's my boss," he said. "Sorry."

Ugh! This was hard enough without an interruption.

He accepted the call and put the phone to his ear. "Hello?"

I couldn't quite make out what his boss was saying, but from the sharp tone and staccato words it didn't sound good.

"You're kidding me." Brett stood reflexively and put a hand in his hair, pushing back until the strands stood on end. "Those trees came from my nursery."

More angry chatter came through the phone.

He grabbed his hair in a death grip now. "Japanese beetles? Damn it! Those bugs don't just kill trees; they eat turf, too. They'll ruin the golf course."

More loud words came through the phone.

"Tell them I'll take care of it. Right away." He paused one last moment. "Right. Thanks."

He jabbed the button to end the call and set his phone back down on the table. He looked at me, his expression part incredulous, part panicked. "Some of the trees I planted in Atlanta are infested with beetles. Shit! I'm always so careful. I inspected every tree that was planted, for God's sake! How could this happen?" He looked around the room as if searching for an answer.

I stood, too. "It's not your fault, right? You didn't grow the trees." The nursery he'd recently started hadn't been in business long enough to grow trees from scratch.

"No," Brett replied. "I got them from another supplier, but I installed them, so it's my problem. It's going to cost thousands of dollars to fix this. The entire nursery stock could be infected, too. Fuck! This could ruin my reputation." He kicked one of his kitchen chairs and it scooted noisily across the floor.

I'd rarely seen Brett so upset, though he had every right to be. He was just breaking out in his career. If news of the Japanese beetle infestation got out, it could take him years to recover. Not only did the bugs make him look bad, but the problem also reflected poorly on Wakefield Designs, the company he worked for. His job might be at stake along with his reputation.

He seemed to remember that we'd been in the middle of a conversation and turned back to me. "Look, Tara. I've got to deal with this now. Can we have our little talk later?"

Our "little talk" wasn't going to be so little. But, hell, how could I break up with Brett now? It wouldn't only be like kicking a puppy; it would be like kicking a sick, crippled puppy, one infested with parasites. Like I said, I'm not heartless.

"Sure. We'll talk later." *Damn those Japanese beetles!* My hopes sank like a navy ship that had been dive-bombed by a kamikaze pilot.

Nick would be a free man a while longer.

While Brett scurried about, hurriedly packing a bag and making reservations on a red-eye flight to Atlanta, I gathered up his dogs' bowls, food, and toys for the pet sitter and tried not to scream in frustration.

chapter seventeen

$\mathcal{S}$pecial Delivery

I left Brett's feeling totally frustrated. Nothing seemed to be going my way lately.

As long as I was out, I figured I'd stop by Zippy's Liquor and speak to the staff on the evening shift, ask them about the wire transfers to Honduras. I drove to the store and parked, retrieving the photos of the terrorists from my briefcase and carrying them inside with me.

Given that it was a Friday night, the store was packed with people stocking up on beer, wine, and hard liquor for the weekend. Heck, as long as I was there I figured I'd snag a couple more bottles of wine. Alicia and I were running low on sangria supplies, and if ever I needed some sangria it was now.

I grabbed the wine and took my place in line. As I waited I glanced around, noting the store's customer base appeared to be largely Latino. Not surprising given that it was located in a neighborhood populated primarily by emigrants from Mexico and Central and South America.

Finally, I reached the checkout counter. The woman

running the cash register was a broad-shouldered black woman with high-curving eyebrows that gave her a constant look of surprise.

"That'll be sixteen twenty-three." She slid the wine into a plain paper bag, the glass bottles clinking against each other as she sat the bag on the counter in front of me.

I ran my debit card through the machine, typed in my PIN, and accepted the receipt she handed to me. Our transaction now complete, I flashed my badge. "I'm Special Agent Tara Holloway with IRS Criminal Investigations. I'd like to ask you some questions about the store's money transmissions."

With her curved brows, the woman's reaction was hard to gauge. She didn't look any more surprised now than she had before I'd told her who I was.

She shrugged. "Okay."

"Are you Dottie or Gloria?" I asked.

"I'm Dottie."

"Do you recognize any of these men, Dottie?" I showed her the three photos. "Have they ever come in the store?"

She looked them over for a moment or two, finally shaking her head. "Hard to say," she said. "We get so many people coming through here I couldn't tell you for sure. Some nights we're so busy I hardly have time to look up."

It seemed like an honest answer.

"Have you handled any wire transfers to Honduras?" I asked.

She chewed her lip and looked down in thought before answering. "Can't say that I have."

"What about your coworker?" I asked, gesturing with my head to a Latino man pushing a dolly loaded with cases of beer. He stopped near the front windows to replenish the rapidly dwindling display.

"Couldn't tell ya." She stood on tiptoe to look over the crowd. "Israel! Come here a minute."

When the man stepped over to the counter, I introduced myself. The two of us stepped aside so Dottie could ring up the next customer in line.

I showed Israel the photographs of the terrorists. "Do any of these men look familiar to you?"

His response was as noncommittal as Dottie's had been. "I don't know," he said, his Spanish accent thick as he spoke. "We have many, many customers every night. We are very busy."

I nodded. "I have some questions about the wire transfers to Honduras. Did you handle those?" It seemed likely. After all, this man spoke Spanish and would be able to communicate with a recipient in Honduras if need be.

"I do not remember," he said.

In my experience, an inability to recall information could mean someone was hedging their bets, not wanting to incriminate themselves yet not wanting to be caught in a lie if the other party had clear evidence regarding the matter under discussion.

"Let's take a look at the wire transfer records," I said. "Maybe that will jog your memory."

We went to the store's tiny, dusty office. Israel retrieved the records and I pointed out the questionable transactions, including the three four-thousand-dollar cash transfers that had been performed on the same night.

Israel shook his head. "I do not believe I did those transfers, but we can look at the schedule to see who worked on those nights."

He pulled a clipboard from a shelf under the counter and we looked it over. Israel had not been scheduled to work on any of the nights in question. Though Dottie had worked on a couple of the nights, Gloria had also worked some of them. The only staff member consistently on the schedule when the suspicious transactions took place was Jesús.

"When does Jesús work again?" I asked.

Israel consulted the schedule. "Monday."

"Great." I thanked Israel and Dottie for their time and left with my bottles of wine.

Had I found him? Was Jesús the man I was after?

* * *

My doorbell rang at nine thirty Saturday morning. Since I was expecting my mother to arrive soon, I was already up and mostly dressed, lacking only shoes and accessories. Still, it was a little early for Mom to have already completed the three-hour drive from Nacogdoches.

I peeked through the peephole. A young man in a FedEx uniform stood on my porch, his white delivery truck visible at the curb behind him.

Hmm. I wasn't expecting a package. Maybe Brett had sent me more of those delicious spiced peaches the country club's chef prepared. With all the peach sangria Alicia and I had been drinking lately, it couldn't hurt to replenish our supply.

I opened the door.

"Tara Holloway?" the man asked.

I nodded. "That's me."

He held out an electronic clipboard and a stylus. "Sign here please."

I scribbled my name with the digital pen and took the shoebox–sized package he offered next. The box was too small and too lightweight to contain mason jars of peaches.

"Enjoy." He gave me a wide, knowing grin, an exaggerated wink, and a hearty chuckle before turning and heading back to his truck.

What was that about?

I closed the door behind me and carried the package inside. I scanned the label for the name of the sender. There it was.

Sensual Essentials, Inc.

I didn't recognize the name of the company. What was this?

I carried the box to the kitchen and set it on the countertop while I rummaged through my junk drawer for a pair of scissors. Anne hopped onto the counter and sniffed the box, her little cream-colored head bobbing up and down as her nose made its way from one end of the box to the other.

I finally found the scissors at the back of the drawer, lodged behind some type of wrench, a flashlight, and a Phillips-head screwdriver. Ten seconds later, I had the box open.

Holy crap!

Lying inside the box were two vibrators, one in my signature red, the other in purple, along with instruction manuals printed in English, French, and, for some reason, Icelandic. I supposed the device could keep someone warm on those frigid winter nights in Reykjavik.

The box also contained a gift card that read: *Men, who needs them? XO, Christina.*

I wasn't sure whether to laugh or cry. But heck, with the way things had been going for me lately I could definitely use a laugh. I let loose with a giggle.

I pulled one of the instruction manuals from the box and perused it over a cup of coffee. Christina had spared no expense in her little gag, ordering us the deluxe model that promised "whisper quiet" sound and came with three speed settings, an oscillating feature, and a "jackhammer" button. The manual also came with warnings, advising those with latex allergies not to use the device and reminding owners that any improper use would void the warranty. Ironic for a device intended for improper uses, huh?

I returned to my junk drawer, dug out a package of AA batteries, and inserted them into the gadgets, giggling once again when I activated the jackhammer button. If nothing else, maybe I could use the thing to pound nails.

Alicia wandered into the kitchen, rubbing her eyes. "What's so funny? I heard you laughing."

I switched the button on the purple device to "oscillate" and handed it to her. The gadget gave off a soft whirring sound and the tip spun around at an angle.

Alicia blinked drowsily at the thing a few times while Anne swatted at it with her paw. "Is this what I think it is?"

"That depends," I said. "What do you think it is?"

She tossed it back into the box. "I think it's way too early for this, that's what I think it is."

I filled out the two warranty cards that came with the contraptions, listing the owner as Trish LeGrande and using the TV station's address. With any luck, she'd be added to their mailing list or maybe there'd be some type of recall and she'd receive an embarrassing notice at her office.

Neener-neener.

chapter eighteen

Retail Therapy

Alicia was sprawled on the couch, still wearing her blue satin pajamas and nursing her third cup of hazelnut coffee, when I heard Mom pull into the driveway an hour later.

I scurried outside and gave my mother a hug as soon as she climbed out of her car.

Mom was dressed in her best country couture, a straight skirt, riding boots, and a long-sleeved blouse. She took one look at my face and knew in an instant something was wrong. "What's the matter, honey?"

I told her about the preceding day's events, about opening my heart to Nick, about Brett and the Japanese beetles. It was enough to make a person consider hari-kari.

Mom gave my hand a squeeze. "It'll all work out eventually," she said, trying to reassure me. Mom was usually right, but nobody had 100 percent accuracy. Sometimes things didn't work out. Sometimes things fell apart instead.

"Let me get that for you." I took her suitcase from her and ushered her inside.

Alicia pulled herself up off the couch and came over to

give my mother a hug, too. "Nice to see you, Mrs. Hollo-way."

My mother hugged my friend warmly and stepped back, a hand on each of Alicia's shoulders. "Now don't you fret, ei-ther, young lady," Mom said. "That boy will come crawling back to you. He just needs some time to sort things out. Trust me. I've been there myself."

Alicia shrugged. "I don't know. Daniel hasn't even called. He texted me once to find out where we keep the ironing board, but that's it."

Mom tsked. "Well, sitting around here moping isn't go-ing to do you any good." She dropped her arms from Ali-cia's shoulders and pointed up the staircase. "March on up those stairs and get dressed," she ordered. "We're going to Neiman Marcus for some retail therapy. Let's do lunch, too. My treat."

Alicia's eyes brightened and she scampered up the stairs. Mothers. They know just the thing to cheer a person up, huh?

My mother set course for the kitchen, probably thirsty after the long drive.

Oh, God! The vibrators were still on the table!

"Let me fix you a drink!" I cried, rushing after her and cutting her off at the doorway. I snatched up the devices and dropped them into the bottomless pit that was my purse. I'd recently upgraded to one of those enormous, shapeless bags when my previous purse could no longer contain all the junk I'd accumulated. Buying a bigger bag seemed quicker and easier than cleaning out my stuff. Before long I'd prob-ably have to upgrade again, maybe to a suitcase or an army trunk.

I moved my purse aside and shoved the box into the bottom of my trash can, pretending that my actions were intended to accommodate my mother. "Here you go," I said, pulling out a kitchen chair for her. "Make yourself comfortable."

She gave me a smile and dropped into the seat. "Thanks, hon."

I snatched a glass from the cabinet, filled it with ice and tap water, and set it on the table in front of her. "So, what's up back in Nacogdoches?" I asked, sliding into the chair across from her.

Mom filled me in on the latest hometown news and gossip. A new boutique had opened downtown. Clara Humphreys, a fellow member of the town's historical society, was recovering from surgery on an ingrown toenail. "The way she was carrying on," Mom said, "you'd have thought she'd lost a limb."

My high school's football team was doing well this season. Rumor had it the quarterback, a senior, was being courted by the coach at the University of Oklahoma, the chief rival to my college.

"Say it isn't so." A graduate from my high school thinking about becoming a Sooner? How could he?

Mom shook her head. "He must've lost his mind."

Alicia came to the kitchen doorway and declared herself "ready to go."

A half hour later, the three of us arrived at Neiman Marcus and headed directly to the cosmetics counter. Both Alicia and I needed under-eye cream to hide the dark, puffy circles we'd accumulated from nights of restless sleep.

When we arrived the clerk took one look at us and cringed. "Might I suggest full makeovers?"

Alicia and I readily agreed. We could both use some attention, even if it was only from a salesclerk looking for a nice commission.

When the makeup artist finished, we eyed ourselves in hand mirrors.

"We might feel awful," I told Alicia, tilting my head to look at the other side of my face, "but we look awesome."

In addition to the eye cream, I stocked up on foundation, blush, and mascara while Alicia purchased eyeliner and shadow.

Properly made up now, we spent two hours browsing the women's, shoe, and lingerie departments. Mom found a cute, clingy dress in a muted pastel print that would be perfect for her upcoming high-school reunion. She firmed, flattened, and rearranged her figure with a strategic pair of

Spanx, slid her feet into a pair of shiny gray sling-backs, and stood in front of the three-way mirror.

"Wow, Mrs. H." Alicia stepped up behind my mother as she turned to and fro. "You've still got it."

Alicia was right. My mother looked fantastic. "Dad's going to love it." Maybe Randall would, too. Candy Cummings could eat her heart out.

We meandered over to the jewelry department and found the perfect pair of earrings and a necklace to complete Mom's outfit. After a light lunch of salads and mimosas at Neiman's café, we headed back to my BMW, shopping bags in hand.

"As long as we're out, do you two mind if I make a quick stop?" One of the MSBs on my list was only a few miles away.

Mom and Alicia said they didn't mind coming along for the ride. None of us had anything better to do that afternoon and it would give us a chance to chat some more on the drive.

The place was a head shop called Huff-N-Puff, located on the back side of a strip center in a seedy part of town. A run-down apartment complex flanked the property, its parking lot filled with beater cars, its Dumpster overloaded and spilling garbage onto the parking lot. Crows pecked at something that had spilled from an open bag.

I pulled into a spot and cut my engine.

Alicia glanced around and crinkled her nose in distaste. "This looks like a questionable neighborhood."

The question being "Why the hell would anyone want to live here?"

"Don't worry," I said. "I'm armed."

We climbed out of the car and headed inside. Thanks to the eighty-six varieties of tobacco the store carried in stock, the space smelled earthy and herby, not unlike the warehouse at Brett's nursery where he stored compost and potting soil.

Alicia waved a hand in front of her face. "It smells like a petting zoo in here."

Mom turned to me. "Remember that petting zoo Dad and I took you and your brothers to when you were little?"

"How could I forget? A goat bit me in the butt." I'd been five years old and traumatized, at least until my dad bought me a grape snow cone. But I'd learned an important lesson. Don't put a box of Cracker Jacks in your back pocket.

I left Alicia and my mother to take a look around while I made my way past a display of colorful glass hookah pipes and down an aisle of natural supplements, including one called Horny Goat Weed that claimed to support sexual vitality. *Not for use by pregnant women,* according to the label. *Hmm.* Maybe I should snag a bottle for Josh.

"Can I help you?" A woman with stringy brown hair that hung past her butt swished up the aisle in her long, loose peasant skirt.

I identified myself and showed her my badge. "I need to look at your records for the prepaid Visa cards."

She gave me a long-suffering look. No doubt she received plenty of hassles from *The Man,* local cops, and whatnot.

I raised a hand to placate her. "I'm not here to give you a hard time. I'm just trying to find out who might have helped some men move funds overseas."

A perplexed look flickered over her face, but she gestured for me to follow her. "This way." She led me past a display of "Legal Highs" to the stockroom. A computer sat on a desk in the corner. Cheap shelves were mounted on the wall over the desk. A series of blue notebooks sat on the shelves, white labels on their spines identifying their contents. *Tobacco Inventory. Pipe Inventory. Miscellaneous.*

She showed me how to access their online sales records and retrieved the *Miscellaneous* notebook, flipping to the section that documented their orders of prepaid Visa cards. "Here you go."

"Thanks."

I spent half an hour looking through the data. Everything appeared to be in order. *Darn!* The lack of progress was eating away at me. Every day that passed without us finding the person who'd moved the funds meant more people might die, more families might be torn apart, more bright yellow school buses might drive over an improvised explosive device.

I returned the notebook to the shelf and wandered back into the store, waiting until the manager had finished assisting a black man with a Jamaican accent who was buying what appeared to be a lifetime supply of rolling papers. I envied how relaxed he looked. A little ganja each day keeps the worries away, huh?

"The records looked fine," I told her once the man had left. "Just one more thing before I go." I pulled the photos of Algafari, Nasser, and Homsi from my purse. "Do you recognize any of these men?"

The woman took the photos, squinting her eyes at them before sliding on a pair of outdated eyeglasses with large, round frames. Finally, she shook her head. "I don't think so. We get quite a few Indians who shop here for their hookah supplies, but I don't think any of our shoppers were these men."

I thanked the woman for her time and walked outside, finding Alicia and my mother standing on the sidewalk.

"Look what I bought," Mom said, reaching into her bag. "A hummingbird feeder." She held up a red glass bong.

Alicia and I exchanged glances. Maybe my mother shouldn't have had that third mimosa at lunch.

"That's not a hummingbird feeder, Mom," I said. "That's a bong."

"A bong?" She looked at me and looked back at the water pipe. "Is that the thing those two guys smoked in those Cheech and Chong movies back in the seventies?"

As teenagers, my brothers and I had watched edited-for-television reruns of the movies on some obscure cable channel. I nodded.

"Well, darn." Her gaze went to a sign in the window.

ALL SALES FINAL. NO REFUNDS.

My mother shrugged. "I'm still going to use it to feed the hummingbirds."

No doubt the birds would be happily buzzed, flying high.

After we climbed back into the car, my mother asked about my other pending cases. I told her about Richard Beauregard and his disappearing act. "It was totally humiliating. He's made me and Eddie look like idiots."

She frowned. "We can't have that. Let's go find him."

We decided to visit a couple of the campgrounds at area lakes and state parks to see if Beauregard had set up base at one of the sites. I used my phone to search the Net and determine which campsites had water and electric hookups for trailers. We made the rounds, looking for a trailer with a Puma logo, but had no luck. This time, the closest I got to a Puma was a fluffy red chow chained to a tree. He gave us a quick bark as we drove past the pop-up camper he was guarding, but quickly realized we posed no threat to his modest estate and went back to chewing on a ratty tennis shoe.

Near sundown we stopped at a campground and removed our shoes, venturing out onto a fishing dock to dangle our toes in the water and watch the pretty orange sunset. The air was cool but tolerable. The site was secluded and, other than the rhythmic chirp of crickets and the occasional croak of a bullfrog, peacefully quiet. I'd have to remember this place. It had all sorts of romantic potential. What I wouldn't have given to have a glass of peach sangria in my hand and Nick Pratt by my side—or vice versa.

We three women sat in silence, each of us thinking her own thoughts. I suppose it would have been impossible for us to think each other's thoughts, though, huh?

Alicia's thoughts were on Daniel. She'd been upset when she'd arrived at my town house Tuesday night. But as the week went on with virtually no contact from him, she'd become withdrawn. She lay back on the pier and sighed, looking up at the dark sky. "I've been a fool, haven't I? Wasting years on a guy who can't even be bothered to call and check on me."

"Sign up at that online dating site," I suggested for at least the tenth time. If it could find a suitable guy for the Lobo, it could surely find a match for Alicia.

"That's not a bad idea," my mother agreed, kicking her toes in the water as she glanced over at my friend. "A girl as pretty and smart as you would have lots of dates in no time."

My thoughts bounced between Brett and Nick, of course. When would Brett return from Atlanta so we could have our talk? Would Nick meet someone special before I could speak to Brett? I lay back on the dock and sighed, too. "Why is fate being such a vicious bitch to me?"

Alicia turned her head my way. "Maybe she's suffering from PMS."

Mom was thinking of Dad, I supposed. Or maybe Randall. Or maybe Candy Cummings. Whoever she was thinking about, Mom was lucky. She and Dad had been contentedly married for nearly four decades. They'd raised three rambunctious kids, worked side by side to fix up the ancient Victorian farmhouse I grew up in, planned to grow old together. I wasn't ready for kids, maybe not even quite ready for marriage, but eventually I'd like to have what my parents had. A fulfilling life with a person I adored, respected, and felt passionate about.

Mom gazed up at a star as if pondering a wish. "I wonder if I could lose ten pounds before the reunion."

"I've heard you can order tapeworms online," I said. "Rumor has it some of the supermodels use them."

"Dear Lord!" Mom replied. "I'd rather be chubby than full of worms."

The hungry mosquitoes eventually became unbearable and we were forced to abandon our refuge lest we be eaten alive. We slid out of our thoughts, into our shoes, and headed home.

Saturday evening, Mom, Alicia, and I lazed around my living room in our pajamas, eating boxed pasta I'd whipped up and drinking peach sangria.

Although a romantic comedy played on the TV screen, none of us paid much attention to the movie. Mom worked her Bedazzler, applying a line of pink sequins around the hem of a tiny pair of jeans that belonged to my five-year-old niece, Jesse. Alicia read through a self-help book that offered advice on rebuilding your life after a breakup. I went through the terrorist file yet again, looking over each item of information carefully, trying to determine if there were any hidden clues we might have missed. Nothing caught my eye.

My cell phone rang. It was Brett calling. I excused myself and took the phone into the kitchen to speak with him.

Our conversation was brief. The weather in Atlanta was unseasonably warm and humid, making his work outdoors nearly unbearable. Fortunately, the club's chef had taken pity on Brett and his crew and brought fresh-squeezed lemonade outside to them. The chef also served them special dinners each night in the club's private dining room, the most recent of which included honey-glazed salmon. Brett might die of heatstroke in Atlanta, but he sure wouldn't die of hunger. The chef had even asked Brett's input on the dishes, using him as a taste tester for new recipes.

"How's everything going back there?" Brett asked.

"Same old same old," I said. "Working my butt off and getting nowhere."

Brett and I used to talk on the phone for hours, about everything and nothing at all. But now I had trouble thinking of anything to say to him and the only thing he seemed to want to discuss was the club's food. Our conversation felt strained and awkward, which didn't go unnoticed by Brett.

"Is everything okay?" he asked, a hint of suspicion in his voice.

No. Everything was not okay. Not at all. But I didn't want to get into it on the phone. "I'm just not in a talkative mood, I guess."

He was quiet for a moment, but he didn't press me for further explanation. Could he sense that things had gone awry? That I was no longer 100 percent invested in our relationship?

"I'll let you go, then," he said. "Stay safe, okay?"

"I'll do my best."

My phone call completed, I turned back to the file. Would we ever find out who had helped the terrorists funnel money overseas? Like my attempts to talk things out with Brett, the case was beginning to feel like a lost cause.

Mom left early Sunday morning so she could arrive back home in Nacogdoches in time to make lunch for the family after church. I dragged Alicia out of bed and to the firing range with me, hoping that putting a few bullets in a man-shaped target would lift her spirits.

"Check out my new gun." I removed the red Cobra .38 from its case and handed it to Alicia.

"Nice," she said, turning it over. She scratched at the bright-orange price sticker with the Strike-it-Rich oil derrick logo, loosening the adhesive and pulling the tag off. She tossed the sticker in a nearby trash can. "Can I try it?"

"Of course," I said. "You're my best friend. Mi casa es su casa." Okay, so that literally translated as "my house is your house." But I didn't know the Spanish word for "gun" and the sentiment was the same.

I offered Alicia some quick pointers and clipped a paper target to the pulley. Once the target was in place, she assumed a shooting stance, narrowed her eyes, and took aim. She emptied the entire clip, her shots hitting the target low, in the general area of the target's crotch.

"Not bad for a beginner," I said. "Your aim was a little low, though."

She gave me the stink eye. "I was going for the gonads."

"Oh. In that case, good shots, then."

I took up residence in the lane beside her, spending several minutes practicing with my Glock. Each of my shots hit the target right in the heart. Yep, the Annie Oakley of the IRS was still in business. Good thing, too. When you were dealing with terrorists, weapon skills could come in handy.

chapter nineteen

*J*ailhouse Rocks

When I arrived at the office Monday morning, Nick stared at me from across the hall, a look of disgust on his face. He'd expected me to call him over the weekend, to tell him I'd put Brett on hold. No doubt Nick felt deceived and betrayed. I tried to explain, but he simply held up his hand.

"I don't want to hear it," he said.

He promptly logged onto the Big D Dating Service site, scrolled through the dozens of new responses, and called one of the women, unabashedly flirting and making a dinner date as I sat within earshot in my office, trying not to burst into tears or hurl my calculator at him.

Josh passed by my office door on his way back from the men's room.

"Hey, Josh!" I hollered. "Get back here."

Josh retreated and poked his head in the door. "What?"

"I need your help," I said.

"I'm busy," he said.

I skewered him with a look. "I helped you land a date with Kira," I reminded him. "You owe me."

He frowned but gave in. "All right. What is it?"

If I told him the specifics, he'd refuse. I strategically kept my words vague. "I need your special skills on a field investigation."

Josh would assume I was referring to his computer skills. What I was actually referring to was his ability to pee standing up. Yep, I needed a man. Why? Because I was heading out to a men's prison. I'd seen what happened to Clarice Starling when she'd gone alone to visit Hannibal Lecter in prison in *The Silence of the Lambs*. I hoped that my being accompanied by a male agent would discourage the inmates from tossing any icky stuff at me.

I would have much preferred Nick's help, but the guy wasn't speaking to me at the moment. Eddie was out on his own rounds of MSBs. That left me with Josh. He wasn't much of a man, but he would have to do.

We piled in a fleet car and drove to Venus, a tiny town of three thousand people located southwest of Dallas. Though named after a planet, the place contained no extraterrestrials, though it was home to the Texas Department of Criminal Justice Sanders Estes Unit. The unit, in turn, was home to approximately one thousand inmates.

Because family members and prisoners needed a safe and secure system for exchanging funds, the unit offered wire transfer services and both sold and cashed traveler's checks and money orders. As a result, the state prison was required to register with the U.S. Treasury Department as an MSB. It was kind of like Big Brother keeping an eye on Little Brother, huh?

As I turned down the road to approach the unit, Josh noticed the high fences and razor wire that harbored groups of men in bright orange jumpsuits. "Wait a minute. We're not going to a prison, are we?"

"Yep," I replied.

"No," Josh said. "No way! I am not going in that place."

I glanced over at him. "I'll tell Kira you're a wuss."

He frowned again. "That's not fair."

"Tough." I was probably being mean to the guy, but fate

hadn't shown me much mercy lately and I was only paying it forward.

I parked the car in the visitors' section and climbed out, donning the cheap plastic poncho I'd purchased at the dollar store on my drive in this morning.

"What's that for?" Josh asked.

"Let's just call it a protective measure."

"Do you have one for me?"

I shook my head. "Sorry."

We headed inside to the *thwump-thwump-thwump* of a basketball being dribbled on the court on the other side of the fence. The sound ceased momentarily when the tall, muscular inmate with the ball wandered over to the fence.

"Hey, baby!" the man called. "You coming for our conjugal visit?" He put a hand under his nards and lifted them. "I'm ready for you."

"Aren't you going to tell him off?" Josh whispered.

"Nope," I said.

"Why not?" Josh asked. I couldn't blame him. It wasn't like me to let a slight pass unaddressed.

I shot Josh a pointed look. "Because he was talking to *you*."

When Josh glanced back at the fence, the man puckered his lips and made a kissing sound. Josh emitted his usual puppy whimper and scampered ahead of me into the building.

We checked in with Security and a warden led us to the administrative offices. He chuckled at my poncho. "Don't worry," he said. "We ain't going to let any of these men within spitting distance of you."

"Thanks," I said, not bothering to mention it wasn't spit I was worried about.

Josh and I settled in at a desk in the jail's financial office. The man currently tasked with the job of maintaining the records was more than happy to let us use his digs in favor of his taking an extended coffee break.

We spent a couple of hours searching through the files. The records were less than ideal, resulting no doubt from the constant employee turnover evident in the files. Seemed nobody stayed at the job for more than a few weeks at a time. Still, though the information was somewhat spotty and incomplete, the data told us enough. All of the transactions were in relatively small amounts and all were to and from other people located within the United States. Nobody who worked here at the jail had helped the terrorists transfer funds to Syria.

We thanked the staff for their assistance and made our way back outside. Josh ran from the door to the car, ducking behind it amid laughter from not only the inmates but also the guards sitting atop a nearby tower.

The same man who'd propositioned Josh earlier stepped up to the fence, lifting his stones once again. "Last chance for love!" he called.

Josh whimpered again.

As I pushed the button on the remote to open the door, a drop of rain fell from the sky. Whaddya know? The poncho had come in handy after all.

chapter twenty

Get Out of Here!

I dropped Josh back at the office, trading him for Eddie and heading to the federal prison located thirty miles west in Fort Worth. Though the federal prison was a low-security facility, the building had a small wing in which violent offenders could be segregated as they awaited trial. Once convicted, these offenders were sent to a high-security prison out of state to serve their sentences.

We checked in at the gate and were directed to park in a designated area. We stepped through a metal detector and endured a thorough pat down before being allowed inside. The staff also searched our briefcases and my purse. Once we'd passed muster, a male warden with a thick neck and thick southern accent led us to the visiting area. The prisoners' three attorneys were already seated in a waiting area outside a private visitation room.

Eddie requested that we be permitted to speak with Karam Homsi first. Homsi was the man who'd earlier offered to talk, the man whose tongue had been later cut out. The warden nodded, pushed a button on his shoulder mic, and turned his head to bark an order into the device. "Bring me Karam Homsi."

A couple of seconds later a male voice responded. "Homsi. Got it. On my way."

Homsi's attorney stood and followed me and Eddie into the small room. While Eddie and I took seats on the near side of the table, the attorney took a seat on the other. I noticed he slid his chair farther away from the empty one, as if he didn't want to get too close to his client. I couldn't blame the guy. Who knew what these men were capable of?

We sat quietly, listening to the hum from the fluorescent lights overhead as we waited. A few minutes later, a door on the back wall opened and a warden led Homsi inside.

Homsi stood around five feet, ten inches, and wore khaki pants and a khaki shirt, the standard federal prison uniform. His hands were cuffed in front of him. He glanced at me and Eddie, then turned his head down as he took his seat. He didn't look up as his attorney identified us and told him why we were there.

Eddie eyed the top of Homsi's downturned head. "We'd like to ask you some questions about how the money was moved overseas."

Homsi didn't respond. He simply sat immobile in his seat, staring at the tabletop.

Eddie and I looked to Homsi's attorney. He merely shrugged as if to say, *I told you he wouldn't talk.*

I figured I might as well take a crack at the guy. Maybe he'd react differently to a woman. "Look, Mr. Homsi. I know you don't want to help the government out and I know the plea deal fell through. But if you give us a break here, share some information, the judge will take it into consideration in your sentencing." I couldn't make any promises, of course, but judges tended to go easier on cooperative inmates.

Homsi raised his head then, looking at me with sheer terror in his eyes. Ironic for a terrorist, huh? He tried to say something, but without benefit of a tongue it came out only as garbled gibberish. "Ay lah my ung lass ime ay awk. Ex ime iss my lie."

Huh?

I slid my legal pad and pen across the table. He snatched up the pen, scribbled on the pad, and slid it back across the table. Eddie leaned over to read the words with me.

I lost my tongue last time I talked. Next time it's my life.

In other words, he'd give us nothing.

The warden led Homsi away and his attorney left, quickly replaced by Algafari's lawyer. A few minutes later, the same warden led Algafari into the room. Unlike Homsi, who'd averted his eyes, Algafari stared straight at me and Eddie, his gaze gleaming with raw rage and hate. He looked like he'd enjoy ripping out our hearts. I was grateful for the shackles on his wrists.

Like his predecessor, Algafari refused to tell us anything. He merely sat there, glaring at us while we all but begged for answers.

Finally, I asked the only question that really mattered. "You're not going to tell us anything, are you?"

He gave me one final glare and a single word. "No."

Damn! The frustration of this case was really starting to get to me. But as they say, the third time's the charm, right? Maybe Nasser would open up to us.

Algafari's attorney left the room and Nasser's came in. I noticed he didn't take a seat. He stood off to the side, one hand holding his briefcase with a death grip, the other nervously jingling the coins in his pant pocket.

When the back door opened again, Nasser shuffled through. He wore shackles not only around his wrists but also around his ankles. He fell back into a chair and kicked out at the table with his shackled feet, shoving the edge of the tabletop into Eddie's gut and my rib cage. *Ouch!* Nasser's attorney had been smart to keep his distance. I rubbed my side and looked at Nasser. Clearly the man was not going to play nice.

So much for the third time being the charm.

As Eddie and I pushed the table back into place, the warden grabbed Nasser's chair and dragged him backward a few feet, out of kicking range of anyone or anything in the room. The distance didn't prevent him from impaling me with his eyes, however. His gaze bored into mine like a heated, pinpoint laser. Heck, he could probably perform LASIK surgery with that stare.

I felt an uneasy prickle along my back, but I did my best to hide my fear. Guys like Nasser feed on fear like beer-bellied men feed on barbecue. I wasn't about to give him the satisfaction of seeing me squirm.

I looked Nasser in the eye. "Mr. Nasser, I'm Special Agent Tara Holloway with IRS Criminal Investigations. My partner and I are trying to determine how you moved funds out of the country. We know you withdrew significant sums of cash from your bank accounts and took the funds to someone who transferred the money overseas. It's only a matter of time before we figure out who that person is."

What a lie. Given the way things had been going, we might not ever figure out who that person was.

"Problem is," I continued, "we're busy people. Our time is valuable. If you would tell us who helped you it would save us some time and maybe knock some time off your sentence." Surely he'd want to get out of jail sooner, right?

Nasser smirked an evil smirk. "You might be busy, Agent Holloway, but me? I've got all the time in world."

Wang and Zardooz had informed us that Syrian officials were seeking to have Nasser extradited back to the country, where he'd surely face the death penalty for his acts of terror there. I supposed it made sense that he'd rather stay in the United States. He might live out the rest of his life in prison here, but at least he'd have a life. Hell, for his own protection the guy was probably hoping for as long a sentence as possible, maybe even additional time for bad behavior.

The odd logic meant we held no bargaining chip, had nothing to offer him in return for the information.

Nasser's attorney jingled the coins again. "We done here?"

I looked at Eddie. He tossed his hand in a gesture of futility.

"Yeah," I told the lawyer. "We're done here."

As Nasser was led out the back door, I couldn't help my-self. "It was such a pleasure to meet you, Mr. Nasser."

He turned back and slid me an icy smile. "The same goes for you, Agent Holloway."

Our futile visit to the federal pen now complete, I headed out to one of the few remaining MSBs on my list, a travel agency called Up, Up, and Away Vacations.

I parked in the strip center's lot, directly in front of the agency's office. Their glass windows boasted colorful post-ers of tropical locales and promised "The Best Bang for Your Vacation Buck!" and demanded that clients "Get the Heck Outta Here!"

Hmm. I could definitely use a vacation.

The Paris poster featured the Eiffel Tower, the Arc de Triomphe, and a street performer with white makeup and a black-and-white-striped shirt. Another featured London land-marks, including London Bridge, Big Ben, and Buckingham Palace. With its beautiful beaches, salt-rimmed margaritas, and cute cabana boys, the poster for Cancún was particu-larly enticing. I'd traveled there not long ago, but the trip had been for business, not pleasure.

That's where I'd first met Nick.

My heart simultaneously fluttered and ached at the mem-ory of him emerging from the ocean, of water droplets glis-tening on his dark hair, broad shoulders, and expansive chest. I'd nearly fallen out of my lounge chair at the spectacle. And when he'd stopped to apply sunscreen to my back, *ay car-amba!* I could still feel the spots on my skin where he'd touched me. God, how they longed to be touched again.

Still, though the women perusing the Big D site were no doubt attracted to Nick's hard candy coating, I knew his yummy exterior was not what truly defined him or why I'd fallen so hard for him.

What was it about Nick that attracted me? It was his drive to see justice done. The fact that he looked out for the little guy, whether it be Josh or a taxpayer who'd been duped in a financial scam. The occasional glimpses of vulnerability, like when he talked about his father suffering a heart attack after losing his entire investment in Enron, the company Nick had worked for years ago.

Nick might look like a badass on the outside, but he was a good guy on the inside. Yep, he could have a hunchback like Quasimodo and his face could be covered in warts and I'd still think he was all that and a bag of chips.

It wasn't just about my feelings for him, though. Part of my attraction to him was how he made me feel about myself. Smart, capable, sexy, even. He never doubted that I could get the job done. He brought out the best in me.

Admittedly, though, Nick was also capable of bringing out my worst. Intense, petty jealousy. Frustration that threatened to cause self-combustion. Longing that made me feel as empty and hollow as a spent shotgun shell.

I climbed out of my car and entered the travel agency. Three women sat at desks configured into a horseshoe shape. Each desk featured a placard indicating that the agency was affiliated with American Express travel services.

All three women were on their phones. One of them wore a head scarf, indicating she was Muslim.

"Up, Up, and Away! Where can we send you today?" another said cheerily as she answered a call.

I took a seat on a padded chair and waited for one of the women to become available. After a moment or two, the woman with the hijab finished making plans for a high-school band to travel to Disney World. She returned her phone to the cradle. "Hi, there," she said in perfect English. "How can I help you?"

I explained who I was and that I was there to take a look at their records relating to traveler's checks, money orders, and money transmission.

She introduced herself as Lilith. "We handle quite a few of those types of transactions," Lilith said, directing me to a special computer apparently reserved exclusively for that purpose. "Is this a routine examination or were you looking for something in particular?"

I wasn't sure whether she was trying to be helpful or digging for information. "A little of both," I said.

She smiled and gave me a knowing nod. "I understand. Just let me know if you have any questions."

I spent a couple of hours digging through their records. Lilith hadn't been kidding. Their agency handled two or three money transfers a day, many of them in significant amounts. The vast majority of the funds were sent to parties in Mexico, Canada, and countries in Europe and Central America. Still, there were a number of transfers to Arab countries. Kuwait, Oman, Qatar, Libya, Lebanon, Bahrain, Djibouti. That last one always made me chuckle. It sounded like "booty." Real mature for a federal agent, huh?

The transactions also included a number of transfers to Syria, though none were to the parties who'd been implicated in the terror plots there and none were on or near the relevant dates. It was possible there had been unrecorded transfers, however.

I pulled the photos of Algafari, Nasser, and Homsi from my purse and showed them to Lilith. "Do you recognize any of these men?"

She looked each one over carefully. She handed Homsi's photo back to me. "I don't know this man," she said. She held up the photos of Algafari and Nasser. "These two look familiar. I believe they pray at my mosque, but I don't think they have attended prayers in quite some time."

My heart halted in my chest.

Lilith was the first person I'd spoken with who recognized any of the men. Was she a possible link? Was this travel agency where the terrorists had transmitted their funds overseas?

I decided to push a little further, eyeing her carefully to gauge her response. "Do you know what might have kept them away?"

She shook her head, offering two raised palms and a smile. "Maybe a vacation?"

I watched her a moment longer. "No. They aren't on vacation. They've been arrested."

Her smile faded and her face became serious. "Arrested? Why?"

I pulled out more photos, including the one of the school bus, and handed them to her. "They were involved in terror plots overseas."

She looked down at the photos, shaking her head. She quickly handed the photos back to me. "I can hardly believe it." She shook her head once. "I didn't know the men personally, but to think that they prayed where I prayed . . . It's . . . upsetting."

"Do you know if these men ever used your agency's services?"

"For travel or financial transactions?"

"Either."

"I don't know," she said. "I never took care of anything for them, but it's possible they came in at a time when I wasn't on duty."

I showed the photos to the other two women. Neither of them recognized the men.

I thanked them all for their time and stepped outside.

I wasn't sure whether Lilith had been completely honest with me or not. But there was one way to find out. I could contact American Express directly and compare their records to those kept at the agency, to make sure there hadn't been undocumented transfers.

I climbed into my car, drove out of sight, and parked.

I called American Express and asked them to provide copies of their records relating to Up, Up, and Away Vacations.

If something was up at Up, Up, and Away, someone would be going down.

chapter twenty-one

*T*here's Neau Stopping Beau

Monday evening I headed back to Zippy's Liquor.

Israel was working again that night. I greeted him and asked to speak to Jesús.

"Sorry," Israel said. "He went home sick."

"Already?" It was only six thirty. He sure hadn't stuck around long. If he was feeling that ill, why had he even bothered to come in? "Did you tell him I was coming to speak with him?"

Israel nodded.

Damn. I should've told the guy to keep that information under wraps. I had a sneaking suspicion that the sudden illness Jesús Benavides was suffering had more than a little to do with my visit.

"You're here alone then?" I asked Israel. Though the customers on a Monday night were not nearly as numerous as the crowd had been on Friday, there was nonetheless a steady stream coming in the door.

Israel took a bottle of vanilla vodka from a customer and rang it up. "Gloria is on her way to fill in."

Good. I'd wait to speak to her. At least my trip out wouldn't be a total waste.

I browsed around while I waited for Gloria to arrive, stopping at the whiskey section and gazing lovingly into a bottle of Jack Daniel's Black Label whiskey, the golden-brown liquid the same color as Nick's eyes. Brett's were the same color as green apple schnapps. I pondered this for a moment, realizing that while the schnapps was fun and could provide a nice buzz, whiskey was a hard-core drink for those who took their alcohol seriously. The whiskey was also far more addictive and dangerous.

"Miss Holloway?" Israel called, raising a hand to wave me over when I looked up. "Gloria is here now."

I made a beeline for the checkout counter, where Israel introduced me to Gloria, a woman with mannish features and short, layered hair dyed a bright copper.

"I didn't handle any of the transfers to Honduras," she said after I inquired about the wire transactions. "That was Jesús."

I thanked her for her time and left the store, knowing now, without a doubt, that I needed to speak with Jesús Benavides.

The rest of the week was pure hell, no two ways about it.

American Express provided all of its documentation relating to the travel agency and it jibed with the agency's records. Nothing was up at Up, Up, and Away. I reluctantly scratched the agency off my list, knowing that the possibility of catching the person who had helped the terrorists move their funds grew smaller each time that the list of remaining MSBs grew shorter.

Brett was busy in Atlanta, repairing both the country club's golf course and his relationship with the club's management. I was stuck in limbo, waiting for Brett to return, agonizing over Nick.

Damn those Japanese beetles!

I spent the next four days visiting money transmitter offices and driving through trailer parks. I even paid a visit to

Madam Magnolia, but she claimed her vision was blocked. I asked if a hundred dollars might clear her vision and she'd been insulted by the insinuation. Hey, I just figured the woman needed to make a living. Despite my profuse apologies, she'd asked me to leave.

I'd returned to Zippy's Liquor on Tuesday, only to learn that Jesús Benavides had phoned earlier in the day and quit his job. I pulled up his driver's license information online and swung by the address listed. The new tenants in the duplex informed me they'd moved in several months ago. They didn't know Jesús, though they recognized his name from a few items of mail that had been delivered to the duplex after he'd moved out.

I tried everything else I could think of to track him down. I contacted his former landlord but was told Jesús had provided no forwarding address. I checked telephone listings and utility company accounts with no luck. Oddly, his previous year's tax return showed an address in Houston and listed his occupation as *History Teacher.* Why would a history teacher leave his job to work at a liquor store? Had he encountered some trouble on the job?

Jesús had failed to update his address with the DMV. That alone could get him in some trouble. I put in a call to the DMV, asking them to flag his license. Now I just had to hope he'd be pulled over for a traffic violation and detained until I could speak with him.

Utterly frustrated, I revisited the quiet spot on the lake, taking a thermos of sangria with me and having my own private *un*happy hour.

Nothing was panning out. Nothing, nothing, nothing! All I got for my efforts was a glimpse of an aged hippy's bare, saggy ass as he hung his dripping tie-dyed T-shirts from a makeshift clothesline strung between two trees at his campsite. Frustration gnawed at my insides, threatening to consume me alive like some type of flesh-eating bacteria. It wasn't just my investigations that were going nowhere; it was my personal life, too. I was stuck in love limbo, with two relationships essentially on hold. I'd been too busy with work to wash my towering pile of laundry and forced to wear mismatched socks today. How much more could a girl endure?

If I couldn't relieve some of this frustration soon, I feared I'd explode. Maybe I should consider the battery-operated boyfriend Christina had sent me. A round or two with the jackhammer would probably rid me of some of this tension. But, alas, I wasn't that type of girl. It was the real thing or nothing. I hoped B.O.B. would understand.

On Friday morning, Lu called me and Eddie into her office for an update on the terrorist case. On her desk sat a huge bouquet of pinkish-orange mums, the exact color of Lu's hair. The card stapled to the ribbon read: *To my gorgeous gal. XO, Carl.*

Looked like things were going well for the Lobo and Comb-over Carl. I was glad things were going good for someone. They sure as hell weren't going well for me.

The flowers' sweet, cloying smell made me think of Brett, of the rosebushes he'd planted in front of my town house. I felt a twinge in my already-aching heart. Maybe I should just forget about Nick and stay with Brett. It would sure as hell make things easier. But I knew that was impossible. Nick wasn't the kind of guy a woman could easily put behind her.

Lu held a Slim Jim aloft between two fingers as if it were a cigarette. Old habits die hard, I suppose.

I gestured to the bouquet. "I take it you and Carl are hitting it off?"

She batted her false eyelashes, smiling like a schoolgirl with a crush. "He's the sweetest thing. We've had dinner three times this week." She reached out and stroked a rose petal before looking back to me. "I suppose I shouldn't settle for the first man I find, though, should I? I've had several more hits. I haven't been this popular since I was the first girl in junior high to grow boobs." She punched some keys on her keyboard, performed a few clicks on her mouse, and turned her computer screen so I could see it, too. "What do you think of these fellas?"

The screen displayed photos and bios for three men. The first man was roundish and totally bald, with a smile as bright as his shiny dome. His bio identified him as Fred, a widower and charter bus driver. The second guy had a head of thick silver hair with a matching full beard. His expression was self-assured but perhaps a tad too serious. His bio identified him as Harry, a divorced upper-level manager at a brokerage firm. It also identified him as a smoker, the last thing Lu needed after successfully fighting lung cancer. The final match was Gerard, a stocky retired high-school basketball coach with wavy white hair. He'd never been married. Perhaps it was presumptuous of me, but if a man made it to his sixties without ever having tied the knot there was probably something wrong with him.

"Try Fred," I suggested. "He looks friendly."

"I thought so, too," Lu said. "Fred it is."

Lu turned her screen away and turned her attention back to me and Eddie, all business now. "The terrorist case. What's happening?"

We gave her an update on the case, which took all of two seconds. It doesn't take long to say, "We've got squat."

She put the meat stick to her lips as if to take a puff but took a nibble instead. "If what you're doing isn't working," she said, "you need to try something else."

No kidding. "But what?" I asked.

"That's for you two to figure out," Lu said. "Put your heads together and come up with a plan." She held out both hands and waved us out of her office. "Scoot. Come back when you've figured things out. But make it quick. We're getting backlogged."

Eddie and I walked back to my office. I plopped down in my desk chair while Eddie took a seat in one of the wing chairs that faced my desk. Nick sat across the hall, talking on his personal cell phone, which meant the call wasn't business related. He chuckled.

How the hell could I concentrate with Nick across the hall setting up dates? I motioned to Eddie. "Shut my door, would ya?"

Eddie stuck out a foot and pushed it closed.

"What can we do that hasn't already been done?" I asked, throwing up my hands.

"I don't know." Eddie leaned his head back and closed his eyes. "We've got to think of something, though."

Viola stepped into my office with a copy of a tax return in her hand. She tossed it onto my desk.

"What's this?" I picked up the document and took a quick look at the front page. It was a tax return for an elderly woman named Ora Bickerstaff. The return had been prepared using surviving-spouse filing status, meaning Ms. Bickerstaff had lost her husband during the tax year. He'd left her well off, through. Her return reported investment income of fifty grand.

"Richard Beauregard is at it again," Vi said, eyeing us over the top of her bifocals.

"How can that be?" Eddie said. "We terminated his e-filing privileges."

Vi pursed her lips. "He filed the old-fashioned way."

"A paper return?" Eddie snatched the pages out of my hand. "Nobody files paper returns anymore." He scanned the first page, then turned to the second. "Beau claimed another fraudulent fuel tax credit."

Which meant another taxpayer defrauded. A widow, no less. Was there no depth too low for Beau to sink to?

Eddie handed the return back to me. I looked it over thoroughly. Sure enough, Beauregard Financial Services was listed in the paid-preparer section.

It was one thing to be outsmarted by well-trained terrorists with college degrees in difficult subjects. It was another to be outsmarted by an idiot with a unibrow.

"Let's pay a visit to Ora Bickerstaff," I suggested.

While Eddie went to his office to retrieve his jacket and briefcase, I gathered up my purse and stepped across the hall to Nick's office.

Nick glanced up from his computer screen. "Hey."

I leaned on the doorjamb. "Another night, another girl, huh?"

He ducked his chin in agreement. "Yep."

"Do me a favor, will you?" I snapped. "Have a horrible, rotten, no-good time." It was a mean-spirited, spiteful, jealous thing to say. I'm human. Sue me.

A knowing grin spread across Nick's lips. "You're eating your heart out, aren't you?"

No sense lying about something that was so obvious. "Yes, I am. If Brett weren't dealing with a beetle infestation in Atlanta it would be you and me going out tonight."

He raised a brow. "Bugs, huh? That's what's kept you from breaking up with him?"

I nodded. "His career's on the line. And not just the landscaping but the nursery business, too."

Nick watched me for a moment, his expression thoughtful, considering. "I suppose it would take a nasty bitch to break up with a guy who's going through a major career setback."

Did that mean he understood why I hadn't been able to move things along with Brett? I didn't have time to find out. Eddie walked up.

"Ready to go?" he asked.

"Yeah." I took one last look at Nick before walking away.

He gave me a soft smile and he gave me a wink. But what he gave me most was hope.

Ora Bickerstaff lived in a newly constructed high-dollar high-rise for senior citizens. The place was gorgeous, with lush gardens outside and Tuscan tile and granite accents inside. The residents enjoyed valet parking, gourmet meals, and maid service. Who said getting old had to suck?

"I'd love to live like this," I told Eddie as we made our way to the security desk to check in.

"No kidding," Eddie agreed. "Did you see the lunch menu posted by the entrance? They're serving mahimahi. You know what I had for dinner last night? Macaroni and cheese, for the third time this week."

Mac 'n' cheese was the twins' favorite. Poor Eddie, stuck with a diet fit for a grade-school palate.

We showed our identification to the guard at the desk.
Once we'd been cleared, we climbed into the elevator and
rode up to the twelfth floor along with a couple of older
women carrying canvases and oil paints.

Ms. Bickerstaff lived in unit 1204, a spacious model
with plate-glass windows and a balcony that overlooked a
park. Her place was filled with expensive high-quality an-
tiques, including an ornate grandfather clock and a baby
grand piano. As for Ms. Bickerstaff, she, too, was a high-
quality antique, dressed in a tailored pantsuit I recognized
as a Liz Claiborne offering. Her silver hair hung in a short,
smooth bob. At her ankles quivered a tiny male Yorkshire
terrier with red ribbons in his hair, a canine cross-dresser.

Ms. Bickerstaff invited Eddie and me to take a seat on
her couch and offered us tea. We both thanked her but declined.

She took a seat in a wooden rocker and used her hands to
lift her legs up onto a footstool with a needlepoint cover.
"Swollen ankles and arthritis," she explained, "but I don't
let it slow me down much."

Good for her.

The dog waited until Ms. Bickerstaff had settled in, then
leaped up into her lap. The woman ran a blue-veined hand
over the dog's back and looked at me and Eddie. "You said
you had some questions about my tax return?"

"That's right," Eddie said. "We've been after your tax
preparer, Richard Beauregard, for a while now. We went to
arrest him at his office last week, but he fled out a window."

"My goodness." Her eyes grew wide and her hand stilled
on the dog's back. "What were you going to arrest him for?"

We explained about Beauregard's fraudulent fuel tax
scheme and the nonexistent insurance and investment companies.

Ms. Bickerstaff sat up in her chair. "Are you telling me I
gave that little bugger three thousand dollars for a gas well
that doesn't even exist?"

The dog looked up at the woman's face, cocking his head
in concern.

"Sorry," I said, "but yes. That's exactly what we're telling you."

She shook her head. "My husband must be rolling over in his grave. He always told me I was too trusting. That's why he took care of all of our finances while he was alive."

We asked her how she'd hooked up with Beauregard.

"I saw his ad in *The Greensheet*," she said. "It caught my eye because it said he'd come to his clients. I don't drive much anymore."

"So he came here?" I asked.

She nodded. "Prepared my return right there at my kitchen table."

"Any chance you've got that *Greensheet*?" I asked. Beauregard's old phone numbers had been disconnected and he hadn't listed a new phone number on the tax return. If we could get a copy of the ad, we'd know his new number and could possibly use it to track him down.

Ms. Bickerstaff gestured toward her pantry. "Check the recycle bin in the bottom. I think it's still in there."

I opened the pantry door and bent down to rifle through her plastic recycle bin. I found a *Greensheet* near the bottom, under a week's worth of the *Dallas Morning News*. I quickly perused it. Beauregard's ad had been circled in pencil. "Found it!" I called.

We thanked the woman for her time and told her we'd let her know when we tracked Richard Beauregard down . . . *if* we tracked him down. Our targets seemed to be doing a good job of staying out of reach lately.

chapter twenty-two

$\mathcal{V}$room-Vroom Kaboom

Eddie and I headed back to the G-ride in the parking lot. As I approached the car, I flipped through *The Greensheet,* perusing the singles section to see if I could find a new love interest for Alicia. One of the pages slipped out, dropping to the parking lot. As I bent to pick it up, I noticed something odd lodged behind the back tire of the car. The thing was plastic, circular, and flat, like the tortilla warmers used in Mexican restaurants. I assumed it was trash, though I wasn't sure how the trash ended up behind the tire and I wasn't sure why someone would throw away what appeared to be a perfectly usable tortilla warmer.

Being the upstanding citizen I was, I grabbed the thing, carried it over to a nearby metal garbage Dumpster, and tossed it over the top of the bin. I turned and was headed back to the car when *KABOOM!*

I dived behind a nearby Impala. Garbage sailed into the air and the Dumpster rocked backward, its metal sides bowing out, the impact blowing a hole completely through the far side.

"Holy shit!" Eddie ducked behind the fleet car and held his briefcase over his head, shielding himself against the deluge of yesterday's cheese tortellini raining down from the sky. "What the hell did you throw in that Dumpster?"

I was guessing it was not a tortilla warmer. I was guessing it was some type of land mine.

Someone had followed us to the high-rise without our knowledge, someone who wanted me and Eddie dead.

That much required no guesswork.

I ran to Eddie, grabbed him, and dragged him away from the car. "There might be more explosives. We've got to call the bomb squad."

Eddie and I put a safe distance between us and the car and called 911. A couple of men from the building's security team raced outside. We waved them over and told them what had happened. They took one look at the blown-out Dumpster and the vehicles splattered with leftovers and gaped.

"Jesus Christ," one of them muttered, shaking his head. "Didn't expect nothing like that on this job."

One of the men stayed outside to prevent cars or people from entering the lot, while the other returned to the building to evacuate the residents. Better safe than sorry.

In minutes, three police cruisers and two fire trucks were on the scene, along with dozens of cops and first responders. Soon afterward, the bomb squad arrived with a frisky black Lab trained to sniff out explosives. The dog put his nose to the ground and set right to work. Looked like we were in good hands. Or should I say good *nostrils*?

A steady stream of residents exited the building, some in wheelchairs, others making their way down the sidewalk as quickly as they could with their walkers and canes. A group of women in bathing suits and rubber swim caps came out together, the bomb having interrupted their water aerobics class. The residents gathered on the far lawn to watch the activity in the parking lot, the sound of their excited chatter drifting across the lawn.

A fortyish plainclothes cop headed our way, identifying

himself as a detective. He whipped out a mini tape recorder and notepad. "Mind if I ask you some questions?"

An hour later, after Eddie and I had provided all the information we could to the detective and the bomb squad had determined there were no other explosives in the vicinity, we were cleared to leave. I demanded that Eddie stand back while I started the car, just in case. If I was blown to smithereens my parents and siblings would lament my death, but if Eddie died he'd leave a wife and two young children behind. I wasn't about to take that chance.

I closed my eyes, held my breath, and crossed the fingers of my left hand as I turned the key in the ignition. The engine started without a hitch. *Phew.* I glanced upward. "Thanks, Big Guy."

Looked like Eddie and I would live to fight crime another day. Of course whoever put the explosives under the tire would no doubt soon be back at work trying to find another way to kill us.

Rats.

As Eddie and I drove back to the IRS building, we tried to make some sense of the situation. I supposed it was possible that Richard Beauregard had planted the land mine, but my money was on the terror network. We knew that the person who'd helped move funds was still on the loose, but was that person the one who'd planted the bomb or were there more of them? If there were more terrorists in the area, how many? When would they strike again? And how did they know that Eddie and I were after them? Had someone at one of the MSBs told the bomber about us? Or had Homsi, Algafari, or Nasser somehow communicated to a cohort on the outside?

"The only thing I can say for sure," Eddie said when I posed the questions to him, "is that you and I had better watch our backs."

chapter twenty-three

*G*irls' Night Out

I kept my eyes wide open on my drive home from work, checking my rearview and side mirrors for a tail. I didn't see one, but just to be safe I performed some evasive maneuvers, crossing three lanes of traffic to make a sudden exit from the freeway, executing several bootlegger's turns at random intervals, backtracking through my neighborhood.

I arrived home to find Alicia in my kitchen slugging back yet another glass of peach sangria. She wore nothing but a black bra, panties, and a slightly buzzed expression. "Put on your dancing shoes!" she called, raising her glass. "We're going out."

After what I'd been through I was in no mood for dancing. But that's precisely when a girl needs to hit the dance floor, isn't it? "You're getting dressed first, right?"

"Of course," she said. "I just wanted to have a drink while I got ready."

I grudgingly bypassed the sangria. Clearly I'd be the designated driver tonight.

We walked upstairs, parting ways on the landing. Alicia

went left into my guest room while I turned right into my bedroom.

It had been ages since I'd been to a nightclub. Frankly, I wasn't all that excited by the prospect. But I was even less excited about the prospect of staying home with Alicia, the two of us sitting on the couch like a couple of old spinsters feeling sorry for ourselves.

Annie hopped onto the corner of my bed, licking her paw and watching as I sorted through my small selection of clean clothes. I searched for something fun and cute that I wouldn't freeze to death in. A rapidly moving cold front had snuck into the Dallas area late this afternoon and the temperatures had plummeted into the forties. I settled on a sweaterdress over tights with high-heeled boots.

Alicia stepped out of the guest room in one of the secondhand designer outfits she'd snagged at the thrift shop several weeks ago. The winter-white dress was cinched at the waist with a wide black belt. She'd paired the dress with classic black T-strap heels.

It had been years since we'd both been single, but tonight, for all practical purposes, the two of us were single again. Though I hadn't yet put things with Brett in a holding pattern as planned, I was miffed he'd only called me twice since leaving for Atlanta a week ago. I knew he was dealing with an emergency situation, but didn't he need me for moral support? I felt left out, cut out. Not that I had any right to feel upset given my plans to put him on the back burner, but the feelings were there nonetheless.

Sheesh. Relationships are complicated, huh?

We piled into my BMW and drove a few blocks to a nightclub in Uptown. We stood in line on the sidewalk for half an hour, shivering and huddling together in a desperate and futile attempt to keep warm. The throbbing bass line reverberated through the wall beside us as we waited.

Alicia reached into her purse, pulled out two lollipops, and handed one to me. "Here. Maybe these suckers will distract us from the fact that we're slowly dying of hypothermia."

I removed the crinkly plastic wrap and stuck the sucker in my mouth. It had an unusual taste, a hint of citrus with something that tasted sort of like a wheatgrass protein shake Christina had once forced on me. "What flavor is this?"

Alicia consulted her wrapper. "Hemp."

"Hemp?" I said. "Where the heck did you get a hemp lollipop?"

"At that smoke shop," she said. "The one where your mother bought the 'hummingbird feeder.'" She made air quotes with her fingers.

After several more minutes we finally reached the front of the line, paid our ten-dollar cover charge, and entered the dark, noisy, crowded club. Bodies packed the dance floor, gyrating under the flashing colored lights. Alicia and I wound our way through onlookers to the bar. We bellied up and shouted our orders to the bartender, who had to lean forward and cup a hand around his ear to hear us over the loud techno music. Alicia ordered a Cosmo while I opted for a Dr Pepper.

A soda.

Ugh.

This was going to be a long night.

As we stood near the dance floor, I wondered about Nick's date tonight. Was he out with a bosomy blonde? A racy redhead? A brainy brunette? Where did they go and what did they do? Did the two of them hit it off? Was he putting the moves on her at this very moment?

I realized then that I wasn't wondering what Brett was doing at the moment, where he was, or who he was with. Should I feel bad about that? I mean, he was still technically my boyfriend. But I supposed I didn't worry about Brett because I knew what Brett was doing. Lying on the bed in his hotel room, watching the late news or maybe David Letterman.

At least I assumed that's what he was doing. For all I knew he was out at a nightclub, too. I mean, he probably thought Alicia and I were at home painting our nails and watching a chick flick. If I could be out doing something unpredictable, so could he, right?

Jeez. Yet another thing to worry about.

Two men in their late twenties came our way and asked Alicia and me to dance. We accepted and followed them onto the crowded dance floor, squeezing between bodies until we found an open spot. My dance partner was tall, dark haired, and undeniably attractive, but he lacked Nick's cocky chipped-tooth smile or Brett's boyish charm. He was fun to dance with, but beyond that he didn't do anything for me. Besides, for all I knew he was the one who'd put the explosive device under my tire. Maybe he'd figured out where I lived, watched my town house, and followed me here with the hopes of kidnapping and torturing me.

Or maybe I was just freaked out by my near-death experience.

The guy attempted to engage me in conversation, but after shouting, "What? I can't hear you!" over the music five times I gave up trying to actually hear him and just responded to everything he said with a smile and a nod.

Smile and nod.

Smile and nod.

I checked my watch. *Dang.* How could it only be eleven thirty? It felt like we'd been here for days.

After several songs, he took my hand and led me off the dance floor. Alicia and her dance partner followed. The men offered to buy us drinks, but both of us girls knew what that meant.

Expectations.

"You're nice guys!" Alicia shouted over the noise. "But we're both coming out of relationships right now and only looking to have some fun!"

The guys gave us the thumbs-up sign and wandered off in search of easier prey.

The minutes passed like millennia as we stood near the dance floor, unable to talk over the music, not really caring whether any other guys asked us to dance. None did. I couldn't much blame them. I'm sure Alicia and I looked like a couple of sourpusses. The loud music jarred my nerves tonight, and the flashing lights were giving me a headache.

It was funny, too. There I was surrounded by hundreds of people, each of whom seemed bound and determined to jostle me as they passed by, yet I'd never felt more desolate and lonely in my entire life.

Eventually, Alicia turned to me. I couldn't hear her, but her expression spoke for her. She was ready to call it a night. *Thank God.* I'd been ready to leave for the past hour.

We ventured back out into the night, which had grown even colder while we'd been in the club. Our teeth chattering, we climbed into my car and headed home. The heater finally warmed up just as we pulled back into my driveway. Par for the course that night, I suppose.

We went inside, changed into our pajamas, and ended up on the couch with glasses in our hands and a pitcher of peach sangria on the coffee table in front of us.

"I thought going out would cheer me up," Alicia said, "but I think I actually feel worse."

"Me, too." I used to enjoy being single, being free to do my own thing, answering to no one. But after dating Brett and enjoying the comfort, security, and companionship a relationship provided, I'd begun to see the upside of being part of a couple.

I wanted to be in a relationship. And I was pretty sure I wanted to be in one with Nick.

Alicia grabbed my laptop off the coffee table and turned it on. "What was that dating site again?"

"It's called Big D Dating Service." I sat up in my seat. "You're going to sign up?"

She sighed. "It's time for me to move on. But I can't stomach the thought of hanging out at another meat market trying to meet a decent guy. This online thing seems way more efficient."

If Alicia was anything, it was efficient. She'd already rearranged my kitchen appliances to put my coffeemaker closer to the sink where it could be easily filled with water and my toaster closer to the pantry where I kept the bread. She'd put a plastic bin under my sink for junk mail so I could carry it out to the larger recycling bin in my garage en masse rather than leaving it stacked around my kitchen until making my usual frantic dash to the curb on garbage day, trying to beat the truck. She'd even figured out how to work my programmable thermostat for maximum energy efficiency. Heck, I'd lived here for years and hadn't gotten around to learning the system yet.

The only thing she hadn't done was my laundry. Maybe if I waited long enough it would drive her crazy and she'd wash it for me. It was a childish tactic, but, hey, it had worked on my mother for years. I had a much higher tolerance for clutter than most people.

Alicia used her credit card to pay her fee and input her basic information. Sex. Height. Weight. Age.

"What are my interests?" she asked.

"Why are you asking me?" I said, realizing I had no idea what her interests were. "They're your interests." How could I not know what my best friend's interests were?

She looked up in thought. "I don't think I have any interests. I mean, I like to shop and go out for drinks and out to eat, but who doesn't?"

I was relieved to know she couldn't identify any interests, either.

Her face clouded over. "I'm boring, aren't I?"

"No!" I said, and I meant it. Alicia might not be into a lot of hobbies or activities, but she was by no means boring. She was witty and smart and fun to be around, not to mention loyal and caring and supportive. She'd always been there when I needed her. What she lacked in interests she made up for in personality.

"I am," she said. "I'm boring. No wonder Daniel doesn't want to marry me."

So we were back to that again, were we?

"Give me that computer this instant." I grabbed the laptop from her. Heck, if I'd come up with descriptions for Josh and Nick, the least I could do was come up with one for my longtime BFF.

I thought for a moment and finally created a bio I hoped she'd like.

Witty and chic CPA seeks a smart professional man who enjoys food, fashion, and good conversation.

"There," I said, turning the screen so she could read her bio.

Alicia pondered my statement for a moment. "In other words, I'm looking for another Daniel."

"Well, yeah, I suppose," I said. "Except with bigger balls."

She snorted. "Yeah. What a wimp, huh? I mean, we've been together forever. He had to know the *m* word would come up at some point."

She answered a series of questions designed to help define her personality type, things like "Would you rather sit by a river or swim in it?"

When she was done, she submitted her information for processing. Three minutes later, the computer had composed a list of eighteen potential candidates for her to screen.

We sorted through them together, eliminating three whose bios seemed excessively arrogant, two with bios that were unnecessarily suggestive, and one who was a former coworker of ours from Martin and McGee who'd left a couple of years ago to take a controller position with one of the firm's corporate clients. He'd been a nice enough guy but never sparked Alicia's interest.

"That leaves a dozen possible replacements for Daniel," I said.

She checked the boxes to indicate potential interest and hit the "submit" key, which would send a notice to the men. If one of the men was interested in Alicia, he'd check his box, too, and the system would then supply the two of them with contact information for each other.

"Why don't you try it, too?" she said.

"No, thanks. I have too much man trouble already."

"Oh, come on," she said. "They let you try it for free. You're only charged if you check the box to show you're interested. It'll be fun."

Since we were only goofing around, she uploaded a photo she'd taken of me on April 15 of last year. I was sitting in my cubicle, my head in my hands, my desktop threatening to collapse under a mountain of tax files. On the computer screen behind me, in easy-to-read 96-point font, were the words "KILL ME NOW."

For my bio she wrote.

> *Feisty federal law enforcement agent seeks well-hung man with significant earning potential. In lieu of said giant penis and earnings will accept a man willing to wash laundry.*

"See?" I said. "You are witty."

"And you really need to do that laundry."

Good. The pile of dirty clothing was already bugging her. If I could muster up enough panties to get me through a few more days she'd cave and wash it for me. It was sneaky and underhanded, but, hey, it's not like she wasn't getting anything in return. I'd given her a free place to live, unwavering support, and, by my best estimate, 243 gallons of peach sangria.

We ran through the personality test next. I answered each question truthfully, curious to see what type of man it would suggest for me. When I finished my responses, Alicia pushed the "enter" button.

The computer churned and churned and churned, the timer in the middle of the screen continuing to circle incessantly as the system tried to find men who would be a good match for me. It seemed to be having a hard time.

"Has it frozen up?" I asked after a couple of minutes.

Alicia eyed the screen. "I'm not sure. Let's give it another minute."

A moment later the screen popped up with just one match. I was as pitiful as Josh, huh?

I clicked on the link to view the file. A photo popped up on the screen, a photo of a gorgeous dark-haired man bearing a mildly annoyed expression.

Nick.

"Wow," Alicia said. "There are thousands of men on this site. What are the odds of him being your only match?"

I had no idea. But I did know one thing. I was definitely interested.

I checked the box and hit the "submit" button.

Alicia held out her hand. "You owe me fifty-nine bucks."

chapter twenty-four

$\mathcal{K}$nock Knock. Who's There?

A knock on the door woke me at nine the next morning. Both of my parents were coming to visit this weekend, having agreed to serve as decoy clients to help Eddie and me nab Beauregard. But their appointment with Beau wasn't until one o'clock and they wouldn't arrive until late morning.

I put a pillow over my head, figuring the person at my door was a salesman who'd eventually give up and go away. No such luck. The knocks were still coming five minutes later, louder and more insistent than ever.

I tossed my pillow aside and went downstairs, bouncing off the stairwell wall in my half-awake state. Annie trotted along after me.

Muttering curses under my breath, I yanked the door open. Not what home security experts would recommend, but with my bed head, no makeup, and wrinkled pajamas I figured I was horrifying enough to scare away any potential solicitor or home invader.

But it wasn't a salesman or burglar on my porch.

It was Nick.

He wore faded jeans, cowboy boots, and a brown cable-knit sweater that brought out his whiskey-colored eyes. He also wore that chipped-tooth smile that had captured my heart.

"Hungry?" He stepped into my foyer without waiting for an invitation.

Not sure what he had in mind, I shrugged and nodded simultaneously, hedging my bets.

"Great. Let's go out for breakfast." He eyed my wild hair and gestured in the general direction of my face. "After you do something about that."

I narrowed my eyes at him and he chucked me on the chin.

"Get moving," he said. "I'm starved."

I went upstairs and rushed through my morning rituals. A quick shower, tooth brushing, minimal makeup. I pulled my hair back in a twist, securing it with a claw clip. A pair of jeans, tennis shoes, a sweatshirt, and I was done.

I went back downstairs to find Annie cuddled in Nick's arms. He was scratching her under the chin and whispering sweet nothings in her ear. Oh, to be that cat.

He set her down in the foyer while I grabbed my purse. Out the door we went.

When I climbed into his truck, I noticed an unmistakable hint of perfume. Once Nick had settled in and backed out of the driveway, I said, "Your date wore Red Door, huh?"

"Yeah. Way too much of it, too." He cracked the windows for ventilation and turned the heater on to fight the morning chill that seeped in. "I dropped her off at ten last night. You'd have thought the smell would be gone by now."

Ten, huh? Sounded like I'd worried unnecessarily about Nick putting moves on the woman. Any date that ended so early hadn't gone well.

Thinking about Nick's date got me wondering about Josh. My coworker and I didn't talk much, but I knew the men in the office routinely shared their conquests over coffee and donuts in the kitchen. Of course 99 percent of it was probably pure bullshit.

"What's the word on Kira?" I asked. "Has she booted up Josh's laptop? Tested his hard drive? Discovered how much RAM he's got?" *Maybe bitten his neck with those pointy teeth and sucked his blood?*

"Josh hasn't logged onto Kira's system yet," Nick said. "But he did get to play with her function keys."

I only hoped he knew how to operate a woman's programs. If not, her entire system could shut down.

Shortly thereafter Nick and I were seated across from each other in a corner booth at a neighborhood café, sipping coffee while we waited for our pancakes to arrive. I'd ordered the short stack with fruit. Nick had gone for a full platter with sausage links on the side.

Nick set his mug on the table. "So, giant penis, huh?"

Oh, God. I'd forgotten Alicia had written that in my bio for the Big D site.

"Alicia signed herself up." I shrugged. "Then we were just goofing around."

"Uh-huh." Nick eyed me. "How many men did the computer match you with?"

I held up my index finger.

"Just one?" The grin quirking about his mouth said Nick found my response amusing. He narrowed his eyes and looked at me, pondering. "I suppose there aren't many men who could keep up with a woman like you."

I noticed he'd said "keep up with" rather than "put up with." That was promising, huh?

"When's Brett coming back?" he asked. "Maybe he could do your laundry." He slid a grin my way.

"I don't know," I said. "I've only talked to him twice since he's been in Atlanta." He'd sent me a few short texts, but those hardly counted as communication, especially when they were primarily rants about the beetles.

Damn bugs are everywhere!
Beetles ate the 9th hole green.
Die, beetles! Die!

He'd also sent me a number of texts about the food.

The club serves a kick-ass mushroom omelet.

I've eaten so much tiramisu I'm growing love handles.
Fiona's homemade peach ice cream is the best!

Fiona? Brett and the chef were on a first-name basis now? He'd mentioned meeting the chef a while back, noted that she'd treated him and his crew to ice-cold lemonade and specially prepared meals, but he'd failed to mention her name. In fact, he'd failed to mention that the chef was a woman. I'd assumed it was a man. Probably sexist of me, but there you go.

Nick cocked his head. "Just two phone calls?"

"Yep," I said, "and short ones at that."

Nick grunted in reply.

The waitress swung by with a coffeepot and topped off our mugs.

I added another packet of sugar, stirred, and took a sip of the hot brew. "How does it feel to be back in the saddle? Having all those women chase after you?" It had to be an ego trip. Then again, while Nick was cocky and confident, he was far from an egomaniac.

"Honestly? I've been underwhelmed. Most of them seem to be gold diggers looking for a sugar daddy." He took another sip of his coffee. "One of them even insulted my truck."

Putting down a man's pickup? That was pure sacrilege. "I hope you put her in her place."

"You know it." Nick raised his mug as if in salute. "That truck brought me back to freedom. I'm going to drive it until the wheels fall off."

I shot him a pointed look. "That truck didn't drive itself down to Mexico, you know."

He shot me a pointed look right back. "I'm well aware of that fact. But all I've got right now is the truck." His pointed look morphed into a sexy grin. "If you were mine, I'd drive you until your wheels fell off, too."

It was a lousy metaphor, but it still gave my nether regions a flutter.

"What about Natalie?" I asked.

The sexy grin turned wicked. "Are you suggesting a threesome?"

I rolled my eyes. Admittedly, though, I felt sexually frustrated. With Brett gone and Nick being the stud muffin he was, who could blame me? "Come on, Nick. I'm serious. I don't want to call things off with Brett only to find out you and Natalie got back together."

Nick let out a long breath. He gave his head a shake. "Natalie and me? That's nothing you need to be concerned about."

"You're sure?"

He gave me a soft, reassuring smile. "I'm sure."

That was a relief.

The waitress plunked my short stack in front of me and Nick's platter in front of him. We took turns with the syrup, grabbed our forks, and dug in.

chapter twenty-five

Taking Another Go at Beau

My dad's pickup was parked in my driveway when Nick and I returned from breakfast. Alicia's Audi was gone. She'd planned to swing by her and Daniel's apartment today while he was working to pick up some more clothes and things. Looked like she'd be my roommate indefinitely. I hated for her to be suffering, but I had to admit that it was nice to have her around. It would be even nicer if she'd wash a load of whites.

I climbed out of Nick's truck and caught a whiff of roses. I glanced over at my town house, at the row of pink rose-bushes Brett had lovingly planted for me. The bushes sported their last blooms of the season, still flowering but fading fast. Soon it would be time to snip them back to bare nubs. Whether they would survive the unpredictable North Texas winter and flower again in the spring remained to be seen.

The bushes were the perfect metaphor for my relation-ship with Brett.

Nick followed me inside to say hello to my parents. We found them in the kitchen.

Mom stood from the table and gave Nick a hug, shooting me a questioning yet hopeful look over his shoulder. "Nice to see you again, Nick."

Dad stood and shook Nick's hand. "How ya doin', son?"

Nick inquired about the purpose of my parents' visit.

I set my purse on the counter. "They're helping me and Eddie today," I said, explaining about the latest developments in the Beauregard case and my plans to deploy my parents as decoy clients.

"If you'd like some extra manpower," Nick said, "I'd be happy to help you and Eddie out."

Given that Beauregard had managed to escape two of the office's best agents before, it couldn't hurt to have another agent along to assist. "That would be great. Thanks."

"No plans for the day, Nick?" Mom asked him, shooting me another look, one that said, *So he's still available, huh?*

"I'm going shopping for a bass boat," Nick said, "but I can do that later this afternoon."

At the mention of a fishing vessel, Dad's ears perked up. "A bass boat, you say?"

Nick nodded. "Lu talked to the higher-ups at the IRS and got me back pay for the three years I was stuck in Mexico. I just received the check. Figured I'd treat myself."

Dad's blue-gray eyes grew starry. He'd always dreamed of owning a bass boat himself. Sending three kids to college had taken precedence, though. He'd had to settle for a john-boat with what he called a "sissy" motor. The substandard boat hadn't affected his fishing, though. He'd held the county record for the biggest bass until last year when an eight-year-old kid had landed one three ounces heavier, with some help from his uncle.

Nick must've noticed my father salivating. "If the women don't mind, maybe you could come along with me, give me your opinion."

Dad looked to Mom for permission. She rolled her eyes but waved her hand. "I'd love to get you out of my hair for a few hours."

A half hour later we headed out, Nick and Dad in Nick's

truck and Mom and me in my BMW. We met up with Eddie at a junior high a mile from the Denny's restaurant where my parents were to rendezvous with Beauregard.

Eddie didn't seem all that surprised to see that Nick had come along. He just looked from me to Nick and back, his brow and lip quirking. "Something going on between you two?"

My "no" was drowned out by Nick's "maybe."

Eddie and Nick chuckled.

"Women," Eddie said. "They're nothing but trouble. Am I right?"

"Amen," Dad said, earning him a "hush" and a glare from my mother.

Beau had arranged to meet another client at the restaurant, too. It was the last weekend before the extended October 15 tax return deadline and no doubt he was busy.

I supplied my parents with phony W-2s and brokerage statements, along with fictionalized sales records from a purported Mary Kay cosmetics business operated by my mother. We had to ensure their return would take sufficient time to prepare so that Eddie, Nick, and I could get into place for the takedown.

Ten minutes before their scheduled appointment time, Nick gave my parents the keys to his truck. We three agents loaded into Eddie's fleet car. Eddie followed my parents at a safe distance. While my parents parked and went into the restaurant, Eddie took a few turns around the neighborhood, looking for Beauregard's beat-up Suburban.

"There it is." I pointed down a nearby side street where the SUV was parked. Beau's camp trailer with the Puma logo was hooked up to it. Looked like he'd been on the move.

Eddie pulled to the curb a block down and the three of us donned our ballistic vests and raid jackets.

Eddie slid his gun into his hip holster. "One of us should keep an eye on his car in case he makes a break for it."

Chances were Beauregard would never make it back to his car, and neither Nick nor I wanted to miss out on the action. We hadn't become special agents to sit on the sidelines and play it safe. The only fair thing was to settle the dispute with rock-paper-scissors. I won, paper over rock. I took advantage of the situation to touch him, wrapping my hand around his fist as if to demonstrate how paper beats rock. It felt good to touch him, to connect with him physically, even if only in jest and for a brief moment.

"Neener-neener," I told Nick. "Have fun babysitting the Puma." With a final *meow,* I climbed out of the car and followed Eddie down the block and across a four-lane road to the Denny's parking lot.

My partner and I crouched behind a utility box on the grass median surrounding the restaurant and used a hand-me-down pair of my father's field glasses to look through the windows. We saw my parents seated side by side at a table in the back. Beauregard sat at the table, too, inputting data into a laptop. A portable printer sat next to the computer.

"It's probably best if we split up in case he makes a break for it," Eddie said.

"Good idea."

I headed down to one end of the parking lot while Eddie headed to the other.

A half hour later, my parents walked out of Denny's and made their way to Nick's truck. Though my mother kept her head aimed toward the truck, her eyes darted around, seeking me out. I peeked out from behind a Volkswagen and gave her the "okay" sign, letting her know things were going as anticipated.

A few minutes later, Beauregard exited the diner, a laptop bag in one hand, his printer tucked under his other arm. His clip-on tie had been crammed into the breast pocket of his white dress shirt now that his work was finished.

As he headed for his SUV, Eddie approached quietly from one direction and I approached from the other. A horn honked in the parking lot behind us and Beauregard glanced back. He did a double take when he noticed my eyes on him. He sped up, his long legs eating pavement quickly. There was no way I could keep up unless I ran. So I did.

Eddie began running, too. "Stop, Beauregard!" Eddie ordered. "You're under arrest!"

By that time Beau had reached the curb of the four-lane road. Eddie and I were nearly on him, closing in from both sides. With heavy traffic in both directions, Beau had nowhere to go. Or at least I'd thought so. He dropped his laptop and his printer and ran into the street.

Beeeeep!

A MINI Cooper narrowly missed plowing Beau down in the street. He continued across the road, dodging cars, getting sideswiped by a city bus, but somehow continuing on. Cursing, Eddie and I ventured into the street, waving our arms, trying to make it across the street after him. Our efforts earned us three honks, two middle fingers, and one shout of, "Fucking morons!"

By the time we'd made it to the other side, Beauregard was already down the block, opening the door to his SUV. In a move that would have made his high-school football coach proud, Nick rushed Beau and tackled him, taking him down to the asphalt.

As the two wrangled on the road ahead of us, a black Dodge Charger came up the street from the other direction, making no effort to slow down as it approached Nick and Beau.

Holy shit! The driver didn't see them!

A scream tore from my throat as I realized Nick was about to become roadkill.

At the last second, Nick and Beau apparently noticed the car and realized the driver had no intention of stopping. They split apart in the nick of time, Beau rolling toward his SUV and Nick rolling to the curb on the other side.

Thank God!

"Idiot!" I hurled my pepper spray at the car's windshield as it approached me and Eddie.

Bam!

The teenage boy at the wheel looked up from the cell phone he'd been texting on, gave me the third middle finger I'd seen in the last two minutes, and continued on. Dumb little shit.

When I turned back to Beau, he'd climbed into his Suburban. The brake lights came on as Nick, Eddie, and I reached him.

Nick banged on the driver's window and Eddie grabbed a door handle just as Beau floored the gas pedal. Eddie was forced to let go as the Suburban sped off. "Damn!"

Screeech. Beau braked to a stop a hundred feet down the road when he realized his camper hadn't followed him. I glanced back at the trailer. Sure enough, Nick had disengaged the trailer hitch.

Smart move.

When the three of us began running after the Suburban, Beau apparently decided it was best to leave his home behind. He floored the gas pedal again, sending up a spray of dust and pebbles.

As I waved the dust out of my face I debated shooting out Beau's tires. Problem was, any unnecessary use of my weapons could lead to disciplinary action. Better not to risk it. My internal affairs file was thick enough already and Lu had a hissy fit every time I shot my gun.

Nick hurried over with the keys to the fleet car and we jumped in to follow Beau. We nearly caught him as he turned onto the four-lane road right in front of a plumbing truck. Unfortunately, we didn't have a siren, so oncoming traffic didn't yield to us. By the time we could safely merge into traffic, Beau's car was no longer in sight.

Eddie banged an angry fist against the door. "I don't believe it! He got away again!"

I called Dallas PD and requested assistance. The dispatcher sent out an APB, but I didn't hold out much hope. The ratio of police cruisers to cars wasn't in our favor.

We drove back to the Denny's parking lot, rounded up my parents, and went to inspect the camper. Looked like it belonged to the IRS now. Beauregard would have to take up residence under a park bench.

The door of the trailer was locked, but one of the windows was open. Nick gestured to the window with his chin, intertwined his fingers to create a stirrup, and gave me a boost up. I tried not to think how firm his shoulder muscles felt under my fingers as I used him for leverage. I reached up, pulled off the flimsy window screen, and wriggled through the small opening. Hey, if Beau could do it, so could I.

I found myself in the RV's sleeping quarters. I dropped to the bed and rolled off, heading for the door. I let Nick, Eddie, and my parents inside.

The trailer was tiny and spare but clean. More oil and gas pamphlets were stacked on the small dinette table next to a plastic bin full of tax returns. A new copy of a tax primer, this one a current version, lay on a cushioned seat.

Dad glanced around the small room. "An RV like this sure would come in handy for my fishing trips."

"Or mine," Nick said, raising a brow in challenge.

The two had engaged in a bidding war over a rifle at an earlier government auction. Looked like they might go head-to-head again when Beau's camper went up on the auction block.

Mom poked a finger in Dad's chest. "You are *not* buying a camper. If you had something comfortable like this to sleep in you'd be hunting or fishing every weekend and I'd never see you again."

Dad looked sheepish. *Busted.*

"Don't worry, Harlan," Nick said. "You can hang with me."

"Booyah!" Dad raised his hand and he and Nick exchanged a high five.

Mom narrowed her eyes at Nick.

"Uh-oh," I said. "You're in trouble now." He'd made it onto Mom's shit list. I'd been on it dozens of times myself. Getting off the list was no easy feat, though I'd learned that asking my mother if she'd lost weight tended to speed up the process.

Nick's truck was outfitted with a trailer hitch, so we hooked it up to Beau's trailer. While Dad and Nick hauled the camper to the government's impound lot, Eddie headed back home to his family and Mom and I headed to the salon for manicures. Afterward, we ran by the grocery store to pick up the ingredients for Dad's Killer Chili and Nick's mother's peach sangria. Heck, I'd need a full pitcher of the stuff to dull the shame of being outsmarted—again!—by Richard "the Unibrow" Beauregard.

chapter twenty-six

Something Fishy Is Going On

Mom and I spent the late afternoon in the kitchen, doing our best to duplicate Dad's Killer Chili recipe. Nick had tried it recently and, once he'd sampled a taste of the caustic stuff, begged for more. The guy must be a masochist. But even though my mother and I used all the right ingredients on the list Dad had given us, our attempts fell short. With six kinds of peppers, onions, and chili powder, the stuff was hot, sure. Still, our batch lacked Dad's usual kick.

"You think he sneaks in another secret ingredient?" I asked Mom.

"It wouldn't surprise me."

If there was anything southerners prized above all else, it was secret recipes. Both Mom and Nick's mother had chicken-fried steak recipes they refused to share, even with their own children. I supposed I should consider myself lucky that Nick's mom had offered me her sangria recipe.

"I bet Dad puts a cup of gasoline in the chili when we aren't looking," I said. "Or maybe some gunpowder." I made a mental note to take a match to the stuff next time he made it to see if it caught fire.

While Mom tended to the simmering chili, I looked over the return Richard Beauregard had prepared for my parents. Sure enough, it reflected his usual MO. He'd claimed a bogus fuel tax credit in the amount of four grand. He'd be in for a big surprise when he attempted to cash my parents' check, however. I'd already notified his bank that the check they'd written for the alleged gas well was bogus. Just like Beau's imaginary fuel and insurance companies, the Bank of Hard Knox didn't exist. The idiot really should have taken a closer look at the check.

Alicia returned from her apartment and brought in the clothes, jewelry, and toiletries she'd rounded up. Once she finished unpacking, she joined us in the kitchen.

I poured another glass of sangria and handed it to her. "Have you checked your responses on the Big D site?"

She nodded. "All twelve responded with interest."

I raised my hand for a high five, but unlike the resounding *smack* my father had given Nick a few minutes earlier, Alicia's slap was less than enthusiastic.

"What's wrong?"

She lifted a shoulder. "Being back in the apartment today was . . . hard. I'm not sure I'm ready to date yet. I don't think I'm over Daniel."

Mom gave the chili another stir. "Want a bowl of chili? This stuff will take your mind off your man troubles."

It would also take the paint off walls.

"Thanks, but no," Alicia said. "Last time I tried Mr. Holloway's chili I was tempted to check myself into the burn unit."

Brett hadn't tolerated the stuff well, either. The chili had brought tears to his eyes. Nick, on the other hand, had spooned up the stuff like it was chocolate pudding. He must have a cast-iron stomach and a high pain tolerance.

Dad and Nick returned at eight o'clock, honking twice from the driveway to roust us from the house. Alicia, Mom, and I ventured outside. The two men stood in the yard, grinning from ear to ear.

Though the night was dark, Dad had turned on his truck's headlights to provide illumination. Attached to Nick's hail-dented pickup was a brand-new, gleaming twenty-one-foot bronze bass boat, complete with padded seats, a large casting deck, and a built-in ice chest. The pointed nose was designed for speed, allowing avid anglers to quickly move from one part of a lake to another where the fish were biting better.

"Check this out," Nick said, opening a compartment in the back. "It's got a forty-four-gallon livewell capacity."

"Sweet," I said, though frankly I was more excited by the ice chest. It would be the perfect place to store pitchers of peach sangria while I sunbathed on the boat's flat deck or water-skied behind it. Fishing wasn't really my thing. I'd worked at a bait shop during high school and gotten more than my fill of slimy worms.

Mom waved the men inside. "Come have some chili."

"Your recipe?" Nick asked my father as we headed in.

"More or less," he said.

I'd bet on *less*. I eyed him, but he quickly looked away, probably to hide the guilty look in his eyes. Yep, he'd definitely left out an ingredient. What was it? Propane? Kerosene? Lighter fluid?

The five of us gathered around my kitchen table. Alicia opted for a frozen waffle instead of my father's chili. Dad might have been insulted if he hadn't considered his hot chili more a test of character than an actual food source.

My cell phone rang in the middle of dinner. Nick watched me while he scooped up another spoonful of chili. I ignored the phone and let it go to voice mail, knowing the caller was most likely Brett. Besides, Mom would have chastised me for taking a call during supper. It wouldn't be proper. She hadn't spent all that hard-earned money to send me to Miss Cecily's Charm School only to have me ignore everything I'd been taught. Besides, if I violated any of Miss Cecily's Ten Tenets of Decorum, my mother would likely sign me up for a refresher course.

When dinner was over, Dad plopped himself down on the

couch to watch the news and Alicia and my mother set about washing the dishes. I walked Nick to the door. He grabbed me by the wrist and pulled me onto my porch, closing the door behind us.

He said nothing, just stared down at me for a moment before swatting away a pesky moth attracted by the porch light. I swatted away another pesky moth, stared at Nick, and said nothing right back. But what was there to say, really? We were at an impasse. Until I could talk with Brett in person, things with Nick would remain stalled.

We stood there, totally still, simply gazing at each other for several moments. I could feel his body heat in the cool night and yearned to press myself up against him. But until I talked to Brett, until we worked out a deal, I knew I'd feel like a low-down, cheating skank if I acted on my desires.

Finally, Nick blew out a long breath, took a step backward, and cracked a smile. "Well, it was good for me. Was it good for you, too?"

I returned the smile. "Best I ever had."

He reached out and put a hand on my cheek. "Good night, Tara."

I put my hand over his and leaned into his touch. "Good night, Nick."

I returned Brett's call later that evening. He told me his crew had been making quick progress. They'd removed the infected trees and other plants, had the entire club treated by an exterminator, and were waiting for replacement foliage from a different nursery supplier. The good news was that the nursery that supplied the infested trees had owned up to its mistake and agreed to pay Brett and Wakefield Designs all costs that resulted from the blunder. Looked like Brett would be able to restore his reputation.

Brett asked about my work, whether there'd been any progress on my cases. I told him how Eddie and I had narrowly missed capturing Beau at the campsite after Madam Magnolia had suggested we look for him there. I also told

Brett about Beauregard's latest escape, how Nick had almost been run down in the street.

"Nick's working the case with you?" Brett asked.

"Unofficially," I said.

Brett and Nick had met before and taken an instant dislike to each other. Admittedly, their problems stemmed from me, from the fact that I was close to each of them, though in entirely different ways. I supposed it was some type of innate, primal male thing. It wouldn't have surprised me if they'd both started beating their chests and grunting.

"Unofficially," Brett repeated. "So you're saying he volunteered to help you out."

"Yeah."

"That's damn convenient."

Fortunately, Brett let the subject drop there. I was glad. I didn't want to discuss this over the phone and apparently neither did he. Besides, if he kept pushing it, I'd have to point out his hypocrisy. Trish had volunteered to help on Brett's Habitat for Humanity projects and he'd gladly accepted her assistance. Heck, I'd once come upon him taking Trish for a ride in his wheelbarrow, her Texas-sized breasts jostling as he rolled her across the uneven turf. The mere thought resurrected the mental image and the sound of her girlish giggle and had me feeling angry and upset all over again.

After a few more minutes of idle chatter, much of it again about the country club's gourmet menu, we bade each other good night and ended the call. It wasn't until I was brushing my teeth a half hour later that I realized neither one of us had told the other that we missed them.

Since my parents had taken over my bedroom, I started the night out sleeping on the futon in my guest room with Alicia. When she threw her leg over me for the third time, no doubt mistaking me for Daniel in her sleeping state, I rolled off the futon and opted for sleeping on the couch downstairs rather than fending off her unconscious lesbian advances all night.

A tongue on my face and whispering voices woke me at the butt crack of dawn.

The tongue belonged to Nick's dog, Nutty, an ancient golden retriever mix with white fur on his snout and cloudy cataracts in his eyes. The whispering voices belonged to Nick and my dad, who were in my foyer packing for an early-morning fishing trip, what would be the new boat's maiden voyage.

I sat up on the couch, rubbing my eyes.

"Sorry we woke you, hon," Dad said.

I noticed it was still pitch-black outside.

"What time is it?"

Nick glanced at his watch. "Five fifteen."

"Ugh." How anyone found pleasure in getting up at this hour and fighting off mosquitoes while trying to track down elusive fish was beyond me. I pulled myself off the couch. "I hope neither of you catch anything."

Nick slid a grin my way. "You sure are grouchy in the morning."

I narrowed my eyes at him. "I take back what I said about the fish. I hope you get eaten by an alligator instead."

The dog and the men left. I returned to sleepy land. They came back at noon with five good-sized fish. By then we women were up and dressed.

"My," said my mother as they brought their catch into the kitchen. "You two had a successful morning."

Mom looked down at the fish and didn't see Dad and Nick exchange glances.

My mother grabbed a large pan, turned the oven on to preheat, and turned her attention back to the fish. She picked up one of the fillets and immediately dropped it back to the counter with a *thunk*. Putting a hand on her hip, she pointed a finger at my father and gave him the evil eye. "Harlan Holloway, this fish is frozen solid." She poked the fish with her pointer finger and took a closer look. "It's halibut to boot. This fish comes from the ocean. *In Alaska*. What do you have to say for yourself?"

Nick came to Dad's rescue, pulling up a photo on his cell

phone. "It was either halibut from the grocery store or this."
I scurried over to take a look. The photo showed my father
holding up a four-inch baby bass. "That was all we managed
to land today."

Mom shook her head. "That's downright pitiful. I hope
you let that poor little thing go?"

Nick nodded. "Gave him a kiss and sent him back on his
way."

Oh, to be that bass.

Mom picked up the fillets and plunked them in the pan.
"I have half a mind to let you men starve to death."

My father made a face behind my mother's back and
spoke to Nick in a stage whisper. "Now you see where Tara
gets it." Dad shot me a wink to let me know he was only
teasing.

The five of us enjoyed the fish along with a salad and rolls
and glasses of peach sangria on my back patio. The meal was
nice, relaxing, comfortable. Nutty made the rounds among
us, begging for scraps and getting more than his share. Hard
to resist an old, sweet dog, especially when he sits patiently
at your feet, happily waiting for anything you're willing to
give.

My parents and Nick left mid-afternoon, my father having wrangled a commitment for another fishing trip out of
Nick.

"You might not be dating Nick yet," Alicia said once the
door closed behind them. "But I think he and your father are
going steady."

Monday morning, Eddie and I stood in a courtroom before
Magistrate Judge Alice Trumbull, trying to convince her to
let us run a triangulation on Richard Beauregard's cell phone
so that we could track him down. Our arguments fell on
deaf ears. Trumbull denied our request, telling us that Beauregard seemed to be on the run now and unless and until we
could show that he was continuing to cause harm, we need
not return.

Dang.

We kept a close eye on our surroundings as we walked back to the IRS office. We had to stay on high alert. If I hadn't noticed the explosives behind the tire of the car the other day, neither of us would still be alive. It was horrifying to think about. If I'd been blown to pieces at least my mother wouldn't have had to worry about what outfit to bury me in. Heck, they probably could have buried me in a Tupperware container.

Eddie stopped in front of a small coffee shop and pretended to read the menu posted on the window. "Stay cool," he whispered, "but we may have a tail."

I pretended to read the menu, too, but saw a dark-haired, olive-skinned man approaching in my peripheral vision. He wore dress pants and a white shirt, typical clothing for a worker downtown, but the running shoes on his feet seemed odd, as if he expected to have to make a quick getaway on foot.

He was about fifty feet from us and heading slowly our way in an odd gait, both hands in the pockets of his dress pants. I shuddered to think what else might be in those pockets. A gun? A knife? And why was he walking funny? Could he be a suicide bomber with explosives strapped to his leg?

My heart began pumping in overdrive. Both Eddie and I had worn our Kevlar vests this morning, but they only protected our torsos. Our heads and legs were still exposed.

The man came closer, only a dozen feet from us now. When he pulled his hand from his pocket, the sun glinted off the metal object in his hand. Eddie and I had our guns trained on him in an instant.

"Put it down!" Eddie yelled.

The man shrieked and dropped the object in his hand, which turned out to be nothing more than a silver money clip. He turned and ran down the sidewalk, his hands in the air, screaming at the top of his lungs.

"On second thought," Eddie said, shoving his gun back into his holster, "maybe the guy was coming to get some coffee."

We retrieved the money clip, called the local police department, and in minutes had turned the clip over to a cop on his way to take a statement from the man, who'd called in an attempted robbery. The cop phoned us back a few minutes later. "He had surgery on a hammertoe. That's why he's wearing sneakers and walking funny."

Oops. Our bad.

chapter twenty-seven

Ring Around the Rosy Nosey

When Eddie and I arrived back at the office, a ruckus in the break room caught our attention. We stepped inside to see what all the commotion was about.

Josh stood in the center of a cluster of male agents. I could only get a partial glimpse of him.

"Did it hurt?" one of them asked.

"How hard was it to get in?" asked another.

"Dude, I think you caught an infection."

Ew! They weren't talking about Josh losing his virginity, were they?

I elbowed my way into the inner circle. Nope, they weren't talking about Josh's virginity; they were talking about his nose. It bore a shiny gold hoop that emerged from a severely inflamed spot on the side of his left nostril, which had swollen nearly closed.

Urk.

The piercing didn't fit Josh at all. He now looked like the Gerber Baby crossed with Pink or Lenny Kravitz. But while Pink and Lenny had the personalities to pull off a nose piercing, Josh simply looked goofy, like a wannabe hipster, like he was trying too hard to be someone he wasn't.

Nick wandered in.

I jerked my head toward Josh and spoke under my breath. "Check out Lord of the Nose Ring."

Nick took a quick glimpse and whispered his reply. "He looks like a fish with a stuck hook."

Yep, Josh looked ridiculous. Still, though the piercing didn't fit Josh, it was nonetheless a bold romantic gesture, his attempt to venture into Kira's world, to show her how committed he was to making their relationship work. Surely she'd be flattered—once the infection cleared up, that is. Until then she'd probably just be disgusted.

Lu stepped into the kitchen to refill her empty coffee mug. As she poured, she glanced my way. "My date with Fred was a bust."

"Sorry to hear it. Not your type?"

She took a sip of her steaming brew. "Too horny. We went to dinner and when I came back from the ladies' room I caught him popping three Viagra."

Three? The guy was lucky he didn't go blind. "What did you do?"

"I told him I was not that kind of girl and if that's all he was looking for he could take me right home."

"How did he react to that?"

"He took me right home."

Sheesh. "Harry had potential. Maybe you should give him a nod."

"Good idea."

After completing a few routine tasks at the office, I dragged Josh to the minor emergency clinic to pay a visit to Ajay. The hole in Josh's nose had begun to seep and the skin had grown more red and swollen. Josh appeared flushed and was sweating, too, as if he was running a temperature.

The things we do for love, huh?

Ajay took one look at the piercing, cringed, and prescribed an antibiotic cream. He also gave Josh a shot of penicillin and suggested he take a couple of ibuprofen for the pain and fever.

I dropped Josh back at the federal building and headed out to visit three more MSBs near the end of my list, keeping a careful eye on the traffic around me in case I was being followed.

Nothing suspicious cropped up at the first location I visited, which was a gold and silver exchange. Every large transaction was properly documented. I knew I shouldn't feel disappointed the staff had actually complied with the laws, but I had grown increasingly frustrated over the days as visit after visit proved futile.

I wanted to find the person who had helped the terrorists move their money.

And I wanted to find him *now*.

My second stop was Cohen & Sons, a combination kosher deli, catering service, and convenience store tucked in a narrow space between a martial-arts studio and a discount dentist office in a working-class neighborhood. The place sold kreplach and candy bars, pastrami and Pepto-Bismol, matzo ball soup and Powerball tickets.

Given that it was now lunchtime, the place was hopping and I had to stand in line with a dozen people from nearby businesses who were picking up lunch for themselves and their coworkers. I inched forward along the refrigerated glass case, peeking inside at the offerings. The case featured a variety of meats and side dishes, including potato salad, coleslaw, macaroni salad, and carrot salad with raisins. I'd never liked carrot salad with raisins. Raisins belonged in oatmeal cookies along with brown sugar and vanilla, not paired up with a vegetable, pretending to be some type of treat. It was unnatural.

Behind the case worked Avram Cohen and his two sons, all three wearing stained white aprons over their clothes and yarmulkes over their dark-brown hair. The men moved quickly and efficiently, the two sons preparing the food while their father rang up the purchases and made change.

By the time I reached the front of the line, the delicious

smells had taken their toll and my stomach was growling. I decided to nosh on a knish while I performed my review.

"Spinach or potato?" Avram asked.

I engaged in a brief mental debate. They both looked good, but I had another stop to make later today and didn't want to risk getting spinach stuck in my teeth. "Let's go with the potato."

He called my order out to his sons, rang up my purchase, and took the cash I offered him. When I identified myself and told him the purpose of my visit, he glanced down the long line of people waiting behind me and gave me a sour look. "Your timing stinks."

"Sorry." But really, is there ever a good time to be visited by an IRS agent?

Avram called to one of his sons in Yiddish and gestured for him to take over the cash register. Then Avram removed his apron, hung it on a wall hook, and led me quickly to a small office at the back of the shop.

While I watched over his shoulder, he quickly logged onto the computer and showed me how to access their money-order sales records. He looked up at me before vacating the chair. "Got it?"

"Got it."

I slid into the seat as he left the office.

While the men finished taking care of the lunch crowd out front, I nibbled my knish and reviewed the entries. Though there were quite a few sales of money orders, all were in relatively nominal amounts, the highest being in the five-hundred-dollar range. Most of the purchases were likely by people with bad credit who couldn't qualify for a credit card or checking account and needed the money orders to pay their bills.

Though none of the sales were in amounts large enough to be immediately suspicious, given the high volume, especially just after payday on the first and fifteenth of each month, I supposed it was possible that the terrorists could have purchased multiple money orders to send overseas.

I peeked out of the office, relieved to see the lunch crowd

had since dwindled and the men were now primarily cleaning up. I called to Avram and he returned to the office.

"Do you recognize any of these men?" I asked him.

He slung his cleaning rag over his shoulder, took the photographs from my hand, and looked over each one. "No. I don't recognize them."

"Can we check with your sons?"

Avram called them back one at a time. Neither of his sons recognized the terrorists, either.

"What is this about?" Avram asked.

"These three men have been arrested here in Dallas. They were involved in acts of terrorism in and around Syria," I said. "We also have evidence that they sent significant sums of money overseas to fund terrorist groups. I'm trying to find the person or persons who helped them move their money."

"These men are Muslim, yes?"

"Yes."

"You thought that a Jewish man would help Muslim terrorists?" His expression said he thought I was too stupid to live.

"We've got to consider all angles," I said. "We can't leave any stone unturned." Even stupid stones.

I thanked him for his time, complimented him on the nice knish, and left.

My final stop for the day was a business called JS Shipping that, despite its name, actually provided a variety of services, including shipping, copying, and lamination services, as well as passport photos. The place sold traveler's checks and money orders, too. JS Shipping was owned and operated by a Pakistani emigrant named Jameel Sakhani, who had dark hair, a thick mustache, and a face I suspected had never cracked a smile.

The place was a bit too warm and smelled of ink and cardboard. As a courtesy, I waited until the customers cleared out before approaching the counter. Sakhani seemed very put off when I identified myself and requested to take a look at his records.

"This is an intrusion. You are disrupting my business. Why do you need to see my files? You must give me a reason." He stepped out from behind the counter and came close as if trying to intimidate me.

He didn't know me very well, did he? I looked up at him and took a step even closer. Two could play the intimidation game.

"Well?" he snapped, crossing his arms over his chest. "What is your reason?"

I didn't owe this man an explanation. His registration as an MSB gave the government the right to inspect his records at any time to ensure compliance. If he'd asked me nicely, I would've simply said it was a routine check. But since he hadn't played nice, neither would I.

"Why don't you want me to see your records?" I cocked my head. "Are you hiding something?"

He narrowed his eyes at me. "It is people like you who give the government a bad name."

And it was people like him who made me want to put a bullet in his foot. "You started it," I said. Real mature, huh?

We stared each other down for several moments. He blinked first. *Ha!*

"You can either show me your records voluntarily," I said, "or I can close this place down, seize your files and computers, and take them back to my office for review." I punctuated my words with a nonchalant shrug.

When the man realized I wasn't backing down, he finally relented. He led me to a small office off to the side, where the store's computer was located. He pointed to the desk. "You can sit there."

I took a seat on the swivel chair and glanced around. On his desk was a framed photo of Sakhani—still not smiling—and a pretty woman I assumed was his wife. They were surrounded by seven beautiful dark-haired girls, ranging in age from toddler to late teens. *Hmm.* Living with eight women couldn't be easy. Maybe I should cut the guy some slack. Or buy him a box of condoms.

I spent all of the morning and most of the afternoon

reviewing the records. My interest was piqued when I noticed various problems, including breaks in the numerical sequences for traveler's checks and money orders. Over fifteen grand in traveler's check sales were undocumented and at least a dozen money orders were unaccounted for.

No wonder he'd been reluctant to give me access to the files.

I called the company that had issued the money orders and requested further data. I needed to know where the money orders were cashed and in what amounts, as well as whether they had any information that might identify the parties who had purchased or redeemed the money orders. Unfortunately, it was late in the afternoon and they wouldn't be able to get the data to me until the following day. Ditto for the company that had issued the traveler's checks.

I called Agents Wang and Zardooz to let them know what I'd discovered. Depending on what type of information the issuers of the money orders and traveler's checks came back with, both agreed it might be worth their time to interrogate Sakhani themselves. So far, he was the only potential lead in the case other than Jesús, and God knows where that man ran off to. I promised to let them know as soon as I received the data.

Despite the suspicious data I'd found, I didn't have enough evidence yet to arrest Sakhani. Nonetheless, I crossed my fingers he was the one we'd been after. Eddie and Agent Wang had finished their visits to the MSBs on their lists and found nothing. There were only two more MSBs on my list.

My cell phone chirped as I stood to leave. I didn't recognize the number but answered anyway.

I was glad I did. Madam Magnolia was on the line.

"I'm afraid I was too harsh with you the last time we spoke," she said. "My apologies."

"No worries," I said, though honestly I'd been quite pissed.

"Do you have time to come see me?" she asked. "I had some visions you might be interested in."

"Great. I can be there in half an hour."

"I'll accept a fee this time," she said. "Without the Tax Wizard's rent, things have been tight."

I ended the call and stepped out of the office and into the shop. Sakhani was behind his counter helping a customer. I pointed a finger at him. "Don't leave Dallas without notifying me first."

The customer looked from me to Sakhani, who was throwing daggers at me with his eyes.

What can I say? Sometimes it's fun to throw my weight around.

chapter twenty-eight

Crystal Balls

Since it was already after five o'clock, I rounded up Alicia from my town house and took her with me to visit Madam Magnolia. Maybe ol' Maggie could give Alicia some hope that things would work out with Daniel. If not, maybe Maggie would give Alicia some hope they'd work out with someone else, maybe one of the guys from the Big D Dating Service who had expressed an interest in meeting my friend. Heck, as long as we were going to see the woman, maybe I should ask her about my love life. Not knowing how things would be resolved was killing me. I could end up with Nick, or I could end up with Brett, or I could end up with neither of them.

When we arrived, Madam Magnolia told me she'd seen glimpses in her ball that seemed to relate to the Beauregard case. She hoped that with me here the visions would gel, become more complete. She led us through the curtain and into her back room, which was painted a deep shade of purple. The dark space was lit only by a single scented candle, sandalwood if I wasn't mistaken. I paid her hundred-dollar fee in cash, wondering if I could deduct it as a legitimate business expense. As the three of us took seats around the circular table I made a mental note to research the matter.

What looked like a garden-gazing ball rested in the center of the table. Madam Magnolia began to make a humming noise and waved her hands over the ball as if to activate it. If she hadn't already provided us with information that was spot-on, I would've laughed at the hokey ritual. Instead, I concentrated on the ball, hoping maybe I'd see a vision there, too. All I saw was my reflection. Definitely time to get my eyebrows waxed.

The humming stopped. "I see Richard Beauregard again," she said. "He's been sleeping in the back of a large SUV in the parking lot of a twenty-four-hour grocery store."

"Which one?" I asked.

She squinted at the ball. "I can't say for sure. The sign is blurry."

Although her information narrowed things down somewhat, Dallas and the surrounding suburbs encompassed over 340 square miles of real estate. There were probably two hundred or so twenty-four-hour grocery stores in the area. It could take days to visit them all. And if Beauregard was constantly on the move as I suspected, we could miss him entirely.

"Anything else you can tell me?"

She shook her head again. "Sorry. That's all I'm getting."

A hundred bucks doesn't buy much psychic information these days.

As long as I was there, I figured I'd ask her about the terrorist case. I told her the basic details. "Can you get me any information on that investigation?"

She gazed into the crystal ball, then suddenly flinched and cried out. "I see what the men have done. They've sent money overseas. It was used by other men in their terror cell to buy bomb-making materials." Tears formed in her eyes. "They've killed hundreds of people, dozens of children. I see some of them being pulled from a school bus."

She turned her head away, as if she didn't want to look at

the ball anymore. I couldn't blame her. I'd felt the same way when I'd seen the photographs of the school bus in the file.

"I need to cut off the terrorists' money supply," I said. "I need to know who helped them transfer the funds." Presumably that person might also be helping other terrorists who had yet to be discovered. "Can you take another look? Can you tell me if it's an angry-looking guy with a thick mustache?" After the rude way he'd talked to me today, I'd really love to bust Sakhani's balls.

Madam Magnolia closed her eyes for a moment, took a deep breath, then opened her eyes and returned her focus to the ball. Her face was intent but unchanging. Finally, she looked up. "I'm not seeing anything now," she said, "but I seem to smell flowers. Roses, maybe?"

My mind immediately went to the pink rosebushes Brett had planted in front of my town house. Their lovely scent welcomed me home after work every day. Well, except when Brett had fertilized them. At those times I was greeted by the stench of composted cow manure. P.U.

"In that case," I asked, deciding to see how far my hundred bucks would get me, "what can you tell me about my love life?"

Madam Magnolia smiled now. "Are you sure you want to know? It might be more fun to wait and see how things work out."

I shook my head. I was tired of waiting. I wanted to know whether Nick and I would end up together or if Brett was the man I should be with. Surely I'd end up with one or the other, right? I refused to accept the possibility I'd lose them both.

She glanced at the ball again. Her eyes flickered up to my face. "Your heart is split between two men." Her gaze lowered to the crystal. "One is boyish, very sweet." A lascivious smile crossed her face. "The other is *hot*." She blew out a breath as if to cool herself.

"Which one do I end up with?" I asked, my voice frantic as I leaned toward her. "I need to know."

She stared at the ball for another moment, blinking several times as if trying to focus her vision. "Sorry. The ball won't give it up."

"What does that mean?"

"Sometimes the ball shows me things; other times it doesn't."

I fluttered my hands around the glass orb. "Can't you reposition it or something?"

She gave me a placating smile. "It's not a television antenna. I can't just move it around to get better reception."

"Dang." I sat back and crossed my arms over my chest. *Ugh!*

"What about me?" Alicia sat up and scooted her chair closer to the table. "Can you see how things will work out in my love life?"

Madam Magnolia looked back into the ball, staring at it for several seconds before speaking. "I see a dark-haired man. He's picking up a pillow from a double bed and holding it to his face."

"Good," Alicia snapped. "Maybe Daniel will suffocate himself."

Magnolia shook her head. "No. He's smelling the pillow. I sense his sadness. The scent reminds him of the person who used to sleep there."

Alicia seemed to choke up a bit. "What side of the bed was the pillow on?" she asked softly.

Magnolia glanced back at the ball. "The side by the ugly silver lamp."

Alicia made a gasping, sobbing sound and turned to me. "He misses me. Daniel misses me." When she'd regained some composure, she turned back to Madam Magnolia. "That lamp cost two hundred dollars at Horchow's."

Magnolia shrugged. "I don't care what it cost. It's still ugly."

I was with her. I'd always thought the lamp was ugly, too.

Though she tried again to conjure up an image, the woman wasn't able to see anything more. We thanked her for her time and the information and went next door for more chocolate coconut cupcakes. We ate them in my car on the way home.

For the first time in days, Alicia seemed happy and optimistic. I hoped the crystal ball was right. If Daniel didn't come back to Alicia soon, maybe I'd have to force fate, kick Daniel in his crystal balls until he realized what a fool he'd been to let Alicia go.

Late afternoon on Tuesday, I received information via e-mail from the companies that had issued the money orders and traveler's checks. They'd also sent images of the back and front of each instrument. All of them had been cashed by the same individual, someone purportedly named Albert Strohmeyer, Jr. All of them had been cashed in the Dallas–Fort Worth area.

"Damn!" The fact they'd been cashed locally rather than overseas meant they weren't related to the terrorist financing. The odds of Sakhani being the man we were looking for now seemed slim to none. I wished the crystal ball had been able to tell me that. It would've saved me some time.

According to both companies, all of the instruments had been reported by Sakhani as stolen. The companies had issued replacements and sucked up the loss.

Had Sakhani committed some type of fraud? Was that why he hadn't wanted me to look at his records?

I forwarded the data to Eddie, Agent Wang, and Agent Zardooz. The next step would be finding out something about this Albert Strohmeyer, if indeed he even existed. For all I knew the name had been concocted as a cover.

I logged into our research system and found out that not only did Albert Strohmeyer actually exist, but also that he was a grade-A loser. He was in his early sixties and had been terminated from dozens of menial jobs over the years. Fry cook at a diner. Elementary-school custodian. Garbage collector. He also had a criminal record, including three convictions for petty thievery at retail stores, two convictions for writing bad checks, and one for theft of services after he'd left a Supercuts without paying for his trim.

The most interesting tidbit I learned about Albert was that he currently worked the evening shift at JS Shipping.

I printed out Strohmeyer's rap sheet and employment history and headed down the hall toward Eddie's office. I passed Josh's digs on the way, backtracking when I realized he had his head down on his desk.

I rapped on his door frame. "Hey, lover boy. You all right?"

Josh lifted his head. He'd removed the gold ring, but his nose still appeared inflamed. "Kira broke up with me."

"What?" I stepped into his office. "Why?"

By all appearances, things between the two of them had been progressing nicely. They'd met for lunch several times, attended a book signing for their mutual favorite spy novelist, engaged in something called geocaching that Josh described as a high-tech scavenger hunt. Heck, they'd even begun to build some type of supercomputer together. If that didn't spell commitment, I don't know what did.

"I don't know why she dumped me," Josh said, his face miserable. "I thought she'd like my piercing, but she took one look at it and said she thought we should move on."

"Is she squeamish?" Maybe she'd been creeped out by his swollen nostril. The thing had been quite revolting. My breakfast had turned cartwheels in my stomach when I'd seen it.

"I don't think so," Josh said. "We babysat her little brother one night and she yanked his loose tooth out with her bare hand."

So not squeamish, then. Hmm.

"Would you talk to her for me?" Josh asked. "I really like her and I thought she liked me, too."

Did I really want to get in the middle of Josh and Kira's relationship? No. But did I want to watch Josh mope around the office for weeks? No. The twerp had grown on me a little bit.

"Okay," I said. "I'll talk to her." I wasn't sure whether it would do any good. I couldn't seem to get my own relationships in order. How was I supposed to help someone else fix his love life?

Josh's face brightened. "Thanks, Tara."

I continued down the hall to Eddie's office and plopped myself down in one of his chairs. I handed him the paperwork and gave him a few minutes to look it over.

"Whaddya think?"

Eddie frowned. "I think there's some monkey business going on at JS Shipping. But I don't think it's the monkey business we're interested in."

My thoughts exactly. Still, MSBs fell under our purview. Might as well figure out what was going on, right?

Eddie grabbed his suit jacket and I grabbed my purse and we headed over to JS. On the drive over, I put in calls to Agents Wang and Zardooz, letting them know Eddie and I were on our way to JS and that it appeared to be a dead end as far as the terrorism case was concerned.

When Eddie and I arrived, we spent several minutes interrogating Sakhani about the missing money orders and traveler's checks. He grew more and more enraged with each question.

"What are you accusing me of?" he shouted, waving his hands wildly. "I do not steal."

"Albert Strohmeyer does," I said.

Sakhani's head snapped my way. "What are you talking about?"

I pulled the rap sheet from my briefcase but held it close to my chest. "Did you run a background check on Strohmeyer when you hired him?"

"Of course I did," Sakhani said. "I run a background check on every new employee."

Eddie jumped in now. "Any chance you've got a copy of it handy?"

Sakhani retrieved Strohmeyer's employment file and showed us the background check report. Sure enough, none of the convictions showed up on Sakhani's document.

We spread the paperwork out on the desk and tried to make sense of the situation.

"Wait a minute," Eddie said as he looked over the reports.

"The clean background check is for Albert Strohmeyer. Our rap sheet is for Albert Strohmeyer, *Jr.*"

Looked like Junior had used his father's Social Security number when applying for the job at JS in order to slip through the cracks. Naughty boy.

Sakhani began shouting in what I assumed was Urdu. I couldn't blame him for being upset. With seven kids to feed, the man didn't need an employee taking advantage of him. He explained that Strohmeyer had claimed someone came into the shop and pulled a gun, demanding he turn over the traveler's checks and money orders. In reality, the man had stuffed them in his own pocket.

"Why hasn't he been arrested?" Sakhani asked.

It was the same question every victim wanted to know. "Police departments are inundated with these types of crimes," I told him. "Dozens of armed robberies take place in Dallas every night. If the issuers even bothered to contact the cops when the checks and money orders were cashed, it's not likely Dallas PD had enough manpower to carry out an investigation."

Now that Eddie and I could hand local law enforcement an open-and-shut case, however, it was far more likely Strohmeyer would be rounded up and justice would be served.

The front door of the shop opened and an older, white-haired man walked in. Sakhani looked up, issued what can only be described as a banshee cry, and flew across the room, launching himself at the man.

Eddie and I exchanged glances.

"I'm guessing that dude would be Albert Strohmeyer, Jr.," Eddie said.

By this time Sakhani had Albert on the ground and was giving the guy what for.

"Yep," I said. "I'm guessing that, too."

We took our sweet time making our way to the door, letting Sakhani exact a little justice of his own before we ordered him off Strohmeyer. The thief deserved a walloping.

Sakhani stood, leaving Strohmeyer on his back on the floor. Sakhani looked at me, ducked his head in a small bow, and thanked me for protecting his business. He offered what was probably his first smile ever.

"Anytime," I said.

chapter twenty-nine

Come Fly with Me

On my way to work Wednesday morning, I received the call I'd been waiting for. Jesús Benavides had been pulled over for a broken taillight. When the police officer had run his license, he'd noted the flag on Benavides' record.

The officer agreed to try to hold Benavides there until I could come question him. Without an arrest warrant, the officer couldn't force the guy to stay put, but, fortunately, most people were not aware of their rights and did what a police officer asked of them without questioning the officer's authority.

I obtained their location, plugged it into my GPS, and drove like a bat out of hell across town.

I pulled in behind the Dallas police cruiser on the side of the highway. The officer had sat Benavides in the back of his car, though he'd put no handcuffs on the guy. Since he wasn't yet under arrest, handcuffs would have been inappropriate.

I slid into the front passenger seat of the cruiser, asking the officer to give me and Jesús some privacy. The cop shot me an annoyed look but deferred, taking his keys and exiting the vehicle. He didn't go far, though, stopping by the front fender and leaning back against it.

"Good morning," I said to Jesús, eyeing him through the metal mesh partition that separated the front seat from the back. He was much younger than I'd expected, hardly more than a kid, and small, only about four inches taller than me and perhaps twenty pounds heavier.

He simply stared at me, fear in his dark eyes.

"I'd like to ask you some questions."

"English not so good," he said, his words thickly accented.

He didn't speak English? I could see that his Spanish could come in handy at the liquor store given that their customers were largely Latino. But if he wasn't fluent in English, how the heck had he taught history in Houston?

I pulled out my cell phone and called Christina, asking her to translate for me. I put the phone on speaker and asked her to ask him if he could tell me about the money transfers to Honduras, who had sent them, why he hadn't filed a Suspicious Activity Report.

He seemed hesitant to answer at first but finally looked into my eyes and said something I didn't understand.

Christina translated. "He says he was the one who sent the money to Honduras. It took him over a year to save it up. He was sending it back home to his family."

I looked at the terrified young man. All of a sudden everything made sense. No doubt the man was an illegal alien using a stolen identity, trying to stay off the grid and under the radar. He hadn't helped the terrorists funnel their money overseas. He'd simply sent money back home to his family and done it in a way he thought would help him avoid detection.

But crap. This put me in a very awkward position. I mean, I felt for the kid, sure, but he was breaking the law by being here. What was I supposed to do? Report him to ICE? I'd never faced this situation before and wasn't sure how to handle it.

My concerns immediately became a moot point. The

young man looked into my eyes and must have read my thoughts. He opened the back door of the cruiser, leaped out, and took off running at warp speed, probably breaking all kinds of records. The officer and I gave chase but quickly lost sight of him when he zigzagged through an apartment complex.

I stopped running and bent over, my hands on my knees as I gasped for air. I eventually caught my breath, but I was beginning to think we'd never catch the person who'd helped the terrorists send their funds overseas. I was nearly to the end of my list of MSBs.

Mid-morning I received a call from an attorney at the Justice Department. Despite the fact that the Tax Wizard had been found wandering the halls of the jail, his cell still somehow locked tight, all charges against Winston Wisbrock had been dropped. His daughter had been contacted and planned to apply for guardianship. Apparently the Wiz was on some type of antipsychotic meds but wasn't good about taking them consistently. When he didn't, he lost touch with reality.

I couldn't much blame him for resisting the meds. What was so great about reality, anyway? My reality had pretty much sucked lately.

Eddie accompanied me on my visits to the last two MSBs on my list. One was a cash-for-car-titles place, the other a precious metals dealer. Both were clean.

"What now?" I asked as we drove back to the office that afternoon. "Lu told us to come up with a new plan."

"Hell, I don't know," Eddie said. "It's frustrating. It's like trying to track down ghosts."

Ghosts, huh? That gave me an idea. Ghost hunters went to the source, right? They set up cameras and looked around the places where the ghosts purportedly lived.

"Why don't we take a look at their houses and cars and workplaces? Visit their mosques? Talk to their neighbors and coworkers?"

Eddie glanced over at me. "Wang and Zardooz have already done all that."

"I know," I said, "but it can't hurt to run a fresh set of eyes over things." Sometimes a small but critical detail that didn't seem important to one person would catch the attention of another and lead to a resolution. That's why cold-case files were often handed over to another investigator for a second look.

Eddie's expression was skeptical, but he shrugged. "What the heck. Give them a call. See what you can set up."

I phoned Zardooz. He was tied up today but said he could take us on the grand tour tomorrow. We arranged to meet at one of the mosques early the next morning when the members would be on-site for their Fajr, or predawn prayer time.

Eddie and I returned to the office. I took advantage of the short lull to catch up on a few things, including my e-mails. As I backed my way through them, I stumbled upon the e-mails I'd forwarded to myself from Richard Beauregard's computer when we'd raided his office. I hadn't bothered to go through them in detail since we didn't have him in custody yet and the terrorism case had taken precedence.

The e-mail from Southwest Airlines confirming his flight to Las Vegas caught my eye. I opened the communication and looked over his electronic ticket. The flight was scheduled to leave in two hours.

Surely Beauregard had abandoned his plans to make this trip, right? I mean, heck, the guy was living out of his car. He had no available credit and little, if any, cash. What kind of vacation could a guy who was totally broke have in Vegas?

Then again, the ticket to Vegas had already been paid for. If he was going to be penniless and sleeping in parking lots, he could do that just as well in Vegas as he could in Dallas, right? At least it would be a change of scenery, and he might be able to finagle his way to a free buffet.

I picked up my phone and dialed Eddie's office. "Beau's flight to Vegas leaves in two hours. Want to see if he's on it?"

Eddie agreed. We met at the elevators, snagged my car from the parking lot, and hurried onto the freeway, trying to beat the looming rush-hour traffic. As we neared the airport, several planes were visible in the sky, many of them circling in a holding pattern, waiting for their chance to land at the busy airport. I supposed that's what I planned to do with Brett, put him in a holding pattern until I decided whether to let him land or divert him to another airport. Okay, so maybe it wasn't the best metaphor ever, but it was how I felt. And I felt damn guilty about it, too.

Eddie pulled up the Southwest Airlines Web site on his phone, keyed in Beau's flight information, and learned the flight was running on time and was scheduled to take off from gate 14 in Terminal C. We exited the freeway, pulled through the tollbooth at the entrance to the DFW airport, and continued on to the short-term parking garage, picking a spot near the doors that led to the C terminal.

Rather than go through the hassle of obtaining permission to carry our guns into the airport, we locked them up in the glove compartment. Ditto for our metal handcuffs and pepper spray. We'd use pliable plastic FlexiCuffs to restrain Beauregard instead. I'd ordered some a while back figuring they'd come in handy someday. Looked like today was someday.

We went inside the terminal and walked through the baggage claim area. People encircled the machines like the Whos in Whoville when they formed their circle on Christmas morning and sang that sweet, sappy song. "Christmas day is in our grasp, so long as we have hands to clasp." However, unlike the Whos, who maintained their spiritual centers despite the Grinch having absconded with their floo-floobers, surely those surrounding the baggage carousel hoped their stuff would arrive intact and stood ready to tear an airline employee a new jing-tingler if it didn't.

One of the machines blasted an obnoxious *eert-eert* sound and, with a lurch, the baggage claim kicked into motion, the metal plates sliding across each other like an oversized meat slicer awaiting a two-ton ham. The luggage began to slide down the chute and clunked onto the carousel. A set of golf clubs in a hard-sided travel case clinked down the chute, followed by a pink polka-dotted suitcase. Someone had been having some fun. It sure as hell wasn't me.

Lord, I needed a vacation.

Eddie and I made our way to the escalators and rode up to the second floor. We checked in with airport police to let them know we were on-site and what we were up to. In case Beauregard resisted arrest and we had to use force to bring him down, we wanted the cops to know we were the good guys. It wasn't always easy to tell when officers came upon a tangle of tussling bodies and, since we were dressed in street clothes rather than law enforcement uniforms, we didn't want to take any chances of being misidentified. The last thing Eddie and I needed was a cop smacking us with a baton or treating us to a faceful of pepper spray. The tear gas at Bulls-Eye had been more than enough for me.

Eddie and I made our way past the row of check-in counters to see if Beauregard might be there, checking a bag. Nope. No sign of the guy at the counters or in the line of people snaking through the belted lanes. No sign of him at those annoying do-it-yourself stations, either.

We walked to the nearest security checkpoint. The man checking tickets had expected us. We showed him our identification and he let us through and into the line awaiting screening. Apparently being a federal agent only got you so far. You could get through Security without a ticket, but you were still required to be screened. Probably not a bad policy given the history of disgruntled postal workers who'd gone on shooting rampages. Being a government employee didn't necessarily mean you weren't a threat.

We waited in line for ten minutes before reaching the pile of rectangular plastic tubs stacked near the belt for the X-ray machine. A young woman in front of me grabbed one of the small jewelry bowls, lifted her tank top, and yanked a silver ring out of her belly button. She dropped the ring into the bowl, set it down on the table, then reached up higher under her top, lifting her bra and wriggling loose a nipple ring. If she put her hand down her pants next, I was changing lines. Fortunately, she seemed to be metal free now and moved forward.

Eddie and I grabbed several tubs, lined them up on the aluminum table, and began preparing for the elaborate screening process. While Eddie unbuckled his belt and slid out of his loafers, I removed my earrings and shoes and stuck them in a tub. My blazer and cell phone went into a second tub.

Ugh. Time to deal with the fifteen-pound portable storage unit I called a purse. I really needed to clean the darn thing out. Carrying the heavy thing around made my shoulder and back ache.

I plopped my purse down on the table and began to sort through the mishmash inside, removing the items that would require special screening. A tiny tube of toothpaste. A small bottle of liquid hand sanitizer. My nephew's metal orthodontic retainer. How the hell did that end up in my purse? I hadn't seen him in weeks. His teeth must be all out of whack by now.

As I pulled my small zippered makeup pouch from the bag, the leather wallet holding my badge fell to the floor. I picked it up and slipped it into the front pocket of my pants so I could continue to empty my purse. Would they want me to remove my solar-powered calculator? It seemed harmless enough, but it did have a battery. *Hmm.* Better to err on the side of caution. Into the tub it went.

I continued to rummage in the purse, my hand wrapping itself around something long and cylindrical shaped and made of latex.

Oh, crap! The vibrators!

I wasn't sure what to do. Should I take them out and put them in a tub? God, that would be so embarrassing! But it would be even more embarrassing to have them discovered by the security screeners.

I looked around for a trash can, hoping I could discreetly ditch the contraptions. No such luck. The closest trash can was way back by the guy checking IDs and tickets.

I decided to leave them in my purse and hope for the best.

Eddie and I glanced around as we inched forward toward the metal detection machines. Still no sign of Beauregard.

Maybe he'd decided to forego his vacation and cashed in his ticket. Maybe we were squandering our time here. I decided if Beau didn't show I'd buy a pretzel at the place by the gates for dinner. Wouldn't want the trip out here to be a total waste, and they smelled damn good.

A man two people ahead of me was pulled aside for further screening. The TSA agent ran a wand up and down his legs, torso, and arms before deeming him worthy of air travel.

I glanced over at the X-ray machine. My purse had made it down the belt and through the screening process. It was sitting on the other side of the machine, waiting for me to pick it up.

What a relief.

The woman in the tank top went right through the metal detector, no problems. I waited for the agent to wave me forward and stepped through the device, expecting smooth sailing, too.

No such luck.

Beep.

"Maybe it's your nipple ring," Eddie teased from behind me.

Had I worn an underwire bra today? I put my hands to my rib cage. Nope, no wire. But I did realize then I was still wearing a silver bangle bracelet.

I pulled the bracelet off and handed it to the attendant. "Sorry."

She gave me an irritated look as she took the bracelet from me. *Sheesh. Cut me some slack, will ya?* I didn't travel much. Besides, the rules seemed to constantly change. Quart bags? Four ounces? Two ounces? The regulations for air travel were nearly as complicated as the Internal Revenue Code. Who could keep up?

A commotion at the X-ray machine caught my eye. A tub had come through after my purse had slammed against it. The impact had apparently activated the vibrator's jackhammer button. My purse gyrated back and forth on the table. A male security screener lifted my purse off the table and began to sift through the contents.

Damn!

"Ma'am!" the woman manning the metal detector demanded. "I told you to step forward."

"Sorry." I felt the heat of humiliation burn my face as I turned back to her. "I was distracted."

I took a step back then moved forward again.

Beep.

What the heck?

The man with the wand motioned for me to step his way. Just as I did, Richard Beauregard sauntered by in the terminal ahead.

The guy had evaded us twice before. There was no way I'd let him get away this time.

I cupped my hands around my mouth. "Beauregard!" I shouted.

On hearing his name, Beau turned toward me. When his gaze met mine, I saw his lips form the words, *Oh, shit!*

He turned back in the direction he'd been headed and took off running. I took off running after him. The distance between us quickly increased. Not only did he have much longer legs than I did; he also had the benefit of rubber-soled shoes. The only things I had on my feet were a thin pair of trouser socks that not only failed to provide traction but were actually quite slippery.

I heard a whistle blow behind me and felt someone shove my shoulders. The next thing I knew, I was flying through the air. But what goes up must come down, right? And I did. Hard. I made a full-on face-plant on the unforgiving tile floor.

Smack!

My teeth snapped shut and my chin felt as if it shattered. *Damn, that hurt!* The impact split my lip, too. And what was the hard, sharp thing in my mouth? Was that a tooth fragment?

Oh!

My!

God!

My teeth would be all out of whack right along with my

nephew's. And while Nick's slightly chipped tooth made
him all the more sexy, I knew it would never have the same
effect on me.

An enormous knee threatened to snap my spine and held
me pinned to the floor while my hands were yanked up behind me by a person I couldn't see. The impact of the fall
had knocked the wind out of me and the pressure from the
knee kept me from taking in enough air to voice a protest.
As handcuffs were slapped on my wrists, I turned my head
to the side to see Eddie dash past me, pursuing Beauregard.

As soon as the person who'd cuffed my wrists climbed
off me, I rolled onto my back. I kicked my legs, trying to
gain some leverage so I could sit. "Release me right now!
I'm a fed—"

Psssh.

I never got to finish my sentence. Instead, I got a faceful
of pepper spray and a swift kick in the thigh. Damn, that
burned! It was like the tear gas all over again. *And shit!* The
spray made my split lip feel like it was on fire.

How the hell did this happen? Hadn't the airport police
informed the screeners that Eddie and I were on location?

Lest I be beaten to death, I lay still on the floor, hoping
that whatever germs had traveled through the airport on
people's shoes weren't crawling into my ear canal with plans
to eat my brain.

I heard shouting and several pairs of feet run past me. I
hoped Eddie wouldn't suffer my same fate. And I hoped he'd
nabbed Beauregard. If that moron escaped again, Lu would
probably make us turn in our badges.

My badge! I'd slipped it into the front pocket of my pants
when I'd been clearing out my purse. That's what had set off
the metal detector.

Ugh. Maybe Beau wasn't the moron. Maybe I was.

chapter thirty

$\mathcal{P}$rincess Charming

A half hour later we sat in the office of airport police. My cuffs had been removed, though I had yet to receive an apology for my rough treatment. Clearly the 240-pound TSA officer who'd manhandled me felt justified in his actions. I just as clearly thought I should be given a crack at his balls to even the score.

Eddie didn't have a scratch on him. Once he'd cleared Security, he'd rushed past me and grabbed Beauregard when he tripped over a rolling carry-on bag being pulled behind a flight attendant. All Eddie'd had to do was cuff him. Lucky duck. Why couldn't things ever go that easily for me?

My purse, blazer, shoes, calculator, and sex toys had been brought to me along with my nephew's retainer, though my jewelry had disappeared. My tooth fragment was also nowhere to be found. I feared I'd swallowed it during the aftermath of the TSA agent decorating my face with pepper spray. I'd probably be the first person in the history of the world to bite herself in the ass. Then again, with my luck, the thing was probably lodged in my gallbladder or appendix and would require emergency surgery.

I blew my runny nose and blinked my burning, teary eyes. I wasn't the only one crying. Beauregard was sobbing his heart out. The prospect of years in the klink tends to bring on the boo hoos.

Given all I'd suffered, Eddie offered me the privilege of reading Beau his rights. I always loved Mirandizing someone we'd nailed. Reading the rights was essentially the legalese way of saying "neener-neener."

"You have the right to remain thilent," I said.

What?!?

I tried again. "Thilent." I looked up at Eddie. "Thit! Thith thucks! I can't talk right with my tooth mithing."

Eddie put a hand over his mouth, but his shaking shoulders gave him away. The bastard was laughing at me!

"Thome partner you are." I glared at him. "Athhole."

"Please." Eddie made an openhanded gesture inviting me to continue, all the while fighting a grin. "Go on."

I wasn't going to give Eddie the thatithfaction—make that "satisfaction"—of seeing me back down. I'd been totally humiliated, but I was Tara Holloway, by God, and I'd power through. And at least I hadn't bitten off my tongue. A chipped tooth and a slight lisp was nothing compared to losing your tongue. Not that I felt at all sorry for Homsi, but still.

I turned back to Beauregard. "Anything you thay can be uthed againtht you in court. You have the right to conthult an attorney and to have the attorney prethent during quethtioning. If you cannot afford an attorney, one will be provided for you."

At least that last one didn't contain any *s*'s. Thank heaven for small favors.

Beauregard's rights now read, I figured it couldn't hurt to see if he'd talk. Besides, I was curious. "Where'd all the money go, Beau? How doeth a perthon thpend theven hundred thouthand dollarth and have nothing to thow for it?"

"Blackjack," he sputtered. "I've got a gambling addiction."

His attorney would probably try to use the addiction in Beauregard's defense, argue for a reduced sentence.

Once the marshals had taken Richard Beauregard off our

hands, I gave Eddie my keys and he drove me to the doc-in-a-box. Ajay suggested I see my dentist about the broken tooth, but my burning eyes and split lip he could handle.

He affixed a butterfly bandage to my lip and flushed my eyes for the second time in a matter of days. "Here," he said, handing me the bottle of soothing saline solution. "Take this with you. It will save you the trip next time."

God, I prayed, *please don't let there be a next time!*

Brett called soon after I arrived home.

"I'm planning to fly back to Dallas this weekend," he said.

"That'th great, Brett." We'd finally be able to have our talk. I was ready. Earlier I'd dreaded it, but now that I'd been forced to put it off for so long I'd had time to prepare myself, work through exactly what I wanted to say.

He was quiet a moment. "Dare I ask why you sound funny?"

"I ate thome tile at the airport. Half of my front tooth ith mithing."

He was quiet another moment. "You remember when I told you that I wanted you to always be honest with me?"

"Yeah?"

"I've changed my mind," he said. "From now on, make something up. Something that won't make me worry."

"Thure," I said. "I'd be glad to."

Brett said he'd be done fixing things at the country club by the weekend. Though the beetles had devoured some plants and eaten parts of the turf on the golf course, the infestation had been discovered fairly quickly, and the damage was not as widespread as they'd initially believed. Chef Fiona had prepared him a special meal to celebrate these happy discoveries, had even taken a break from her duties to join him at his table while he enjoyed her delicacies.

"That'th good newth," I said. "Tho now that the beetleth are taken care of you won't have to go back to Atlanta, right?"

He didn't respond to the question, but it didn't really require an answer. Of course he wasn't going back to Atlanta.

What reason would he have to go back once he'd completed the repairs?

His voice became soft. "I really need to see you, Tara."

Ugh. Why did he have to be so sweet all the time? Just once couldn't he be a jackass so I wouldn't have to feel so bad about my attraction to Nick?

We talked for a few more minutes about nothing in particular. When we finished, I poured myself a tall glass of peach sangria and slugged it back. The ice-cold liquid sent a shock through my broken tooth. *Yee-ouch!*

I went to my miscellaneous drawer and rummaged through take-out menus, plastic silverware, and packets of ketchup, mustard, and soy sauce until I found a drinking straw. I tore off the paper wrap, plunked the straw in my sangria, and took a sip.

Aaah. The straw worked. No pain.

Alicia hadn't come in yet by the time I went to bed. Martin and McGee always threw parties for their weary, exhausted staff after the April 15 and October 15 deadlines and gave everyone the day off afterward. The parties were one of the things I missed about working at the firm. The partners spared no expense, renting a fancy hotel ballroom with a dance floor, serving a scrumptious buffet, hosting an open bar.

Alicia wouldn't be home until late. Too bad. I wanted to freak her out with my broken tooth.

My alarm buzzed at 4:00 AM and I nearly knocked the clock off the night table in my attempts to put an end to the infernal noise.

What the . . . ? Oh, yeah. Time to get up and prepare for the early-morning trip to the mosque.

I groaned. Seemed everyone was being hard on me lately. Beauregard. Nick. The TSA agent. Even Allah.

"Why are you getting up so early?" Alicia called from the guest room across the hall. "Are you finally going to do your laundry?"

I told her of our plans to visit the terrorists' stomping

grounds today. "We're thtarting with one of the mothqueth. We have to be there for predawn prayerth at five forty-five."

It was her turn to groan now. I heard rustling from her room as she apparently threw back the covers. I was a little surprised she didn't notice my new lisp, but Alicia didn't notice much before her first cup of coffee.

"I'll start the coffeepot," she said. "It's the least I can do for you after you've put up with me the past few days."

I took a quick shower, wrapped my wet hair in a towel, and ventured down to the kitchen in my bathrobe. Alicia stood at the counter, pouring hazelnut creamer into a mug. She topped off the creamer with the fresh-perked coffee.

She stirred the coffee with a spoon, turned, and handed me the mug. "Here you go."

"Thankth."

Her eyes flickered to my mouth and her hands reflexively went to her face. "Holy hell! What happened to you?"

I explained how I'd been tackled by the TSA officer at the airport after stupidly leaving my badge in my pocket, setting off the metal detector, and taking off after Beauregard before they could clear me.

I sighed. "I look horrible, don't I?"

"I don't know," Alicia said. "It has a certain white-trash charm. All you need to go with it are a banjo, a baby bump, and a dozen mangy dogs."

"Thankth a lot."

"It's four thirty in the morning," she said. "You can't expect more from me at this ungodly time of day."

"I hope my dentitht can thqueeze me in today." I didn't want to go around looking like this for long. I also wondered whether I could talk Lu into reimbursing the cost of the cap for my tooth. They didn't come cheap. Since the injury had taken place on the job, it seemed only fair for Uncle Sam to cover it, right? Maybe I should go for a gold cap, like Johnny Depp wore in his role as Captain Jack Sparrow in the *Pirates of the Caribbean* movies. Or maybe caps with diamonds imbedded in them. I'd look like Nellie or that other rap star, Waka Flocka Flame.

I took a sip of my coffee. *Dang!* The hot liquid shocked my tooth as bad as the cold sangria had last night. I went to the drawer and fished out another straw, hoping the coffee wouldn't melt the plastic and poison me.

Alicia and I headed back upstairs.

"You'll need to cover your head if you're going into a mosque, right?" she asked.

I hadn't thought of that. "You're right."

"I've got just the thing." She dashed into the guest room and returned with the beautiful Hermès scarf she'd scored at the thrift shop along with the discounted wedding gown.

"Perfect." While Alicia returned to her bed for more sleep, I dried and styled my hair, dressed in a business suit, and wrapped the scarf around my head. The stylish accessory almost made up for my redneck tooth.

Almost.

But not quite.

chapter thirty-one

Home Ain't Necessarily Where the Heart Is

I met up with Eddie and Agent Zardooz in the parking lot of the mosque. Although the sun had yet to come up and the morning was still dark, the parking lot was well lit. The building was large, with a dome in the center and decorative minarets at the corners. A steady crowd of people, mostly men, streamed inside. Was one of them the person who'd helped the terrorists send their funds to Syria undetected?

Zardooz had brought his wife, Dorri, with him.

I shook her hand. "Nice to meet you, Dorri." Finally! A name I could not only pronounce but also remember. It was the name of the fish in *Finding Nemo*, the one with the voice of Ellen DeGeneres. I'd watched the movie at least a gazillion times with my young niece.

Dorri Zardooz looked nothing like a fish, however. She was a pretty woman, with the kind of naturally thick, dark lashes I could achieve only with three coats of mascara. She glanced up at the scarf covering my hair and dipped her head in gratitude. "I see you have prepared yourself. Thank you."

While Zardooz gave Eddie and Wang a quick primer on mosque etiquette, Dorri did the same for me. "Remove your shoes when you enter," she advised, "and walk behind those who are praying."

I nodded to let her know I understood.

We spent several minutes in the mosque. It was plain inside, without the distractions of stained-glass windows, oil paintings, statues, and candles that I was used to.

While Azad led Eddie to the men's prayer room, I followed Dorri to the women's room, standing at the back and merely observing. Women were lined up, heads bowed in prayer. I noticed Lilith among them.

When the ritual ended, Zardooz spoke to the imam, asking if he would be willing to talk to me and Eddie. He agreed and we stepped outside to the parking lot.

Zardooz introduced us to the imam and informed us that the two had already engaged in an extensive discussion about Algafari and Nasser.

"They prayed here," the imam said, "but this is a large mosque and I did not know them well."

Two young men walked past us on their way to their cars and the imam called out to them, reminding them about the upcoming youth group trip to Six Flags. The youth group from my family's church back in Nacogdoches took a trip to Six Flags each year, too. Nothing like ascending twenty-five stories high on a roller coaster to bring you closer to your God, huh?

"Can you think of anyone who might have helped them move money?" I asked, hoping the question would not cause offense. "Maybe someone with a job at a bank?"

The imam shook his head. "I wish I could help you," he said, "but I can't think of anyone. The men kept to themselves and did not interact much with the others."

I thanked the imam for his time and he went back inside.

Zardooz shrugged. "I interviewed the imam at Homsi's mosque in Fort Worth," he said. "Homsi didn't socialize much, either."

It was typical of radicals, I supposed. They tended to be loners or associate mostly with others of like mind.

The four of us went to a nearby waffle house for breakfast. I fortified myself with gravy-covered biscuits and cheese grits while Eddie opted for scrambled eggs and an English muffin. Dorri headed home after breakfast while Eddie and I followed Azad to Algafari's apartment.

Yellow crime scene tape stretched across the front door. Agent Zardooz pulled it back to allow us to enter.

Eddie flipped on the lights and we looked around. The place looked like a typical bachelor pad. The living room contained a comfortable couch, coffee table, and a big-screen television. Two tall wooden stools stood at the breakfast bar.

I opened the pantry to find canned vegetables, a moldy loaf of bread, and a jar of peanut butter. A bag of Oreos sat in the pantry, too, half of them already eaten, the rest surely stale by now. I checked the freezer and refrigerator next. Typical bachelor foods there, too. The only thing missing was the usual six-pack of beer.

The small bedroom contained only a twin-sized bed and a dresser. The closet housed the usual trappings of an urban professional. Slacks, loafers, dress shirts, belts. Ditto for the dresser. Underwear, socks, pajamas.

We returned to the living room. Eddie retrieved the remote from the coffee table and turned on the television. It was tuned to Al Jazeera, which showed video footage from yet another bombing.

Would the madness never end?

Algafari's apartment was an end unit, so he had only one neighbor. We spoke to the woman who lived there, a butch and bulky fortyish woman who drove a forklift on the graveyard shift at a local warehouse.

"Hardly ever saw the guy," she said. "I once gave him a jump start when his car battery died, but that was the extent of our interaction."

We thanked her and made our way down to the apartments' mailboxes. Zardooz stuck a small key in Algafari's

box and retrieved his mail. He'd received a cable bill and
credit card solicitation, along with a postcard depicting a
beach. Though the address was written in English, the rest
of the postcard was in Arabic.

Zardooz translated for us. " 'We had a wonderful time at
the shore. Hope you can come visit again soon. Love, Aunt
Sabeen.' "

We left Algafari's apartment and drove to Nasser's, located a few miles farther west. His apartment was a virtual
duplicate of his cohort's, though Nasser had a treadmill in
his living room. I'd been thinking about getting one myself,
for those days when I couldn't make it to the YMCA. I
looked the machine over. It was a nice piece of equipment,
though it had accumulated some dust while Nasser had been
in jail.

I noticed a small orange spot near the digital readout and
instinctively scratched at it, assuming it was a speck of paint.
It wasn't paint, though. It was a tiny remnant of an orange
sticker that had probably been the manufacturer's warning
label. Really, weren't some of the warnings they put on exercise equipment ridiculous?

Do not place treadmill in water. Gee, I can't use my electric treadmill in water? How shocking!

Wear proper athletic shoes during use. Darn! I so wanted
to take a run in my stilettos.

*If you feel faint, stop exercising immediately and consult
a doctor.* If I want to drop dead, isn't that my own business?

The warning label might as well say: *Do not use this machine if your head is up your butt.*

Nobody was home at the apartments located on either
side of Nasser's digs. His neighbors were probably at work.

While Eddie and Zardooz grabbed some lunch, I made a
quick stop at my dentist's office. He was able to use some
type of composite to repair my tooth. Thank goodness. I
was tired of sounding like Daffy Duck.

We three agents hooked back up and visited Texas Instruments next. Eddie and I searched through Algafari's
desk and spoke with his manager and coworkers, but none

had anything of interest to offer. We had the same results at the small biotech company where Nasser had worked. Apparently both men had kept their noses to their respective grindstones and had interacted with their coworkers only on business matters.

By that time, it was late in the day. We decided to make the rounds of Homsi's mosque, home, and workplace the following day, though we suggested visiting the mosque after the daytime prayers. I didn't think I could handle another 4:00 AM muster.

chapter thirty-two

ℳatchmaker

It was nearly seven that evening when I made my way into
the drive-through at the same coffee shop where Nick,
Josh, and I had met up with Kira a couple of weeks ago. I
ordered a decaf this time, hoping to get a decent night's
sleep tonight given the early morning I'd had. I snagged
another double espresso for Kira. Josh had told me she was
a night owl.

I drove to her office a few blocks away. She leased a
small space on the second floor of a trendy strip center. She
was still at work, just as Josh had assured me. When you're
your own boss, you get to set your own hours. Kira generally worked noon to ten. Then, presumably, she stalked the
streets looking for victims with good veins.

Her office was dark, lit only by her computer screen and
a black light that made the velvet Mad Hatter poster behind
her glow. Once my eyes adjusted to the dim, I could see that
the walls of her space were decorated with enlarged prints
of Web sites she'd created. Her desk wasn't actually a desk
at all but rather a space-age-looking glass-top structure with

spiderlike chrome legs. Today, Kira's blond almost dread-locks were pulled up into a sort of ponytail on top of her head and hung down, surrounding her head as if she were a modern-day Medusa. She wore a sweatshirt with a picture of a smiling Justin Bieber on it.

I gestured to her sweatshirt as I handed her the espresso. "You're wearing that ironically, right?"

She took the espresso, glanced down at her sweatshirt, and shrugged. "Actually, I think the little dude is kind of cute."

Huh. Who would've thought it?

Some type of chrome and canvas contraption sat in front of her desk. I assumed it must be a chair and took a seat on it, changing positions several times in a futile attempt to find a comfortable position.

Kira took a sip of her drink and eyed me. "I'm guessing Josh sent you."

"He's heartbroken, Kira. He thought things were going well. He doesn't understand why you broke up with him."

She sighed. "You saw the nose ring, right?"

I nodded. "He did that for you."

"I don't know why." She rolled her eyes. "I never asked him to do anything like that. That was the last straw for me, honestly."

"What do you mean?"

She set her cup down on the desk. "When we met he was this adorable little dork, all shy and geeky. Then he changed. It started with a leather jacket and a chain on his wallet. The next thing I know he's putting holes in himself."

"Wait a minute. You liked Josh better when he was a dork?"

She threw her hands in the air. "Yes!" She leaned forward over the glass. "I don't want to date a guy like me. If I did, I wouldn't have responded to his ad on the dating site. I want someone different, someone who will keep me grounded, someone who might make a good husband and father some-day."

Wow. "What if he was just himself again? The annoying little dweeb you fell for?"

She skewered me with a look. "I didn't say 'annoying little dweeb.' I said 'adorable little dork.'"

"Right. Sorry." My ass had fallen asleep and I shifted on the chair. "So, what about it? What if he goes back to being the old Josh again?"

She grabbed her cup and tossed back the remainder of her espresso. "I guess I'd be willing to give him a second chance. I've been out with a few other guys I met on the dating site and it's been brutal." She jotted something down on a notepad, folded the paper, and stapled it shut. "Here." She handed it across the table. "Give this to Josh."

"Will do." I wiggled myself loose from the chair and stood. "See you around."

On my drive home from Kira's office, my cell phone rang. The readout indicated it was Daniel calling.

I jabbed the button to accept the call. "Hey, jerkface." I might be rude, but I'm also fiercely loyal. He deserved to be called names after hurting my best friend the way he did.

Daniel ignored my insult. He was a lawyer, after all. He was probably used to being called names. "How's Alicia?"

I chuffed. "How do you think? She wasted the last three years living with a guy she thought she'd be with forever only to learn he's a weenie."

"I'm not a weenie, Tara."

"Oh, yeah? Prove it."

"That's exactly what I plan to do," Daniel said. "But I need your help."

He sounded not only sincere but desperate, too. Still, I wasn't going to give in easily. I was going to make him work for it. "Why should I help you?"

"Because I love Alicia," he said, "and so do you."

Damn! He'd gotten me. Alicia and I might not agree on everything, but we shared a tight bond. She was the sister I never had, minus the sibling rivalry, hand-me-downs, and childhood illnesses most real sisters shared.

I changed lanes to ditch the eighteen-wheeler that had been riding my ass for the last two miles. "What do you want me to do?"

"Bring me one of her rings," he said. "I need to take it to a jeweler to figure out the size of her ring finger."

I nearly sideswiped the concrete barrier that divided the regular road from the car pool lane. "Daniel! Are you saying what I think you're saying?"

"Yes," he said. "I'm having an exact replica of Alicia made and I need to make sure I get her measurements right."

"Bullshit," I said. "You're going to ask her to marry you!"

He chuckled. "I am." He was quiet a moment before speaking again. "Being without her has been pure torture, Tara. That whole thing about not knowing what you've got until it's gone is true."

Whoa. A rare moment of emotional honesty from a man. Would wonders never cease?

Daniel's words got me thinking. Brett was gone now and, though I was aware of his absence, I didn't feel tortured. Sure, I missed our dinners out and missed watching BBC America with him by my side, imitating the actors in a horribly faked accent. I also missed the sex. I hadn't had an orgasm in days. I think I was going through sex withdrawal. I'd felt shaky and light-headed. But did I feel tortured? No. Then again, maybe I'd been too busy with my investigations and the arrests and my parents' visits and Alicia shacking up with me to have time to feel the pain.

"So?" Daniel asked. "Will you do it?"

"All right," I agreed. Stealing her ring would be sneaky, but all in the name of love, right?

"Thanks, Tara."

"No problem," I said, feeling myself tear up at the thought of losing my best friend, once again, to this man. "Alicia's a pain in the butt anyway. She uses up all the hot water, complains about the cat hair in her food, and refuses to wash my dirty laundry. I'll be glad to see her go."

Lies. Every word of it. It had been great having her around, and not just because she cooked and cleaned and generally served as my surrogate wife.

Daniel knew it, too. "You're a good friend to her, Tara. She's lucky to have you."

I blinked to try to keep the tears at bay. "Once you get her back, you won't have to sniff her pillow anymore."

"Wait," Daniel said. "How did you know I'd been doing that?"

Let him wonder. "Gotta go," I said, disconnecting the call and slipping the phone into my cup holder.

I eyed my rearview mirror again. Given that it was nearly full dark now, drivers had turned on their headlights and it was difficult to distinguish one car from the next. Still, there was an SUV behind me with a set of fog lights on in addition to the headlights. If I wasn't mistaken, the car had been behind me before the eighteen-wheeler had cut in between us.

Was I being followed? I wasn't sure. But there was one way to find out, wasn't there?

I put on my signal and eased over two lanes to the right, as if preparing to take an upcoming exit. A few seconds after I'd made my move, the SUV moved over, too, though the driver failed to signal the lane change and seemed to have slowed a bit, putting a little more distance between us as if to avoid detection. A freeway interchange came up shortly, and I exited from the north–south highway onto another running east–west. The car with the fog lights exited, too. *Hmm.* Still, it could be mere coincidence, right?

I took the first exit and, so as not to look suspicious, pulled into a fast-food drive-through. I stopped at the menu board and ran my eyes over it. The place served seasoned curly fries. *Score!*

I placed my order for a large fries and a soda at the drive-through speaker and pulled up to the service window. As I waited for my food, the SUV turned into the dark parking lot of an adjacent donut shop that was closed for the night. The driver parked at the back of the lot and cut the lights on the vehicle, though the exhaust cloud told me he'd left the engine running.

No doubt about it now. The car was following me.

Given that the last time I'd been followed someone had tried to end my life and Eddie's with a bomb, I wasn't going to take any chances. Once I received my food, I drove back onto the freeway. I pulled my Glock from my purse, inserted a clip, and laid the gun in easy reach on the passenger seat. The next step was putting in a call to 911. I was tough, sure, but I was also smart. The smart thing to do when followed by a violent terrorist was call for backup.

When the dispatcher answered the phone, I explained who I was and told her I was being followed, very possibly by a terrorist adept with explosives.

"We'll get someone out there right away," she said. She took my cell number so the officers en route could communicate directly with me.

A minute later an officer called. "I hear you've got a tail. What's your exact location?"

I activated the cell's speaker and set the phone in the cup holder. "I-Thirty heading west," I told him, "approaching the Westmoreland exit."

"Keep heading west," he said. "Don't exit unless absolutely necessary. We'll see if we can sneak up on the guy." He explained he'd approach from the rear while another patrol car would lie in wait ahead to assist.

I continued driving, keeping an eye on my rearview mirror. Yep, the SUV was still behind me. A mile later, a wall of red brake lights reflected off the road ahead. Highway construction caused several lanes to be closed, forcing all of the traffic into the two right lanes. I slowed and moved into the right of the two open lanes, while the car with the fog lights pulled into the lane on the left. With a concrete barrier to my right and vehicles both in front and behind me, I was trapped, a sitting duck.

Damn.

We approached the work zone, bright overhead lights illuminating the dusty air and men in hard hats working heavy machinery. A green sign overhead indicated the next exit would come up in half a mile. A potential means of escape should I need one, assuming I'd get that far before the terrorist pulled up and attempted to turn me into flesh confetti.

"I'm in the construction zone," I told the cop on the

phone, feeling myself grow warm with adrenaline. "The car that's been following me is coming up on my left."

"Uh-oh. That's not good."

Not exactly what I wanted to hear.

I rolled down my window and grabbed my gun, holding it ready on my lap in case I'd need to put a bullet in the bastard. My lane slowed to a complete stop, but the lane next to me was still moving. With me trapped in traffic and the exit ramp only twenty feet ahead, my follower would have the perfect opportunity to take me out and make a quick getaway.

Better beat him to the punch, huh?

My breaths came fast as the SUV inched up next to me. A quick glance told me the driver had unrolled his passenger window. Clearly he planned to lob an explosive at my car or shoot me. With cars and construction boxing me in, I'd have no way of escaping an explosive. And what about collateral damage? I'd been crazy enough to sign up for this job, but the people in the cars around me didn't deserve to be injured—or worse.

I crossed my fingers, hoping for a gun rather than a bomb. I hoped, too, that if I was blown to smithereens Nick would wait a respectable amount of time after my demise—say a decade or two—before returning to the dating scene.

As the car drew up beside mine, I looked over to see a thirtyish Arab man at the wheel. He raised a semiautomatic, but I'd raised my gun faster.

Neener-neener.

The man emitted a cry of surprise and reflexively threw up his hands to shield himself while simultaneously pulling the trigger. A stupid move.

Pop-pop-pop-pop-pop!

He ended up shooting out his own windshield and sending a few bullets through the top of his car. As the shattered glass rained back in on him, he involuntarily jerked the wheel, swerving head-on into the blunt end of a concrete barrier protecting the construction zone. His hood crumpled with a metallic *crunch* and the air bag deployed with a powdery *poom!*

"Shit! Was that gunfire?" the cop hollered through my phone speaker.

Sure as shootin'. "Yep."

The cop activated his siren, the *woo-woo* coming both through my phone and from his spot in traffic somewhere behind me.

Taking advantage of what would be a short window of opportunity, I whipped into the lane ahead of the SUV, shoved the gearshift into park, and ran to the driver's window. The guy flailed in the seat, fighting the air bag and screaming in Arabic. I yanked my cuffs from the pocket of my blazer, grabbed his left arm, and snapped the cuff onto it, jerking his arm up and out of the window, clicking the other end of the cuffs to the vehicle's luggage rack. Unless this asshole could drag the entire car with him, he wouldn't be going anywhere.

The air bag deflated and sagged down now, revealing my stalker. A quick glance inside told me he'd dropped the gun onto the floorboard at his feet during the chaos. Cursing, he yanked on his shackled arm and, when he realized he'd have no chance of escape, turned a death glare on me.

I gave him a big smile as I aimed my gun at him. "Howdy!" I hollered over the approaching siren.

He threw an ineffective swing at me with his right hand, managing only to get his body turned cockeyed in the seat.

"Sit still," I ordered.

He didn't obey. Instead, he righted himself and jerked his head around, desperately seeking his semiautomatic.

"If you reach for your gun," I warned him, taking a step closer, "I'll shoot you."

He ignored me again, apparently spotting his gun and reaching down to the floorboard with his free hand.

At this point, I had a couple of options. One, I could do as promised and shoot the guy, fill out yet another firearm discharge report, and face yet another internal inquiry. Or two,

I could figure out another way to keep the guy from reaching his gun.

I went for option two. I'm nothing if not resourceful.

With his left arm cuffed to the luggage rack, the man's armpit was exposed. I reached out and tickled him. He shrieked, twisted in his seat, and slapped my fingers away. The instant he reached down for his weapon again, I tickled him a second time. He shrieked and slapped again. Say what you will about this rudimentary method, but tickle torture was an effective technique and far less controversial than waterboarding. Maybe they should add the tickle torture technique to the special agent manual.

The cruiser pulled to a screeching stop behind the wrecked vehicle, lights twirling. The officer cut the siren and leaped from the car, his gun drawn.

As he approached I cut my eyes his way for a quick second. "I'm good here. We just need to get the gun out of his reach. It's on the floor by his feet."

"I'm on it."

While I continued to offer the driver an occasional corrective tickle, the cop exchanged the gun in his hand for his baton. He opened the passenger door and leaned inside, exhibiting his nightstick at my would-be killer. "No funny business or this baton goes up your ass. Comprende, kimosabe?"

The officer reached across the space to retrieve the gun. Despite the threats of a baton enema, the man kicked at the cop and stomped down on his hand as he grabbed the gun. The officer treated my stalker to a well-deserved elbow strike to the gut, followed by a nightstick to the face. The seasoned curly fries in my stomach churned when I heard the unmistakable *thwop* of metal meeting flesh.

Our captive grimaced in pain, a diagonal red welt forming on his cheek. "Death to you!" he cried. "Death to you all!"

How rude. Clearly he had never attended class at Miss Cecily's Charm School.

* * *

An hour later, I was sprawled out on my sofa, the man who had planned to end my life was on his way to jail, and the man who made my life worth living was on the phone, congratulating me on a job well done.

"You're quite a woman, Tara Holloway," Nick said. "Are you sure you don't have a big pair of balls hidden somewhere?"

"Quite sure," I replied. "Just a pair of steel-plated ovaries."

Nick was quiet a moment. When he spoke, his voice had become serious. "Need some comfort?"

I'd have loved nothing more than for Nick to come over and hold me all night like he did the last time I'd faced down a violent attacker. Hell, I could barely hang on to the phone with my hand shaking so uncontrollably. But no, I shouldn't take him up on his offer. Not until I gave Brett fair warning. If Nick took me in his arms, I'd have a damn difficult time resisting him. "I'll settle for a big glass of sangria instead."

"All right," Nick said, frustration in his voice. "But if you change your mind, the offer stands. Just call me back. It doesn't matter what time it is."

"Thanks, Nick. You don't know how much that means to me."

"You're right," he said. "I don't."

I let his dig slide. Under the circumstances, I couldn't much blame him for feeling frustrated and unsure. Hell, I felt the same way.

I phoned Eddie next and gave him the rundown.

"A semiautomatic?" my partner said. "I would've shit myself."

"Ew," I said. "But, yes, I managed to remain unsoiled throughout the encounter." Thank heaven for my outstanding sphincter control.

"You sound exhausted," Eddie said. "Want me to get in touch with Wang and Zardooz for you?"

The adrenaline crash had indeed kicked in, leaving me totally wiped out, physically and mentally. "That would be great."

We ended the call and I headed for the pitcher of sangria in the refrigerator.

chapter thirty-three

Petty Theft and Heartbreak

Friday morning, I took a shower and rummaged around in my nearly empty underwear drawer for a pair of clean panties. The only remaining pairs were my Monday and Thursday panties. I opted for the Monday pair, slipped them on, and finished dressing.

As Alicia took her shower shortly thereafter, I snuck into my guest room and looked around for her jewelry. I found it in a small case on top of the dresser.

She often wore a gold birthstone ring her grandmother had bought for her birthday years before. I rummaged around in the case until I found it and slid it into a small cardboard box that had earlier contained a pair of costume jewelry earrings I'd picked up at the mall. I went downstairs, slid the box into the inside pocket of my purse, and zipped the pocket safely closed.

My petty theft now completed, I wandered into the kitchen to make coffee. I found a brand-new canister in the pantry, between a fresh loaf of bread and a large can of organic tomato soup. Alicia had been grocery shopping again,

God bless her. Now if I could just convince her to do my laundry before she moved back in with Daniel . . .

Alicia wandered down a few minutes later while I was feeding my cats. "Good. You found the coffee I bought."

"I did. Thanks."

Alicia was far more organized and domestic than I was. While I made do, she made beds and lists.

I set a bowl of tuna pâté on the floor in front of Henry. He shot me a look of disgust and angrily swished his bushy brown tail back and forth to let me know he wasn't impressed by either the speed of my service or the quality of food I served.

"Oh, yeah?" I told the cat. "Bite me."

He did, damn him. Luckily it was only a warning bite, a quick nip to let me know who was boss.

Him.

Alicia shook her head as she poured a mug of coffee. "I don't know why you put up with that brat. You should send him to obedience school."

"They don't have obedience school for cats."

"Really?" She took a sip of coffee. "They should."

I retrieved a loaf of bread from the pantry. "Want some toast?"

She declined. I loaded two slices into the toaster and pushed the button down.

"Have you happened to see my ring?" Alicia asked, checking the pockets on her bathrobe. "The one with my birthstone in it? I can't find it anywhere."

Uh-oh. Afraid my eyes might give me away, I peeked into the toaster so she couldn't see my face. "Nope, haven't seen it. It's probably back at your apartment."

"No, I'm pretty sure I brought it here."

I shrugged. "Maybe you left it in your desk at work."

"I suppose that's possible," she said, though she looked skeptical. "I hope I didn't lose it. That was my favorite ring."

I fought a smile, knowing she'd soon have a new favorite.

When the toaster ejected my breakfast, I slathered the

bread with apricot jelly and took a seat at the table across from Alicia.

"So, tonight, huh?" she said.

I nodded. I knew exactly what she was referring to. My talk with Brett.

"I'm guessing you want me to make myself scarce?"

"I'd appreciate it."

"No problem. A couple of the girls at work suggested we try a new martini bar in the West End tonight. I'll take them up on it. I've heard the place makes a fabulous lemon drop."

A lemon drop martini sounded almost as good as the peach sangria.

An hour later, Daniel met me in front of the IRS building.

"What happened to your lip?" he asked.

Though I'd removed the butterfly bandage, the darn thing was still swollen and sore. "A TSA agent tackled me in the airport. I did a total face-plant." Of course the TSA agent was nothing compared to the crazed terrorist who'd come after me last night.

"You're insane," Daniel said. "I don't know why you stay in that job. It's too dangerous."

Staying at Martin and McGee would have been riskier. If I had to explain the concept of depreciation recapture to one more client, I would've jumped out the window.

I pulled the ring from my purse and handed it to him. "Alicia already noticed it's missing. I hate to make her worry."

"I'll stop by the jeweler's today," he said. "I can have it back to you by tonight." He stuck the box in the inside pocket of his coat jacket and removed a glossy page he'd torn from a Tiffany's jewelry catalog. He unfolded the paper and held it out to me. "This is the one I've been looking at."

The ring was platinum, featuring a brilliant-cut diamond with baguettes encircling the remainder of the band. The price tag was fourteen grand.

"Whoa!" I said. "That's more than I paid for my car." I'd gotten a sweet deal on my BMW at a government auction.

"Think she'll like it?" Daniel asked.

"Like it? Are you nuts? That ring is gorgeous! She'll *love* it."

He grinned.

Nick came up the walk then.

"Gotta go," I told Daniel.

I fell into step next to Nick and flashed him a smile. "To-night's the night."

The hot look Nick gave me nearly melted my Monday panties. Really, I needed to get on that laundry.

"What happened to your lip?" he asked.

Both of us had been out of the office a lot lately and he hadn't seen me since before the airport incident. I told him what happened. Unlike Brett, Nick took my on-the-job injuries a little more in stride.

His eyes flickered to my lip again and his own lip quirked up in a small smile. "It's kind of sexy all red and swollen like that."

I felt a rush of heat to my girlie regions.

We made our way through the security checkpoint and into the elevator. A woman rode up two floors with us, then stepped off, leaving us alone.

Nick glanced over at me. "You look nervous."

No wonder. My mind was thinking of Nick, of his lips kissing mine, of what it would be like once he and I could finally be together.

He cocked his head. "You feeling guilty about breaking up with Brett?"

I shook my head. "Not really. Telling him we need to take a break and explore other options is the right thing to do."

"What?" Nick's eyes flashed. "What did you say?"

Uh-oh. The fire in Nick's eyes told me he was royally pissed, but I wasn't sure why. "I said that taking a break is the right thing for me and Brett to do."

"'Taking a break'?" He grunted. "So not breaking up outright, then."

"Well, not yet," I said, giving Nick a knowing smile. "But I expect that's coming."

Nick turned away, staring at the back of the elevator door,

his jaw flexing as he ground his teeth. "You told me you were breaking up with him, Tara. Now I find out that you're keeping your options open with him. What the hell?"

I stepped in front of Nick, forcing him to look at me. "There's no real difference, Nick. If you and I work out—"

"*If* we work out you'll break things off for good with Brett?"

"Right."

Nick closed his eyes and shook his head. He opened them back up and pinned me with his gaze. "Dammit, Tara, this is not what we agreed to."

I racked my brain, trying to recall the exact wording of our previous conversations. Heck, I had no idea how I'd phrased things back at Bulls-Eye, when Jimmy John had his guns trained on us. I'd been more than a little flustered. "Why are you so upset, Nick? I'm telling you that I'm giving us a try, that I hope things work out with us."

"You know what you're also telling me?" he boomed. "You're telling me that you still have feelings for Brett. That I might be your first choice at the moment, but that you care enough about Brett to keep him in a fallback position. That's what you're telling me."

What could I say? He was right.

The doors opened onto our floor and Nick stormed out.

Viola looked up from her desk by Lu's office down the hall, eyeing me and Nick over her bifocals.

I gave her a friendly wave and forced a smile. "'Mornin', Vi."

She jerked her head toward Lu's office behind her. "The Lobo wants to see you."

Damn. So much for trying to make Nick see things my way.

While Nick continued on to his office, I hurried down the hall to Lu's digs, hoping we could get our conversation over with quickly so I could go speak to Nick.

No such luck.

chapter thirty-four

Another Day, Another Case

I entered Lu's office to find Eddie already seated in one of her wing chairs. Lu gestured for me to take a seat in the other.

"I've already busted Eddie's balls this morning," she said. "It's only fair I bust yours, too."

I was tempted to point out, once again, that I had no balls, but didn't want to say anything that would drag things out unnecessarily. I really needed to finish my conversation with Nick, make him see that my feelings for Brett in no way diminished how I felt about him. I supposed it seemed odd, but it was true. I mean, it wasn't like I had a limited amount of feelings to allocate and had to decide on a ratio, giving a certain percentage to Nick and the remainder to Brett. I could care about both of them, deeply and simultaneously.

The Lobo used her teeth to rip a bite off yet another Slim Jim. I could virtually see her arteries clogging in front of me. "Eddie says you two still haven't made any real progress on the terrorist case."

"I brought in another member of their ring last night," I pointed out. And nearly got shot doing it.

Lu waved her hand dismissively. "The guy you nabbed is as tight-lipped as the others. He's not going to give you anything new to go on. Besides, bringing in the terrorists is the CIA's and Homeland Security's job. Your job is to find the money trail."

Would I really get so little credit for my near-death experience? "We've made the rounds of all the MSBs," I said, adding that we planned to make a trip out to Homsi's mosque, apartment, and workplace today.

"When you're done with today's visits," she said, "you're done with the case. You two have spent a lot of time spinning your wheels with nothing to show for it and we've got a backlog I need to assign. I can't loan two of my agents out indefinitely. Our tax cases have to take priority."

I slumped in my seat in shame. I knew it was unrealistic to expect we would nail every bad guy we went after, but in the months I'd been with IRS Criminal Investigations I had yet to leave a case unresolved. It wasn't in my nature to give up or give in.

But, hell, what else could we do? Agents Zardooz and Wang hadn't been able to find the terrorists' accomplice and they had received just as much training as Eddie and I. I had no new ideas short of rounding up a bloodhound and seeing if the dog could sniff its way to the person who'd helped them move their money.

"A bloodhound?" Lu repeated after I made the suggestion. Her false eyelashes accentuated her look of incredulity. "You've got to be kidding me."

I supposed I shouldn't mention that I'd consulted a psychic about the case. The Lobo would probably send me packing on the spot.

Lu pointed to a large stack of files on her desk. "Those are for you, Tara. Some new cases." She gestured for Eddie to take another stack. "You two take a quick look. Let me know if you have any questions."

I picked up the heavy pile, plunked them on my lap, and

began to work my way down through them. The first was a routine tax evasion case against a divorced community college professor who'd claimed to be exempt from income taxes after having renounced his U.S. citizenship and declaring himself a personal corporation, as if such a thing actually existed. The goofball taught political science, including a course called Anarchy in Action. The audit department had already built a complete case against the professor and issued him seven demands for payment, all of which he'd refused. The only thing I had to do was arrest the guy. It should be a slam dunk.

The second was a high-dollar case involving a slew of people who'd conspired in a mortgage fraud scheme. According to the notes, the case involved building contractors, appraisers, Realtors, and mortgage brokers. Everyone involved was pointing fingers at everyone else. *Ugh.* That case would be a certain pain in the ass.

The final case involved alleged unreported earnings by various people who worked at a topless bar. Because the case involved both drugs and prostitution, the IRS would team up with agents from the DEA and Dallas PD's sex crimes unit. I skimmed over the list of contacts and saw the name Christina Marquez. Knowing I'd be working with Christina again was the only good news I'd had this morning.

Nick's name was also on the list, I noticed. At the moment, I wasn't sure whether that was good or bad. Normally, I'd be thrilled to work side by side with him. But with the mood he was in now, I wasn't so sure that would be a good thing. After all, the man was armed and I could admittedly be a royal pain in the ass. I couldn't much blame him if he decided to bust a cap in my butt.

"Nick's assigned to the bar case, too?" I asked.

Lu nodded. "That's a sleazy case if ever there was one. The investigation has the potential to become dangerous. I wanted to put some muscle on it."

"I've got muscle," Eddie said, holding up his arm and flexing it.

Lu cocked her head. "Your muscles have two little girls that need a daddy."

Eddie sighed and lowered his arm.

I supposed I should have felt insulted that Lu considered me more expendable than my partner. After all, if something happened to me, my cats would be orphaned. But as long as someone fed them they'd likely get over my loss in a day or two. Hell, I bet Henry wouldn't miss me at all, the furry little brat.

I crammed the paperwork back into the file. "Have you gone out with Harry yet?" I asked Lu.

"Yes." She pursed her lips. "Another bust."

"What was it this time?"

"He's still hung up on his ex-wife. She was all he talked about. Raylene this and Raylene that. But I suppose I can't complain too much. I got a lobster dinner out of it."

"Gonna give the coach a try?"

She lifted a shoulder. "Might as well. What have I got to lose?"

Armed with our new files, Eddie and I returned to our offices to drop them off. When I glanced across the hall, I noticed Nick's office was vacant. He was probably in the kitchen snagging a Red Bull. *Damn.* I'd hoped to have a chance to smooth things over before Eddie and I headed out. Again, no such luck.

This really wasn't turning out to be my day.

Before leaving, I stopped by Josh's office and gave him Kira's note. He ripped through the staple and read the page, a big grin spreading across his face. I had no idea what she'd written, but it was clear she was giving Josh a second chance.

Josh looked up at me. "Thanks, Tara."

I waved my hand, letting him know I'd been glad to help.

As I left his office, I had to wonder. Why was I so good at helping other people fix their relationships and so bad at handling my own?

Both Agent Zardooz and Agent Wang accompanied us on our rounds today. We struck out at Homsi's mosque and apartment. One of his Islamophobic female coworkers said the guy had always creeped her out, spoke too loudly in his "gibberish language" on his cell phone, and had taken his coffee with two sugar packets, but that didn't really give us anything workable to run with.

Our final stop was the government impound lot, where we searched through the men's cars. Nothing incriminating or suspicious there, though I noticed Nasser's auto insurance card had expired since his arrest.

By mid-afternoon, we were done. The four of us stood at our cars and shook hands, saying things like "it's been nice working with you" and "you can't win them all." We promised to contact each other if any of us came up with a sudden bright idea, though I doubted any of us really expected to ever hear from the others.

I looked up at the sky. The sun was shining. Shining on us and shining on the person who'd helped fund the terrorists, too. Yep, somewhere out there, someone was getting away with aiding and abetting murder and mayhem.

I dropped Eddie at the office and decided to pay a visit to the community college where Larry Horst, the tax-evading college professor, taught classes. I was tired of feeling frustrated and incompetent. I needed an easy arrest and Horst was just the ticket.

After the events that had taken place at the airport, I decided it was best to make sure campus security knew I was on-site and that I'd be arresting Professor Horst. I phoned the campus police and told them of my plans.

"Good luck," said the officer on the phone. "That Horst is one bizarre bastard."

I sent Nick a text next. *Plz don't B mad.*

I didn't receive a reply. *Damn.*

I parked in a visitor spot and ventured onto the campus. An enormous concrete fountain graced the entrance, a cascade of water billowing from the top, its huge bowl filled with pennies, nickels, and dimes students had tossed into the water as if it were a wishing well. If I had to hazard a bet, I'd say each and every one of the coins represented a wish for an A+. Or maybe to get laid. I wondered how many of those wishes had come true.

After a few minutes of aimless wandering around the campus, I eventually stumbled upon a dark brick building with a sign outside identifying it as the shared home of the poetry and political science departments. Looked like they'd chosen to divvy up space by alphabet rather than discipline.

A glass-enclosed bulletin board near the elevators contained a list of the professors and their office numbers. According to the list, Horst's space was in room 214B. I took the elevator up with two skinny college boys who were discussing the basic tenets of Marxism, apparently for an upcoming test next week. They climbed off on the second floor and I ventured out behind them.

I found room 214 with no problem. Not easy to miss a door spray-painted with a red circle A, the symbol for anarchy.

The room was divided into two cubicles, one for Horst, another for a poetry professor, judging from the framed portrait of Maya Angelou hanging on the wall on that side of the space.

A large black flag was draped over the wall of Horst's cubicle. Blue books, potato chip wrappers, and paper coffee cups, many still containing liquid, were scattered haphazardly over the desktop. His in-box overflowed with unopened mail, some of it having fallen to the floor.

Clearly, Horst had attained tenure.

On his bookshelf rested copies of classic political science books. Writings by Plato, Aristotle, John Locke, and Friedrich Nietzsche. *The Communist Manifesto.* Even an English translation of *Mein Kampf.* While his desk and bookshelf were cluttered, the chair in his cubicle remained empty.

I stepped over to the other cubicle. "Hello," I said to the black woman sitting there. "I'm looking for Professor Horst. Any idea where he might be?"

"Where he might be," she repeated, raising a hand and

sweeping it through the air. "He might be here; he might be there." She clenched her fists in front of her chest and boomed, "What might he be if he be mighty?"

Although I was glad to have inspired this woman's free-style flow, I had a job to get done and no time to dally in sonnets or iambic pentameter. "So, yeah," I said. "That poem was inspiring and all, but can you be more specific about Horst's whereabouts?"

She hiked a thumb, indicating I should continue the way I'd been headed. "Professor Horst is in class now. Three doors down. Room Two-Seventeen."

chapter thirty-five

You've Been Schooled

I walked down the hall to room 217, stopping to peek through the vertical pane of glass in the door. At the front of the class stood a man with wild salt-and-pepper hair, gesticulating flamboyantly and ranting loudly about the tyranny of big government.

I quietly opened the door and slipped inside.

There were only ten or so students in the class. Rather than sitting in neat rows, the students had arranged their desks at haphazard angles, apparently placing them wherever they chose. One student had turned his desk sideways so that he faced the window. Another student was asleep in his seat, his face slack against the fake wood fold-down desktop, a string of viscous drool hanging from his open mouth. A third student, this one a girl, had totally foregone a desk and was lying on her back on the floor, her legs stretched up the wall, earbuds in her ears.

Professor Horst stopped ranting as I entered. "What are you doing in my classroom?" he demanded, sounding quite

like the tyrants he'd been condemning only seconds before.
"Are you a student?"

I ignored the second question, figuring I'd wait until class
was complete before approaching Horst about his overdue
tax returns and payments. No sense tipping my hand now.
As for the first question, wasn't it ironic for him to be asking? Excluding me from the class would go against everything he was ranting about, wouldn't it?

The students all turned to look at me. Well, other than the
drooling guy, that is. He just continued to sleep and produce
mucus.

"This is a class on anarchy, right?" I said, letting a student-
like hint of sarcasm sneak into my voice. "I'm here to learn
about anarchy."

I continued on, walking with self-assurance. I'd learned
long ago that if you act like you have the right to do something, few will question your actions. I snagged an empty
desk at the back of the room and plunked myself down. As
expected, no one questioned me further.

I looked around as Professor Horst resumed his ranting
and gesticulating.

A quote attributed to Mahatma Gandhi was written on
the chalkboard. *The ideally non-violent state will be an ordered anarchy. That State is the best governed which is
governed the least.*

Gandhi advocated anarchy? Huh, I never knew that.
Looked like I had learned something from going back to
college. I had to admit the quote surprised me, though. It
seemed pretty radical for a guy who went around wearing
a bedsheet like a diaper.

The class wrapped up at thirty-seven minutes after the
hour. A random time but, hey, anarchy.

The students streamed out into the hallway. Well, all but
the sleeping guy, that is. He continued to doze on at his desk.
I stepped out with the students, waiting by the door for Professor Horst. Unfortunately, when he walked out he was
talking on his cell phone, arguing with his ex-wife about

who was legally obligated to pay for their teenage son's six-hundred-dollar speeding ticket.

"What do you mean I encourage this type of behavior?" Horst barked. "Need I remind you that you're the one who took him to get his driver's license!"

I followed Horst down a set of stairs and out onto the quad. He continued arguing with his ex, eventually saying, "Fine. We'll split the cost." He snapped his phone shut and muttered "bitch" under his breath.

By this time, we'd nearly reached the fountain at the edge of campus.

"Professor Horst!" I called. "Wait a minute!"

The man stopped, turned, and shot me an irritated look. "What do you want?" he spat. "Besides a free lesson in government."

I pulled my badge from my purse and flashed it at him. "I'm Special Agent Tara Holloway with the IRS. You're under arrest for willful tax evasion. I need you to come with me."

"As if," he said, sounding like the eighteen-year-old students in his class. He turned and took off running. He was remarkably fast. Either he jogged on a regular basis or he had experience running from law enforcement.

I took off after him. When he neared the fountain, he was forced to turn to avoid colliding with a large group of students. I ran around the fountain from the other direction, hoping to head him off. When he saw me coming around the other side, he reversed course. For several seconds, the two of us played a ridiculous game of cat and mouse, each of us running first one way, then the other, around the fountain.

A chubby campus police officer on a golf cart saw the commotion and headed over at full speed, which was approximately three miles an hour. He braked to a stop. "Are you the IRS agent?" he called out to me.

"Yes!" I shouted. "Horst is resisting arrest!"

"I'm not resisting!" Horst hollered. "How can I be resisting you when you aren't even touching me?"

By this time, a large group of students had noticed the cop arrive and gathered around to watch the antics taking place. Fortunately for me, the crowd served as an effective fence, preventing Horst from escaping.

The officer joined in my chase, though he stayed in his golf cart, driving forward and back in the tiny vehicle like a dog herding a maverick steer. Eventually I was able to grab Horst in a bear hug from behind.

He wrapped his fingers around my wrists and tried to wrench my hands off him. "Now I'm resisting arrest!"

We wrangled next to the fountain for several seconds before Horst lost his balance and toppled over sideways into the water, taking me with him.

Splash!

Damn. I'd expected this case to be a slam dunk. Instead, it was just a dunk.

Both of us came up sputtering.

Horst hoisted himself over the side and back to the pavement. The campus cop was waiting for him, Taser at the ready.

Zzzap!

The taser delivered fifty thousand volts of electricity into Horst. His wet clothing no doubt aided in effective conductivity of the electrical charge. Horst stood, rigidly convulsing for a few seconds like a monster being animated in one of those cheesy old horror flicks. When the cop released the charge, Horst crumpled to the ground.

I pulled myself out of the fountain, scooping up a handful of coins as I did so, aiming for the quarters. After this debacle, I deserved a cherry limeade from Sonic. Hey, I'd earned it.

As I shoved the coins into the pocket of my jacket, a student nearby raised his fist in the air and shouted, "Surf's up!"

The next thing we knew, students were throwing themselves into the fountain, laughing and shouting and splashing. The cop blew his whistle but still didn't stand from his golf cart. The kids ignored him and continued their romp.

The poetry professor walked by, took one look at my wet, dripping clothing, and improvised a verse on the spot. "The droplets sparkle with prisms of color, millions of tiny rainbows, bringing beauty to us all."

A half hour later, Horst had been hauled off to jail by a marshal and I was dressed in an oversized pair of sweatpants and a long-sleeved Dallas County Community College T-shirt I'd purchased at the campus bookstore. Though I'd ditched my hopelessly soaked padded bra in a trash can, I'd been able to dry my Monday panties under the air dryer in the ladies' room, so at least I wasn't forced to go full-on commando.

A barrage of thoughts assaulted my mind as I headed back to my car.

How angry was Nick? Should I try to talk to him again before I spoke with Brett? How would Brett react when I gave him the news?

How fast had Horst's son been driving to get a six-hundred-dollar speeding ticket? *Sheesh!*

Could that orange speck on Nasser's treadmill have been the remains of a price sticker from Strike-it-Rich Pawn?

chapter thirty-six

Roses Are Red.
So Is Blood.

Brett's flight wouldn't arrive until eight o'clock. By the time he had claimed his bags, retrieved his car from the long-term parking lot, and driven home, it would be nine thirty or so. In other words, no need for me to rush home.

I stopped at a Sonic and ordered an extra-large cherry limeade. It wasn't nearly as good as the peach sangria I'd become addicted to, but it wasn't a bad substitute and would pose no risk of a DUI conviction.

I handed the carhop all of the coins I'd collected from the fountain at the college. "Keep the change."

Her face lit up when she glanced down at the heavy pile in her hand and realized her tip would be at least three dollars.

I sat in the stall for a moment, sipping my drink and using my phone to log onto the Internet. Once I was connected to the Web, I accessed the MSB registrations and searched for one in the name of Strike-it-Rich Pawn.

I shook my head, chastising myself. Shame on me. It was ridiculous to think a sweet grandmother like Margie Bainbridge could be involved in a terror plot. Right?

Then again, I'd been up to my eyeballs in crazies for the past two weeks. Hell, I hardly knew what normal behavior was anymore.

The circle at the top of the screen spun while the phone accessed the data. After a few seconds it stopped spinning and displayed the information I'd sought.

There was no current registration listed.

I experienced an odd feeling then, part frustration, part relief. I'd been hoping this could be a lead in the case. At the same time, I'd hate for the information to lead me to a seemingly nice person like Margie. I liked my bad guys to be, well, *bad*.

To make sure I'd done a thorough job, I tried several variations of spelling for Strike-it-Rich Pawn, leaving out the hyphens, spelling it as one word, removing "Pawn" afterward.

Still nothing.

Hmm. If the store only made short-term pawn loans and didn't transmit funds, engage in significant cash-for-gold transactions, or sell money orders, traveler's checks, or stored-value cards, it would need only a state license and wouldn't have to be registered with the Treasury Department. Given that there was no current registration, maybe the store did none of those things and I was barking up the wrong tree here.

Then again, Margie had seemed overwhelmed by record keeping at the store and was far from computer savvy. It was possible she'd failed to register as required or perhaps had inadvertently let the store's registration lapse.

I searched the records for lapsed registrations, holding my breath as the data processed. The circle spun again for a moment or two before the information flashed up on the screen.

Bingo.

Strike-it-Rich had been registered decades ago by Margie's husband, Ronald Bainbridge, and had maintained its registration until last year, when no renewal had been received. Because her husband had registered electronically, any renewal notice would have been sent to the e-mail address on file. Margie probably didn't have access to her husband's e-mail account and therefore would not have received the notice. Or even if she did have access to his e-mail account, she probably hadn't bothered to check it since he'd run off with the floozy.

I was beginning to feel that little buzz of anticipation, the one that said maybe I was on to something here. I tried not to pay too much attention to it. Just because the pawnshop had been registered as a money transmitter at one time didn't mean it had continued to provide money transmission services. Heck, it was doubtful Margie would even be able to handle a wire transfer. The transactions could be complicated. Besides, even if the place had continued to wire funds, it didn't necessarily mean she'd helped Algafari, Nasser, and Homsi move their money. Still, it couldn't hurt to check things out. Like I said before, leave no stone unturned, even if Lu had ordered me to stop overturning stones. She couldn't very well complain if I continued the investigation on my own time, though, could she?

I dialed Eddie's cell phone to let him know of my plans. The phone rang several times and, when Eddie didn't pick up, put me into voice mail. I couldn't blame him for not answering. It was Friday night, after work hours, and he was probably enjoying some long overdue family time with his wife and daughters.

"Yo, bro," I said. "I know this is a total long shot, but I noticed an orange sticker on Nasser's treadmill yesterday. I went gun shopping at a place called Strike-it-Rich Pawn a few days ago and they use orange price stickers. They carry a lot of used exercise equipment. They were also previously registered as a money transmitter, but their license lapsed a while back. Anyway, I'll call you later tonight, let you know what I find out."

I dropped my phone into my purse, backed out of the stall, and set out to Strike-it-Rich.

* * *

Other than Margie's ancient station wagon, the only car in the Strike-it-Rich lot was a Jeep Grand Cherokee outfitted with headlamps and gun racks, obviously a hunter's vehicle. I parked near the door of the shop and stepped inside, once again greeted by the scent of roses from the bowl of dusty potpourri by the door.

I made my way past the guitars and televisions and treadmills to the back of the store, where Margie was assisting a customer with a Smith &Wesson rifle. She looked up and offered a smile when she saw me approach the counter. "Be with you in just a bit."

While I waited, I looked around. I noticed the official Major League Baseball bat signed by Josh Hamilton was still available.

I clutched the manila file folder to my chest and eyed the space around the cash register, looking for a sticker or placard indicating the shop provided wire transfer services. I saw colorful stickers affixed to the register, indicating the store accepted Visa, MasterCard, and American Express.

And I also saw one in brown and yellow.

Western Union.

That little buzz I'd been feeling increased from one errant bee to an entire swarm. Could this seemingly innocuous store be the place where Algafari, Nasser, and Homsi had wired their funds to the terror groups abroad? Had the seemingly sweet grandmother behind the counter played a role in the deaths of thousands of people, including children?

The customer stood at the counter for a moment, his fingers rubbing his chin as he considered the Smith & Wesson. Finally, he stepped back. "Let me sleep on it."

"Okay," Margie said, "but you know what they say. If you snooze, you lose." She gave him a smile to let him know her words were intended primarily in jest, not as a high-pressure sales tactic.

Margie returned the gun to the case as the man left the store. She pulled the stretchy coiled key ring from her wrist and used it to lock the case back up.

"Hi, there," she said as she made her way toward me. She was wearing her pink plastic reading glasses again, and again they kept sliding down her nose. She put a finger to them and pushed them back into place. "You're the gal who bought the Cobra, right? Back for something else? I'll make you a great deal."

"Actually," I said, setting the file down on the counter, "I'm here on official IRS business this time."

"Uh-oh." Margie tilted her head. "Is there some kind of tax problem? I'm not sure how much help I'd be with that. I turn everything over to my CPA."

I narrowed my eyes at her as if trying to see into her soul, determine whether this woman was a bloodthirsty, evil bitch. But, God help me, I just didn't see it.

She stared back at me with friendly, innocent eyes, blinking as she waited for me to respond.

"I'm not here about a tax problem per se," I said. "It's about your money services business registration."

"My money business . . . my . . . what was that you said, dear?"

The woman seemed to have no idea what I was talking about.

I pointed to the Western Union logo. "I see you offer wire transfer services here."

She nodded. "We do. Have for years. Not many takers anymore, though. With online banking it's easy for people to transfer funds themselves these days."

"Did you realize that your business is supposed to be registered with the Treasury Department? That the registration for Strike-it-Rich lapsed last year?"

She looked taken aback and instinctively put a hand to her chest. "I had no idea. My husband always took care of those things." Her brows drew together and she began to look worried. "I always read through the mail. I know I sent in the forms to register our shop with the state, but I don't recall receiving any forms from the Treasury Department. I suppose it's possible I could have missed them somehow."

"Your husband registered electronically in the past," I told her. "The renewal notice would have been sent to his e-mail address."

Now the woman appeared equal parts worried and angry. "That darn man. He's caused me no end of grief, running out on me like he did, leaving me to try to run this shop on my own. Now I'm the one left holding the bag, aren't I?"

I held up a palm, hoping to calm her. "The registration can be sorted out," I said, "but what I really need to know is whether you recognize any of these men."

I removed the photos of Algafari, Nasser, and Homsi from the file and laid them on the glass countertop.

Margie pushed her glasses back again and looked down at the photos. "Well, sure," she said, picking up Nasser's photo. "I know this man."

My heart began to pound in my chest, so loud I could barely hear. I felt warm as the increased blood supply raced through my veins. "You do?"

"If I recall correctly, his name's Nassau. No, wait. That's the place in the Bahamas, isn't it? Anyway, it's something that sounds like 'Nassau.' Nasher, maybe? At any rate, he's come in here several times. He's one of the few people I mentioned who have used our Western Union service." She set the photo back down on the glass. "Nice man. Did you know his family runs an orphanage overseas? He's sent thousands of dollars over to help out, sometimes fifteen or twenty thousand at a time. Isn't it wonderful? He's like that man, what's his name, the *Three Cups of Cocoa* guy who started the schools for girls?"

She was referring to Greg Mortenson, the famous coauthor of the book *Three Cups of Tea,* a man whose veracity had also come under question.

I shook my head. "No, Margie. The man's name is Hani Nasser. If he claimed to be running an orphanage, he lied to you. This man doesn't take care of orphans. He *creates* orphans."

She stiffened and her eyes grew wary. "What are you talking about, Miss Holloway? I'm not following you."

I pulled the remaining photos from the file and spread them across the countertop. "This. This is what I'm talking about. Buildings destroyed. People executed. Families torn apart. Children killed on their way to school."

She looked down at the photographs, tears forming in her eyes. "This is . . . this is horrible." Her voice shook. "But why are you showing this to me? I don't understand."

"The man in this photo," I said, pointing to Nasser's picture, "is a convicted terrorist. He and his cohorts have been linked to a number of bombings and other violent acts in and around Syria."

Her eyes grew wide.

"The money you helped Nasser send overseas wasn't used to fund an orphanage. It was used to buy weapons and bomb-making supplies."

Margie stepped back, as if losing her balance. She reached a hand out to the wall behind her to steady herself. "Oh, my goodness. Oh, my." She looked at me and shook her head. "I had no idea." She seemed to have trouble catching her breath. "I . . . I thought I was helping him do something good."

That was precisely the problem.

In many cases, the so-called bad guys were actually nice people who wanted to do good, who wanted to help those who came to them seeking assistance. Unfortunately, they were unable to see past the person in front of them, unable to see the bigger picture, unable to realize the potentially devastating consequences of their seemingly benign actions.

"I understand your motives were innocent," I told Margie. "But you still broke the law. You aided and abetted terrorism and violated banking laws by failing to report the wire transfers as required. I'm going to have to take you in."

"Are you saying you're going to arrest me?" Margie's eyes went wide and wild with fear.

"Yes, Ms. Bainbridge. But given the circumstances—"

I'd been about to tell her I believed the prosecutors would

go easy on her. I'd been about to tell her she'd likely walk away with nothing more than a fine and probation. I'd been about to tell her I was sorry she'd been duped.

But she didn't give me a chance to finish.

Margie reached above her, seized the official Major League Baseball bat autographed by Josh Hamilton, and swung the bat with all her might.

CONK!

A shooting pain raced through my head and the world went black.

chapter thirty-seven

*G*rand Slam

Damn, my head hurt.

I heard voices. A woman's soft voice telling my parents that there was no way yet to know the extent of my brain injuries, that only time would tell.

I heard my mother sob and I wanted to tell her that it would be okay, that I'd be fine, that I just needed . . . to sleep . . . a little longer.

Damn, my head still hurt.

Why did my scalp feel so tight? It felt as if my skin were trying to strangle my skull.

Eyes closed, I reached up a hand to touch my pounding head. My fingers didn't meet hair as I'd expected, though. Instead, they came in contact with a gauze bandage.

"She's awake!" I heard Alicia cry.

I tried to force my heavy eyelids open. I caught a glimpse of sunlight between the miniblinds on the window before they closed again. Corralling my will, I tried a second time. This time I managed to keep them partially open for three seconds or so, long enough to catch a glimpse of my mother's grief-stricken, tearstained face.

I felt my mother take my hand. "Tara," she said. "Tara, can you hear me?"

I tried to answer her, but the words in my head couldn't seem to make it to my mouth. I settled for giving her hand a soft squeeze instead.

"Get the doctor, Harlan!" my mother cried. "Now!"

I heard a scuffling sound as my father apparently left the room in search of the doctor.

He returned a moment later.

"Tara?" said a woman's voice I didn't recognize. "Tara, this is Dr. Ling. Can you hear me?"

My brain said, *Yes,* but my mouth just opened and closed again.

"This is a good sign," I heard the doctor tell my parents. "She's responding. But it may take some time before she completely comes around."

I must have lapsed back into unconsciousness, because the next time I was able to force my eyes open my parents and Alicia were gone, the world outside the window was dark, and Nick, Lu, and Eddie were in the room.

Eddie and Lu sat in chairs at the end of the bed. Lu was watching a *Golden Girls* rerun on the wall-mounted television and nervously sucking on a Slim Jim while Eddie fooled with his cell phone, probably checking e-mails. Though his movements were routine and casual, the way he gnawed his lip told me he was worried.

Nick had pulled a chair up next to my bed and was manipulating my fingers, wrapping them around his stress ball and gently squeezing them, as if subtly encouraging me to move on my own.

I wouldn't have thought it possible, but Nick looked like hell. His hair was unkempt, his clothes were wrinkled, and at least three days' growth of beard shadowed his face.

Whoa. The last time I'd seen him, when he'd told me my lip looked sexy and then became angry with me over Brett, Nick had been clean shaven.

Had I been in the hospital for three days?

"You lied," I said, my voice coming out airy and breathless as my eyelids drooped closed again. "You lied about the fish."

Lu leaped from her chair. "What did she say?"

Nick emitted a sound that was half choke, half chuckle. When he spoke, his voice was raspy with emotion. "I'm not sure."

"Was it something about a fish?"

I opened my eyes again.

Nick still looked like hell, but his devilish grin had returned. He gave me a discreet wink. "Hey, there."

"Hey."

"You think you're good and awake now?"

I nodded.

"All righty, then. I'll go round up your parents."

"Thanks, Nick."

He gave my hand a final squeeze and released it, pulling his chair back to give Lu access to me.

Lu stepped up next to my bed. "You gave us a real scare, you know that?" She blinked her false eyelashes, trying to hold back her tears.

I offered a feeble smile. "Sorry."

She wagged a meaty finger at me. "You learned your lesson, right? That you can't trust anybody? That you can never let your guard down?"

"Yes, Lu. I did." Yep, I'd learned that lesson well and I'd learned it the hard way.

"Good." She yanked a tissue from a box on the bedside table and dabbed at her eyes. "Because I don't want anything like this to ever happen again. I don't think my heart could take it."

Neither could my head.

Eddie stepped up next to me. "It's like déjà vu all over again, huh?"

"Yeah," I said. "Except last time you were the one with a bandage on your head."

"Maybe we should start wearing helmets."

"It couldn't hurt."

Eddie exhaled a long breath. "Thank God you left that voice mail telling me where you were going. Otherwise we wouldn't have found you until it was too late."

I asked Eddie what had happened after Margie tried to hit a home run with my head. He gave me a quick rundown. When I hadn't called him back by eight o'clock, he'd begun to worry. He'd called my cell phone several times with no success. When he couldn't get an answer on my mobile, he tried my home number and got in contact with Alicia. She hadn't heard from me, either, and had been worried, too.

Eddie had phoned Nick and the two of them headed to Strike-it-Rich. Though the lights were off inside the store, my car was still parked out front. Fearing something bad had happened inside, Nick picked up one of the concrete parking stops and smashed it through the front window.

"But the windows have metal bars on them," I said. Even if he'd managed to shatter the glass, there was no way a grown man could squeeze through the bars.

"Nick ripped them off like some kind of rabid gorilla." Eddie acted out the scene, raising clenched fists and pretending to wrangle with invisible bars. "I've never seen anything like it."

Nick must have been terrified for me. At the thought of him coming to my rescue, my heart gave a little flutter and the beeping monitor sped up slightly. Lu glanced at the noisy machine, then at me, one pinkish-orange brow raised.

"We drew our guns," Eddie continued, "and charged the place."

They'd found me sprawled unconscious on the floor in front of the cash register, my head resting in an expanding pool of blood, the autographed bat lying nearby. After assuring themselves I was still alive, Eddie had immediately called 911 to summon an ambulance while Nick searched the store, looking to see if my attacker was still around.

"Whoever did this to you is lucky Nick didn't find him," Eddie said. "Nick would've ripped him limb from limb."

"It wasn't a *him*," I said. "It was a *her*."

Eddie's brows drew together. "What are you talking about?"

"It was a woman named Margie Bainbridge. She owns the place."

"Seriously?" Eddie and Lu exchanged glances. "She and her car have been missing since that night. The police assumed you'd been injured in a botched robbery attempt and Margie Bainbridge had been kidnapped and probably killed. They've had search and rescue teams out looking for her in empty fields near the pawnshop."

Fury flared in the Lobo's eyes. "It's been three days. That woman could be anywhere by now." Lu pulled her cell phone from her purse and stepped into the hallway to call the detective at Dallas PD and give him this new information.

Eddie continued his story, telling me that my cell phone had rung in my purse while he and Nick waited for the EMTs to arrive. It had been Brett calling. Eddie told him what had happened, that they'd found me with a head injury in a pool of blood and were waiting for medical help.

"He totally freaked," Eddie said.

I felt a twinge in my heart. "Has Brett been here?" I asked, glad Nick wasn't in the room at the moment.

Eddie nodded. "Several times. He waited with the rest of us in the ER while they ran your MRI. He's the one who called Alicia and your parents after we told him what happened. Alicia's been around a lot, too. In fact, they're both here at the hospital now, getting coffee with your parents in the cafeteria."

Both Nick and Brett were here, at the same time. This could definitely get awkward.

The doctor, a petite Asian woman, came into the room. "Your coworker caught me in the hall. He said you'd come to. How are you feeling, Tara?"

"Like I've got a major-league headache."

Eddie groaned at my lame joke. "She's back. God help us."

Dr. Ling gripped the ends of a stethoscope draped around

her neck. "Your skull is fractured, and you've lost a lot of blood. But you're lucky—"

I interrupted her with a soft snort. *Lucky? Good one, Doc.*

"Your coworkers found you fairly quickly," the doctor continued. "There are no other broken bones, your vital signs have been stable, and the MRI showed little swelling in your brain."

Thank heaven for small favors.

The doctor shined a flashlight into both of my eyes and asked me some questions to check my memory. I gave her my date of birth, current address, hometown, and high-school mascot, passing the rudimentary test with flying colors.

Though things were looking good so far, she said head injuries could be tricky and sometimes unpredictable. They'd need to keep me a few more days for observation. I thanked her and she patted my leg, leaving the room.

I found the controller to adjust the bed and raised the top half until I was in a more upright position. I glanced around the room. Several houseplants and bouquets of flowers rested on the tables and countertops. A trio of Mylar balloons filled with helium floated above one of the bouquets, the inscription inviting me to *Get well soon!*

When Lu saw me eyeing the plants and flowers, she rounded up the cards for me to read. The huge bouquet of mixed flowers was from everyone at the office. The greeting card was signed with various sentiments, most of which expressed surprise at my skull fracture given that I had a reputation around IRS Criminal Investigations for being extremely hardheaded.

The peace lily was from my two brothers and their families. *Dear Itty Bitty, Sorry to hear you're feeling shitty.* Yep, my brothers got the smart-ass gene, too. Nice rhyme, though.

The card accompanying Christina and Ajay's ivy suggested I *keep my head together,* while the one attached to the orchid sent by Agents Zardooz and Wang read: *Hooray for ovaries!*

Aw, shucks. They'd remembered.

Nick's mother had sent a vase of lavender gladiolus with a matching bow. *Dear Tara, You're in my thoughts and prayers, Bonnie Pratt.* What a caring, thoughtful woman.

Nick had brought me an enormous white azalea in a pale-blue decorative tin. His card read only: *Nick.* It didn't need to say anything else. Ripping burglar bars off a building said much more to me than words ever could. I bet his muscles were damn sore afterward. I should probably treat the guy to a professional massage.

Brett's offering was a beautiful bouquet with greenery, baby's breath, and red, pink, and white roses.

Roses.

When I'd asked Madam Magnolia who had helped the terrorists move their money, she couldn't summon a vision, but she'd said she smelled roses. My thoughts had immediately gone to Brett back then, to the rosebushes he'd planted at my house. But the pawnshop had a bowl of rose-scented potpourri by the door.

Ugh. Too bad I hadn't put those clues together earlier. I could've saved myself a real headache.

"How'd the date go with the basketball coach?" I asked Lu.

"Gerard?" My boss grimaced. "He was another winner. He bent over to tie his shoe and what did I see sticking out of the back of his gym shorts? Ladies' panties. Pink lace."

Definitely a deal breaker. "So Carl gets the prize, huh?"

The Lobo nodded and pointed to the gold Sigma Chi pin on her blouse. "He pinned me."

"He *pinned* you?" Eddie chuckled. "What's next, a sock hop?"

Lu narrowed her eyes at him. "What's next is I assign you all the crummy cases; that's what's next."

Eddie held up his hands. "I take it back."

My parents arrived, rushing through the door of my room, both of them looking as if they'd aged twenty years since I'd seen them mere days earlier. Both had dark circles under their eyes and appeared pallid, feeble, and utterly exhausted.

My mother gave me a gentle hug, though she had a death grip on my thin hospital gown. "Don't you ever put us through anything like this again," she managed in a choked-up whisper. "You hear me?"

She spoke as if I'd asked for this. Still, I knew better than to argue with her. "Sorry, Mom."

Dad gave me a kiss on the cheek. "How many times do I have to tell you? *Shoot first and ask questions later.*"

Alicia couldn't talk. She just fluttered her hands around her face, made little kitten-like mewing noises, and cried.

I reached out, grabbed a fluttering hand, and gave it a squeeze. "See if you can get the nurse to put some peach sangria in my IV."

Alicia laughed through her tears, nodding and brushing at her eyes with her bare hands, smearing mascara all over her cheeks. I handed her the box of tissues.

Brett had been hanging back. He stepped forward now, his face drawn and pensive. He looked tired and spent, too, but not nearly as bad as my parents and Nick looked. Then again, Brett hadn't actually seen me lying in a pool of blood like Nick had.

Brett gazed down at me, as if unsure what to say. I felt awkward, too. Odd, that two people who'd been so close and intimate could suddenly feel uncomfortable with each other, as if they were worlds apart.

Brett gave me a soft smile. "I had to cancel our dinner reservations for Saturday night. I'd planned on taking you to The French Room."

It crossed my mind that even if I hadn't been whacked upside the head, he would have had to cancel those reservations after we had our talk. Too bad. The food at The French Room was darn good. Far more appetizing than hospital food. No doubt a nurse would soon bring me a meal of meat with congealed gravy followed by lime Jell-O with mushy pears inside.

Eddie and Lu prepared to leave.

"Stay in touch," Lu said. "Let us know when the doctors give you the all clear."

"Sure, Lu. I will."

Nick didn't return to the room. He simply stood outside the door and took one final look in at me, as if he needed to reassure himself that I was okay. I met his gaze, picked up the blue stress ball he'd left tucked among my covers, and held it tight to my heart. He flashed a small, chipped-tooth smile and followed Eddie and Lu down the hall.

When I returned my attention to those still in the room, I noticed Brett looking at me with a strange expression. Had he noticed the exchange between me and Nick?

chapter thirty-eight

$\mathcal{N}$egotiations

I woke bright and early the next morning when the nurse brought my breakfast of runny eggs, soggy toast, and color-less oatmeal. Oh, how I missed my Fruity Pebbles.

My mother had brought me some things from home. My toiletries. The mystery novel I'd been reading. My house slippers and my Thursday panties, the last clean pair she could find.

I threw my covers back. Whoa. Nick's face wasn't the only thing that bore three days of stubble. My legs looked like they belonged on a cavewoman.

The nurse helped me into the shower. I bathed, sham-pooed, and shaved for the first time in days. When I was done, I slipped into a fresh hospital gown and the fresh pant-ies. I felt nearly human again.

Ajay and Christina came by shortly thereafter, before regular visiting hours. As one of my regular doctors, Ajay could come see me at any time. Christina slipped in with him.

I thanked them for the ivy they'd sent. "The vibrators, though, that's a different story."

"Ooh. I want to hear that story." Ajay looked from me to Christina.

"None of your business," she said.

"We're engaged," he said. "Everything you do is my business."

Christina gave him a pointed look. "Oh, yeah? Then you tell me what happened at that medical convention in Reno."

"Okay! Okay!" He held up his hands in surrender. "You can have your vibrators if I can have Reno."

"Deal." Christina plunked herself down at the end of my bed. "Are they going to put a steel plate in your head? That would be cool."

What could possibly be "cool" about having a steel plate in your head? Then again, I supposed it would make me less vulnerable. Maybe I could even use it to my advantage should an occasion arise in which I needed to head butt someone. "Nah. The fracture was actually relatively small." Thank goodness Margie hadn't been any stronger than she was or she probably would have killed me instantly.

My back hurt and my muscles felt as if they were beginning to atrophy. I suggested the three of us take a walk around the hospital.

"Good idea," Ajay said. "It will get your blood flowing, reduce the risk of clotting."

When I climbed out of bed, Christina shrieked. I turned to find her eyeing the gap where the back of my gown hung open. "You've been wearing those underwear for almost a week?"

I rolled my eyes. "No. I just put them on this morning."

She gestured at my ass. "But they say Thursday."

"Yeah, and my high-school yearbook says I plan to marry Keith Urban." I rolled my eyes. "Don't believe everything you read."

The first thing I'd do when I was released from this hospital would be to wash my dirty laundry.

Ajay, Christina, and I made only three rounds of the floor before returning to my room. Amazing how quickly I tuckered out after having spent several days in bed. The two left with a reminder about their Halloween party. Hard to believe it was only a week away.

My parents came into the room not long after Ajay and Christina had gone. Mom had brought a box of Fruity Pebbles. She sent Dad to the cafeteria to get me a pint of cold milk.

"You look much better," she said.

"I feel much better." The shower had done wonders for me.

"I washed your laundry." She pursed her lips in disapproval. "All thirteen loads of it. Took me hours."

I gave her a big smile. "I love you, Mommy."

My parents stayed for a half hour or so, then headed out. Dad planned to return to Nacogdoches to check on things back home, but Mom insisted on staying in town a few more days until I'd been released and she'd convinced herself I'd be okay on my own.

Alone now, I raised the miniblinds and looked out my second-floor window. Nick's truck pulled into the parking lot below. My heart gave a little flutter. When Brett's Navigator pulled in directly afterward, that little flutter turned into a major flurry.

No good could come from the two of them showing up here at the same time with no one else around to run interference for me.

The two pulled into spots not far from each other. Nick stepped out of his truck, doing a double take when he saw Brett climb out of his SUV. He hesitated a moment but then stepped toward Brett, his mouth moving to form words I couldn't hear. Brett said something back, his posture becoming rigid as Nick removed the white felt cowboy hat I'd bought him and approached.

The two stood a few feet apart. As Nick spoke, his fingers worked the cowboy hat in his hands. I supposed I should've returned his stress ball to him. Brett crossed his arms over his chest and stood with his feet slightly apart, a defensive stance.

Oh, no. Nick wasn't telling Brett about my plans to bench him, was he?

I rapped on my window, hoping to interrupt their conversation. Unfortunately, my window was too far away for them to hear me.

Dammit! What was going on? What were they talking about?

The two spoke for several minutes, Nick doing most of the talking. Eventually Brett's shoulders relaxed. His arms moved from his chest to his sides and he shoved his hands into the front pockets of his jeans.

When Nick finished, he stepped forward and held a hand out to Brett. The two shook hands. Nick returned to his truck, started it, and drove away while Brett came toward the building.

What the hell had just happened?

I was still standing at the window when Brett entered my room.

"Thursday?" he said.

I turned to find his eyes on my butt, his lip curled back in mock disgust.

"Hi, Brett."

He sighed, cocked his head, and looked at me for a moment. "You and I need to talk."

I went to the door of my room and closed it before taking a seat on the edge of the bed. He opted for one of the chairs, putting some space between us. Under the unclear circumstances, I wasn't sure whether that was a good sign or a bad sign.

He looked down at the floor for a moment before looking back up at me. "I saw Nick in the parking lot."

"I know. I saw you two from the window."

Brett looked at me for a moment. "He asked me to step aside."

My heart pounded in my chest. "Step aside?"

Brett exhaled a loud breath. "He wants a chance with you, Tara."

And I wanted a chance with Nick, too. I only wished I wouldn't have to break Brett's heart to get it.

Brett stared at me another moment, as if waiting for me

to say something. Finally, he looked down at his tennis shoes. "I'm going to give it to him."

My head swam. I had no idea what to think about all of this. I hadn't wanted to hurt Brett, but hell, here he was shredding my heart like a rototiller. Despite my attraction to Nick, I still had deep feelings for the guy. Who was Brett to say he'd give Nick a chance with me, as if the choice were his to make, as if I were something he owned and could give away? And who did Nick think he was, asking Brett to step aside, butting in on my relationship with another man?

The thought of the two of them haggling over me as if I were a fish at a market left me hurt and angry. But I was getting what I wanted, wasn't I?

Tears welled up in my eyes, partly from the heartache, partly from the relief that this issue was finally out in the open.

Brett looked back up at me now. "Do you have feelings for him, Tara?"

No sense denying it. I could tell he suspected I did. "I'm sorry, Brett."

He raised a hand. "No need to apologize. People don't have control over their feelings, only their actions."

It sounded as if he was speaking from experience. Wait, *was* he speaking from experience?

I eyed him closely. Sure, part of him looked heartbroken. But I saw something else there. Was he also feeling relieved?

He looked at me. "I've got feelings for someone else, too."

It felt as if the earth had shifted under me. I hadn't expected this.

I gripped the bed rail. "Is it Trish?"

If he said, *Yes,* I'd strangle him with the blood pressure cuff. Please let it be anyone but that big-titted twit!

He shook his head and thus would live to see another day. "No, it's not Trish."

I didn't want to think of Brett with someone else, but at the same time I knew I had to know. "Who, then?"

"The chef at the country club in Atlanta."

"The one who made the spiced peaches?" I racked my bruised brain for her name. "Fiona?"

He nodded.

Huh. Looked like the way to a man's heart really was through his stomach.

I supposed I shouldn't have been surprised. Thinking back, I realized there had been some fairly obvious signs. During our phone calls, he'd rambled on incessantly about the food at the club, how good everything tasted. Heck, I'd even noticed he'd put on a pound or two while working in Atlanta.

"Has anything happened between you two?" I asked. If he'd cheated on me, I'd never forgive him. I'd make sure he was audited every year for the rest of his life.

"No." Brett's voice was emphatic. He looked me in the eye. "I'd never do that to you, Tara."

I believed him. "Nothing's happened with Nick, either."

"I know that, too. You wouldn't make a fool of me like that."

We were both quiet a moment as we tried to sort our thoughts.

"When were you going to tell me?" I asked finally.

"I don't know," he said. "Soon. I was still working through my feelings."

"And what do you think now?"

"Honestly, Tara? I'm still not sure. Sometimes I can really see me and you having a future together."

"And other times?"

"Other times I think a life with you would be an absolute pain in the ass."

We shared a laugh.

"So, what now?" I asked.

Brett shrugged. "I guess we work out some parameters for a trial separation."

It seemed so formal and legalistic, but it was the right thing to do. It was the only way to ensure that if things didn't work out with Nick or Fiona, neither Brett nor I crossed a line from which there could be no return.

We talked things out and finally reached an agreement, the terms of which were fairly straightforward:

> *Number one: a total break for one month with no communication between us.*
>
> *Number two: no nooky with the new partner during the trial period.*
>
> *Number three: On an agreed Saturday one month from now, if either of us wanted to reconcile, that person should go to the children's pool at the arboretum at noon and see if the other showed up. If we both showed up, we'd get back together, no questions asked. If not, well, it's been great. No regrets.*

Brett leaned in and gave me a soft, sweet kiss on the cheek before leaving. I grabbed his hand and held it to my cheek for a moment, yet more tears welling up in my eyes.

Willie Shakespeare got it right. Parting really is such sweet sorrow.

chapter thirty-nine

$\mathcal{N}$ick + Tara = ♥

As soon as Brett left, I texted Nick. *U R in big trouble, mister.*

A reply came instantly, as if he'd been waiting to hear from me. *On my way.*

Twenty minutes later, Nick stepped into the doorway of my room. He crossed his arms over his chest and leaned back against the jamb. "You're angry that I spoke with Brett?"

"Furious." It was a lie. Although part of me didn't like the fact that Nick had taken charge of the situation and fought my battle for me, so to speak, another part appreciated the fact that he'd taken the heat off me, made things easier. Besides, seeing him standing there made it impossible to maintain any anger I might have felt.

"I got tired of waiting, woman. Besides, I have a feeling you won't be furious for long." He flashed that chipped-tooth smile that never failed to send me reeling.

I felt a blush warm my cheeks. "Cocky son of a bitch."

He chuckled. "You wouldn't have me any other way."

It was true. He really did understand me, huh?

Nick stepped over to the bed and took a seat facing me,

reaching out his hand to entwine his fingers with mine. God, his touch felt wonderful. After weeks of yearning for contact, I didn't think I'd ever want to let go. He raised my hand to the smooth cheek he'd recently shaved and held it there, closing his eyes and releasing a long breath as if our physical connection brought him some sort of spiritual release. Heck, I felt the same way, like my restless soul was finally at peace.

A moment later he opened his eyes. "Should we get naked and do it right here in the hospital bed? It's adjustable. We could probably come up with a really interesting position." Still holding my hand, he took one of my knuckles between his front teeth and gave it a playful bite.

If not for my agreement with Brett, I'd have been willing to try. But until the one-month probationary period was up, there'd be no nooky with Nick.

When I told him the details of my agreement with Brett he released my hand and frowned.

I grabbed his hand back and held it to my cheek this time. "Please don't be mad. I'm crazy about you, Nick. You know that."

He gave a grunt of displeasure, but when he eyed my face his frown melted. "I'll never understand how you can be so tough at your job and such a chickenshit about your personal life."

If he hadn't nailed me so perfectly, I might've been angry again. "Guns are much easier to handle than men," I said, shrugging. "They don't go off unexpectedly, I can control them, and they're easier to clean."

"I suppose you've got a point." He pulled his phone from his pocket and began punching buttons. When he finished, he held the phone up to show me the screen. On the Saturday after Thanksgiving, the day when Brett and I were to either part for good or meet at noon to reconcile, Nick had scheduled a date with me for the evening. He'd titled the event ROCK TARA'S WORLD. Clearly he, too, believed things would work out between us, despite this somewhat inauspicious start.

I picked my phone up from the bedside table and marked my calendar, too. *ROCK NICK'S WORLD RIGHT BACK*. I held up the phone. "It's a date."

Dr. Ling released me from the hospital the following day with strict orders to take it easy. And what better place to take it easy than on a boat?

Nick played hooky from work in the afternoon and we took his boat out to one of the area lakes. The day was cool, so we wore windbreakers. Given that it was not only late October but also a weekday, we virtually had the lake to ourselves.

It felt like we were the only two people in the world.

Nick fished while I lounged on the deck with a glass of peach sangria and a new mystery novel. Nutty lay on his back at our feet, his tummy turned toward the sky, basking in the meager sunshine.

Though Nick hadn't been especially thrilled to know our relationship was a trial run and that Brett and I had kept each other in a backup position, he'd acquiesced. Of course he'd kept his account at Big D Dating Service active, too. It was his way of letting me know that he wasn't a pushover, that two could play this game. He was keeping his options open, too. Still, I was cautiously optimistic that things would work out between us.

In late afternoon, as the sun began to wane, Nick eased his boat into the cove that contained the quiet dock where my mother, Alicia, and I had stopped the evening after we'd gone shopping at Neiman's. Nick tied up to the side of the dock and we stepped off the boat, Nutty trotting up the wooden pier to dry land and sniffing around for the squirrels that so easily eluded his nearly blind eyes.

Nick and I sat on the dock and looked out over the water. I recalled the night that I dreamed of having a glass of peach sangria in my hand and Nick sitting next to me.

My dream had come true.

chapter forty

Fairy Tales

Things were looking up all around.

Daniel phoned Alicia and the two met for lunch. Though she was happy he'd called and thrilled he wanted to resume their relationship, she wasn't about to go rushing back into either his arms or his apartment. I told her she could stay at my place as long as she wanted to. It was nice having her around, even if she refused to do my laundry.

Though Margie Bainbridge had hidden out at the home of her cousin in nearby Rockwall for five days, she'd been overcome with guilt and turned herself in the day after I was released from the hospital. She'd been relieved to learn she hadn't killed me. She'd panicked, she said. She'd been overcome by the horror of learning she'd facilitated the terrorists and thought she'd face life in prison. Her actions earned her five years in the federal penitentiary. If only she'd let me finish talking before taking the bat to my brains. When will people learn to listen?

Richard Beauregard hired a sleazebag lawyer who was giving the attorneys at the Department of Justice all kinds of unnecessary hell. Hiring the bastard had been yet another bad decision in a long line of bad decisions Beau had made. The government attorneys quickly revoked the relatively generous plea deal they'd offered and planned to go for the jugular.

But I had better things to do than think about Margie or Beau. It was Halloween now and my first official date with Nick.

He carried a gallon-size jug of peach sangria into the rec room at Ajay's condominium complex while I carried a stack of plastic cups. Christina had decorated the place with fake spiderwebs and black streamers, along with a skeleton model on wheels that Ajay had ordered from a medical supply outfit. A strobe light flashed while a fog machine provided an eerie haze. Ajay had connected his iPod player to the room's built-in speakers and dance music reverberated through the space, the windows rattling with each throb of the bass line.

I wore the cute fairy costume I'd bought a few weeks ago at one of those specialty stores that pop up before the holiday. Nick was dressed as a cowboy. He already owned boots, spurs, chaps, and a hat and hadn't needed to go shopping. Heck, for him the costume was hardly a costume at all. He'd brought a rope from his boat to serve as a lasso. The yellow nylon was hardly authentic, but it had been handy.

Christina wore a skimpy Dallas Cowboy Cheerleader costume. Ajay wore an oversized toy stethoscope over a white lab coat and carried a gag pill bottle filled with Skittles, which he dispensed freely. Eddie and his wife, Sandra, had been invited to the party, but parental duty called, requiring them to take their twins trick-or-treating instead. Oh, well. Every party needs a pooper.

Alicia had teased her blond hair until it stuck straight up on top of her head. She'd sprayed the updo black, leaving platinum lightning bolts along the side. She'd loaded on dark eye shadow, dark lipstick, and dark rouge. In her poofy secondhand wedding dress, she made the perfect Bride of Frankenstein. Little did she know just how appropriate the costume would be tonight.

Josh and Kira arrived shortly after me and Nick. The two had reconciled and Josh's infected nose had cleared up completely. My coworker was once again the annoying little dweeb—make that "adorable little dork"—Kira had fallen for.

Kira was dressed in her Sailor Moon costume, while Josh wore a classic tuxedo under a black cape with red satin lining. His costume also included a top hat and a white eye mask. He actually looked quite dashing, nothing like his normally nerdy self. What's more, his usual stiff gait had been replaced by a smooth and confident swagger.

"Who are you?" I asked, gesturing to his getup as they approached.

"Tuxedo Mask," he said, his voice sounding deeper, more manly than I remembered. "He's a character from the Sailor Moon show."

Kira looked at Josh with affection before turning to me. "Tuxedo Mask is the guy Sailor Moon is hot for."

Nick looked from Josh to Kira and back to Josh again. "You lost it, didn't you?" It was more a proclamation than a question.

Josh glanced at Kira as if seeking permission to answer. She slid him a sly smile and Josh looked up at Nick, beaming proudly. "Yeah. I lost it."

Nick raised his hand for a high five. "My man!"

Josh slapped Nick's hand with a resounding *smack*.

"He's a natural," Kira added.

"Drinks?" I asked before Kira could elaborate. My mind had already produced a number of mental images, including one involving the creative use of a wireless mouse on Kira's etherport. *Damn my vivid imagination!* "I'll get them."

Nick followed me to the makeshift bar.

"Josh, a natural?" I said. "I have a hard time believing that."

Nick cut a grin my way. "I might have given him a few pointers."

"Really? You said earlier that teaching Josh your tricks would be like letting a kid play with dynamite."

"True," Nick said. "That's why I only taught him the basics. The equivalent of a firecracker."

Apparently whatever Nick taught him had been enough. Kira looked happy and content, as if the firecracker had provided more than enough *bang* to satisfy her. I could only imagine what it might be like to be treated to the full range of Nick's skills. Of course I wouldn't find out for at least another month. Per the terms of my contract with Brett, I was prohibited from engaging in nooky with Nick until the thirty-day trial period was over. But, heck, I was getting way ahead of myself, wasn't I? Nick and I hadn't even kissed yet.

But surely it would happen tonight.

Nick filled four plastic cups with peach sangria and I carried two of them back to Josh and Kira.

The party was in full swing when Daniel arrived. He and I had conspired to make tonight a special event. I'd told him about Alicia's costume plans and he'd dressed accordingly as Frankenstein, with green face paint, torn clothes, and plastic bolts affixed to his neck.

"Look!" one of Ajay's medical school buddies called out as Daniel walked by. "It's the Incredible Hulk."

"I'm Frankenstein," Daniel said.

"Are you sure?" the guy said, his words slurred thanks to six Jell-O-Shots. "You're green and your clothes are torn. I think you're the Hulk."

I pointed my fairy wand at him. "Trust me, dude. He's Frankenstein."

Alicia looked up from the bar, where she'd been fixing Kira a second plastic cup of sangria. She immediately realized it was Daniel in the Frankenstein costume. A surprised yet tentative smile spread across her face. "What are you doing here?"

I knew exactly what Daniel was doing here. I grabbed Nick's hand and dragged him with me. My best friend had been waiting years for this moment. I wasn't about to miss it.

Frankendaniel made his way to Alicia in jerking, monster-like movements, stopping in front of her. They stared into each other's eyes for a long moment, their gazes communicating wordlessly yet perfectly.

I love you so much, Daniel's eyes said. *I'm sorry for being such a wimpy jackass.*

I'm sorry for pressuring you, Alicia's eyes replied. *And I love you, too, you wimpy jackass.*

He took her left hand in his and got down on one knee in front of her.

Christina ran as fast as her white go-go boots would take her and yanked the plug on Ajay's iPod player. The room immediately went silent. There were a few shouts of protest from those dancing in the center of the room until they realized that Frankenstein was about to pop the question to his bride.

"Oh, my God," Alicia said softly, breathlessly, her chest heaving as if she were beginning to hyperventilate. "Oh, my God!"

When Daniel pulled a signature blue Tiffany's box from the pocket of his torn jacket, Alicia's eyes grew wide and she wobbled. I rushed over and grabbed her arm, stabilizing her in case she fainted. Nick came around, too, ready to catch her if she swooned.

Daniel opened the box, revealing the beautiful diamond ring from the catalog.

Staying in character, Daniel proposed to Alicia through a series of monster-like grunts. What it lacked in romance it made up for in originality. "Hnh hn hnh-hnh hn?"

Alicia squealed, lifted the skirt of her dress up a few inches, and performed a happy dance.

Looking up at her, Daniel emitted a questioning grunt. "Hnh?"

"Yes!" she cried, grabbing his green face in her hands and planting a big kiss on him. "Yes! Yes! Yes!"

Daniel slid the ring onto her finger, stood, and took her in his arms, giving her another big kiss. Cheers and applause erupted from the crowd.

I stepped over and gave Alicia a hug. "I'm so happy for you two!"

She hugged me back, then pushed me away, holding me at arm's length. "You knew all about this, didn't you?"

I raised my hands, palms up. "Who, me?" I asked innocently.

She laughed and held up her hand to admire her gorgeous new ring. "It fits perfectly."

"About that." I looked at Daniel and he reached into another pocket and pulled out her birthstone ring. I took it from him and handed it back to my friend. "I borrowed this so Daniel could get the size right."

She slid the ring onto her right hand and pointed an accusing finger at me, smiling all the while. "You're a naughty little fairy. I'll have your wings for this."

The party was an absolute blast, just what I needed after the stressful, frustrating weeks I'd recently endured. Nick and I danced until we could dance no more. At the end of the night, the last remaining partygoers leaped into the apartment swimming pool. I hoped the alcohol in their blood would prevent them from freezing to death.

Nick and I helped Ajay and Christina round up stray cups, bottles, and cans and take down the decorations.

"Now that your skull is in one piece again," Christina said as she took some empty beer bottles out of my hands, "will you be ready to start working the bar case?"

"Sure. Have you worked out a strategy?"

"Yeah." She dropped the bottles in a recycling bin. "I've met with an officer from Dallas PD's sex crimes unit. You, Nick, and I will go in undercover along with him. The DEA and Dallas PD have been after the bar owners for years, but they run a tight ship and use scare tactics to keep their workers quiet and in line. We've never been able to gather enough concrete evidence to arrest anyone."

"So we'll have to gather evidence ourselves?"

"Exactly. It won't be easy. The bar owners trust no one. It's going to take some effort to wiggle our way into their inner circle."

What the heck. I was always up for a little wiggling.

When the room was clean, Christina and Ajay thanked us for the help and Nick drove me home.

I felt giddy with anticipation the entire drive. Nick had yet to kiss me and it was all I could do not to grab the steering wheel, force his truck to the side of the road, and lay one on him. I'd waited for this moment for so long, since the first time I'd laid eyes on him, truth be told.

He parked in my driveway and came around to help me down from his truck. I laughed as he swept me up in his arms and carried me to the porch.

He set me down and I looked up at him. He looked back down at me, fire burning in his whiskey-colored eyes.

I could wait no longer. I stood on tiptoe, wrapped my hands around his neck, and pulled his face to mine, closing my eyes and eagerly anticipating the touch of his mouth on mine.

Our lips met and everything else ceased to exist.

There was only me and Nick.

And that was all that mattered.

When my work was done, Clean, Christine, and Abby thanked me for the ride and told them they are home.

Led quietly with aspiration to come drive Dick but ... her, and it was ... I could do not reach the ... He came from his truck in the shoe shine I told and he one-time, I waited for his turmoil by a long since he first ... I had seen all that, must be told.

He picked at my driveway and turn around to kiss my slow front he might. I motioned as he swept me upon his arms and gathered me to the ninth.

He set me down and I loved to paralipin. He wished her down as her fingers in his clothes collected to ... I couldn't help my fingers. I stood far under wrapped my hands around his heck and pulled him near to me, kissing his tears and caught, whispering the tumult of my wished up time.

"This life and I even gotta be just waited to ever. There was only me and Niall."

And that was all that mattered.

Read on for a look ahead to

Death, Taxes,
and Hot-Pink Leg Warmers

—the next Tara Holloway novel from
Diane Kelly and St. Martin's Paperbacks!

The Informant

"Officer Menger?" came a female voice from the doorway.

We turned to find a thin woman waiting in the hall. She stood around five foot seven, with a smooth, wrinkleless face that had been botoxed into immobility, giving her a porcelain doll look. Her body was likewise firm and pert. Anything that could be enlarged, liposuctioned, or lifted had been, probably several times over. Even her teeth looked perfect.

Despite these obvious cosmetic enhancements, the woman was nonetheless attractive, elegant even. Her champagne-colored hair was swept high into a classy, classic updo and her makeup, though heavy, was of subtle shades. She slipped out of her coat to reveal a sleeveless black dress accented with a gold brooch in the shape of an autumn leaf. Very tasteful.

Given the surgical enhancements, her age was impossible to guess. I'd put her somewhere between forty and four hundred. She might even pass for younger if not for the slightly loose skin on her neck and under her arms. On most women the underarm flaps looked like chicken wings. On this elegant woman they seemed more like skin ruffles.

Menger waved the woman into the conference room. "Hi, Bernice. Thanks for agreeing to meet with the team."

He introduced the woman to us as Bernice LaBerge. According to the information in the file, Bernice performed at the strip club. Although she wasn't onstage at the moment, she carried herself with a grace, sensuality, and self-assurance that said she'd have a fantastic stage presence. No wonder she'd been able to continue her exotic dance career into her . . . what?

Fifties?

Sixties?

Seventies?

As Bernice shook Nick's hand, her gaze roamed over his face and a smile played about her enhanced lips. "My, my. Don't you look like Burt Reynolds from back in the day?"

Nick returned the grin. "I'm a big fan of *Smokey and the Bandit.*"

Bernice took a seat at the table. After Menger gave us some brief background information, she filled the rest of us in.

"I was a showgirl at Caesar's Palace years ago," she said. "Long before those conglomerates moved into Las Vegas and built those tacky theme hotels."

If she told me she'd done vaudeville or worked with Shakespeare I wouldn't have been surprised.

Her voice took on a wistful tone as she continued. "I loved performing in Vegas. But when I ruptured my Achilles tendon my dance career was over, at least as far as those types of shows went. I'd grown up in Dallas so I moved back here and auditioned at Guys & Dolls. Back then the place was a dinner theater. I was a triple threat so I landed a role in nearly all of their shows."

My brows scrunched. "A 'triple threat?' What's that?"

"Showbiz term," she explained. "It means I can act, sing, and dance."

I supposed I was a triple threat, too, though in an entirely different way. I couldn't act, sing, or dance my way out of a paper bag, but I could handle a pistol, rifle, or shotgun with equal skill.

"I starred in several plays," Bernice said. "*Death of a Salesman. Mary Poppins.* I was even featured as Maria in a production of *The Sound of Music.*"

I'd seen the movie at least a dozen times as a girl. At the reference, my mind instantly brought up the scene in which the Von Trapp children performed their puppet show. Great. Now I'd hear yodeling in my head the rest of the day, while still mentally undressing Nick, of course. It made for a really odd imaginary striptease. If I ever actually saw Nick naked, though, I had a feeling I'd emit some high-pitched yodel-like sounds. *Yodel-ay-hee-hoo!*

With the yodeling now going on in my head, my mental faculties were reduced to 85%, luckily still enough brain-power to keep up with the conversation taking place in the conference room.

Bernice went on to tell us that when dinner theater went out of style, the owners of the establishment tried running bur-lesque shows. That worked well for a while, but then it became clear that the way to eke the most money out of the place would be to perform some simple mathematics—add some poles to the stage and subtract some clothing from the girls.

"I'd danced topless in Vegas," Bernice said, "so stripping wasn't much of a stretch for me. I was their featured dancer for years. Brought in quite the crowds."

She was clearly proud of her career accomplishments. I had been proud of mine, too. Until the damned baseball bat, that is. Getting knocked out by a grandmother had been humiliating. Would I ever get over it?

Bernice steepled her long, pink-tipped fingers. "The three men who owned the place back then took good care of us girls. They paid us a generous base wage, provided health insurance, tossed out any customers who got too handsy. We had quite a few good years."

How many? I wondered. Really, exactly how old was this woman? Forty-seven? Seventy-four?

Bernice's shoulders hunched slightly with tension. "Every-thing changed a year ago when the former owners decided to retire and sold out to a guy named Donald Geils." She pursed her lips as if merely uttering the man's name left a foul taste in her mouth. "Mr. Geils made a lot of changes. He re-duced the dancers' wages to the legal minimum, canceled our health insurance, and hired a bunch of thugs to work security. He even turned the employee lounge into a V.I.P. room."

Nick and I exchanged glances. I had an inkling what went on in that V.I.P. room. Very Icky Perverted stuff.

"I've never been asked to perform in the V.I.P. room," Bernice said. "Only a small number of the dancers work the room and it's by invitation only. The girls are very tight-lipped about what goes on in there."

Their tight lips might explain why they were chosen to work the room in the first place.

Aaron chimed in now. "We've sent undercover agents to the club. So far, none have been granted access to the V.I.P. room."

"Mr. Geils is very selective about which men he allows in there," Bernice added. "Only regular customers with a lot of money to throw around are given access. He keeps a couple of men from his security team stationed at the door at all times."

I pushed my brain's image of a naked Nick aside and men-tally filed away this information. "That explains the prostitu-tion, but what about the drugs?"

Bernice's face clouded over. "As I'm sure you've guessed, I'm the most experienced dancer at the club."

Most experienced did sound better than *oldest*, didn't it? While it seemed sad when people couldn't accept their ad-vancing age and enjoy what each phase of life had to offer, Bernice obviously enjoyed performing. What was wrong with making the most of it and extending her career as long as possible?

Bernice leaned forward in her seat. "Some of the girls look up to me, ask me for advice. They think of me as their big sister."

Or their mother. Or maybe even their grandmother.

"A few weeks ago, one of the cocktail waitresses, a girl named Madelyn, went through a rough patch. Maddie attended paralegal school during the day and was hoping to make a better life for herself and her daughter. She'd grown up in less-than-ideal circumstances and wanted more for her child."

Admirable goals.

"Her boyfriend abandoned her and their two-year-old daughter and moved in with another woman." Bernice explained that the errant boyfriend had paid no child support since he'd left. Between household expenses, child care costs, and tuition, Maddie quickly found herself in dire financial straits. "Maddie had never planned on dancing," Bernice said, "but she realized it was the quickest way for her to make the money she needed, a means to an end. She planned on quitting the club as soon as she finished school." With her boyfriend gone, Maddie had to work more hours to make ends meet. "The poor thing became exhausted, came in with bags under her eyes, nearly fell asleep standing up at her pole."

Bernice went on to tell us that Geils' henchmen had summoned Maddie to Geils' office one evening when her performance had been particularly lackluster. "Maddie came out of the office acting like a new woman. She took the stage and spun around that pole like a tornado."

A knowing look passed between Christina and Menger. Christina cut her eyes to me and Nick. "Crystal meth'll do that for ya. They don't call it 'speed' for nothing."

After that night, Bernice noticed that when Maddie showed up at work, her pupils appeared dilated and she seemed to have an excess of nervous energy. She became agitated and withdrawn and stopped speaking much to her co-workers. "She began working in the V.I.P. room. Not long afterward, I saw her one night and she was acting very strange. She was jittery and paranoid. She even shoved me and accused me of stealing her tips."

Christina gave a knowing nod. "She was tweaking."

"Tweaking?" Nick repeated.

I had no idea what the term meant either. I could define

cross collateralization, debt leveraging, and uniform capital-
ization, but when it came to street drug lingo my knowledge
was sorely lacking.

Christina filled us in. "Tweaking is when a drug user has
a bad reaction, freaks out."

Bernice blinked. "Well, whatever you call it, she got up
on stage to dance, twirled around the pole a few times, and
collapsed. I held her in my arms until the paramedics took
her away. A few days later, when she still hadn't returned to
work, I asked Mr. Geils what had happened to her. He
claimed he didn't know."

Worried, Bernice had gone to Maddie's house to see if
she could find her. A neighbor told Bernice that Maddie
remained in the hospital, undergoing treatment for a methamphetamine overdose.

Bernice's eyes grew misty. "Her daughter had been taken
away by Child Protective Services."

My heart contracted. "That poor little girl." She must've
been so scared and confused. *Suffer the children.*

Christina sighed. "People think they can use speed on
occasion for an energy boost, but meth isn't exactly like
caffeine or an energy drink." She explained how the drug
affected levels of a brain neurochemical called dopamine.
Dopamine acted as the brain's reward system and was released during pleasurable activities such as sex and eating
food. Methamphetamine caused high amounts of dopamine
to collect in the brain, resulting in a euphoric rush. The sub-
sequent depression when real life returned reinforced its
use, leaving the user craving more. "It's not a drug that's easy
to walk away from."

Bernice told us that she went to the hospital to visit Maddie but the girl refused to see her. "That wasn't like the
Maddie I used to know. She and I had been close." Fortunately for Maddie's sake, Bernice was persistent. "Eventually I was able to sneak past the nurse's station and get to her
room. Once she saw me, she burst into tears and told me she'd
only used the drugs to stay awake on the job. She never intended to get hooked."

Christina cocked her head. "Did she say she got the drugs from Geils or one of his men?"

"I asked," Bernice said, "but she wouldn't tell me where she got the drugs. She wouldn't tell me what had gone on in the V.I.P. room, either. But one thing was clear. She wanted out."

Though Madelyn had yet to finger Geils, it seemed obvious he had supplied her with the meth. When she'd overdosed, she'd been terrified Geils would do something to keep her from being able to talk to law enforcement or testify against him.

"She was ashamed and scared," Bernice said. "She doesn't have any family, at least none that care enough about her to help her out, so I used some of my savings to send her to a rehab center. She's still there now. I managed to convince CPS and the foster parents to allow me to take her daughter there for short visits once a week. God willing, Maddie will stay clean and get her daughter back. She regrets ever trying the stuff. If she hadn't been so exhausted she never would have taken drugs."

I'd probably never understand what drove Bernice to a career as a stripper, but one thing was obvious to me. Her heart was as big as her silicone-enhanced breasts.

Moonlighting

Aaron leaned forward and looked around the table. "Maddie won't talk to law enforcement even though the district attorney offered her immunity. I'm hoping she'll eventually break and agree to turn state's witness. Until then, we've got to work on obtaining more direct evidence."

Nick cocked his head. "Why isn't Dallas PD handling the drug case, too?"

"The drugs go way beyond Dallas," Christina said.

The DEA suspected that Guys & Dolls, while making some sales locally, served primarily as a distribution center for meth on its way to dealers in Oklahoma. When a dealer in Oklahoma had recently been arrested by state troopers, the phone number for Guys & Dolls was found in his cell phone's contact list. The cops probably wouldn't have thought much about it if not for the fact that the address for Guys & Dolls had appeared in the GPS of another dealer who'd been arrested several months before. The local cops figured the two connections to Guys & Dolls had to be more than coincidence. Because they didn't have jurisdiction beyond the

Oklahoma border, however, they'd turned the case over to the DEA. Presumably a new dealer had taken over after the arrests. Who that new dealer might be was anyone's guess.

"There might even be multiple dealers," Christina said.

She went on to tell us more about the drug. Crystal meth, also known as speed, chalk, ice, and glass, was very popular, especially among the twentyish crowd. After a rash of explosions at meth labs in Oklahoma and the deaths of several law enforcement officers at the hands of meth producers and users, the Oklahoma legislature was the first in the country to enact laws restricting the sale of pseudoephedrine, the drug's key ingredient. The impact was profound and the state's illegal labs dried up virtually overnight.

Unfortunately, the demand for the drug didn't dry up with the supply. Colombian and Mexican drug cartels stepped in to fill the void, as did entrepreneurial east Texans who could easily and inexpensively manufacture the drug in trailers hidden in the thick and difficult-to-access woods of the Big Thicket.

Our goal was to obtain evidence that Geils and his cohorts at Guys & Dolls were moving drugs, pimping out dancers, and cheating on their taxes. All in a day's work, right?

"What's the plan?" I asked. I knew we'd be going undercover, but that was all I'd been told so far about the operation.

Menger glanced my way. "Employee turnover has been high since Geils took over the club."

Not surprising. The guy sounded like an A-1 A-hole.

"I've already landed a job there, tending bar. The rest of you will apply for jobs, too. Once we're inside, we'll try to get closer to Geils and his goons, the dancers, too. Whatever it takes to gather evidence."

Wonderful. Now I'd be working two jobs. As if my special agent position didn't keep me busy enough.

Menger continued. "The club is looking for dancers—"

"No way!" Christina said. "I am not shaking my boobs for a bunch of horny men."

Menger rolled his eyes. "Nobody's asking you to."

Nick chuckled. "I might."

Apparently he didn't want to live much longer. I kicked him under the table. He shot me a wink back, giving another to Christina, letting us know he'd only been joking.

"They've got an opening for a cocktail waitress." Aaron pointed his pen at Christina. "That's where you come in."

"Much better," she said.

"Nick," Aaron continued, "you'll apply for a job as a bouncer."

Nick cracked his knuckles. "I'm on it."

"What about me?" I owned a perky but small pair of breasts, 32As. Surely they wouldn't expect me to take a job as a dancer. Besides, the only formal dance experience I had was a year of ballet when I was five. My parents still had the home video of my recital. I spent half my time on stage scratching my ass. Damn itchy tutu. And while I could mix up a mean batch of Nick's mother's peach sangria recipe, my mixed drink repertoire was severely limited. I'd make a lousy bartender. "Will I apply for a waitress job, too?"

"No," Aaron said. "They're looking for evening help in their cash office. That seems more up your alley."

Bookkeeping. No problem. The job would also put me in a better position to determine if there was any financial hanky-panky going on. But I had to admit I was a little miffed they hadn't mentioned the possibility of me dancing. My A-cups were offended. I might not be able to fill a bra, but that had never stopped guys from trying to get in my pants. I suppose my unconventional, rebellious ways made them think that what I lacked in boobage I'd make up for in enthusiasm.

We all stood to go.

Bernice offered us a weak smile. "See you all at the office."